THE SHIP IN THE HILL

In 1904, an elaborate Viking ship was discovered inside a hill. miles from the ocean on a farm at Oseberg, in southern Norway.

Published by the Navillus Press
1958 Onyx Street
Eugene, Oregon 97403

www.oregonhiking.com

Front cover: dragonhead post from the Oseberg ship, and a photograph of the Norwegian excavation in 1904, altered to include a suffragette from Oslo in 1905. *Spine:* the restored Gokstad ship in Oslo. *Back cover:* figurehead from an Oseberg sledge, and the restored Oseberg ship at the Vikingskipsmuseet in Oslo.

This book is a work of fiction. Although many of the characters from the Viking Age are based on descriptions in historical sagas, all other characters are strictly products of the author's imagination.

THE SHIP IN THE HILL

BY
WILLIAM L. SULLIVAN

ILLUSTRATIONS BY
KAREN SORENSEN SULLIVAN

NAVILLUS PRESS
EUGENE, OREGON

FOR
JANELL ELAINE SORENSEN

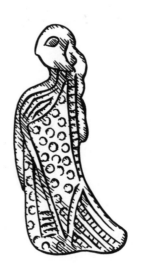

CHAPTER 1
SUMMER, 825

Asa was running barefoot in a short white dress.

As she ran through the grass above a gravel beach, a cluster of sheep parted before her, bleating. Then she cut across a headland and ducked through a row of pole racks. Old slave women cutting down dried codfish there threw up their hands.

When she emerged from the last of the pole frames she suddenly stopped. Ahead of her on the beach was a dragon-prowed longship—the ship that was to take her away.

Men at a smoky fire on the beach stirred a cauldron of pitch to caulk the ship's lapped planks. Other men atop the long boom straightened the rigging of the blue-and-white-striped sail. Still others carried tubs and bundles up the gangplank.

She gave her head a shake to arrange her long blond hair. Then she strode onward at a dignified gait.

"Asa!" A red-bearded man called to her impatiently from the row of shields along the ship's gunwale. "Where have you been?"

What could she tell her father? That she had wanted to make flower chains and ride the brown mare beyond the fields one last time? That she had needed to run barefoot with short dress and loose hair, knowing all these things would be forever forbidden to her after today?

"I was saying goodbye."

Her father blew out an exasperated breath. "There will be time to tell everyone goodbye at the feast tonight. Don't you want to see what's sailing with you?"

"Oh yes," she said, brightening again. Nordic tradition forbade unmarried women from owning property—even their own clothing. But what treasures would she be given as a bride?

She rounded the ship's prow, running her hand along the carved dragon's head as if she were stroking the forehead of a familiar horse. At the gangplank two massive men with axes, swords, and metal caps grunted, "Hail, Princess!" They held out hairy arms as impromptu railings, but she balanced up the narrow ramp on her own.

On the deck her father stopped her at arm's length and held her chin to examine her. "Asa, Asa. My little troublemaker." He shook his head, wondering if even as proud a man as Eirik of Horthaland could tame her. The woven belt pulled casually about the waist of her pleated white shift accented her womanly form, but her feet were sandy and a daisy clung to her loose hair.

Asa looked up at her father, realizing this would be the most difficult good-bye of all. As he stood there, shaking his head, Harald Granraude of Agthir seemed everything a Norwegian king should be. A purple cloak, pinned with an inlaid silver clasp, draped his powerful shoulders. His features might have been hewn from oak, with stern, bushy eyebrows, but gentle brown eyes.

In a way she hardly looked his daughter, for her own eyes were blue and her blond hair straight. But she owed him her high, white forehead, her tall frame, and a certain commanding demeanor that—so people said—had won her so many powerful suitors.

"Come and see what I have loaded," Harald said.

"Do you have the looms?"

"Yes, yes. All your weaving things." He led her across the cluttered deck to a hunchbacked older man who was assembling a large square structure of carved boards. "You see, Orm has been busy."

The stooped man stood with some embarrassment. "Princess Asa."

Asa suppressed a smile, for the old artisan had always been a favorite of hers. "So what have you made now, Orm?"

"Why, since I did the carvings on your ship in honor of your birth, it seemed only fitting that I carve the vessel for your next voyage."

"But what is it?" The framework seemed too flimsy for a sleigh or a wagon, although it was about the right size.

The old woodcarver fit a post through a chiseled slot and tightened the joint by tapping a wedge. "Why, it's collapsible. Easier to take along, such as now. Look at these fine horsehead figures."

Asa rolled her eyes. "But what does one *do* with it?"

"Do?" Orm chuckled. "Why, Princess, I thought you knew what

one does with a bed."

Asa flushed and the king roared. When Harald's laughter finally subsided he kicked an oak chest and handed her a heavy key. "Look in there, child. That will lift your spirits."

She held the bronze key in her hands a moment, admiring its heft. Receiving the key was a rite of passage she had looked forward to for years. Every woman of consequence in Norway's kingdoms wore a key or two at her waist. A key was a wife's badge of office, symbolizing her right to possessions of her own. It meant she no longer had to endure the frustration of being as powerless as a thrall, but rather was chieftain of her home.

Asa fit the key into the chest's slot, turned it, and slid it to one side. Springs creaked inside the chest's iron rim. When she lifted the heavy lid, metal glinted at her from inside. Handfuls of silver coins lay heaped amidst filigreed gold brooches, a silver chalice, and a massive, twisted gold necklace she guessed might weigh three pounds. Beneath the treasure were rare Arctic fox furs and folds of scarlet Frisian cloth.

She looked at her father, a lump in her throat. "This is wrong,

7

father," she said.

"Wrong? Why wrong? A princess deserves to take a royal fortune into her marriage."

"But if you give me gold, it means you are not giving me land."

The king looked at his daughter blankly. Then he slowly turned away, beginning to growl like a prodded bear. He banged his fist against a cask. "*Why* must you be so cursed political? I thought I was through with plotting, ambitious women when your mother died."

He shook a finger under her nose, but she did not flinch. " What did you imagine, child? That *you* would be heir to Agthir instead of your brother? He turned away again. "I should change my mind and give you to Guthroth the Viking. Then you could *be* a cursed king each summer while he's off pirating."

At this threat Asa felt a sudden chill. She had gone too far. "I'm sorry, father," she said, lowering her eyes. "I was ungrateful. You have been very generous."

Of all her suitors she feared Guthroth most. She had never met the man, just as she had never met her future husband or most of her suitors. But she knew them by their reputations. The court poets, the skalds, invented verses about everyone of consequence.

Guthroth was both the most powerful king in southern Norway and the most brutally unpredictable. He ruled Vestfold from an island in a small but dreaded fjord called the Vik. His red-sailed ships terrorized the Norwegian coast, using the slightest provocation as an excuse to raid and loot. The only season without attacks was summer, when Guthroth's longships disappeared across the sea. They returned to Norway each fall with strange slaves and unbelievable treasure.

Harald had once ridiculed the pirates from the Vik with the disparaging name "Vikings," and now, out of sheer defiance, Guthroth's men used the name themselves with pride. As a result it had seemed unlikely that Asa's father would accept Guthroth's marriage offer. On top of everything else Guthroth was an old man of forty-five winters, with a grown son. But she had been relieved when the official messengers had been sent to tell Guthroth no.

"Well, it is a bit late to refuse Eirik," Harald said, softening his tone. "I suppose you'll do well enough with him." In fact, Harald had chosen Eirik partly because he thought Asa's ambitious nature might thrive in Horthaland. Though Eirik had nowhere near the metal wealth of the Vikings, he stood to inherit his aged father's huge kingdom in the northern fjords. Harald had decided to give Asa silver only because he knew Eirik's matching marriage gift could be nothing else but land.

"Is Eirik really as quick-tongued as the verses say?" Asa couldn't help asking yet again about her husband-to-be. She had been pondering a poem in which the young Eirik gave his best horse to a shepherd when the horse refused to cross an ice-covered stream. She wondered, did that kind of impetuousness mean he might scold a wife with independent ways? Would he find her at all attractive? And would she like him? The poets never said outright if a man was handsome or not. It seemed she couldn't ask anyone the questions that worried her most.

"A wife should be glad if her tongue isn't quicker than her husband's. Then she always has the last word." To hide his smile, Harald turned to help direct four men carrying a wooden sledge past the mast.

When he looked back and saw his daughter lost in thought, turning the bronze key over in her hand, it suddenly struck him how much he would miss her. Perhaps he shouldn't have married her off so far from home? Since his wife had died, Asa had been his greatest comfort. He wondered if he had spoiled her, giving her half the honors of a queen, yet allowing her to dress and act with the freedom of a girl. She was fifteen, and still running about in a short linen shift. A mother would have been stricter. The thought made him gruff.

"It's time you prepared for the feast, Asa. Get a decent long dress and cloak out of the chest. And have one of the thralls tie up your hair. Eirik of Horthaland's wife will have to bear herself with proper dignity."

"Yes, Father." She started to open the chest again, but he stopped her.

Slowly he touched her blond hair, and his lips tightened. "Remember me, Asa."

CHAPTER 2
SUMMER, 1904

The train's whistle startled Kirstin Williams from yet another unsettling dream. But when she looked out the window of the railway carriage, the dream had already dissolved. As usual, all that remained was a disturbing trail of emotion—a heart-aching loss. Or was there something else this time? Something she had wanted to remember?

The low, red sun of the Norwegian summer evening flashed between half-timbered houses and log buildings. Suddenly Kirstin realized the train was slowing down. Could this already be the town near the excavation? Finally she would be able to see the legendary Viking dragonship for herself.

Kirstin sat up and rubbed her temples, hoping to clear away the weariness of the week-long voyage from New York. The two other archeologists from the excavation had telegraphed that they would meet the train. She knew it would be important to make a good impression. This would be her first major archeological expedition without her father. Glancing at her reflection in the polished metal beside the window, she straightened the blond hair she had put up into a professional-looking bun. She was glad she hadn't worn a hat—this wasn't a garden party. Her high, white forehead made her look quite a bit older than twenty-eight. Most women would have been glad to look young, but right now Kirstin wanted all the extra years she could get.

"Tønsberg!" a conductor called. Metal brakes screeched on metal. Kirstin stood, pulled her traveling bag from the overhead rack, and smoothed her long, dark blue dress. She lugged her bag to the end of the line of passengers at the car's door.

Suddenly she felt a flush of terror. Perhaps she should have insisted that her father come with her after all. Dr. Leland Williams, the grand old man of archeology at Cornell—he was the one they had really wanted as co-leader.

When the invitation had come, her father had leaned back in their Ithaca home, set down his pipe, and run his hand through his thin gray hair. "But this is your specialty, Kirstin. You're the one who's studied Norse sagas. It was in your mother's blood, and it's in yours. Besides, I'm too old to run about the globe for every excavation. You go instead. If you want, you can tell them I might come later."

"I would like to go," she had admitted, "But so far the only excavations I've been welcome at have been ours. Everywhere else, a woman with a Ph.D. is just a woman."

"Kirstin, this is 1904, not the Bronze Age. You've got what it takes to be a great field researcher. They need your help at that dig. Or would you rather spend the rest of your life working in museums?"

Still she had hesitated. "Scientists in Europe can be old-fashioned about these things."

Her father had laughed. "If they're fossils, you're just the one to put them in glass cases where they belong." Then his eyes had twinkled mischievously. "I tell you what. I'll send them a telegram explaining things. See if they don't fire back a welcome."

She had agreed, and he had touched her chin with his hand. "I'm so proud of you, Kirstin. When you're out there in Norway, remember me."

Now that she really was in Norway, her heart was pounding in her throat. All she could see beyond the car's doorway was steam, billowing white across the platform. It almost seemed she might be stepping out into mere clouds. Would she even recognize these men? Would they treat her as if she were a student? And what if her theory about the burial ship's importance was wrong? She had studied Nordic myths for so long that they almost seemed like genuine history to her.

Gripping the bag tightly for courage, she stepped down through the fog, her head held high.

Three men appeared almost directly before her, standing in front of the station—a large workman in rough clothes and two middle-aged men in suits and shiny black top hats.

The taller of the two gentlemen squinted past her as though she were invisible. The man frowned and spoke in such clear Swedish that Kirstin understood every word. "Well, that's the last of the passengers.

Looks like Dr. Williams must have been delayed."

The shorter gentleman stroked his full beard and replied in a thick German accent, "Missed our boat, so to speak?"

Kirstin almost smiled at their misunderstanding. She set down her bag in front of them. "No, gentlemen, I'm here as promised."

The taller man stared at her, obviously baffled. "I beg your pardon, Miss?"

The word set Kirstin on edge. "Miss" did not hit the professional tone she had wanted. Politely but firmly she announced, "If you are Dr. Carl Söderfelt, then I believe you are waiting for me."

When the gentleman still looked confused, she added, "I am Kirstin Williams."

"Ah! Leland's daughter." The man's fine-featured face lit up with an understanding smile. He doffed his hat and bowed slightly, a courteous gesture that suited his elegant handlebar mustache and blue eyes. "Forgive me, Miss Williams. A pleasure to meet you. Of course you are quite right. I am Dr. Söderfelt. And allow me to introduce my colleague, Dr. Otto Hoffmann, from Heidelberg University."

She offered the German a handshake. To her dismay he picked up her hand and kissed it instead. "Charmed, *Fräulein*," he murmured.

An awkward silence followed. Despite their chivalry — or perhaps because of it — Kirstin suspected something was very wrong.

Carl cleared his throat. "I must admit you have caught me off guard, Miss Williams. You see, I had understood that your father would be traveling alone." He turned to the workman by his side. "Magnus, could you go see if Dr. Williams needs help getting his baggage?"

Kirstin flushed. "You were expecting my father? But he won't be able to join the expedition for weeks, perhaps months."

"*Ach, Gott,*" Otto said, shaking his head. "This is difficult news indeed. Is Leland ill?"

"No. Surely you received his telegram explaining all this? Why else would you have met the train?"

Carl put his top hat back on and took a paper from his vest pocket. "Here is the only message I received. It was rather short. Perhaps there was some misunderstanding?"

Kirstin took her father's telegram and read it through.

CHAPTER 2 ~ 1904

PLEASED TO ACCEPT POSITION AS CO LEADER STOP MAY
BE DELAYED STOP CANNOT ARRIVE WITH DAUGHTER
AS PER EARLIER PLAN STOP EXPECT DOCTOR WILLIAMS
JUNE 15 ON TRAIN 2115 HOURS STOP GOOD LUCK STOP

She nearly groaned out loud. This was exactly her father's style of mischief. He had known perfectly well that they would misread the message. Expect Doctor Williams indeed! She couldn't help feeling a flash of anger at her father for tricking them all. But at the same time she could understand his ruse. He had wanted to give her a chance to pry her way into a leadership role at a major excavation. Wasn't that what she wanted too?

Carl frowned at the pavement. "This is most awkward. We were counting on Leland's advice. The excavation is proving more difficult than anticipated—finances, logistics, everything."

"Yes, and that's why my father wanted me to come," Kirstin said, feeling bolder by the man's admission. She was not surprised the excavation might be in trouble. Her father had warned her about Dr. Söderfelt. An art historian from Stockholm, the man had somehow risen to a post of importance at Kristiania University. It would be easiest, and a bit satisfying, to leave him stumbling toward failure. But now that she was actually in Tønsberg, how could she turn her back on the Viking ship? The discovery of a gigantic burial ship with a dragon-shaped prow had made headlines around the world.

Carl looked at her uncertainly. "I'm sorry, exactly why is it that you've come? It's a terribly long trip for a young woman, all by herself."

"Perhaps you don't understand, Dr. Söderfelt. I am here to join your excavation."

"What?"

"Did you or did you not send a telegram welcoming Dr. Williams to your team?"

"Yes, but—"

"I am the Dr. Williams my father asked you to meet." she said. "Dr. Kirstin Williams, associate professor of archeology at Cornell University."

Carl looked at her blankly. "You're not suggesting that you could take Leland's place? That's preposterous."

13

But his German colleague, Otto, burst out with a laugh. "No, it's marvelous! She's caught you, Carl. You invited a Dr. Williams, and now, *bei Gott*, you've got one."

Kirstin looked down. "I don't claim I can take my father's place. But he couldn't have taken my place either. My father accepted your invitation only because he knew this was my field of expertise. He's asked me to serve as his representative in the interim."

"As his representative." Carl studied her uncertainly. "I suppose you were one of Leland's students?"

"No, my doctorate is from Columbia. I published my dissertation on Scandinavian legends." It was during her doctoral studies that she had stumbled onto the stories of dragons. One legend claimed that Harald Fairhair, the king who united Norway in the ninth century, had been aided by a dragon with the power to build empires. When she first published her work, it had been largely ignored. But now even the newspapers were openly speculating that the newly discovered Viking warship might be Norway's long lost, invincible "dragon."

Suddenly Otto snapped his fingers. "You're the one who came up with that business about dragons, aren't you? Someone brought it up at the German Academy's last meeting. The Kaiser is very interested in anything to do with empires, you know. Have you done any more research along those lines?"

Kirstin nodded, heartened by this more sympathetic response. "I've been comparing Old Norse sagas with archeological finds. I'm hoping it may help identify the ship."

There was another awkward pause. Carl cleared his throat. "Well, at least you speak Norwegian better than your father ever managed."

It was not much of a compliment, but Kirstin accepted it, hoping to calm the troubled waters. "I'm a little rusty. I learned from my mother. She grew up in Norway."

Suddenly the train's whistle blasted across the platform. Steam hissed from behind the great iron wheels. With a deep-throated puff, the locomotive clanked the cars' couplings tight and began to pull away from the station.

The brawny workman brought Kirstin's trunk on a dolly. He touched his sailor's cap, gave Kirstin an oddly probing look, and said in the crisp local dialect, "Where to, doctor? You staying?"

Carl stepped in. "Thank you, Magnus. Just put the trunk in the buggy. We'll take Miss—excuse me, *Doctor* Williams to a hotel before returning to the dig."

"A hotel?" Kirstin asked with some surprise.

"Well yes, until we get things sorted out. You know our tents at the dig are really quite primitive. We don't have proper accommodations for ladies."

"Dr. Söderfelt, I am quite used to camping at excavations."

He shook his head slowly. "I just don't think it will work out. You'll be wanting to get back to America before long, I'm sure."

This would have been the moment to back away gracefully, to avoid further confrontation. A part of Kristin wanted that escape. But the man's patronizing tone made her all the more determined to stand her ground. She crossed her arms and aimed her words straight at him. "You offered Dr. Williams a position at this excavation, Dr. Söderfelt, and I intend to fill that post until my father arrives."

For a moment she and Carl glared at each other. She hadn't traveled this far to back down.

"Do you two want sabers?" The German archeologist broke the standoff with a wry smile. "I love duels, but it seems a shame to slaughter an American professor just when we need help. An accident like that might prevent her father from joining our excavation altogether, you know."

Carl cleared his throat. "I suppose you're right, Otto. As long as she's here, we might as well find out if she can be of use. Lord knows, we need the help." He frowned. Then he looked askance at Kirstin and extended his hand. "Sorry if I seemed a bit brusque. As I said, you caught me a little off guard this evening."

"I understand," Kirstin shook his hand firmly. She had won her first battle at the excavation. But she knew she had only gained enough ground to stay and face the many battles that obviously lay ahead.

"Good, then if that's settled for the time being," Otto said, leading the way to the buggy, "perhaps we could show you the ship?"

Kirstin smiled. "Yes, I'd like very much to see it."

"Actually, Carl brought a sample along." Otto pulled a valise from behind the seat and set it on the running board.

Kirstin turned to Carl with surprise. "You brought a piece of the ship?"

Carl gave a small shrug. "It was meant as a sort of welcoming gesture for your father."

Otto chuckled, "I think you were just afraid to let it out of your sight."

"A little, perhaps," Carl admitted. "This was one of the first artifacts we found, and the most valuable so far. It must have broken off from the ship long before our time." He unsnapped the valise's clasps, lifted the lid, and pulled back white rags that had been used as packing.

Kirstin caught her breath. From inside the valise, three fragments of a carved wooden spiral the size of a dinner plate were leering up at her with beady eyes.

A distant memory rippled through her, and the haunting sensation of loss she had felt in her dream. She whispered, "The head of the dragon."

CHAPTER 3
SUMMER, 825

With its back to the sea, the longship stretched on the beach below the great hall of Agthir, as if even the fierce-looking dragon at its prow had wanted to forget the worries of the world and join the evening's revelries.

Inside the straw-roofed hall, King Harald Granraude raised a silver-mounted horn to a crowd of merrymakers. "A toast!"

Women with glinting brooches and necklaces quickly ladled up hornfuls of ale and brought them to their assigned drinking partners of the evening. Men in brightly colored cloaks waited impatiently on the wall benches along the sides of the hall.

Only Princess Asa had the honor of being served by a man tonight — by the skald Kalf, a handsome, sandy-haired young man. Even more unusual was that she sat on the Dragon High Seat at the middle of the north wall, between the hall's elaborately carved central pillars, directly before the hearth fire. Her mother had been the only other woman of Agthir to sit in the high seat, and then rarely. It was an honor reserved for the hall's host or the king himself.

Tonight the young princess was dressed as a queen with the treasures from her marriage chest: a daringly low-cut Frisian red dress, with filigreed gold brooches securing the dress's delicate straps above each breast.

"A toast for the princess, Kalf," the king commanded.

The young skald turned toward the king's voice, but looked over the heads of the crowd, as if he saw something far beyond the smoky hall.

"Hear my words
And heed them well.

Fell wood in the winter;
In fair weather set sail.
Choose a shield for strength,
A ship for speed,
A sword for keenness —
And a girl for kissing."

The crowd laughed its approval. The young poet went on.

"But laughter leaves many
A promise unproved.
Praise no ice till crossed,
Praise no ale till drunk . . ."

Suddenly a shadow crossed his face and he stopped. He held his hand to his forehead. The crowd began to murmur impatiently. Only Asa knew why Kalf might do such a thing, and she felt uneasy.

"Well, and then what?" Asa's brother, the lanky Prince Gyrth, spoke from across the hall. "Here, let me try:

"Praise no sword till sheathed."

"Good!" It was Orm the woodcarver. The hunched old man stood and winked,

"Praise no wench till bedded."

The king laughed at Orm's typical wit and called out a line of his own:

"Praise no verse till finished."

The men roared, and only then did Kalf appear to return from wherever his thoughts had been. Somberly, he spoke the last line of his poem:

"And praise no day till done."

The strangely forboding words left the audience quiet. But then the king called out, "To the future queen of Horthaland!" and the toast was drunk with renewed good cheer.

Asa drank from the bitter, amber ale, and gave the horn to Kalf. She was dying to know what Kalf had learned when he stopped his poem, but this was no night to display girlish haste. After he had emptied the horn, she spoke low over the cup's lip. "What did you see?"

"I don't know, Princess. How can I ever know what the visions really are? There were many things moving — square things, outside the hall, I think." Kalf's glazed eyes stared past her shoulder into the darkness.

He sighed with frustration. "Odin may give skalds their inspiration, but he is a troublesome god indeed. It is just like Odin to have granted the gift of second sight to me, a man born blind."

Asa had first learned of the blind poet's visions when they were children. Even then they had kept it secret, fearing the reprisals of the jealous wizards who traveled the countryside. Many a time she had tried to help him interpret the strange, infrequent pictures. Once, when he had seen two overlapping circles, she had guessed at an eclipse a day before it occurred. But usually they failed. Kalf's eyes had known only blackness, or at most spots when he pressed them in anger. He knew no colors. He could hardly describe, much less understand his prescient visions from the gods.

"Square, moving things?" She asked. "That could be the square weaving cards of my hand loom. Perhaps I'll weave a new belt."

"No, the squares were scattered. And they seemed to be growing." Kalf frowned. He loved her too much to tell her the whole truth tonight. The squares had exuded a sense of evil so powerful that he could hardly put the feeling in words. But whatever danger it represented would surely come only after she was gone, and he did not want to spoil the evening's mood. He shook his head quickly, trying to clear the memory of the brilliant image.

He raised his eyes again, just missing hers, and smiled with an effort. "This is selfish of me to waste your last evening here with such talk. Tomorrow you must go to Horthaland. Let's talk of you."

Asa sighed, thinking of the trip. She had once visited distant relatives in the gentle islands of Denmark, but she had never been to Norway's stormy, rocky northlands. Horthaland bordered the desolate Horthangr Wastes, the legendary realm of the frost giants feared even by the gods. Would she ever feel at home in the north? She knew Kalf himself had been to Eirik's homeland twice, accompanying her father as court skald.

"Tell me about Eirik," she begged.

It was a subject Kalf disliked. If only he had been born sighted! Then, perhaps, he would have been the one who was marrying Asa. He cleared his throat and began stiffly,

> "Bearer of the eagle banner,
> Sailor of sword's steel,

19

Eirik, the coming king—"

"I've heard the verses so often," Asa interrupted impatiently. "But you've met him. Can't you simply tell me if he's ugly or handsome or—"

She caught herself. Kalf had been her friend for so long that she sometimes forgot he was blind. Worse yet, a future queen should not ask such questions at all.

Kalf reddened. "Princess, I miss much because I was not born whole."

"Not at all, Kalf! Where others see with their eyes, you see with your heart. That's why you are a skald."

The blind poet reached out tentatively, as if to touch her, but then dropped his hand. It was true, he thought, that he had learned to read emotions with his heart, where even his beloved Asa evidently could not. Perhaps it was as rare a skill as learning to read runes. But what use was seeing with his heart if it meant he could never see the beauty of her face or the grace of her walk as others did?

Finally he took a leather pouch from his belt. "I have brought you a farewell present, Princess," he said. It's only bronze, I'm afraid, but the workmanship is very fine. Please accept it as a memory of one who would please you."

Puzzled, she opened the pouch and took out two elegant, oval brooches cast with an intricate fishnet pattern. Though they were merely bronze, she knew they must have cost the blind poet dearly. What was he imagining? "Kalf, you know girls can't own presents. And as a married woman I'll only be able to accept gifts from my husband."

Kalf lowered his head. "I thought tonight, when you are no longer a girl and not yet a wife, you might take them. Please, if only because of my father."

Before Kalf was born, his father had died defending King Harald from an ambush in the forest. The king had promised, if the child were a boy, to train him as a warrior and to raise him as the king's own foster son. But once they had discovered Kalf's blindness the promise had not been entirely kept.

"They're beautiful, Kalf. I'll treasure them," Asa said. She leaned back into the shadows and quickly replaced her dress's gold brooches with the bronze gifts. "See, I've put them on."

She took his strong hands in hers. She could feel his fingers trembling as she drew them to her and touched them to the curved clasps above her breasts. The trembling in his hands gave her a strange thought. Could it be that he loved her?

"A toast to Eirik!" the king called.

Kalf pulled his hands back with a start, his face pale and his breathing shallow. "Yes!" he cried, jumping to his feet. "A toast to Eirik!" The blind young man stumbled along the bench to the ale vat and returned with a dripping horn.

Asa's head was spinning as she drank. She needed to calm her thoughts and order her emotions. When she returned the horn to Kalf she said, "The smoke's so thick in here. I need to go outside a while for the air."

She walked to the low, wooden door, ducked through to the vestibule lined with axes and shields, and ducked again onto the pillared breezeway. The evening wind felt like a splash of cool water in her face. She leaned against one of the log pillars and closed her eyes, breathing deep the vibrant scents: salt air, hayed meadows, split wood, home.

She did not want to leave the people she loved—her father, old Orm, her brother Gyrth, and yes, Kalf. Had she unknowingly been hurting her childhood friend all these years? And wasn't the tenderness she felt for him more than merely friendship? But a princess could never marry a blind skald.

For the second time that day, she looked with a touch of bitterness for the blue-and-white-sailed ship on the beach, the ship that would take her away.

But this time when she turned toward the sea she saw the moving squares. Red squares, growing. Terrifying, blood-red sails.

"Asa, are you out here?" Harald asked, ducking out the doorway. In an instant he had seen her frightened, silent look and followed her eyes.

The red sails of the Viking longships billowed in the fjord. A dozen sixty-man serpents. The first were nearly at the beach.

"Guthroth," the king growled. "That worthless Viking! I told him I'd chosen a better man to marry my daughter. Get inside, Asa. By all the gods of the north, he'll not take you easily. To arms!"

The hall erupted in shouts and clamor. Hastily armed men rushed out of the doorway in such tumult that at first she could not go in. When she did, she cast a last look at the beach. Hundreds of men with the round, red shields of the Vik were leaping into the water, splashing ashore, and running up the slope. The swiftness of the Viking ships and the suddenness of the attack were every bit as terrifying as their reputation. A chilling, prolonged cry rose from the Vikings' throats. It seemed impossible that they could be coming for her, a mere girl.

Inside the dark hall, a handful of armed men herded the women toward the back door. "Where's Asa?" Prince Gyrth shouted, striding through the confusion.

Asa silently took her spot on the Dragon High Seat, struggling not to show the fear boiling within her.

Gyrth spotted her with relief. "Good. Stay there. We can defend you best in the hall." He turned to the other women. "The rest of you, run! Spread out so they'll take fewer of you, and warn the men in the settlements!"

Kalf was standing in the middle of the floor, his arms partly outstretched to protect himself from the jostling crowd. Gyrth took one of his hands and put it in the hand of a passing woman. "Follow the women, Kalf. Run as best you can."

Kalf shook his hand free. "I wish to stay and fight."

"I said go! You can't help here."

The skald crossed his arms defiantly. "I will die with my king."

The last of the fleeing women closed the hall's back door behind them. Gyrth was just motioning to two men to remove the blind man by force when they were stopped by a commanding voice from the Dragon High Seat.

"Let him stay!" Asa's white-knuckled hands gripped the carved dragon heads of the throne. "Give him a weapon, Gyrth!"

Gyrth stared at his sister, baffled.

Suddenly an enraged growl came from the front doorway and King Harald burst in, followed by Orm and five wide-eyed men. Asa paled to see the king apparently unaware that an arrow was protruding from his left forearm. "Prop the doors closed!" the king bellowed. "They won't burn the hall as long as Asa's here."

The heavy front door thudded shut, suddenly dampening the cries of battle from the beach.

In the ominous stillness that followed, Asa realized with a terrible certainty that most of Harald's men must already be lost, or the king would not have barricaded the hall. The others in the room knew it too and exchanged silent glances. The goddesses of fate had ended their luck, and they would meet Odin.

A thin curl of smoke slowly rose from the embers on the open hearth, weaving into a pall among the dark beams. Kalf felt his way to the edge of the high seat. Asa touched his arm. Like all women she carried a short, hidden dagger at her waist. Now she put the hilt in his hand and squeezed his fingers gently around it.

Suddenly there was a splintered crash and the watering trough that had crushed the door skidded across the dirt floor. Asa watched, frozen with horror, as the defenders beside the broken doorway swung their broad axes two-handed, hacking through the red, wooden shields of the screaming attackers until the door was half blocked with bodies.

After a moment, spears suddenly jabbed up through the doorway, impaling the shieldless axemen there. Then other spears sailed across the room, felling two more men before the hearth. Finally the Vikings stormed through the breach single file, swords swinging before them. Still Asa gripped her chair, unflinching.

With a shriek, Orm sprang from a bench upon the foremost attacker, sinking his long-handled adze into the man's back. But when Orm stooped to pull the tool free, a second swordsmen lopped the old woodcarver's head.

Now Harald let loose an unearthly roar. One-handed, he skewered Orm's killer and battled three other Vikings back to the doorway, meeting their blows with such strength that he broke one of their swords and knocked a man to the floor. Gyrth finished the fallen man with a thrust from the side, and the others retreated to the shadows.

Backlit by the doorway stood two square-shouldered men. They wore inlaid metal helmets and shirts of shiny chain mail, such as no man in Agthir had ever owned.

Harald turned his sword to the taller of the two armored men. "Come and fight, Guthroth. Until you are dead, and all your kind, there will never be peace in Norway."

"It will pain me to see you die," Guthroth replied. "But I am not a man lightly refused." He sliced his glinting sword at the king, but Harald dodged and parried.

"Gyrth!" Harald called, parrying again. "Take Olav."

Harald landed a glancing blow on Guthroth's shoulder. Somehow the sword refused to bite and Harald fell back. Meanwhile, Guthroth's armored son, Olav, began driving Gyrth backwards with dazzling agility, thrusting and slashing so quickly that Gyrth could scarcely block the blows in time. When they reached the low stone border of the hearth, Olav's sword slipped through Gyrth's chest, a red fish-shape out the back of his tunic. Harald glanced at his son, and Guthroth's shiny sword flashed.

"No need to look," Guthroth said. "The leg is gone."

With a frozen, incredulous expression, Harald toppled to one side.

Asa screamed silently: "Father! Gyrth! Get up! You can't die!" It had happened too fast. Her spirit bridled within her as if her body would burst. But still she clenched the high seat silently, refusing to give the Viking murderers the satisfaction of seeing her blazing anger and fear.

Guthroth thrust his sword into Harald's jerking, red body. Then he sized up Kalf. "So, the last defender before my queen carries a girl's knife."

The skald lunged forward, but the Viking deftly stepped back and swung his bloody sword.

"No!" Asa cried aloud.

The sword clanged against Kalf's dagger and sent it flying. At once

Kalf ripped open his shirt, baring his chest to receive the Viking's death blow.

"No indeed?" Guthroth asked, poising his wavy-edged sword for the final thrust.

"He's blind!" Asa said.

Guthroth paused. "A blind swordsman?"

"He's a skald. You'll gain no fame for murdering him, too." Asa held her head high, eyes flashing with hatred.

The Viking king met her gaze and slowly lowered his sword. She was even bolder and more beautiful than he had heard. Her golden hair was tied back in a loose knot. Her red, low-cut dress suited her fiery spirit. He knew she was a dangerous prize. Now that the sword battle was won, a more delicate battle lay ahead.

"Olav!" the king called to his son. "Tell the men to stop the attack. There will be no looting. And kill any man who lays a hand on a woman."

Guthroth tapped Kalf's tensed arm. "Your name, skald."

"Kalf, son of Ottva the Bold."

"My queen would spare you, and I enjoy a tale well told. Would you choose to serve as my retainer or to die?"

Kalf's eyes stared straight ahead. "I would serve the princess."

Guthroth smiled. He pulled off his acorn-shaped helmet, revealing matted, shoulder-length hair that was dark for a Norseman—nearly black—with strands of gray that matched his frost-streaked beard. He knew Asa would think him old, and he could see the blind skald was young and handsome. A defiant young queen might be more tractable if she were allowed to keep such a man.

"Very well. The skald may live as your servant," Guthroth announced to Asa.

She closed her eyes with relief that Kalf would live. But then the precise meaning of Guthroth's words registered. A servant was not a free-serving retainer, but rather a thrall. Kalf would be allowed to live only with the same rank as a slave stable hand.

"You will find I am known as Guthroth the Generous for more than the gold I give." Then Guthroth turned abruptly to the crowd of swarthy men that had assembled in the hall. "Arinbjorn! Prepare the first three ships to sail. Jarl Grim! Stay to secure the kingdom and send me a score of prominent hostages. Bjorgolf! Have proper burial mounds raised for the king and his son. Thorstein! See the princess to her ship. I think a draught or two of mead awaits us all at the Vik."

The Viking king clapped the shoulders of several of his men good-naturedly, and they left the hall together, laughing and wiping the blood from their weapons.

Asa stared after them in stunned silence. In the time it would take for a haystack to burn, her father's kingdom had fallen—and it was only because of her. Her brave family was dead, strewn before her on the blood-soaked dirt. Suddenly her hopes and fears of Eirik seemed like a faintly remembered girlhood dream. Now she had no one but Kalf. Now she had nothing left but revenge.

"Queen Asa." An older man in an embroidered tunic approached with respect. "I am Thorstein. My crew is skilled at night sailing."

She drilled the man with a fierce gaze.

Thorstein continued, "It is time to go." He held out his hand patiently.

Slowly Asa's fingers unclenched from the carved dragonhead posts of the high seat. She stood, scorning his hand.

Promptly the Viking captain gripped one of the dragonheads and yanked it free. The chair's cloth seat flopped to the floor.

"Stop!" Asa cried, aghast. "How dare you touch the royal high seat!"

Thorstein shrugged. "Don't Agthir's high seat pillars travel? They're built to come apart like others."

"But they may never be used outside the hall of the kingdom's sovereign!"

The old Viking glanced at the bodies on the floor. "So, Queen Asa?" He began pulling out the second dragon head. "I think the royal pillars had best follow you."

* * *

In the dark of the rocking ship, huddled in a blanket beside a barrel at the prow, Asa could finally cry. Finally, beneath the creaking of the ropes and the sloshing of the wake and the jesting of the crew, no one could hear her sobs. No one would know that she was just an exhausted, frightened, orphaned girl instead of a stoic queen. She bit into the blanket and drenched it with tears. This had been her ship—the dragonship for her maiden voyage to Eirik in Horthaland. Now it was sailing in the other direction, in the worst possible direction, deeper into the Viking terror.

"Shh, Asa!" a voice whispered.

She stifled a cry and looked up. The stars were faint, blurry balls in the glowing midnight sky. Above her rose the dark coil of the ship's dragon prow.

"Asa?" the voice came again. This time she looked toward the stern and recognized a shape groping behind a barrel. Kalf had somehow made his way from the crew's portion of the deck to the forecastle, reserved for nobility. She crawled to his side, buried her head in the comforting cloak on his chest, and sobbed. "Oh, Kalf! And they've even made you a slave. We're slaves together."

He stroked her hair, torn between despair and happiness. "No, Asa. You are a queen, and will be one of the highest women in Norway."

She pulled back her head. "I don't want to be a queen for Vikings. I want them to taste the suffering they've given us."

The blind skald quoted,

"The coward never takes revenge;
The slave, at once."

She studied his stern features. "You were right when you told me about the moving squares. Have you seen another vision, Kalf?"

"No, but I think you have."

She looked out across the gunwale at the islands of the Vestfold frontier—great, low shapes surfacing like fearsome thoughts in the near-night. She felt the slap of waves against the planks at her side. Did she remember a vision?

When she let her mind drift back, she only saw her father's red-bearded head shaking at her: "Remember me, Asa."

And then she knew.

"I will put an end to the Vikings," she said solemnly. "I swear before Odin, I will stop them forever."

Kalf opened his mouth, but could not speak. He had not meant to suggest the impossible! Did this fifteen-winter-old girl imagine her vengeance could somehow dissolve the world's most powerful fleet?

"Will you swear to help me, Kalf?" She took the blind poet's hands and held them to her lips.

Suddenly a heavy leather belt whacked in the dark and Kalf's head thudded against the planks. "Thrall!" a voice bellowed. "Back to the aft. Did you think you were the king's forecastleman?"

The crewman leaned back laughing, joined by a dozen rough Viking voices. The belt whistled in the dark again and cracked on the blind man's unprotected face.

Instead of crying out, Kalf put his hand to the bleeding slash across his cheek and replied, "Yes."

The Viking roared again. "The slave says, 'Yes!' He's our blind battle king." The crewman dragged Kalf by his tunic from the forecastle and dropped him on the boards. Another Viking pushed a bow and an arrow at Kalf, jeering, "To arms, to arms!"

But while the men laughed, Kalf rose to his knees. He could see each man by his voice as clearly as if he were touching the tips of a dozen racked spears. He could feel Asa's pity as clearly as the glow of a hot hearth. And he soared with a new, unbelievable freedom. He could even feel the wing-beats of a white seagull—a token of peace from the gods?—that had banked out from the islands to turn its curious eye on the ship and now sailed alongside, screaming.

Asa held her breath as Kalf cocked the arrow beneath his cloak. The crewmen had carelessly turned away to tell other jokes. Asa's heart was beating so hard in her throat she could not summon the words to tell Kalf to wait.

With his head bent forward in concentration, the blind poet slowly lifted the bow toward the stars. For a painfully long moment he bent there, poised. Then there was a sudden swish and a faint thud.

In an instant the Vikings had jumped to their feet and wrenched the bow away. But Asa alone knew they were too late.

Broken, the gentle white bird had fallen dead into the waves.

CHAPTER 4
SUMMER, 1904

"Dr. Williams?" A voice prodded Kirstin loose from her dream. Jolting in a buggy through the Norwegian night, she felt for a moment that she might still be sailing. Had she really only dreamed that dark sea? The fading vision left powerful new emotions: vengeance, fear, and challenge.

"We're almost at the Oseberg farm."

The Swedish accent held just a tinge of disdain. Suddenly she recalled her arrival at the train station and was wide awake. How could she have fallen asleep on the way to the excavation site? This was no way to impress Dr. Söderfelt with her professionalism. She quickly sat upright on the buggy seat and straightened the sleeves of her long dress. "I—I must have drifted off for a moment."

"You've had a long trip," a voice with a German accent consoled her. Otto had turned around from the carriage's front seat, beside the driver. "Still, I don't think you'll want to miss seeing our dragon's lair."

Ahead the carriage's shivering lanterns veered toward a broad hill. It took Kirstin a moment to realize that this was no natural landform, but rather the burial mound itself. The looming shape seemed large enough to cover half a village. Why had the Vikings needed such an enormous mound to entomb this particular ship?

As the carriage slowed, one of the horses snorted nervously.

Suddenly a flame flickered atop the mound, followed by a thin trail of orange smoke.

Carl twisted around in his seat. "What are the workers doing? Lighting torches in the middle of the site?"

"No, damn it." The burly Norwegian driver tied up the reins, grabbed the whip, and leaped to the ground. "The workers are down in camp."

Otto frowned. "Then who the devil is up there?"

"Don't you leave a guard?" Kirstin asked. Could these men have overlooked security—the first rule of any excavation? The discovery of the burial ship had been so widely publicized that it could easily attract looters.

Carl began, "I brought along the most valuable artifact—"

But Kirstin had already climbed out of her seat. She grabbed one of the carriage's kerosene lamps. Then she held the embroidered hem of her long dress in one hand and followed the driver uphill past piles of dirt and jumbled crates.

When Kirstin crested the mound's top, she stopped short at the chilling sound of a woman's scream. Before her, smoky torchlight lit a hundred-foot-long rectangular pit excavated into the summit. The outline of a sixty-foot Viking ship stretched from end to end of the dig, as if the great vessel had simply sunk into the top of this hill, leaving only the stub of a mast and the pointed prows free on either end.

Near the mast a stooped, old woman in a gray farm dress held a torch in her shaking hands. Before her, as if frozen by the scream, the driver held an old man by his arms. Patched trousers hung loosely on the man's withered frame. He wore the wooden shoes of a poor farmer and held a simple wooden spade.

When Kirstin came closer she was outraged to see that they had already dug a crude hole in the middle of the site. Obviously they had been looking for treasure. But Kirstin couldn't help feeling a little sorry for the old farm couple as well. She had heard that times were hard in Norway—1904 had been another year when ships took a seemingly endless stream of desperate emigrants to New York. Famine had ravaged Norway's provinces. The hunger must have been terrible indeed if it had driven the people here to loot their own history.

As soon as Carl and Otto caught up with her, Carl waved a hand to the driver. "Let Mr. Hansen go."

Kirstin turned to the excavation leader with raised eyebrows. "You know these people?"

"I'm afraid so." Carl walked down a ramp into the pit and stepped across the strings dividing the site into squares. The driver slowly dropped his grip.

"Damn right he knows me," the old man said, shaking his arms free. "I own this farm."

Kirstin had read Söderfelt's preliminary reports, but now she realized how incomplete they had been. "I thought the Oseberg farmer had already sold you the excavation rights."

"Sold, ha!" The old man hitched up his baggy pants by his suspenders. "It's my hill till you pay for it."

Carl's voice betrayed a strained patience. "It takes time to get that kind of money budgeted, Mr. Hansen. I'm still paying my workers half wages. Our primary goal here is to finish excavating the ship before winter sets in."

"And my goal is not to be robbed by some Swede." The farmer nodded once emphatically. "Here I've got three acres of bottomland covered with dirt piles and what have I got to show for it?"

"Did you expect to dig up your payment?" Carl asked. "Any gold or silver treasure unearthed within the Kingdom of Sweden and Norway belongs to the king."

"The *Swedish* king." The farmer spat. "But even your damned king pays a reward. So now you've had the grave room uncovered for a week, but instead of fetching up the treasure you waste your time fiddling around with little brushes."

The farmer's wife pulled on his arm. "Thorvald!"

"You've found a grave room?" Kirstin asked. "There's actually a burial structure on the ship?"

Carl waved to a broken, tent-shaped arrangement of boards protruding behind the mast. "Yes. We estimate it was originally two and a half meters tall, but the weight of the mound has crushed the oak planking, making excavation difficult."

"Difficult, hell!" The farmer held a torch out over the hole he had dug. "If you'd leave me alone I'd have the treasure chest up in an hour."

"Treasure chest?" Suddenly intent, Carl knelt beside the hole. "Good Lord, it really does appear to be some sort of trunk." Carl peered even more deeply into the pit. When he finally looked up again he seemed at a loss for words. "Even the lock—it all looks intact."

For a moment the three archeologists exchanged silent looks. The German raised his bushy eyebrows. Carl ran a hand over his smooth jaw. The chest in the grave room was a time capsule from a lost world of saga heroes, swords, and sea empires. Kirstin knew that a Viking grave of this scale might well contain a royal treasure—and the peculiar thing was, she could already picture it. She could envision the trunk's lid agape, revealing a pile of silver coins and a gold cup. Where on earth had that unbidden image come from?

"Well?" the farmer asked.

Carl appeared to gather his wits. "We'll open the chest at a public ceremony after the grave chamber has been excavated. You'll be invited, Mr. Hansen, and you will be paid your due. If I'm not mistaken, unveiling an artifact like this for the newspapers should help us come up with the funding we need." He stood and faced the farmer. "Now you may go."

"Wait!" The farmer's wife stepped before them, her eyes gleaming in the torchlight. "We didn't come just for the reward." Kirstin noticed with a start that one of the woman's eyes was blue, while the other was an eerie, deep green.

"What then?" Carl asked.

"The bones." The farmer's wife crooked her finger toward the hole. "The remains of the one buried in there."

"First looters, now grave robbers?" the German archeologist chuckled.

At once the old woman wheeled toward him. "No! You are the grave robbers. The one buried there is our ancestor, not yours." She fired a withering look at Carl.

"I am the Director of Norwegian Antiquities, Mrs. Hansen" Carl replied stiffly, his Swedish accent suddenly obtrusive. "It is my job to

exhume unidentified remains in Norway."

The old woman cast her eye on Kirstin. "A powerful grave harbors powerful spirits." She laughed to herself. Then she whispered, "Fear your dreams if you should find the bones!"

Before Kirstin could respond, the old woman tossed her white hair and spun on her heel. Then, using her husband's shovel as a walking stick, she led him along the buried ship and out of the mound.

Kirstin was left wondering if she had heard the woman rightly. Were her cryptic words a warning or a threat? The only other person close enough to have heard the whisper was the Norwegian driver. Kirstin noticed he wore a worried look.

"These damn farmers have been nothing but trouble," Carl sighed.

"They found a nice chest though," Otto said. "A little treasure never hurts if you want publicity."

Carl nodded. "My thoughts exactly. Almost everything else we've got is wood."

"Is it too dark to show me what you've done so far?" Kirstin asked.

Otto picked up a lamp. "Actually, Carl's work looks better in the dark. Come on, I'll show you where we found the dragon prow."

Kirstin followed him toward the ship's upcurved stem, a monumental arc of fluted planks and intricately carved reliefs. The artwork was among the finest she had ever seen—far more elaborate than on the smaller burial ships found at Gokstad and Tune.

Otto confided to her in a stage whisper, "This is where the first looters got in."

"You've had other looters?" Kirstin asked, surprised. "And you still didn't leave a guard?"

Carl quickly explained, "The other break-in was a thousand years ago, not long after the burial itself."

"Oh. Well, did they take much?"

Carl shrugged. "We don't know. They must have tunneled in from the front, since they hacked off the prow ornament on their way." He opened one of the crates beside the ship and took out a shiny oval clasp. "We also found this. Apparently a woman's hair ornament. An odd artifact to find with a ship, isn't it?" The curved surface was cast in a fishnet pattern like an elegant Easter egg.

Otto passed the fist-sized piece to Kirstin. "Just bronze. Not much for treasure hunters."

Kirstin handled the oval ornament. Somehow it seemed faintly familiar. Had it really been a hair clasp? And if so, whose? The thought brought her back to the vague warning of the old farmer's wife. "Have you found any human remains?"

Silently Carl reached into the crate and held up a thin, greenish bone in the lantern light.

A cold shiver ran up Kirstin's back. She rubbed her arms for warmth. She had helped excavate burial sites before. Why should this one cause a flicker of fear?

Carl said, "An ulna, from the forearm of our Viking king. Even a thousand years ago, grave robbers must have wanted the bones of the powerful. They dropped this one as they tunneled out."

Otto added, "We've been debating which king it was." He winked to Kirstin. "Of course I know your dragon theory favors Harald Fairhair."

"The newspapers can speculate as they like," Carl said, "but leaping to conclusions would be irresponsible. In the early 800s Norway was divided into thirty-one warring kingdoms, each with its own Viking chief."

"Nonetheless, Carl," Otto replied, "you must admit that the burial looks rich enough for an important king, and Oseberg is in Vestfold, Harald Fairhair's original realm."

But as the men stood talking, Kirstin had taken the bone in her hands. A chilly tingling began to run through her body. Unsteadily she laid the bone alongside her own white forearm.

From elbow to wrist the bone and her forearm were precisely the same length.

A cold wind swept across the meadows, shaking the creekside willows and whipping the folds of her dress. The distant cry of a gull drifted through the luminous dark blue already portending the Norwegian dawn.

"This bone is short for the arm of a king," Kirstin said quietly.

Carl nodded. "Yes, we know that men were shorter a thousand years ago."

"Have you considered that this may in fact be the burial of a *woman?*"

"A woman?" Carl wrinkled his brow skeptically. "The Vikings were led by men. Women weren't even allowed on warships like this."

Kirstin handed Carl the bone. "Does your university have a

laboratory that could analyze this ulna?"

"Well, yes," Carl hesitated. "But—"

"Then have it analyzed." The firmness in Kirstin's voice surprised even herself. Yet she didn't want to be treated as a student for the rest of the dig, and the ulna had given her such a strange chill. She aimed a steady smile at the excavation leader. "As you say, leaping to conclusions would be irresponsible."

Otto chuckled. "Touché, Carl. You lowered your saber and she's drawn first blood."

Carl's blue eyes flashed. "I think we're all a bit tired. Certainly Dr. Williams has had a long day." He motioned to the Norwegian driver. "Magnus, could you fetch the doctor's trunk and show her to her quarters?" Then he turned to Kirstin. "I hope you'll be comfortable in the tent we set up for Leland."

"Of course," Kirstin replied.

Carl gave her a slight bow. "Until tomorrow then."

Otto added, "It has been enchanting making your acquaintance." He caught up her hand and kissed it lightly. "Sweet dreams."

But as Kirstin followed Magnus down from the mound she was not at all sure her dreams that night would be calm. So many new worries had arisen: the lack of money to pay for excavation rights, the unfortunate friction between her and Carl, and the disturbing emotions this ancient burial site somehow aroused within her.

She slipped a small, smooth piece of ebony from her dress pocket, as she sometimes did when uneasy. The wooden burl's polished black curve had a comforting feel. It brought back memories of her last expedition with her father to India, when the British archeologists had entertained her with sightseeing side trips and dinners in Delhi. One of them had even proposed.

Of course she had turned down that offer, knowing marriage would have ended her career. Pleasant though the young man had been, he had imagined she wanted nothing more than to manage his home in Devonshire. Nor had it been the first such offer she'd refused.

Her father, the man who had fired her with ambition in the first place, had begun dropping hints that she was sacrificing too much for archeology. His warning, "Don't end up working in a museum," could be taken two ways. And the truth was, she did sometimes wonder, as she read of the tumultuous passions in the old sagas, how much she had missed.

"Here we are," Magnus announced, pulling her trunk from the buggy's rack.

Kirstin returned from her thoughts with a start. "Be careful, it's heavy."

"So it is," the Norwegian replied, but hoisted the load to his shoulder as if the trunk were a sailor's laundry duffel. He smiled as he balanced the weight. "What did you pack, your whole library?"

"Nearly, I'm afraid. You can't tell which sagas might prove useful at a dig like this." She picked up his lantern, lighting a trampled path about the base of the mound.

"I like Njal's myself," Magnus said.

"Pardon?"

"Njal's saga. Where Gunnar holds off twenty attackers with his arrows, defending his clan's honor. Then he finally dies when his bowstring breaks and his wife refuses to replace it with a few strands of her hair. She's splendid when she tells Njal, 'I would just remind you of a slap you once gave me.'"

Kirstin knew the epic, but was surprised that this laborer did too. She looked more carefully at Magnus. In his seaman's cap and work clothes he hardly seemed a scholar. His short, reddish beard, craggy features, and unruly blond hair gave him a ruggedly attractive look. Had Carl introduced him as the excavation's labor manager? She had been barraged with so much information since her arrival at the train station, she'd forgotten.

"How do you know the sagas?" she asked.

"I picked up a little Icelandic the season I shipped out on a cod boat from Reykjavik. The men I bunked with read the old stories out loud like newspapers. They'd argue half the night about heroes a thousand years dead."

Kirstin nodded at the explanation. She had heard that Icelanders still read the sagas during their long winter nights. Unlike the Norwegian language, Icelandic had hardly changed since the days when all the North spoke Norse.

When they reached the first of a cluster of tents, Magnus swung her trunk inside and lit a candle. "Best I could do here at camp."

She glanced about at the simple cot, straightback chair, and shelves made of boxes. The grimness was broken by a few touches: a wildflower bouquet in a beer bottle, a little mirror hung on a tent post. Tired as she was, she appreciated the effort. "Thanks. It'll do fine."

"Then sleep well," he said. But before leaving he paused in the opening of the tent. "And I'm sorry about your dress. I haven't seen embroidery like that for years."

As the tent flap closed behind him she looked down at her long dress. The stylized pattern of eagles about the hem was torn and spattered with mud from the site. She had worked so hard reconstructing the pattern from childhood memories of the embroidered Norwegian aprons her mother had once worn, before she had learned to dress like an American. No one else had even noticed.

Wearily Kirstin unbuttoned the dress and put on a white flannel nightgown from the trunk. Then she paused, studying herself in the little round mirror.

She knew she was not beautiful—her unfortunately high, white forehead saw to that. But she did have many of the features of a classic Nordic beauty: clear blue eyes, high cheekbones, and full blond hair. She undid the bun and shook her hair down about her shoulders.

She remembered how Otto had kissed her hand. He was a jesting sort, and she hadn't attached any particular significance to the kiss. But Carl had been watching with a stern look.

She leaned forward and blew out the candle.

The sudden darkness reminded her how alone she was. In the tent beside the ancient grave, fear fluttered like a shadowy moth.

She lay down on the stiff cot and pulled the comforter to her lips. She watched the snuffed candle's smoke curl up toward the canvas roof, faintly lit by the ghostly glow of the night dawn.

And she drifted toward a fitful sleep, thinking again of the farm wife's strangely mismatched eyes.

CHAPTER 5
SPRING, 827

A wild-eyed Viking appeared before Asa, his long hair and tunic dripping with salt spray. "Eirik is coming!"

Asa caught her breath. After two winters as Guthroth's queen, she had almost stopped expecting Eirik's help. She glanced to her husband.

The king merely spun the hand ax he used as a walking stick. "How many ships? When?"

"Twenty longships under the black eagle banner. We turned after sighting them by Hafrsfjord. They could be here as early as tomorrow."

"So slow?"

The Viking proudly wiped the strands of hair from his face. "Horthalanders do not dare to sail on moonless nights."

Guthroth smiled. He slipped a gold ring from his finger for the man. "Well done. Have the lookouts on the headlands ready bonfires. And tell Olav we'll drink to the coming victory tonight at the Vik. But do not alarm the townspeople." Then he extended an arm to Asa, indicating with a nod that they would continue.

"Shouldn't we return to the Vik?" Asa asked. Suddenly she felt an urge to check on the baby. She also wanted time to rethink her plans. No foreign fleet had ever attempted to attack the Vikings in their home fjord. Could Eirik's daring armada succeed?

"Your old suitor is always late. I came to Skiringssal to buy clasps for your cloak, and I intend to do it."

"But—"

"Come. I know you enjoy the town."

She knew there was no arguing with Guthroth. The real reason he

38

would not change plans, she guessed, was to show his troops how little fear he felt. Perhaps, Asa thought, Guthroth's stubbornness would give Eirik a much needed advantage.

And it was true that she found Skiringssal exciting. There was nothing else like it in Norway—a village of independent craftsmen, merchants, and scoundrels, all thriving under the protection of the Vik. In the thatch-roofed houses jammed along the narrow streets one could buy Italian glass beads, Irish harnesses, Arabian spices, and dozens of other luxuries unknown in the rest of the North.

Along the bayfront, fishermen repaired their nets while washerwomen thumped linen with wooden paddles. Away from the docks, the tangy smell of fish blended with wood smoke and the insidious redolence of unseen privies. Rich farmers in pleated pantaloons trotted through the streets on short Norse ponies. Scar-faced men gambled in the corners with dice. A one-armed drover bumped a wagonload of soapstone cooking bowls down a lane paved with logs. Women with their hair in tall, complicated knots fetched well water in buckets.

One and all, the people stopped as Guthroth's bodyguards filled the street five abreast. Everyone craned their necks for a glimpse of Asa, the beautiful young queen, resplendent in her ivory headdress and trailing crimson cloak.

Suddenly Guthroth laughed. "Bjorgolf!" He held out his hand to a Viking buying a slave from a street merchant. "Is this what you do with the gold I give you?"

The slave merchant started so violently at the outcry that he jangled the little balance scale he had been unfolding. Bjorgolf seemed nearly as surprised. "King, I did not sail this summer, and need a slave."

The king sized up the bound slave, a fine-featured, square-shouldered blond man with glistening eyes. Then he asked Bjorgolf, "How much does the merchant want?"

"A pound." Bjorgolf showed the mark on his spiral silver bracelet where he had already begun to cut off the payment. "But it is a fine ware."

Guthroth ran his hand through the slave's blond hair. Yellow powder clung to his fingers. "We took red-haired Skirings like this from the Isle of Man. This one's been given drops for shiny eyes and has a painted face as well. Go on, open the tunic. You'll find shoulder pads."

Outraged, the Viking ripped the slave's shirt from the neck down.

Not only did a wad of cloth tumble from the shoulder, but a pink-tipped breast sagged loose.

"A woman!" Bjorgolf exclaimed. " It's not worth half a pound."

Guthroth motioned for his retainers to stay with Bjorgolf. "See that they settle fairly. The queen and I will be in the metalsmith's hall. Alone."

As the king led her toward the nearby hall, Asa couldn't help looking back. She had been raised to take slaves for granted. They were fated to their work as naturally as horses were fated to fields. But the unmasking of this silent, foreign woman, who now proudly clutched her torn tunic to her breast, stirred Asa's sympathy. Asa herself had been stolen. Kalf had been unjustly enslaved. The Vikings brought hundreds of fresh captives from their voyages each summer. What did Guthroth really know about the people they sold?

Guthroth kicked open the door of a blacksmith shop and glanced inside, his hand on the hilt of his sword. The reek of charcoal, wax, and sweat met them like an invisible wall. "Thorleif!"

The smith stood silhouetted in red by the glow of the coals, an old man with stringy, sweat-glistened muscles. He laid his hammer and tongs on a stump beside his anvil. When Asa's eyes adjusted to the hall's murk, she realized the man was grinning. Short whiskers bristled like nails pounded into his jutting jaw. Behind the coals a decrepit, bald servant dropped the handles of the bellows and moved his hand repeatedly between his forehead, chest, and shoulders in the cross-shaped motion peculiar to slaves of the Skiring faith.

"Do you have the clasps?" Guthroth asked.

"Have I ever failed you?" The smith nodded to the slave, who scurried across the room to fetch a bundle wrapped in cloth.

Guthroth reached out for the bundle, but the smith caught the king's hand. "Don't touch them!"

Asa expected Guthroth would strike the insolent man dead. No commoner spoke to the king in such a tone. To her astonishment the king withdrew his hand.

Thorleif's beard bristled again as he grinned. "They have been wrought for woman, not man. Look at them, Queen Asa. They are for you."

Uncertainly, she lifted a corner of the cloth. Blue, red, and green gemstones glittered at her from swirls of beaded gold filigree. With a murmur of surprise, she uncovered two heavy rectangular gold clasps, studded with luminous jewels she knew could never have been mined in the North. Each clasp had two parts that snapped together with a click. "They're beautiful," she whispered.

"There is a hidden spring," the smith said. "Press the blue stone to unhook them."

"Ingenious! This must have taken months of work."

Guthroth smiled, obviously relieved by her reaction. "Will you wear them?"

She looked up at the aging king, moved. For the first time she saw him as a man she might have loved. "So this is why you would not turn back to the Vik. You are a generous husband, Guthroth."

He nodded to the smith. "Thorleif's work has no equal. It was Thorleif himself who forged Fenris."

"Fenris?" She knew the word only as the name of the fearsome Nordic wolf-god.

Guthroth quoted to the smith,

> "Let one know and none other.
> If three know, thousands will."

Then he slid his sword from its leather scabbard and flexed the blade in the red glow of the coals.

Asa tensed, as she always did at the sight of the sword that had killed her father. As long as she lived with this man, she would never forget the vengeance she had sworn. The hated sword was not straight, but had a wavy edge. The metal itself was banded with damascened patterns of silver and dark gray. Now for the first time she noticed the outline of a wolf and a line of runes engraved on the blade.

"Thirteen rods of iron and steel," the smith said proudly. "Twisted, welded, and beaten thin, until they became so strong the blade can be bent double."

Guthroth said, "I had seen thirteen winters when my great-grandfather Halfdan Whiteleg ordered Fenris forged to accompany me on the first great sea crossing of warriors from the Vik. We captured the treasures of the Lindisfarne monastery and returned to build Skiringssal. A clever goldsmith slave wasn't all I brought back to reward Thorleif's skill."

"But Fenris is an evil god," Asa objected.

41

"And a dread sword," Guthroth added. "Just as the wolf-god will live to slay Odin at Ragnarök, this sword will still be wielded in the final battle, the twilight of the gods."

As Guthroth held the ripple-edged sword, it seemed to Asa the manifestation of the rapacious Viking spirit upon which she had vowed vengeance. In that moment it almost seemed possible that the evil she despised might be separated from her brash husband as easily as a sword is knocked from a man's hand. If only!

The king slid the sword into its sheath. "I wanted no lesser smith than Thorleif to forge your clasps. Remove the old ones and fasten the new."

Self-consciously Asa gathered her trailing red cloak onto her arm and unpinned the oval bronze brooches that held it at her shoulders. No sooner had she laid them aside than Guthroth gave them to the smith with the gruff command, "Melt them down."

"No!" Asa cried.

"And why not? A queen deserves better than bronze."

Asa hesitated, afraid to admit she cherished the oval brooches because they had been a gift from Kalf — an improper gift to be sure, and from a man who was now a slave.

The old smith carefully ran his fingers over the fishnet pattern on the bronze, looking from the king to the beautiful young queen. "I have aided you a long time, Guthroth," he said slowly. Was there a touch of regret in his voice? "These old brooches are finely wrought. I believe the queen should keep them."

Again Asa was surprised by the smith's daring.

"But you can hardly wear both at once," the old smith added. "The new ones are made to be sewn onto the cloak itself. Bhaldec will take you to my wife for the sewing while I speak with the king."

Asa nodded her gratitude to Thorleif. Then, gathering the jewelry in her cloak, she followed the stooped slave through a back door.

The doorway did not lead outside, but rather to a corridor between the building's walls — a mud-plastered inner wall of woven willow branches and a solid outer wall of wooden staves. She began to ask where the corridor led, but Bhaldec only turned to her and gurgled, demonstrating all too clearly that his tongue had been cut out.

Asa knew such gruesome mutilations were common only to the oldest of the Vik's slaves — those taken before the Vikings learned that

the Skirings' gibbering holy men were not only harmless, but also worth more if taught to speak Norse.

"Then you are the goldsmith from Lindisfarne that the king mentioned."

Bhaldec nodded, watching her warily.

She thought of this man, who had no doubt spent the first half of his life creating treasures for the gods of his own temple. Now he was condemned to spend the second half of his life recasting his people's gold for his captors. She held up the clasps. "Did you make these?"

He shook his head quickly, making cross-shaped motions on his chest. Then he pointed urgently down the corridor and hobbled ahead.

Soon the corridor branched. The bald slave led Asa down a narrow stone stairway to a chamber lit only by a smoke-hole in the straw roof. In the middle of the room, a white-haired woman was lifting a dripping red mass of wool from a cauldron suspended above a fire.

"Come in, Queen, come in. I am called Groa."

Asa stopped at the old woman's glance, for her eyes did not match. One was blue while the other was a chilling green.

"Don't be afraid, child. I am a weaver like yourself. A friend. Give me the cloak." Her bony fingers took the cloth and spread it on a broad bench along the stone wall. Nimbly she began measuring for the clasps' placement. "My husband sent you without the king?"

The woman's calm voice did not reassure her. Asa replied, "He spoke against Guthroth without fear. How does he dare?"

"We forged Fenris," the old woman said, as if this explained everything.

"The sword that killed my father?"

43

The old woman frowned. "Yes." As she stitched she kept time with an old verse,

> "An ax-age, a sword-age,
> Shields are sundered.
> A storm-age, a wolf-age,
> While the world crumbles.
> The sun grows black;
> Earth sinks into the sea.
> Stars fall from the skies.
> Fire roars and smoke rages.
> The leaping flames
> Lick Heaven itself."

Asa watched her cautiously. "Guthroth said the sword would swing at Ragnarök."

"He said no more?"

Asa shook her head.

The old woman sewed the clasps tight. Then she lowered her voice to a hoarse whisper. "Dark powers were welded in that weapon's making. The runes on Fenris hold the bearer invulnerable to the steel of warriors."

Suddenly Asa recalled how her father's sword had struck Guthroth on the shoulder during their battle, but had mysteriously slid off without cutting. Sorcery! She struggled against an inner voice of panic that told her to flee. To save Eirik she would have to face this old woman, even if the witch changed herself into a dragon.

"Then the men of the Vik do not win their battles fairly," Asa said, her chin high.

"That is true." The old woman lowered her unsettling gaze. "We have begun to regret what was unleashed. But neither Thorleif nor I can undo such a curse. The sword carries a debt to the gods invoked in its making."

"Eirik is coming, perhaps tomorrow," Asa said. "If you have regrets, spare him the fate of my father. Give him a weapon against Fenris."

"No one can win the coming battle but you," the old woman said.

"Me? I have no skill with swords."

"The greatest battles are not won by swords." The old woman lifted the finished cloak and wrapped it about Asa's shoulders. "Look carefully at the clasps, child."

Asa looked again at the ornamentation. This time she began to discern a picture in the patterns of gold wire between the jewels. There was a filigreed man with staring eyes. The figure held a hammer above a large wire braid. "It's Thor forging the chain to bind the wolf-god."

She stopped, weighing the significance of the legend. She too needed to bind the wolf-god, the evil that Fenris represented. She looked to Groa. "But in the story, Thor's chain broke. The only leash ever to hold Fenris came from the dwarves of Hel."

"Yes," Groa nodded. "And what else do you know of the evil god's leash?"

"It was said to look like a mere wisp of thread. It was woven from the footfalls of cats and the breath of fish."

The old woman snapped the clasps in place. "Learn from this, Queen."

"How—"

"Learn. There is little time."

CHAPTER 6
SUMMER, 1904

Kirstin jerked upright with a small cry. Her nightgown twisted across her damp body.

A man's voice outside the tent asked, "Are you all right, Kirstin?"

It was Otto, in his own tent a few yards away. She breathed a little easier. "Yes. I'm all right. It was just a dream. A bad dream." Then she closed her eyes and sank back with a sigh. Every morning at the excavation she had awakened from dark struggles just beyond her consciousness. Lack of sleep left her drained.

She could hear Otto's cot squeak as he sat on its edge, no doubt trimming his beard, or perhaps tying the ridiculous bow tie he insisted on wearing, even when working on his knees in the dirt. He had gotten into the habit of talking to her through the canvas to help her wake up in the mornings, partly because she had no alarm clock and partly because she really did tend to oversleep, given a chance. At some point he had started calling her by her first name, and she had allowed it.

"I haven't slept very well since I came here either," Otto remarked. "Of course I've got Carl's tent on the other side, and he snores like a buzz saw."

She smiled and dabbed the perspiration from her face with the corner of a sheet. "At least you have an excuse. You'd think I'd sleep like a rock after staying up so late."

"But that's just it, Kirstin. You've been working too hard."

He was right, of course. With the strain she had been under, cataloging thousands of wooden fragments, it was no wonder her mind followed strange pathways at night. But she wasn't about to admit her ambition to Otto. He would think she was just trying to prove herself to Carl—and that wasn't her point at all. She wanted to prove herself to herself.

"Haff you had zese nightmares before?" The German accent drifting through the tent wall was suddenly much thicker.

She laughed. "A few times, Dr. Freud."

"Vell! Vould it help if you talked about it?"

"I wish I could." She sighed. "All I can remember are the feelings that went with them." There had been anger and loss. And fear too — genuine fear.

"Can't you recall anything else?"

"Not really."

Except possibly . . . the chest.

The trunk from the grave room was still sealed shut with the rust of a millennium. So how was she able to picture it wide open, glittering with mounds of silver coins, a silver goblet, and a thick gold necklace? The haunting image seemed to have come from one of the dreams.

Kirstin wrinkled her brow and stared across the tent.

"Then ve need to continue ze therapy." Otto dropped the heavy accent. "But first I think it's time we showed up at the dig for Carl's little fundraising scheme. They'll be opening the chest in a few minutes."

"What!" Kirstin gasped. How could she have forgotten that this was the day of the ceremony? "Why didn't you tell me?"

Otto sounded bewildered. "But that's precisely why I came to —"

"Enough! I've got to get ready." She leaped to the wash basin. Her skin stiffened at the shock of the icy water, and then burned as she hurriedly toweled off in the chill morning air. Time was short and the work dress was wrinkled beyond hope. She pulled on her new, more practical khaki pants. Then she slipped on an embroidered blouse and jacket, brushed her hair before the frustratingly small mirror, tied her hair up into a bun, and strode out toward the dig.

Otto, waiting just outside his tent, raised his bushy eyebrows when he saw her outfit.

Kirstin shook her head. "You'd think a man had never seen pants before."

"Well, bicycling perhaps, but here?"

"My work at the dig is every bit as demanding as a bicycle tour."

Otto shrugged and followed her to the far side of the mound, where a crowd of reporters, townsfolk, and curious farmers had gathered. She pushed her way through the throng of jostling men in vests and bowler hats. Magnus, the labor manager, waved them past a rope railing that held the crowd away from the excavation itself.

A bespectacled gentleman in a top hat stood beside the unopened chest, addressing the crowd. The onlookers were fidgeting or looking at the ground. As soon as Kirstin heard the dignitary's lilting Stockholm dialect, bristling with Swedish words, she understood the audience's restlessness.

"On behalf of His Majesty, King Oscar II, I wish to thank Kristiania University for undertaking the excavation which now is about to relinquish the treasure of one of the earliest Norwegian monarchs— quite possibly the great Harald Fairhair—to our current monarch in Stockholm."

Amid the thin applause that followed were several jeers.

The gentleman's eyes flashed at the crowd. "Because of the significance of what we may uncover here, the Ministry of Defense has provided an honor guard to assure safe transit to Sweden. Dr. Söderfelt?"

While Carl stepped forward, Kirstin noticed that there actually were half a dozen soldiers at the periphery of the crowd. Though apparently unarmed, they wore the crisp, blue-and-gold uniforms of the Swedish military.

Carl took out a paper and began, "Thank you, Mr. Dödkvist. First let me—"

"Louder!" a voice called out.

The archeologist reddened and raised his voice. "First, let me emphasize that the ship burial most likely is not that of Harald Fairhair, reports in the press notwithstanding. At the suggestion of our American advisor, Kirstin Williams—" he glanced to Kirstin. When he saw her pants outfit he stopped a second, obviously taken aback. But then he continued, "At Dr. Williams' suggestion we have analyzed the bones and learned that they belong to not one, but to two incomplete skeletons."

"Can you tell which one's the king?" a harsh-voiced reporter shouted.

Carl frowned. "If we are to believe the initial lab report, based on the shape of the individual bones, both of the skeletons are *female*."

For a moment the audience was silent. Kirstin looked out at the crowd of men, hoping to register their surprise. The faces she saw, however, revealed only puzzlement and doubt. Finally a tall reporter

CHAPTER 6 ~ 1904

aimed his pencil at Carl. "Are you trying to say this whole ship belonged to some kind of Viking *queen?*"

"Of course the lab may be mistaken. But the initial tests indicate one female aged sixty to seventy and another female about thirty."

The harsh-voiced reporter called, "Well, which one's the queen?" The audience laughed.

Carl sighed. "Dr. Williams. Could you explain your theory?"

Kirstin stepped forward, fighting stage fright. Although she had spoken to large groups of men before, this crowd seemed particularly unruly. She raised her hands for silence. "I understand your skepticism, gentlemen. But the skeletal remains suggest two hypotheses—either that the grave was raised for an aged queen and her handmaiden, or that it belonged to an aged serving woman and a queen who died young."

A grinning reporter called out, "Do you think this queen of yours was a suffragette, too?" While the crowd laughed, a photographer's magnesium pan flashed and smoke billowed. A second cameraman yelled, "Take a step, Doc, so we can see the Bloomers!"

Kirstin flushed, but did not flinch. Her best hope, she decided, was to ignore the hecklers and sally onward. The thought of the Viking queen added to her conviction. Surely that woman, a thousand years before, had faced even less tolerant men. Kirstin's voice rang across the crowd. "Whether the queen died young or old, it appears she was given a larger ship burial than any known Viking king. I believe this should change how we view the role of women in the Viking age."

Otto held up his hands in front of the photographers. "Save your film for the treasure chest, gentlemen." He glanced to Carl. "Can't we move on?"

"Yes, yes, of course." Carl cleared his throat and motioned Magnus to his side. As they bent over the ancient trunk the onlookers finally quieted. The chest's curved oak lid was encased in iron bands, studded with heavy rivets. The lock, however, had rusted to almost nothing. Cautiously the two men began to lift. A ring of powdered rust fell about the chest's sides.

Kirstin held her breath.

As the lid slowly rose, three photographers set off brilliant fireballs, each with the whoomf! of a cannon's salute. But when the smoke cleared, there was no heap of glinting silver. Instead the chest was

49

neatly packed with a variety of dark objects of wood and iron.

For a moment Kirstin was dumbfounded that her dream had been wrong. In the back of her mind she had wanted to believe her tantalizing vision.

But wrong it was. Where Kirstin had pictured the gold neckband, Carl lifted out a simple wooden bowl. Where she recalled a silver goblet, he removed an iron lamp. One by one, Carl examined and gently lifted the artifacts onto a nearby table. Kirstin cataloged them in turn, and as she did, her disappointment faded. Instead she began to marvel at the variety of thousand-year-old objects emerging from the chest. There was a foot-long comb. A hazelnut. An awl. A small wooden club. A spindle with rotted thread. A wooden bucket filled with the shriveled skins of what appeared to be apples.

The reporters began putting their notepads away. "No treasure?" one of them asked.

Carl looked at them blankly. "Don't you understand the importance of this?" Reverently, he lifted a pair of U-shaped shears from the chest.

The Oseberg farmer—for he too had come to the ceremony—jutted his weathered face from the crowd and mocked, "I got three pairs of sheep shears better than that in my barn!"

The crowd roared.

"You're laughing because these are everyday things," Kirstin said, her voice strong. "But until this moment we didn't know the Vikings even *had* shears—much less that they could make spring steel. Museums are already full of swords and jewelry from Viking graves. She pointed to the chest. Here is a *scientific* treasure. Everyday tools and wooden artifacts that can finally show us how Vikings actually lived."

Meanwhile, Carl was peering into the trunk again, but with a puzzled frown. "Can we get a photographer here? I want to record this final artifact *in situ*."

"What is it?" Otto asked, but Carl held him back. The reporters, too, seemed to have regained their interest.

Only after a picture had been taken did Carl reach into the chest again. He withdrew a stack of thirty square wooden cards. Each of the little wooden plates had holes drilled in its rounded corners. Carl examined them uncertainly. "I've never seen anything like it."

"Neither have I," Otto said. "Is it some kind of riddle?"

A reporter leaned out. "Dr. Söderfelt, what do you think the riddle means?"

Carl shrugged. "Perhaps they're for record-keeping. Or gambling, maybe."

Kirstin had been stifling a smile at the men. "Actually, they're weaving cards."

"Weaving cards?" Otto asked.

"Of course. I myself once had a set. Every girl from Hordaland does. You thread strings through the holes and then twist the cards as you weave. I'm sure you've seen patterned belts made with them."

"Ah," Carl said. "As in peasant dresses. A tradition evidently much older than we thought."

"Yes. And it shows the grave really does belong to a woman. The shears, the spindle, the loom—all weaving tools."

A reporter scoffed, "A weaving woman, then. But no queen."

There was a silence as the obvious truth of this statement sank in. There were no royal robes, no golden crowns, and no jewels. The chest contained the mundane possessions of a farmwife.

Kirstin looked to Carl. "If this isn't a queen, why on earth was she buried in a fully-equipped Viking warship?"

Carl sighed. "I know how important the queen theory was to you."

His gentle tone made Kirstin wonder if he disliked her less than he let on. Or was this more of his patronizing chivalry? He had given her a chance to take credit for her startling theory, even though he must have developed alternative ideas of his own. She asked, "If the ship wasn't buried for a queen, then who do you think it was buried for?"

"A god."

Several reporters began asking questions at once. Carl motioned for them to be silent. "In light of what we've seen, the women in the grave chamber were probably slaves, sacrificed with the ship as part of a Nordic cult ritual."

Otto stroked his beard thoughtfully. "But the ornamentation of the ship itself is so extraordinarily rich for a cult sacrifice."

"Then consider the origin of the name *Oseberg*," Carl said. "Of course, berg means 'hill' in Old Norse. But Ose derives from Aesir, the name of the race of Nordic gods. In short, Oseberg was the 'hill of the gods'—a holy site."

Kirstin's heart sank at this devastating argument. Why hadn't she thought of *Aesirberg* herself, before making a fool of herself with her talk about queens?

Otto commented, "Odd that no one has found other cult mounds with such treasures."

"Liars!"

All eyes turned to the Oseberg farmer, who had ducked under the rope railing and was aiming his withered finger at Carl as though it were a gun. "You stand there bickering, but the truth is, there's no treasure here at all. You promised to pay the lease on this land with the reward. Where's my money?"

Carl reddened. "This is not the time to —"

"Then when?"

Carl glanced to the gentleman in a top hat. "Very well. Let's ask Mr. Dödkvist himself. The university has spent nearly all of its archeology budget and is waiting for funding from the Ministry of the Interior. When can we expect government support?"

The dignitary nodded seriously. "As I said, we'll provide everything you need for transportation. Of course the king can only offer a finder's reward for precious metals." He hesitated. "Shouldn't the Norwegian parliament be helping with the on-site expenses?"

Magnus strode forward. The red-bearded Norwegian stood a head taller than the official. "Our parliament has no money because our taxes go to Sweden."

Several voices in the crowd called out, "That's right!"

Magnus continued, "I've been supervising a dozen men who've worked here almost a month at half pay. They've got families in Tønsberg. They don't need honor guards. They need wages."

Mr. Dödkvist frowned. "I understand. Times are hard throughout the kingdom. That's why the Interior Ministry wants to share the financial burden. You people handle the local costs and we'll pay for freighting the major artifacts and the ship itself by rail to Stockholm, where they can be displayed properly."

"But Mr. Dödkvist," Carl said, obviously dismayed. "This excavation is under the auspices of the university in Kristiania. Naturally, I had hoped to bring the finds there." He glanced to Otto and Kirstin as if for help.

Kirstin asked, "Doesn't the king's right to archeological finds extend only to gold and silver? Since we haven't unearthed any precious metals, I'd think the artifacts could remain in Norway."

The dignitary smiled. "Yes, of course. A sampling of the artifacts should stay in Tønsberg and Kristiania. But a find of this scale is simply too important to waste in provincial museums. The Minister of the Interior has assigned me to see the Oseberg ship brought to Sweden."

Suddenly Magnus gripped the front of the man's suit in his massive fist. "The hell you will. You've taken our freedom and our taxes, but you'll not get our history, too." He let go with a small push. "Now get out."

"Of all the—!" Mr. Dödkvist flushed. "This is an assault on the authority of the Swedish crown. Guards!"

But as the uniformed men pushed forward, the crowd broke into shouts. Fists flew when the workers tried to hold their ground at the rope. Townspeople and reporters ducked for cover or joined in. The Oseberg farmer gave a terrifying battle cry, swinging a shovel indiscriminately. Kirstin noticed Otto standing helplessly in the midst of the fracas, looking dazed. She managed to grab him by the arm and pull him toward the safety of the tents.

Her last glimpse of the ceremony was of Magnus, his sleeves rolled up, wading through the brawl.

* * *

That afternoon Kirstin slowly turned the weaving cards over in her hands. After the crowd had dispersed and quiet had returned to the camp, she had taken the ancient chest to a work tent for closer study. Now, as she ran her fingers over the wooden cards, worn smooth with use, she found herself wondering about the Viking women who had held these tools a thousand years ago. What would they have told her if they could?

Kirstin sighed. With a touch of loneliness she realized that she felt closer to the shadowy Viking women than to any of her real colleagues at the excavation. She had wanted the challenge of proving herself in a world of men, and instead she had found isolation. Had the Viking women felt the same? She wanted to ask them what they had woven, what they had dreamed. And who had they been?

"Ah, Dr. Williams." Carl pushed past the tent's flap. "Forgive me for interrupting."

"That's quite all right, Dr. Söderfelt." Since the ceremony she had begun to feel a little more sympathetic toward Carl. Even he hadn't deserved such a debacle. "Actually, I was hoping we could talk. Do you have time for coffee?"

"Coffee?" He looked at his watch. "Yes, if you like."

She closed her catalog book and led the way across a dusty opening to the dining tent. How could she get him to talk more openly? Since the disastrous chest-opening ceremony, the excavation's problems would only be worse. They needed to work together. As she poured them each a cup from the pot on the woodstove, she said, "I'm sorry about this morning."

"Is that what's bothering you?" he asked, taking his cup to a table.

"Partly, yes."

"You know, for a while I almost believed in your dragon legends. If this had been a famous king's grave, we might have convinced private donors to fund the rest of the excavation."

His words cut. Kirstin had come to Norway hoping the ship was the legendary "dragon" that built Harald Fairhair's empire. When they learned the burial's bones belonged to a woman, Kirstin had jumped at the theory of a Viking queen. Now even that seemed wrong. At every turn, her intuition seemed to be leading her astray.

"How much money do we have left?" Kirstin asked.

"Not much."

Why wouldn't he tell her outright? It irked her that Carl insisted on keeping a wall around his power. "Maybe we should talk with Otto," she suggested. "The German Kaiser always seems to have money for archeology."

Carl sat back. "Well, since you bring it up, it turns out Otto has already contacted the German Science Academy on his own."

"Oh?"

"Yes. After the press conference he showed me a telegram from Berlin. They're offering five thousand crowns."

"Excellent," Kirstin said. "That should be enough to buy the farmer's rights and pay the workers full wages."

Carl shook his head. "Actually, it's hardly half what we'll need. And there's a catch."

"A catch?"

"Oh yes. Don't be misled by Otto's sense of humor. He and his Kaiser have a competitive streak."

"What do they want?"

"The ship, of course. We'd have to display the artifacts permanently in Berlin."

"I see." Kirstin felt her sympathy subtly shift at this news. Was this why Otto had been so friendly with her? To win Oseberg's archeological treasures for Germany at a bargain price? She remembered how boldly Magnus had defied the Swedish official earlier that day, insisting that the artifacts should stay in Norway. Apparently Otto saw the excavation as an opportunity to move the ship to Germany. And where were Carl's loyalties?

"Would you accept the offer?" she asked, looking at him squarely.

"It puts me in a difficult situation," Carl sighed. "The German Academy wants to buy the ship. The Swedish government claims to own it. And the Norwegians want to keep it."

"So what will it be?" Kirstin asked. "German money, Swedish responsibility, or Norwegian honor?"

"Those are the choices." Carl frowned. He turned the coffee cup in his hands. Finally he said, "In my opinion, Otto should never have asked for the German money at all. It's simply not right to take artifacts out of a country."

Kirstin was glad that he had chosen the honorable path. Perhaps she would yet be proud to be working with this man. "I think you're right. The ship belongs in Norway."

"Then we finally agree, Kirstin," he said, brushing her hand with his as he set down his cup. He added, "You don't mind if I call you Kirstin?"

"I suppose not. Otto does." But it did give her an odd feeling. She moved her hand to her lap. Carl had treated her with an aloof, formal manner for so long—and she had encouraged it, if only to make him pay for his earlier disrespect. Could she have been mistaken about his arrogance? At the chest opening ceremony he had given her more than a fair chance to make a case for her unlikely queen theory. Obviously he did understand her ambition.

"Good. Then I hope you'll call me Carl." He glanced up at her with a smile.

She tilted her head. She had wanted more openness, but she wasn't sure she wanted—or trusted—the familiarity that had come along with it. "Very well, Carl."

* * *

That evening a haunting melody floated out on the evening sea breeze. Eyes closed, Kirstin leaned against a tree, pursing her lips to play the tune. The hollow tones of her wooden flute fitted the slowly lilting, melancholy music well. She couldn't remember where she had first learned the old melody. Certainly it had no words.

When the verse broke off—she could hardly say it ended, for it stopped, seemingly unfinished, on the second tone of the scale—she opened her eyes. Above, through the leaves of a beech tree, rose the red brick towers and green copper steeples of Slagen church. To the south a few white sails still dotted the dark blue stripe of Tønsberg fjord. Below the church hill stood a flock of board-and-batten farmhouses, red with white trim, peering from the broad valley's fields like stray cattle. To the north, near the meandering curve of willows marking a creek, was a brown hill: the Oseberg mound.

Kirstin often played her flute to settle her thoughts. The comforting old music seemed to put her worries in perspective. But now it was time to return. Night was already falling.

Slowly she put away the flute and walked back along the dirt road toward Oseberg. The tents were dark, so she knew the others must already be in bed. To her surprise, however, a lantern glowed faintly from the top of the excavation's hill. Who could it be? Surely not more looters.

Alarmed, she hurried toward the mound to check on the ship. Her heart sped when she made out the shape of a man crouched near the grave chamber.

The man suddenly wheeled about, a digging trowel in his hand.

"Magnus?" She asked, incredulous. Could their own labor manager be a thief?

"Dr. Williams! Look at these carvings."

"What on earth are you doing?"

The big Norwegian looked straight at her. "Working."

"Alone? At night?"

"I have to stand watch anyway. Look. What do you make of these?" He held the lantern over an area marked by strings, where two arm-length posts lay partly buried.

Kirstin's suspicions retreated somewhat. After all, Magnus was the one who had caught the Oseberg farmer digging for treasure the night she had arrived. And now she recalled that he really was supposed to be on watch. But something still bothered her about the thought of him working without supervision at night.

"All right, let's see what you've found." She pulled back a loose strand of hair and knelt to examine the artifacts more closely.

The wooden posts were densely covered with carved patterns of abstract curls and grotesque beasts. "These are exquisite," she said quietly, running her finger over the wood. For a moment Kirstin was so captivated by the intertwined patterns that she missed the larger representation. Then she raised her eyebrows. The curved posts were arching necks. At their heads were bulging eyes and toothed jaws.

"More dragons!" Kirstin whispered.

"Looks like it. Think they tie in with your dragon legend?"

"Unlikely, I'm afraid," she said. "Slave women would hardly have been building empires."

"Still, dragon sculptures are valuable."

Did he really know how salable such carvings would be in the art market? Kirstin found the thought disturbing. Dragon statues were just the sort of Viking artifacts a looter might seek out.

Magnus knelt beside her, pointing with a camel-hair brush. "This one has the same style of biting beast motif as the ship's prow."

"Possibly made by the same person," Kirstin mused, watching him from the side. "It must have taken a first-rate artist months to carve."

Magnus nodded. "And look here." He carefully dusted a twisted iron bar in the dragon's mouth.

"A sort of bridle," Kirstin said. He seemed so genuinely enthused — so sincere — that it was hard to doubt his honesty. Kneeling beside

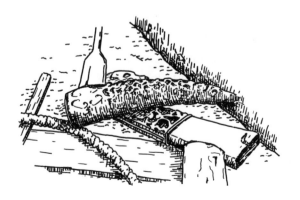

THE SHIP IN THE HILL

him in the shadowy excavation gave her a strangely conspiratorial feeling. "I wonder if these could be ship's figureheads? Sometimes prow ornaments were removed when ships beached so they wouldn't frighten the land's spirits."

"I doubt they'd fit on a prow." He pointed to a peculiar, broom-stick-like shaft protruding from the statue's blunt base.

"Then what were they for?"

For a minute neither spoke. Magnus gently brushed the carvings. His sleeves were rolled up nearly to his shoulders, and Kirstin found herself watching his powerfully muscled arm, with its sheen of reddish-blond hair. The closeness of such a strong, ruggedly handsome man gave her a flutter of warning.

She stood up. "Whatever the posts are, they're obviously important. Please don't excavate them any further until I can help tomorrow."

"Tomorrow? But as long as you're here now —"

"I'm sorry, I'm tired. I haven't been sleeping well."

"I have trouble sleeping too sometimes. Nightmares, I guess." Magnus's blue eyes gave her a piercing look.

She nearly mentioned her own disturbing dreams. But she caught herself in time. Certainly the labor manager did not need to know about her personal life. And besides, now that her vision of the trasure chest had proven false, she knew the unpleasant dreams would be ending soon. Even as a girl she had been able to end a dream by confronting it with the knowledge that it wasn't true.

She gave him a firm smile. "Good night, Magnus."

"Here, let me accompany you with the lantern."

"I'll manage alone, thank you." It was not yet pitch dark, and she didn't want to be seen returning to her tent this late with one of the working men. In a small camp, rumors had wings.

Magnus held up the lantern after her. "Sleep well."

As she walked up from the excavation's pit she thought: Yes. Now that the troublesome nightmares had been discredited, the dreams would finally end.

At last she would spend a night in peace.

CHAPTER 7
SPRING, 827

"There'll be little sleep in the Vik tonight," Guthroth chuckled to Asa on their return trip from Skiringssal.

How could he treat Eirik's impending attack so casually, Asa wondered? He had ordered the captain to lower the mast and row — the usual way to keep the sailors' backs to any revelries in the forecastle. Then, before the longship had even cleared the stone jetties separating the town's harbor from Viksfjord, he had lifted a decking plank and fetched up a foreign earthenware jug. Asa had dutifully poured two horns of the wine.

The king drank deeply and leaned against the gunwale. "It has been five winters since Alfhild died. I thought I would never marry as well again."

Asa avoided his eyes, uncomfortable that he would bring up such a topic now, with the fleet of Horthaland on its way. She worried about Eirik and his plans. She knew frustratingly little about her former suitor. Why had he waited two years before setting out to help her? Did he know about the Vikings' defenses? And even if he defeated Guthroth, what kind of husband would Eirik be?

"You have changed over the past two winters, my queen," Guthroth said.

"Have I?"

"Greatly. Once there was hatred in your every word, like an angry girl. It seemed you might never love me."

Unsure how to respond, Asa tipped her horn to drink.

"But then you ordered Agthir to submit. And you turned my Agthir hostages into one of my most zealous fighting crews."

Asa shrugged. She had done these things for her own reasons.

"At first I doubted your suggestion to raise Sigurth Hart. Why should I stoop to foster the son of a land-bound king like Hring? But I had overlooked the danger of our Viking expeditions. Every summer Vestfold itself is undefended. Now, with Sigurth at the Vik, the inland border is secure. You are a rare woman with a sense of power."

"Do you trust a wife with a sense of power?" She poured Guthroth another horn of wine.

"I trust no one. I believe in assuring myself of people's motives. That is why I have never forced you to my bed." He leaned forward and kissed her on the forehead.

The kiss, the foreign wine, Guthroth's words—Asa was alarmed by a sweet confusion beginning to spread through her thoughts. Of course she had first gone to his bed as part of her larger plan. Even later, she had only wanted to allay his suspicions. And all the political suggestions—how could she deny the ambitious nature that had been her curse? But taken together, could it be that her resolve to defeat the Vikings had weakened?

She remembered that first night, when she had stood before his bed, naked and unsmiling, to ask curtly if he would sleep with his wife. She had never hated him more, and that night had felt nothing but pain under the press of his flesh. But since then two winters had passed. She had borne his child, and he had persevered in treating her with a puzzling gentleness belying his Viking reputation. Never in that time had he touched her without her permission. Gradually she had grown accustomed to his solid warmth in the chilly hall's bed. Gradually she had begun to anticipate the nights when the slow stroke of his hands, from her shoulders to her thighs, would tell her he was ready.

Guthroth believed she loved him. Was there a kernel of truth to it?

* * *

That evening in the Vik's royal hall Asa could hear the distant chants and laughter of the Vikings on their ships at the beach, preparing for tomorrow's battle. For a time she kept her spirits up by playing hide-and-seek behind the shadowy pillars with little Halfdan. The child had learned to toddle nearly all the way around the hall by holding onto benches. She always watched him carefully at this favorite game. If an ax were lying about he invariably grabbed it, and if a door were open he promptly crawled off through it. His hair had grown out even blacker than Guthroth's. It looked particularly valiant against the tall white forehead he had inherited from her.

When Halfdan finally crawled to her lap and she nursed him to sleep, she heard again to the disquieting battle chants echoing faintly through the hall.

"Take Halfdan to his bed," she told the three servant women waiting by the hearth. "And stay by him tonight, all of you. I wish to weave."

"Alone, Queen?"

Asa made a point of hesitating, as though she were thinking better of the decision. "Send Kalf, then."

When they were gone Asa took a stick from the hearth and lit the oil lamps in her weaving corner. The walls were hung with her work, foot-wide tapestries of wool on linen, sewn end to end. Memories from Agthir marched along that narrow woven road. There were bearded chieftains on strutting ponies, red-robed women with drinking horns, wagons loaded with golden grain, and soldiers with blue tunics and spears. The zigzag patterns of the top and bottom borders had been made with her weaving cards and added later. Visitors invariably praised the fineness of detail and richness of color. Many asked why the woven panorama included no ships. In reply she would shrug. Only Kalf understood. He shared the memory of the Vikings' terrifying red sails.

She pulled the woof-threads of her tabletop loom tight. Then, lifting every other thread with a comb-like device in her left hand, she

passed a shuttle of blue thread across the loom with her right hand. This time she was not weaving another tapestry. The only design on the blue cloth was a black dragon's head. She had told the women of the court that it was to be a runner.

The door creaked faintly. Quickly she turned, but the fire had burned too low to see the far end of the hall. Kalf came through the dark silently. As he emerged into the lamp's ring of light, Asa marveled that the young, broad-shouldered man could ennoble even the simple brown tunic he was forced to wear. He stopped when he felt the lamp's warmth.

"Queen?"

"There is no one else here," she said, watching for his reaction. For over a year the skald had not been allowed in her presence alone. She regretted her aloofness during their first months at the Vik, when Guthroth had often left her and the handsome young poet alone. She had kept a distance between them then, fearing a trap. After the night she had gone to Guthroth's bed, the king had suddenly put a stop to Kalf's private audiences. Since then they had been able to talk only in whispers of the subjects that mattered most.

Kalf smiled cautiously. Even now that this barrier between them was briefly lifted, he was unsure how many other barriers might remain. They were sworn conspirators and he loved her above all else, but she was a queen and he was a slave. "I heard the king has called all his retainers to the ships."

"Eirik is finally coming," Asa said.

The blind poet sighed. "I have known since yesterday."

"Oh?" Asa's hopes rose. "Have you had a vision? Can you tell what will happen?"

"No, no. I'm afraid Odin has lost interest in teasing his blind skald." Kalf found it troubling that his prophetic glimpses had apparently ceased. The visions had become less frequent since he arrived at the Vik. He did not like to think the poetic god had withdrawn his favor. But the alternative was to believe that the visions were continuing— and that the future was black.

"Then how did you know Eirik had sailed?"

"From a shepherd. He rode from the border fjells and swam the strait, hoping to plead a complaint before the king. Last night I entertained him with a verse, and in payment he told me what he'd heard from the shepherds in the north. They said Eirik had waited two winters for his revenge because, as prince of Horthaland, he did not yet command enough ships to challenge Guthroth. But they also said Horthaland's old king died two months ago. Eirik began conscription at once."

"Then Eirik is king. Did they say anything else?"

Kalf hesitated. He had not wanted to tell her. She would need to concentrate her will tonight, without distractions. But she had asked outright, and he loved her too much to lie. "There—was a garbled verse."

"About Eirik?"

"Yes. It's said to be a continuation of the Eirik Saga, composed by Eirik's own skald, the great Horth. But the shepherd who told it was no poet, and it must have passed through several other untutored mouths before his."

"Retell it in prose, then."

Kalf began uncertainly, "According to the story, Thor angered Odin by helping the Vikings capture you."

"As if the gods would be fighting over me!"

"Perhaps they are," Kalf said, lifting his head. "Vestfolders worship Thor, while Horthalanders worship Odin. And everyone knows the gods have an eye for beautiful women."

Asa was glad he could not see her blush. "Go on with your story. Does the saga say if Odin took revenge?"

"Yes, he ordered Thor to attend Eirik's coronation feast. The thunder god disguised himself as a farmer. He arrived in the evening, bringing the two goats he uses to drive the sun across the sky each day. He offered to slaughter his goats for the feast. But he insisted their bones be returned to him intact before daybreak. The meat was so savory it was soon gone. At that point Eirik secretly cracked open a leg bone to see if the marrow was as good as the meat.

"The next morning Thor waved his hammer over the bones and the goats sprang back to life. But one had a broken leg. Thor was furious. All that day he struggled with the lame goat trying to get the sun across the sky on time. By evening he was so angry he called a council of the gods.

"That night a great eagle lifted Eirik from his dreams and carried him over the fjords to a forested island. There, in a clearing, twelve gods sat in a circle of twelve chairs to judge him. First Thor stood and spoke, 'Since Eirik has acted so contemptuously at his own coronation, I ordain that he will be the last king of Horthaland.'

"One-eyed Odin, however, rose to Eirik's defense. 'Then I ordain he will be the most esteemed of kings, and rule over fifty winters of prosperity.'

"'But I say he will die in despair,' Thor decreed.

"Odin said, 'Then I grant him the gift of poetry, that he will be able to create verse as fast as he can speak.'

"'But he will never remember what he composes.'

"Odin was outraged that Thor had diminished each of his gifts with a curse. Odin added, 'I grant Eirik three courageous sons, each of whom will be the pride of Norway.'"

"'And I ordain that they will all die childless.'

"Odin glared at the thunder god and spoke with a gale that bent the trees. 'Then I give him the greatest of all mortal gifts: he shall have one true love, that will last all his life.'

"But Thor countered, 'And I give him this curse: that his one great love shall remain forever unconsummated.'

"With that Odin angrily ended the trial. The gods agreed the judgments would come to pass nonetheless, and the eagle carried Eirik back to his hall."

When Kalf had finished he lowered his head, waiting for the tone of her response. Long silences troubled him. A sighted skald might read from an expression if his listener was confused, or doubtful, or defiant, or resigned. Kalf needed a spoken word to know.

"If the verse is true, it tells us Eirik will survive tomorrow's battle, but not how," Asa finally said.

Kalf noted her tone was calculating, but disturbingly cool. "Perhaps it depends on what we do. Do you have a new plan?"

"I'm no longer sure." She leaned back, suddenly wishing that harm would not come to any of the three men who loved her: Kalf, Eirik, and Guthroth. Yes, even Guthroth was a man who could love. "Did I tell you Guthroth gave me some new jeweled clasps today?"

"Clasps?" Kalf asked, bewildered by the new topic.

"He wouldn't turn back from Skiringssal without them, even after hearing Eirik was underway. Oh, I've kept yours, too, on my dress. The new ones are for my cloak. I'll show you."

As Kalf felt her take his hands, a memory flamed before him of the evening two summers ago when she had first learned of his love. How many times since then had he trembled at the thought of touching her again! When he felt Guthroth's gemstones on the new clasps, however, they were hard and cold — uglier by far to the touch than his bronze brooches. Then he ran his fingers about the edge of the clasp, and he froze.

"Are you all right?" she asked.

"Take them off," he said.

"What?"

"Take off the clasps, if you still can. There are runes on the back."

She turned them over. At first she thought jealousy had spurred his imagination, for she saw no runes. But when she slid her finger under the clasp's edge, she did feel a peculiar row of hidden scratches. "Are you sure these are runes?"

"I cannot read, but I know the shapes. The gift is charmed." Now Kalf recalled the troubling coolness in Asa's tone that evening, and he feared the runes' sorcery may have already begun to take effect. "Take off the cloak, Asa!"

Asa's hand hesitated above the clasp. She knew the metalsmith and his wife could have wrought runes into the clasps, but hadn't they been trying to help? The old woman had told her to use the clasps to find a way of binding Fenris, the evil behind the Viking sword. A charm could as easily be helpful as hurtful. And what of Kalf's bronze brooches? Had they been charmed all this time, too?

"Asa! Fight the sorcery! Have you forgotten who Guthroth is — the monster who slaughtered your family, crushed your homeland, and raped you? Together we swore vengeance. The time is at hand! Eirik is on his way! Take off Guthroth's cloak!"

With a touch of sadness, Asa pressed the clasps' blue gemstones. The cloak slid from her white arms.

Kalf breathed a sigh of relief. He asked, "Do you still seek the destruction of the Vikings?"

"There are many methods," she said.

"Then you have chosen a plan for tomorrow?"

She paced across the room to think, and stopped with her hand on the carved post of the royal bed. She had mentally woven many different plans in the past two winters, but the trip to Skiringssal that day had left them all badly frayed. Groa had hinted that there was an indirect way to her goals. Was there?

"Asa?" Kalf asked.

Quickly she made up her mind. "Guthroth will return from the ships at dawn, when the battle ceremony ends. As soon as he is asleep, I will take his sword." The Vikings relied on violence, but her strengths lay elsewhere. Groa, the old metalsmith's wife, had suggested she must rely on cunning.

"His sword?"

"It is named Fenris. I have learned that whoever holds the sword is invulnerable to the steel of warriors."

Kalf followed her voice, moving his hand from pillar to pillar as he approached. Asa's story, even if true, confirmed his fears that the clasps posed a far greater danger than she realized. She had already been influenced by them. No wonder Guthroth had made sure she was given the clasps today — of all days. "In the past, Asa, your plans were aimed at the king and not merely his weapons."

"The sword is controlled by an evil power. Only if we remove it can Eirik succeed."

"It is well that you know of Guthroth's sorcery," Kalf said, far from reassured. "He is more dangerous than we had thought." Kalf wanted more time to think. There would never be another opportunity like tomorrow. Why had she never utilized him in any of her plans? If only he were not blind!

"Our escape remains the same," she said, touching his fingers to show she was near.

Impulsively he cupped her hand, as if it were a forbidden treasure. Even without the visions he knew tomorrow held promise only for his wounded honor — not for his love. If Guthroth won the battle, Kalf knew he would never be allowed alone with Asa again. If Eirik won, he would forever be a helpless bystander to another man's happiness. And still she spoke of escape! He closed his eyes, caressing her silken palm, her narrow fingers adorned with rings, and her warm wrist pulsing with life.

Asa felt a warmth melt through her as the blind young man greedily explored her hand. He had loved her steadfastly, yet she had always forced herself to hold back. She had wanted to return his love for so long! In the early months at the Vik, when she and Kalf had been permitted to be alone together, she had been afraid of losing him to Guthroth's jealousy. The blind poet had been her only grip on her shattered childhood. Tonight, before the battle, was as narrow and poignant a gap in her life as the evening of her wedding feast in Agthir. Then she had dared to accept Kalf's gift because she was no longer a girl, nor yet a wife. Tonight she was neither Guthroth's queen nor Eirik's. Tonight she would rule her own heart.

Kalf sensed the warmth even before he felt the kiss on his lips, softer and more longing than he had ever dreamed. It was impossible madness—the king could appear at any minute! But already desire was swelling within him, shutting out reason. As the miraculous kiss lingered, nothing mattered but the touch of the woman he had wanted for so long.

Then Kalf felt her pull away. "Asa!" he called out, grasping after the dream. But he caught only air. He froze, listening with agonized intensity. She had vanished into silence. If the kiss had been a dream it was a dream he would gladly die to dream again. Finally he heard a sound to his right: the rolling clink of a bronze brooch on a wooden bench. His heart raced. He didn't understand.

There was an almost inaudible sigh of linen. His mouth was dry. His chest pounded.

Out of the unbearable stillness that followed, a gentle fingertip touched his burning cheek. Slowly the arousing touch slipped down his cheek to his beard, to his collar, and to his chest, releasing the pin that held his simple tunic. His broad, bare shoulders shivered. Narrow hands slid about his waist, pulling him effortlessly toward the furs of the royal bed.

Inflamed with desire, he sank forward into the heaven he had never seen but long sensed. Desperately he searched out her moist mouth, her firm-tipped breasts, and the honeyed skin that now at last he could know through eager lips and delirious hands, a single word welling within him as though it were the only poem he had ever known: "Asa," he said, "Asa, Asa, Asa . . ."

CHAPTER 8
SUMMER, 1904

Kirstin awoke with a name ringing in her head.

Then she opened her eyes and testily threw the sponge across the tent. She had fallen asleep in the bath.

Curse the dreams that kept her tossing all night! It was bad enough that the camp had just one washtub, so much in demand for soaking artifacts and laundry and sweaty men that she could only reserve it on the occasional morning. Now she had slept her time away. Her legs had grown stiff, buckled up in the little wooden vat. The water was so cold her skin was tight with goosebumps. But she was not going to get out yet.

Kirstin used baths to make decisions. She had read of others who smoked pipes or played the violin to help coax answers to troubling questions out of weary minds. But she had found most problems were soluble in hot water—and the rest dissolved in cold. Few puzzles could survive a bath if she adamantly stuck to her rule not to leave the tub without an answer.

Remembering the question now, she shivered. She had been sketching artifacts yesterday when Carl had approached from across the dig, an oval bronze ornament in his outstretched hand. "How did you know?" he had asked. In the first weeks of the dig, when they had been talking about the bronze hair holder found at the site, she had casually told Carl to keep an eye out for the other one. He had laughed then that hair holders didn't come in pairs, and she had shrugged at her error.

But now Carl really had the other. A second little pin-backed bronze dish, cast with the same elegant fishnet pattern. It too struck a faintly sorrowful chord within her. Did she somehow know it?

Her teeth chattered as she drove her mind backwards, searching museums, texts, and catalogs for bronze patterns. She hugged her knees for warmth, wishing she had not wasted so much time that morning in dreams.

And then suddenly she saw. The room was murky. The dress was deep red. The bronze ovals glinted from the young woman's shoulders. And the woman had a name.

* * *

"What on earth has gotten into you, Kirstin?" Carl asked, shaking his head. "We've already agreed the ship is a religious sacrifice. Everything points to the fertility goddess: the buckets of fruit, the weaving tools, the horse skeletons, the two women—even all this cooking equipment."

Kirstin had joined the other archeologists removing dirt from a collection of iron pots on the foredeck. She did feel different—more assertive, as if some of the emotions from her dreams had lingered into the day. She put down her tools and met Carl's gaze. "When you say 'fertility goddess' you mean Freya?"

"Of course. Freya."

"But Freya was one of the Vanir."

Carl shrugged. "So?"

"You've been telling us that 'Oseberg' means 'hill of the Aesir.' Freya wasn't one of them. She came from the other race of Nordic gods, the Vanir."

Otto, who had been listening nearby, chuckled. "*Mein Gott*, she's right. If the mound were built for one of the Vanir it would be Vanirberg, not Oseberg."

Carl ran his hand over his chin. "Well, then who do you think was Oseberg named for?"

"Asa. *Queen* Asa from the Yngling Saga."

Otto laughed. "Bravo! The queen theory rises again."

Carl sounded more skeptical. "It's a thin lead to follow. If I recall, that saga is about Norwegian kings—not queens. And all but a fragment was lost."

"That's true," Kirstin admitted. "It was an oral verse, and wasn't written down until the twelfth century. But it does mention an Asa from Agthir. She was captured by King Guthroth and made queen of Vestfold in the early 800s."

"So you're saying Oseberg was originally Asaberg?"

"Asa's Hill. Why not?"

"Dr. Söderfelt!" a worker called from the far edge of the dig.

"Later!" Carl replied.

The worker shook his head. "Sorry, sir, but it's about the crates. There were fifteen last night. I think one's missing."

Kirstin gave Carl a sharp glance. "I thought you tightened security."

Carl frowned. "I ordered a twenty-four-hour watch. Otto, you take over here. Come on, Kirstin."

She and Carl hurried across the site and down the hill, where the workman had already flipped back the tarp from the stack of crates. Only fourteen of the large wooden boxes remained. And although the crates were roughly the same size and shape, it took Kirstin only a moment to check the stenciled codes on the sides and realize which was missing.

"It's the dragonhead posts," she announced grimly.

"Of course." Carl turned away, tight-lipped. "Precisely the most marketable artifacts."

Kirstin dismissed the waiting workman with a nod. When he was out of earshot she suggested, "Could the Oseberg farmer have slipped in again?"

"Hansen wouldn't come near the dig without a fairly obvious

torch," Carl said. "He seems to believe fire keeps the evil spirits at bay."

"He told you that?" Kirstin asked.

Carl nodded. "He wouldn't know which wooden artifacts are valuable anyway."

"Then he either he took a crate at random," Kirstin considered, "or it was someone who knew more."

Carl studied her carefully. "You mean someone at the dig?"

"Yes." Kirstin remembered her suspicions the night she had found Magnus working alone. "We owe the workers back wages. One of them might have been tempted to take a crate as payment."

Carl raised an eyebrow. "Now that you mention it, there's Otto, too."

"Otto?"

"It's just a feeling I've had," Carl said uncertainly. "Since we turned down his offer to buy the ship for the German Academy he's acted — well, not like his usual self."

"You don't think he'd steal?"

"Have you ever been to the Reichsmuseum in Berlin?" Carl asked. "I sometimes wonder how the Germans manage to acquire rare artifacts from so many temples and tombs."

Kirstin didn't like the feeling of mistrust that was already spreading through her. "We need evidence, not conjecture."

"Yes." Carl sighed. "I'll report the lost crate to the police in Tønsberg, though I doubt they'll be much help."

"We should start our own investigation first." Kirstin was already examining a confusion of wheel ruts in the grass. "Look at this. Whoever took the crate obviously used a wagon."

Carl knelt to inspect the ruts. "The ground's so dry the tracks aren't very detailed. These could have been left by almost any wagon — even our own."

"That crate weighed at least sixty kilos," Kirstin said. "It must have taken two people to lift it onto a wagon. A night watchman really should have noticed them. Who was on duty last night?"

"It was supposed to be Magnus's turn."

Kirstin had not wanted it to be the Norwegian labor manager. It strengthened her earlier suspicions about him. Still, she wondered if a thief would be so obvious as to steal artifacts when he was on guard duty. "Well, we'd better go see what Magnus has to say."

Carl nodded agreement. He led the way around the mound to a cluster of gray tents. Carl stopped in front of one of the closed tents. "Magnus?"

When there was no reply, Carl pulled back the entry flap.

The burly Norwegian lay half-naked on his cot, his mouth open. His heavy arm hung into the mud.

Kirstin caught her breath. "Good heavens. Is he—?"

"Yes," Carl said, bending closer to the prone figure. "He's drunk."

Slowly Magnus's muscular chest rose and fell. A tattoo of a wide-eyed serpent stared from the thick reddish hair curling above his right breast.

Carl nudged the man. As Magnus rolled to one side, bottles clanked from the blanket. "Cheap beer and Norwegian akvavit. No point even trying to wake him. If he's this drunk he won't remember much about last night."

Kirstin was taken aback. "Perhaps he got drunk after his shift was over."

"Perhaps. But that wouldn't explain why he missed the thieves." Carl paused for a moment. Kirstin could almost see his thoughts catching up with her own. "Unless Magnus was the thief. He's probably the only one in camp who could lift that heavy a crate by himself. And he needed money as much as any of the workers."

"That's just more conjecture," Kirstin warned, trying to slow Carl down. "Remember how protective Magnus was of the ship at the chest-opening ceremony? He was proud of discovering the dragon-head posts. It doesn't make sense that he'd turn around and sell them." She stopped, hit by another thought.

Carl looked at her quizzically.

Kirstin lowered her eyes. "But he might hide the crate to keep the Swedish government from confiscating it later."

"Now you're the one doing the conjecturing."

She nodded, surveying again the tousled figure in the tent. What did any of them really know about Magnus?

CHAPTER 9
SPRING, 827

Asa stretched in the deliciously warm feather bed, her eyes half closed. Though Kalf had left, she was still glowing like a Yule fire. Where Guthroth was heavy and quickly quenched, Kalf had been lithe and tireless. He had devoured her with a hungry passion, exploring every curve of the body he could only know by touch. Their love had been all the more intense, knowing that at any moment the king might burst through the door and they could die.

Afterwards, when she had clung to Kalf's side like a robe, he had surprised her by putting his hands behind his head and speaking just as if all were at peace. He had smiled and quoted,

> "The halt can ride;
> The handless can herd;
> The deaf can deal
> A swordsman defeat.
> Better to be blind
> Than burnt on a bier."

The tension she had felt within him over the years had suddenly been replaced by a fearless calm. "Everyone has second sight," he had said. "It's just that some recognize it more easily. Even you must have the visions, I'm sure of it. To capture them you need only clear your mind of ordinary sight."

Could it be true? She closed her eyes and let out a long breath. The battle chants had long since ceased. The ships' decks would be full of men sleeping men beneath cloaks and tents. Even Guthroth, who no doubt had stayed to prove he could outdrink them all, would soon return, Fenris clanking at his side with each lurching step.

There was a faint flutter of wings. A tiny voice from above called, "Slip! Slip!" Without opening her eyes, Asa knew that the first of the fork-tailed swallows had left its rafter nest to perch in the hall's smoke-hole, beckoning the dawn to come.

Asa sighed. However much she tried to clear her mind of images, she still could not foresee what the day would bring.

Suddenly a man's distant howl of rage sent a chill through her.

She sat bolt upright. The flicker of her single bedside lamp shivered dark shadows across the empty hall. And then, faintly at first, an even more terrifying sound rose through the night. It was a sound she had not heard since Agthir fell: the dread battle cry of the Vikings.

At once she threw off her comforter and began putting on her clothes. Somehow her plans had gone very wrong. The hall was so cold her breath made ghostly puffs. She considered the crimson cloak with Guthroth's clasps, but left it on the bed. By the time the slave boy burst into the hall she had just managed to throw on her dress and set her royal headdress in place.

"Eirik's men have landed!" the boy gasped, terror written on his face.

Asa wrinkled her tall brow. "Are the bonfires on the headlands lit?"

"No! The fleet must have slipped past the lookouts in the dark. No one thought Eirik could sail by night. The king—" the boy lowered his head, "King Guthroth is dead."

The words hit Asa like a wintry wind. She had plotted her husband's death for two winters, yet suddenly she felt desolated. After the niceties of the day and the pleasures of the night, she had almost convinced herself that no one need die. And she had begun to think Guthroth was not killable at all. His casual disdain of danger had given him an aura of invincibility even before she hard heard the story of his charmed sword. Evidently Eirik was a bolder and cleverer warrior than anyone had thought.

"How did the king fall?"

"By treachery."

Asa watched the boy cautiously. "Go on."

"Eirik's ships beached secretly on the island. His men spread through the forests while King Guthroth was still on his ship drinking mead. When the king came down the gangplank singing a verse—a verse about you, Queen—Eirik's men attacked."

Her throat tightened to think that the crusty old Viking had sung of her while she was lying in bed together with Kalf. "And then?"

"Then the king was felled by a spear, thrown in darkness across the beach. Our warriors drove the attackers back to the forests. Scores have already been killed."

"So many?"

"With my own eyes I saw one with his head cut clean off."

Asa quickly stood and walked several paces away so the messenger could not see her expression of distaste. The battle would evidently not be fought with the footfalls of cats, but rather the blades of Vikings. The old metalsmith's wife must have lied about the magic power of Guthroth's sword, for Fenris had not saved him from the steel of warriors. The rune-charmed clasps were undoubtedly harmless as well. Asa turned again to the boy, phrasing her question with care. "Did Guthroth have time to draw his sword?"

The boy shook his head sadly. Falling in an undefended attack was one of the basest Viking deaths. "The old king's sword was in its sheath until Olav drew it to lead the return attack."

The mention of the crown prince made Asa remember how little time she had left to marshal her thoughts and rework her plans. Olav had become the new king of the Vikings, and he had already made his first error. By setting out to avenge Guthroth's death, he was forgetting why Eirik had come: to fetch Asa, a stolen bride. When Olav remembered, he would swiftly barricade Asa in her hall, where she could be defended. Asa knew she had little time to plan her escape.

The slave boy, worried by the queen's silence, added, "We should be happy for the king. Already the Valkyries are riding to meet him with horns of mead. In Valhalla he can battle every day, and every night his wounds will heal."

Asa strode to the far end of the hall. She stopped, raised her head, and deliberately drew the small dagger she wore at her waist.

"Queen!" the boy cried. "Do not rush to Odin!"

With a sudden sweep, Asa slashed the blade across the strings of her loom. Then she gathered up the blue weaving that had been cut loose. She held it out to the slave boy. "Take this to the ship with the dragonhead prow. Give it to the warriors there."

The confused boy stammered, "But—the battle—"

"*You* will be safe."

She spoke the words with such force the boy shivered. "Yes, Queen."

"And tell my serving women that they are to bring me Halfdan at once." Asa slipped a filigreed silver ring from her finger to his. "If you are questioned, show them this."

The boy goggled at the treasure on his stubby brown finger.

"Now run!"

He nodded, clutched the weaving under his arm, and sprinted out the door.

Alone again, Asa quickly began taking down the narrow tapestry she had woven. Now that her plans had changed, she could take a few precious belongings. There would be time—providing the messenger boy proved as fleet-footed, and Olav as slow-witted, as she suspected.

She dared not misjudge Olav. Though legally her stepson, Olav was actually older than her by one winter. From the first she had known he was jealous that his father had chosen such a young queen. What rankled Olav even more, Asa guessed, was her sense for power. Olav had trained his sword arm to lightning speed, obviously believing that this was more important to a Viking leader than political intrigues or complicated poetry—for which he had little aptitude. But as Guthroth aged, Olav had not been given more responsibility. When the independent jarls of Vingulmork began clearing forests on the Vestfold border for farms, Olav had pushed for a retaliatory raid. Guthroth, however, had heeded Asa's suggestion to bargain, gaining both timber for ships and a subtle authority over the jarls.

Another instance, closer to home, had seemed to shake Olav even more. When the Vikings returned from their summer raids last year they discovered Asa had brought a herd of goats to the island, installed them in the servants' run-down huts, and built a large new servants' hall. Olav had complained that the big hall was wasteful and the noisy goats demeaning. But Guthroth had let Asa's decision stand. When Olav still grumbled, his father ordered him to silence. It had become clear to Olav that the old king trusted a young woman's judgment above his own son's. Nothing could have enraged Olav more.

Olav's hatred made him dangerous. Perhaps, Asa thought, he would not barricade her in the hall, but would simply kill her to spite Eirik.

"Slip! Slip!" Two swallows swooped through the roof beams. The smoke-hole was already light gray. Dawn had come. Asa hurriedly tucked the roll of tapestries under her arm and rushed to the door. But she couldn't leave without the high seat! Orm himself had carved the dragonhead posts. She ran back to the center pillars beside the hearth and tugged on the first of the wooden statues. The slot that held it in place had swollen tight.

She yanked harder. Suddenly the first statue came free, nearly staggering her into the hearth. She had just managed to pull the second post loose when the hall's door creaked open. She spun about to face Olav.

But it was Halfdan. The black-haired child toddled toward her with a sleepy squeal. Thanking the gods, she scooped him up into her embrace. Then she issued orders to the three serving women waiting fearfully by the door. "We will sail. Bera, take the high seat posts. Thora, carry the tapestries. Sigrid, carry Halfdan. Quickly!"

As Asa passed the royal bed she hesitated at the sight of the beautiful cloak with Guthroth's gold clasps. On an impulse she flung it about her shoulders and snapped the clasps as she ran.

"This way!" Asa veered from the shortest path to the beach, her cloak fluttering like a crimson banner in the cold dawn. Ominous shapes shifted at the far edges of the fields. Out of breath, she burst into one of the slave halls and cried, "Kalf!"

Frightened faces stared at her from the murk. "Kalf! Now!" she called again. By the plan, he should have been waiting. "Kalf?" Perhaps he had gone ahead to the ship, though she'd warned him impatience might give them away. But he had always been impatient. Yes, that was it.

She turned again and ran on toward the beach. Already she could see the blue-and-white shields lining the gunwales of her familiar, dragon-prowed ship. For a moment she regretted wearing her cloak, knowing Kalf would dislike the gold clasps even though Guthroth's death had proven the runes powerless.

But as she passed the last building before the beach, the heavy clasps suddenly jerked to Asa's throat, choking her viciously. The sorcery! She fell back with a strangled cry.

When she managed to turn she saw Olav, in blood-spattered armor, standing on the train of her crimson cloak.

"Were you looking for this?" the young king asked. He held out a grisly red head and dropped it at her feet.

The bloody ball rolled on its side, exposing a severed neckbone, a shock of blood-matted blond hair, and the whites of blank eyes. Asa gasped, her stomach in her throat. She looked away, pressing her lips together to keep from retching.

"Eirik's men did not attack," Olav said icily. "We searched the island and found neither ships nor warriors. My father's only assassin was the slave we killed at the first. When dawn came, I recognized his face. It was your lackey Kalf."

Shock left Asa spinning on the edge of consciousness. Distantly she fought against the swirling, downward current. Just before she reached the black tunnel, it dissolved into a shattered tingling. She struggled to catch her balance and her thoughts.

It seemed just moments ago that she had lain beside Kalf's comforting warmth. Now he was dead. Both her lovers were dead. Kalf must have gone to the beach directly from her bed, and—yes. The boy had said a spear felled the king in the dark. Who could see a king in the dark? To Kalf, a man singing on a gangplank would be as clear by night as day. But why?

Her mind raced back to images that now were lit by new explanations. When they had both vowed vengeance on the Vikings, had they meant the same thing? She had pledged to extinguish a rapacious spirit—to crush the entire Viking way of life before its barbarity infected the rest of Norway. But now she could see Kalf had set his aim lower. He had always targeted only the king. Kalf had thought the charmed clasps had weakened her resolve. He must have felt he alone retained the will to kill Guthroth.

"Do you deny it is your slave?" Olav demanded. He unsheathed Fenris with a clang.

When Asa saw the wavy-edged blade her fear mounted with a horrifying revelation: Fenris' curse was real after all! That's why Kalf had sacrificed his life—because he knew only a person who was not a warrior could kill Guthroth. Now Olav held the cursed sword. But did he realize the power of the evil in his hands? When Guthroth told her the secret yesterday he had hinted that no one else knew.

"Have you forgotten that Kalf was blind?" Asa asked, her chin high. She needed time—a few moments more time.

"I asked if you deny him!" Olav thundered.

"Kalf and I both sought to chain the wolf before the final battle."

78

Olav gaped at her. Then he reddened with rage. "You know! Guthroth told you the sword would swing at Ragnarök! You've been whoring for his secrets. I'll not let a girl push me aside anymore." Olav raised the glinting blade.

From Olav's words, she guessed Guthroth had told him only half the sword's charm—not that it made him invulnerable to warriors' steel. Asa's voice was steady. "Slay your mother and the gods will turn against you."

"You are not my mother!" Olav cried, his sword still raised.

"I gave birth to your brother. You know the blood kinship laws. If you harm me you will be ruled an outlaw, banished from Norway, and stripped of your kingdom."

Olav paused, for he understood little of law. The people's tribunals—courts known as Things—had lost much of their importance under Guthroth's rule, but they still judged disputes between free Norsemen. Verdicts of outlawry were possible. Could Asa really be considered his mother by the blood kinship laws?

It was all the pause Asa needed. Behind Olav's back the serving women had finally reached the ship and spread the alarm. Asa pointed toward the beach. "Put Fenris away, Olav."

The young Viking turned and his jaw dropped. Forty armed men were advancing against him from one of the Vik's own red-sailed ships. Or was it one of their ships? A peculiar blue banner with a black dragon emblem flew above its deck. And the men carried the blue-and-white shields of the Agthir crew. With a single-minded precision that bespoke months of secret organization, the Agthir warriors flanked Olav with a semi-circle of drawn bows and poised spears. Asa had obviously convinced the former hostages from her homeland to turn traitor.

Olav's face quivered. For the second time that day, Asa had caught a Viking king without his bodyguard. He aimed Fenris at the ring of men. "Come fight me then, cowards. I will die with Guthroth's blade in my hands."

Asa motioned the warriors not to attack. "No. I wish to sail unpursued. And I wish Kalf to be cremated on a warrior's bier. Promise me these things and you may have your life."

It was a bluff. Even if her men attacked with forty-to-one odds she knew they would fail against Fenris' sorcery. But as long as no Viking knew the sword's true power, she had an advantage — and time to lay a new, more intricate plan.

Olav glared at her. "And do you think I would bargain for my life with a *woman*?"

"Yes. Because if you choose to die, the only rightful heir to your kingdom is Guthroth's other legitimately born son. *My* son, Halfdan."

Slowly Olav's sword sank. She had outmaneuvered him once more. Allowing her to leave the island without a fight was a dishonor he could never live down. But if he fought, she would become king in his place through her son. Olav spoke through gritted teeth, "What you ask will be done. And then I suppose you will run to Eirik?"

She lifted her head. "A widow may choose her own destiny. I am sovereign of Agthir in my own right. And my son will one day be more, for even if you should live to beget your own heirs, Halfdan remains your brother. When he comes of age you must split the kingdom of Vestfold with him by law."

Olav slammed Fenris into its sheath. "Treacherous woman! You have planned this all."

Without reply Asa turned and strode toward the ship. She did not want Olav to see the trembling that had come over her. The Vikings must never learn how badly shattered her plans had been, or how narrow her escape. Fear of an enemy's luck was a powerful weapon — a weapon she would yet need to fulfill her vow to end the Vikings' ways forever.

* * *

Black smoke drifted from the signal bonfires on the Viksfjord headlands as Asa's ship tacked toward the open sea. Gusts of cold rain swept the pitching deck. The sailors battened the oar holes against the choppy waves and huddled beneath dripping shields.

Asa pulled up her cloak to cover her head. She knew she should feel triumphant, but she did not. She had lost the two men who loved her most. Only now that they were both gone did she realize how much she had loved them both in return. A ragged hole had been torn in her life. And what did she really know of the quick-tongued king she was sailing to find? Only what Kalf had told her. She ran her finger guiltily over the delicate curve of Kalf's bronze brooch beneath her cloak.

The sigh of wind about the luffing sail and the splash of waves along the strakes conjured haunting voices. Long ago she had sailed in

this same ship with her mother on an autumn progress. She recalled how tall the queen had seemed, with shining, golden hair, a dimpled cheek, and always a conscience pebble in her hand, rubbed smooth by nimble fingers. "Nothing is more important than the family's honor," the voice sighed, then slipped into a silvery laugh. "But if a woman would have power in the North, she must be widowed." It was a common jest among wives, but it held much truth. Girls were thralls. Wives lost their dowries after a year. Only widows had the rights of men, and then only until their sons were grown.

"White sails!" a voice cried. Asa returned to the present with a start. She had nearly nodded off after the sleepless night. Gray clouds still churned overhead, but the drizzle had ceased. She looked anxiously at the sails rounding a rocky island ahead. The ships were deeper than hers, better suited to the open sea. Already she could see the prows — blunt, practical stubs. A pole on the foremost deck lifted Eirik's black banner against the billowing white. She strained to make out the figures on the deck.

The men on the deck were archers, with bows drawn. Of course: Eirik had seen the signal fires and expected war-bent Vikings to meet him at sea. Asa spun about. "Lower the red sail!" She wished she could fly Agthir's blue-and-white striped sail in greeting, but the Vikings had long since dumped it in the woods to rot. Instead she beckoned forward the white-haired Agthir warrior who carried her homemade blue banner on a shortened oar. Then she struck a proud pose, her heart beating wildly.

Eirik's longships lowered their sails and rowed closer.

"Surrender, Vikings!" a voice bellowed. Now Asa could see the beards and leather armor of the men crowding the deck. A volley of arrows sliced the waves before her.

"We come in peace!" she called, but her high voice was lost in the sea wind.

"Prepare to board!" A giant, black-bearded forecastleman leaned from the prow of Eirik's flagship, swinging a long-poled halberd. The hooked blade crunched into the carved gunwale directly in front of Asa.

She held her ground. "Stand off! We are not Vikings!"

The two ships collided with a shudder. Eirik's men grappled the gunwales and surged onto Asa's ship, swords swinging.

"Hold — they have a woman on board!" a man cried, startled.

For a minute the blows of swords still thudded against wooden shields. But one by one the attackers lowered their weapons. The boats creaked against each other in the swells.

"Aside," a trim-bearded man ordered in a stern baritone voice. A path opened before him through the crowd on Asa's deck. "Who commands this ship?"

The Agthir warriors lowered their shields and looked toward the prow. The white-haired banner bearer there stood aside, lowering his head to Asa.

Eirik stared at her, dumbstruck. Could this be the charmed ship of the Vanir, unfolded from a goddess' pocket? Freya was said to be so fair that all men who looked upon her fell instantly in love. An ivory headdress bound this woman's golden hair above her tall, white forehead and piercing blue eyes. Magnificently jeweled gold clasps above her breasts held a crimson cloak that draped damply about her body. Her features had the flush of youth, but her poise was that of an empress.

"Who—?" he managed to ask.

"I am Asa."

"Asa?" he echoed incredulously. "But—how did you escape Guthroth?"

She lowered her eyes before his frank gaze. He was an inspiringly handsome, bright-eyed man, though shorter than she had imagined. He wore embossed leather armor with bronze studs—not rich, but a practical, well-fitted battle uniform. Judging from his halting questions, he was not nearly so quick-tongued as the poems told.

"My servant killed Guthroth in the night," she said simply. "At dawn I raised a force and left the Vik. I saw to it that there was no pursuit."

Eirik stroked his beard, looking about at the ships he had sailed three hard days from Horthangr Fjord. Somehow, this seventeen-year-old woman had accomplished what he had nearly despaired of achieving with Horthaland's entire fleet and army. The long-dreaded battle was unnecessary. He had already won. And the goddess who had performed this miracle was to be his bride! Where was the thunderbolt that would disrupt all of this stormy morning's unbelievably sunny news? Was it possible he had caught Thor napping?

He smiled, and a daring verse sprang to mind. Since his coronation he seemed to have discovered the skill of a skald, and could miraculously shape his words as in the sagas.

> "A pity that poets
> May praise only men,
> Else Eirik might earn
> A word-smith's reward
> By weaving a verse-cloak
> For the Viking vanquisher—
> The comely queen
> Who's conquering this king too."

Asa smiled appreciatively. Eirik's verse ingeniously sidestepped the taboos on suitors' love poetry. "Does that mean you'll accept no payment for your pretty words?" Though she still felt cold from the loss of Kalf and Guthroth, she could imagine that one day she might warm to this new king. Encouraging Eirik's ardor would be the easy, pleasant first step of her next plan. She cocked a shoulder and cast him a questioning look.

At once his arm swept about her and pulled her close. She offered no resistance as he pressed her against the full length of his powerful body, kissing her with passionate fury. Dimly she heard the cheers of men.

When Eirik finally stepped back, breathing quickly, he turned to the warriors. "A queen who can outwit the Vikings deserves a warrior's fame and a title of honor. Hail Asa, the *Little Chieftain!*"

The men roared back, "Hail Asa, the Little Chieftain!" The white-haired banner bearer held the dragon emblem high, the cloth snapping in the breeze.

She felt a lump in her throat. Only the most famous of the nobility received second names. "But a title is only valid if there is a proper naming gift," she reminded Eirik.

"And you shall have a gift befitting a warrior," he replied. He took off his helmet, nobly decorated with a ring of silver plates. "You have avenged your honor well. Would you replace Guthroth's headdress with one more suited to you?"

The morning's tumultuous events had brought so many changes that she had forgotten to remove her marriage headdress. She pulled out the long ivory comb and shook her head, loosing a cascade of hair over her shoulders.

Eirik lifted his helmet triumphantly and set it on her head like a crown. "I have thought of you every day for the past two years."

"And I you," Asa said.

"In all that time I never guessed how beautiful you would be." He smiled. "The verses mentioned other traits."

"Oh? And what was said about me?"

He laughed. "That there once was an ambitious young princess who convinced an old woodcarver to whittle wooden copies of her mother's keys."

She reddened at the tale. The keys had broken in the first lock she tried, confounding the king's metalsmiths for hours.

"And I seem to recall a verse about an impetuous prince who challenged an entire troop to an archery contest — before realizing that the barrel he used as the target was full of the king's mead."

He lifted an eyebrow. "Perhaps we know each other better than we thought. Would you have me as your husband nonetheless?"

She would rather have waited to answer Eirik's question. She still had much to mourn. But with kingdoms teetering on her decision, she knew she had to reply at once. "If you would have me, yes."

Eirik approached her more gently now. Her blue eyes, framed by the long, golden hair and the shining helmet, drew him like a spell. He touched her shoulders lightly and drew her to him until her heart beat softly against his chest. When his lips touched hers, it seemed this time he might never let her go.

Finally he leaned back, his voice husky. "Little Chieftain, you shall have all the keys you could possibly desire. The wedding gifts intended for you two winters ago are still waiting. Estates in the east. Trinkets I think may catch your eye. In Stavanes we'll have the grandest wedding feast the North has ever seen."

After the torments of the day, the handsome young king's comforting words sounded almost too good to be true. "And a proper wedding verse," she insisted. "The Vikings are unbearable poets. Promise me we'll have your skald Horth tell our story in grand style."

For the first time, Eirik's expression darkened. "My skald has been banished. But what of Kalf, the famous blind poet of Agthir? Surely he is the one worthy to make our verse."

"No." Asa shook her head. "Dead."

Eirik pursed his lips. "Then by the gods I'll do it myself. It's time we put the tragedies of the past two winters behind us. I've waited long enough for this moment. Nothing now stands in my way."

But even as he spoke there was a cry from the deck—a tiny, squealing cry that even Eirik did not at first recognize as the fateful clap of Thor's delayed revenge. Eirik glanced irritably toward the sound.

An anxious serving woman stood out from behind the mast. "A hundred pardons, king. The babe is hungry."

Eirik stared at the child. Little Halfdan was waving a stick as though it were a sword. In his Vik-red tunic and startlingly black hair the toddling boy was a miniature Guthroth. Eirik dimly recalled that a child had resulted from Asa's forced marriage, but he could not imagine how—or why—it had been allowed to survive her flight. "I'm afraid it can't be fed any longer," he said with a calm but firm voice. "We'd best put it overboard at once."

"What!" Asa exclaimed.

He put his hand on her arm. "Misbegotten children should be put out to a natural death. A husband has that duty."

She yanked her arm free. "You are not yet my husband. Nor may a child be exposed once it's suckled. Halfdan has lived two winters."

"Consider your words, woman. No one is bound to nurture the product of rape."

She nearly replied that there had been no rape, that she had gone to Guthroth of her own will. But she caught the words in time, realizing that Eirik would not understand. Instead she answered stiffly, "I choose to raise Halfdan as my own nonetheless."

"Asa! I cannot—I will not—foster a sworn enemy's son. Guthroth stole you when you were to become my bride. Shall I raise his black-haired ghost as if it were my own first-born heir?"

Asa folded her arms stubbornly. "If you wish to marry me you must accept my child."

Eirik glared at her. Now he recognized the malevolent meddling of Thor. Raising this child was politically impossible. Guthroth had killed Asa's family and had been justly killed in return. Obviously the hated tyrant's seed must not be cultivated. Yet Asa clung to the infant. Who else but the gods could have devised such a cruel stalemate?

Even more unsettling for Eirik was the attraction he felt for this woman. Her beauty, her proud poise, even her defiance were an elixir pounding in his veins. He wished she were not a widow so he could bargain for her marriage contract with a reasonable man, as he had years before with her father. He considered taking her by force. With the fleet of Horthaland behind him, he had the power to do it. But then he would be as dishonored as Guthroth and as vulnerable to her revenge. What then could he do? The knowledge that his dilemma doomed their love only increased his anger.

"Then keep your bastard! But you won't be my queen. You will never find a husband."

Asa held her head high. Kalf's verses had been right about Eirik after all. The man had too quick a tongue and too rash a temper for his own good. "If that is your decision, leave my ship."

The two glowered at each other in frustration.

Finally Eirik turned away. He signaled to his men with a sweep of his arm. "Let us leave this stubborn girl to her folly. We'll sail on to the Vik."

Asa felt a spark of hope. "Then you will attack the Vikings?"

"And why should I? You say Guthroth is already dead. I plan to celebrate the peace now that our grudge is erased." He climbed over the gunwale and gave the order to cast off. Then he turned and called to Asa, "I also intend to negotiate with the Vikings about the future of Agthir. If you hold Guthroth's marriage valid, then you lost your rights to property after the first year. Agthir is legally theirs."

"Agthir is Halfdan's!" Asa exclaimed. If Eirik's logic prevailed, she would be a homeless pauper.

Eirik's grim expression seemed to soften. The proud queen's beauty still tore at his heart. "I might argue your case. But even if I could convince them, the Little Chieftain will face challenges from untold directions. And I shall never help her again."

The wind was rapidly carrying Eirik's white-sailed ship away. Before she lost sight of him, he turned his head sharply toward the Vik—a gesture that sent a pain through Asa's chest. She had not wanted to lose him at all, especially not on a day when she had lost so much. But no man could take her child. Perhaps he was right that she would never marry again. Did it matter? The men who had fought over her had seen her as a prize to win and own. Had any of them really understood who she was?

Waves slapped against the hull of the drifting ship. The wind whistled in the mast's stays. A dark wall of rain approached. Little Halfdan hid from the cold in the skirts of a serving woman, obviously frightened by the uproar he had unknowingly caused.

The old banner bearer, wearied from his task, quietly lowered the dragon emblem. "Queen? What now?"

Asa turned with a start. When she saw the blue banner's tip dragging in the waves, a defiant surge of energy coursed through her. She grabbed the pole and held the banner aloft. "Raise the sail and set course for Agthir!" she commanded, with a voice that shook the sailors from their dejection.

Then, facing the storm clouds ahead, she added quietly, "The Little Chieftain has much to do."

CHAPTER 10
FALL, 1904

"Set course for Tønsberg!" Magnus commanded as he pulled in a tiny pair of oars. Then he straightened his sailor's cap over unruly blond hair and saluted back to himself, "Aye aye. Prepare to raise the mast."

Kirstin, at a miniature tiller, could not suppress a smile. When she had determined to find out what the suspicious labor manager did with his free Sundays, this was hardly what she had expected. Magnus had not gone on a drinking spree. Nor had he met with accomplices to sell looted artifacts. Instead, after she had stealthily followed him to an anchorage on Oslo Fjord, she had seen him untying an astonishingly detailed, sixteen-foot replica of a Viking longship. Curious, she had ventured so close that he had finally hailed her and invited her for a sail.

At first she had refused, embarrassed that she had been such a clumsy sleuth. Evidently the light green summer dress and straw hat she had chosen from her limited camp wardrobe as camouflage had not enabled her to blend in after all. When Magnus persisted with his invitation ("Come on, we'll just sail around the headland to Tønsberg"), the temptation had been too great. Here was a chance to investigate Magnus and to study the workings of a miniature Viking ship at the same time.

"It would have taken half a dozen crewmen to lift a full-scale mast," Magnus explained, inserting an eight-foot pole into a slot in the deck.

"It looks awfully short, even for a model," Kirstin objected. No one had ever unearthed a complete Viking mast. Even at Oseberg the top of the mast had rotted off. But she had always pictured them taller.

Magnus secured the mast to the sides of the ship with guy ropes and cinched them tight. "Masts had to be short."

"What makes you say that?"

"Try putting up a tall mast on a boat like this sometime. You have to dangle it overboard. It weighs so much you could capsize. With a short mast you can raise and lower it fast, right on the deck."

It was a refreshingly practical argument, unlike the dry, academic theories Kirstin usually confronted. And now that she thought about it, the speed of raising the mast might well have been critical. The Vikings had been renowned for hair-breadth escapes, rushing to their beached ships to spread sail.

Magnus shoved up his sleeves and pulled a rope, creaking a pulley atop the mast. A long boom lifted from the deck, unfurling a blue-checked sail. Guy ropes strained taut as the canvas billowed. The little ship slid forward across the sunny sea like a skate on ice.

"About the steering—" Kirstin had never handled anything larger than a rowboat.

Magnus grinned and came aft on his knees, keeping his center of gravity low. He put his big hand over hers on the tiller. "Keep right about Jersøy. We'll run with the wind south to Nes, then tack up Tønsberg fjord. Here, let me make a place for your feet." He lifted out several of the decking planks so she could stretch her legs into the shallow hold.

"Foot room. I suppose you'll say that's why the Oseberg ship's decking was left loose."

"Why not?" Magnus asked. "There weren't any benches. Makes it easy to bail, too. Steady now, the wind will freshen past the island."

As the sleek ship sliced across the water Kirstin felt an oddly familiar exhilaration. The tang of the salt air smacked of summer beaches. The sun, caught in the rays of the rigging, flashed liquid fire across the water. Through her feet the thin wooden hull vibrated with the ocean's life.

All about her the Viking ship lore she had only known from numbered archeological remnants was straining with use. Waves sloshed against the oar holes' circular hatchcovers. Ropes tautened on the W-shaped cleats that clung like bats in the rigging. Seaweed draped from a slender, wrought-iron Viking anchor in the forecastle. A bronze windvane on the stubby prow swiveled forward, a gleaming horse pawing ahead.

"This is the Gokstad ship, isn't it?" she asked, suddenly recalling the suspicions that had made her decide to investigate Magnus. Even a replica of the famous burial ship from 1880 would be worth a small fortune. How did a Norwegian laborer come to possess such a marvel? Every detail on the ship was a functioning treatise on Viking ship-wright skills.

He nodded, shading his eyes as he peered ahead. "At one quarter scale. Not as ornate as the Oseberg ship, but a better sailer, I'll wager."

"But how could you afford it?"

"Me?" He glanced at her, a chuckle widening his red beard. "I built it."

She looked again at the graceful curve of the hull's strakes. As in the Oseberg ship itself, each plank bore ax marks proving it had been split and painstakingly hand-hewn from oak. The lapped strakes were joined by rivets whose irregular square heads had clearly been hand-forged from iron. "It must have taken years."

He shrugged. "When I was twelve my father helped excavate the mound in Gokstad. Most of that summer I watched and learned what I could. Then in the winters I worked on *Skiblathnir*, copying what I'd seen."

The significance of the model's name did not escape Kirstin. *Skiblathnir* had been the Vanirs' pocket-sized ship — a magic vessel that could unfold to hold all the gods at once. In a way, Magnus himself seemed almost as mysterious as that mythic ship. At the Oseberg dig she had seen him as a rough laborer and a drunken thief. But here she was seeing a quiet, complex man who read sagas and built longships. Which Magnus could she believe?

"A lot was missing from the Gokstad ship," Magnus continued. "But I didn't have to look far to fill in the details. Twenty years ago every dock in Vestfold still had a couple of old clinker-built dinghies made the same way."

She ran her hand along the polished gunwale. "You obviously put a lot into your work. Collectors would pay well for a model like this."

For an instant his blue eyes flashed. "I've had offers. *Skiblathnir's* not for sale."

The fact that he would not sell his model made it seem less likely that he would steal artifacts. Yet he hardly seemed in a position to scorn income. All the workers were still only receiving half pay. "Are you a boat builder by trade, then?"

"No, just a sailor. Aground for a while, like most of the whalers in Tønsberg. That's one reason we're working for you at the dig."

"Are times that hard in town?" Kirstin had been struck by the poverty in the farming villages around Oseberg, but had imagined fishermen would be better off.

"Since summer, two of my friends have had to emigrate to support their families."

"And what about you?"

"Guess I'm lucky—no family."

She was not heartened by his wry smile. "Why is it so difficult for sailors to find work here?"

Magnus nodded toward a cluster of brick smokestacks on the island of Jersøy. "See those buildings? For forty years that's where they rendered whale blubber. Most of Norway's whaling fleet docked in Tønsberg. Every summer the ships would hunt the North Atlantic. But the price of whale oil dropped fifty percent last year."

Magnus shoved the tiller aside. "Hold her there a minute." The ship canted precariously as it swung crosswise to the breeze. The burly sailor sat on the uphill side, and his weight gradually leveled the ship. He continued talking, as if to the waves ahead. "I guess folks don't want whale-oil lamps when they can get cheap kerosene from oil out of the ground, or even buy electric lights. And now parliament's banned whaling altogether off the north coast of Norway."

"Why would they do that?"

"Not enough whales. We've cleaned out the best grounds in the North Atlantic."

Kirstin had never before considered that an entire ocean could be depleted. Whales were so large, and the North Atlantic so enormous. "What will the whalers do?"

"Well, with the price of oil so low, the renderers say the only way to turn a profit is to sell thirty times as much. So they've built a factory ship—a gigantic floating cookery that can render whale blubber at sea. They're signing up the old whaling ships to sail with them to Antarctica to fill the factory ship in the South Atlantic, where no one's whaled before."

"That's half way around the world. Will you go?"

Magnus took a pipe from his pocket and began thoughtfully filling it with tobacco. "I think I'll give the whales a rest, maybe try cod again. Guess I'm too damned independent. Couldn't stomach working for someone else's factory." He lit the pipe and puffed. "Almost as unpleasant as paying taxes to someone else's king."

His words reminded Kirstin of another troubling thought—that Magnus could have taken the dragonhead statues to keep them from the Swedish authorities. She had noticed the flag fluttering behind her on the stern: a blue-and-white cross on a red field — *without* the Swedish coat of arms. Flying the "pure" Norwegian flag was technically a criminal offense. Only firebrands showed such a banner in public.

She decided to risk a direct question. "Magnus, did you hide the dragonhead posts?"

He blew out a thin stream of smoke, squinting into the sun. "I wish I had." Pointing his pipe stem at Kirstin he added, "This country's been oppressed by foreign kings for six hundred years. Six hundred years! Your mother was born here. You must be able to feel how Swedish rule has turned Norway into a loaded cannon. All that's needed now for independence is a spark—a symbol to remind the people of Norway's greatness." He puffed on his pipe again. "The Oseberg ship could be that spark. No, I worry a lot about who has those dragonhead posts now."

"Then you know who has them?"

He shook his head grimly. "Just guesses. No evidence."

"Magnus, it doesn't look good that you were drinking the night they disappeared."

He pushed back his sailor's cap. "So you believe that? Look, I never drink alone, and I sure as hell don't know where those bottles in my cot came from. You can't even buy that brand of beer in Tønsberg."

She wrinkled her brow. "You *looked* drunk, Magnus."

"Did I? What did you see? A man asleep at noon? I'd been awake for thirty straight hours."

"Then why didn't you notice someone taking the crate of artifacts?"

Magnus sighed heavily and lowered his eyes. "That *was* my fault. I was working on the excavation during my watch again. I know you told me not to, but it's so damned dull pacing the rounds at night when there's a whole ship to unearth. The problem is, you can't see the stack of crates when you're working inside the dig. I guess I thought whatever was crated would be safe." Then he gave her an unflinching gaze. "I was wrong, that's all."

Kirstin studied him carefully. There was sincerity in his voice, yet she still sensed he wasn't telling her all he knew.

He asked, "Do you think I stole the crate?"

She sighed. "No." He lacked a solid alibi, to be sure. But intuition shouted to her that he was not lying. Unfortunately, his innocence would only complicate the mystery, casting more suspicion on Otto, the Oseberg farmer, and the other workers.

He touched her hand on the tiller. "You won't regret your trust."

Suddenly the tiller jumped from their hands. The boat rocked sharply.

"Damn!" Magnus jerked the tiller free. At once the boat steadied, drifting through reeds near shore.

"Is the rudder damaged?" Kirstin asked.

"No, it's designed to come loose in shallow water."

She looked over the starboard gunwale. The rudder was indeed unharmed, bobbing on its pivot alongside the boat like a big wooden butter knife. She should have known a side-mounted rudder would do that. But it was one thing to study a Viking ship at an excavation and something else entirely to sail one.

Magnus lowered the sail and rowed toward deeper water. He nodded toward a thicket on the marshy bank. "No wonder we ran aground. That's the mouth of Oseberg Creek."

She surveyed the willow-choked opening. "Not much of a creek, is it?"

Magnus chuckled. "If we ran out of water here, how the devil did the Vikings get a full-scale ship through?"

Kirstin was glad to push the matter of the stolen crate aside for a while. She preferred mysteries she could solve. "The creek was bigger then because the sea was higher."

"Seriously? The ocean's been going down?"

"No. The land's been going up. All of Scandinavia has been rising a centimeter a year since Viking times."

"So Oseberg was the head of navigation back then?"

"More likely Slagen church." She stopped a moment, musing. "I suppose that explains why it was a battlefield."

Magnus raised an eyebrow. "I've lived here all my life and never knew Slagen was a battlefield."

"It must have been. Slag means battle in Old Norse. And churches were often built on the sites of older heathen burial grounds. You'd expect a burial ground at a battle site."

"Then the Oseberg queen you talk about died in a war?"

She frowned at the thought. The skeletons were too incomplete to tell much about how Asa had died. But her brief dream of the proud young woman made the thought of a battle death unpleasant. "I'm afraid even the Yngling Saga doesn't give very many facts about Asa — or any Viking women, for that matter. The poets were trying to tell the story of Vestfold's kings."

Magnus had secured the edge of the sail with a small pole, allowing the ship to pick up speed while tacking against the breeze. "I never read the Yngling Saga," he said, emptying his pipe with a tap on the gunwale. "Just how does it fit in with your theory of the Oseberg queen?"

Kirstin leaned back against the stern. "The saga says Asa was captured by an old Viking king named Guthroth. She waited two years for revenge, until she had a son. That way she'd have a male heir. Then she had her servant kill Guthroth with a spear."

Magnus whistled. "A dangerous woman."

"A courageous queen. I don't think her life was easy. After Guthroth died she had to wait sixteen years before her son came of age. Then they still divided Vestfold in half, because Guthroth had another son. Asa's son Halfdan was given the part of Vestfold near here."

"Halfdan?" The brawny sailor looked at her uncertainly. "You mean this son of hers was *Halfdan the Black* — the king who founded Tønsberg?"

"I believe so."

"And he's the one who built the burial mound?"

Kirstin tilted her head. "I'm not so sure. The saga doesn't say what happened to Asa. Maybe the excavation will give us an answer."

Magnus smiled. "I almost think you prefer excavating words to excavating ships."

"Well, it's a different kind of digging."

"Not many Americans would know the language well enough to do it. You're a Norwegian at heart."

"Do you think? My mother left Norway before I was born."

Magnus looked out across the waves. "And I left at the age of three."

94

"I thought you said you'd always lived in Tønsberg."

"My father was a sailor."

"But didn't you stay behind with your mother?"

"For the first three years, I suppose." He stared at the waves again. His voice dropped a note. "All I remember of my mother is a pair of thin, white arms and a faraway voice—as if she weren't of this world at all. My father said she gave him something to remember her by whenever he set sail. A sentimental present. One time the present was me."

Kirstin gave him a sympathetic look. "It must have been hard for you, so young."

He shrugged. "I sailed the world with my father. Cape Town, São Paulo, New Orleans. Had the run of the ship, learned all I could from the crew. One old-timer had me memorize the multiplication tables in German. Another man taught me the balalaika. Still another showed me how to whittle wooden chains out of driftwood, link by link. I was ten before my father decided I needed more organized schooling. That's when we came back to Tønsberg for good."

He frowned. "By then I'd missed the tests that might have put me on track for the university."

"Honestly, Magnus. That doesn't make any difference."

"Doesn't it, doctor?" His penetrating blue eyes caught her off guard.

She flushed, for with three words he had cut to the heart of her aloofness. She had been treating him as a common laborer. And it wasn't simply because he swore and had rough hands—she had known many archeologists with these traits. Obviously, he had a mind capable of scholarship. His grasp of Old Norse and his work on *Skiblathnir* proved that. But he lacked the polish of a university education. He wore pewter buttons on his jacket. He ate from the back of his fork. Could it be that such trivialities had subconsciously allowed her to suspect him as a thief? The thought made her angry with herself.

"Of course it doesn't matter, Magnus," she said. "And please don't call me doctor. My name is Kirstin."

"Very well," he smiled. "Kirstin."

While they were talking, the ship sailed under the arch of an iron bridge near the head of the Tønsberg fjord. A forest of masts and smokestacks loomed from the colorful fishing ships moored along the docks. Beyond were red warehouses of hewn logs, and steep streets

95

packed with white clapboard houses. The rock face of a hill crowded the town toward the fjord. Magnus steered the little Viking sailboat past the great, curving, barnacled hulls of the fishing fleet.

Kirstin found she was sorry they had reached the dock so quickly. She let him help her up from the deck. "Thank you, Magnus. Oseberg's not far. I can hire a hansom cab."

He tied up the ship's prow. "Don't you want to see Halfdan the Black's old fortress? It's just up Castle Hill."

She hesitated. She had planned to spend the day spying on Magnus, rather than going on outings with him. And while sailing *Skiblathnir* might be considered a scientific exercise, searching for Halfdan's mythical fortress sounded more like a wild goose chase. Generations of archeologists had searched in vain for the Viking fort that the original name 'Tunsberg' seemed to promise. The word *tun* in Old Norse meant a log stockade. In England, similar village stockades had been known as *towns*.

"I thought the digs on Castle Hill didn't reveal buildings of Viking age," she countered.

"Professors never know where to look. Come on, I go there all the time."

His disarming tone won her over. "All right then, if you're sure."

As they walked together along the waterfront several rough-looking men nodded and waved to Magnus. Kirstin mused, "You seem to be well known here."

Magnus shrugged. "Whalers. When they're not in the taverns or in the jail they're generally down here by the Seaman's Center. Between sailings I spend a lot of time there myself."

She smiled. "In taverns and jails?"

He seemed not to have heard. "How about a *krumkake?*" He stopped at an umbrellaed pushcart in the narrow cobblestone street. He bought two of the crisp waffle cones filled with whipped cream.

Kirstin let him shift the conversation, partly because she really did like krumkake. "It must have been fifteen years since I tasted one of these." They each bit into their cones with a crunch, and she laughed when Magnus looked up, his mustache white.

At the upper end of town the cobblestone streets gave way to a steep path through an ancient grove of gnarled oaks. Kirstin held the hem of her dress to keep it free of brambles. When they finally reached a hilltop meadow, surprised sheep tumbled away, neck bells jangling. Curves of granite bedrock rose from the field like whales surfacing amidst the wildflowers.

Kirstin stopped to catch her breath at a crumbling stone wall near the top of the field. The town and the docks lay hidden at the foot of the hill, leaving an uncluttered sweep of blue fjords and green hills. "The view really is wonderful," she said. A large, tile-roofed manor house on a hill caught her eye. "What farm is that?"

"Jarlsberg," Magnus replied. "An old estate. They make Vestfold's best cheese."

"'Jarls' Hill,'" Kirstin mused. "I wonder if Viking nobles really settled there. If so, they were awfully close to King Halfdan's town. And Jersøy was on the other side of town."

"Let me guess. Jersøy came from *Jarlsøy* — 'Jarls' Isle.'"

"Precisely. I expect Jersøy was the original home of the Vikings who settled the English Channel Islands of Jersey."

"Jersøy's small and rocky. They made a good trade."

Kirstin tilted her head noncommittally. "Where's this fortress of Halfdan's you promised?"

"Behind you."

She turned to the tumble-down wall of granite blocks. "This can't be it. Vikings didn't build with stone."

"It's just a bit farther. Come on." He led the way through a breach in the wall. Inside, the stone walls were higher, divided into a confusion of rooms and corridors. The curved remnant of a window opening told Kirstin the building's tale all too plainly.

"I'm afraid this was an eleventh-century church, not a Viking fortress."

Without reply Magnus continued through the grassy ruin to a tall portion of the wall. There he gripped a granite boulder. Straining until the veins stood out on the muscles of his arms, he shifted the stone aside. Sun streamed in through a small archway. Silently he swept his hand forward, indicating that Kirstin could go first.

Cautiously she ducked through the opening. On the far side was a small, garden-like enclosure without other doors or windows. A crooked ash tree grew in the ruined room's grassy middle, its orange berries and red leaves flaming in the sunshine. Magnus hung his cap on a branch in passing, then sprang up a narrow flight of uneven stone stairs against the garden's far wall. He sat on the top of the stone wall. "You can only see the fortress from here."

Kirstin paused, suddenly aware that what Magnus wanted was for her to sit beside him. The realization was both enticing and a little frightening. In her heart, she knew she had followed Magnus for more than his knowledge of Viking lore. He was an attractive man. On *Skiblathnir* she had been able to tell herself she was merely studying sailing techniques—merely traveling to Tønsberg. But in this remote ruin she was entering Magnus's private domain. Either she was going to climb the stairs or she must turn back to Oseberg at once.

With her heart beating faster, she stepped up the broken stairway to the wall. The meadow spread below her like an overturned green bowl. There was no fortress in sight.

"There." Magnus pointed about the edges of the field below.

She leaned forward. "I don't see—or wait. Maybe." Was there a faint discoloration in the grass? By squinting she could imagine a straight, delicately shaded line angling across the sheep trails.

"You said yourself that Vikings didn't build with stone. The old wall of Halfdan's fortress probably rotted away long before the church was built. You can't see anything when you're in the field, and digging won't help. But up here, at the right time of day—"

"Of course! The grass is a fraction greener where the wall disturbed the ground. The rotten wood made the soil more fertile." Kirstin marveled at the discovery. Magnus had hit upon a way to see something that no longer existed. Archeologists gave up when they found nothing in the ground. Who would have thought to look from the air? "Then the fortress really was surrounded by a wooden palisade after all." As she looked out across the field she could almost visualize the curved Viking halls and the parapet of sharpened wood staves.

"This is the view your Queen Asa once had," Magnus said.

"Yes. To a fjord full of red sails."

Magnus added, "And blue. Only the warships were red."

It took a moment for the significance of the words to sink in. No records existed of Viking sail colors. She had seen them only in her dreams . How did Magnus know?

"Do you—do you remember dreams?"

He shook his head. "Sometimes I have the nightmares of a boy."

"A boy? Who?"

He shrugged. "I thought you might tell me. We were together when the talk of spells began."

She half laughed. "Dreams are nothing more than the fantasies of overworked minds."

"When I'm with you, though, I wonder," Magnus said. "I watch you when we work together, and it almost feels like we're somewhere else. As if we both know how the dream we're in will end."

A tingling ran through her—the same dizzying rush she had felt the first night at the dig. She opened her lips but could not speak.

Slowly Magnus touched her chin and leaned to her. His lips touched hers.

Kirstin's head swam with the fiery thrill of the kiss, unlike anything she had felt before. Broad hands slid from her shoulders to her back, pulling her close. Her heart pounded against his muscled chest. For a moment she felt she really was swirling in a dream—a dream she could not possibly remember when she awoke.

But then he gently loosened his hold.

She swayed, looking incredulously at the sailor she had kissed with such passion.

CHAPTER 11
FALL, 856

A thin man with sharp cheekbones rolled a feathery leaf between his long fingers. Slowly he walked across the garden of the Tunsberg fortress and held out the pungent herb to Asa. "Yarrow may be what you seek, Queen." The words had the staccato accent of a Lapp. He quoted,

> "Against flu use fire,
> Against quarrels, elderberry,
> Against hate, the moon,
> Against rabies, alum,
> Against ill luck, runes,
> Against cruelty, yarrow."

"There's no poison in it, is there, Paalo?" Asa trusted her friend's skill with herbs, but wanted no misunderstanding. She had learned of the death of Sigurth, her foster son, only the week before, and the tragedy left her acutely aware of the precariousness of growing old. She herself had already seen 46 winters.

Paalo shook his silvery blond head.

"Is it distasteful?"

"On the contrary, yarrow adds a pleasant bitterness to ale."

"To ale? Perhaps—"

She was interrupted by the baying of dogs in the halls' breezeways. The curs streaked down the yard, tearing through the garden of cabbages, garlic, and herbs. Paalo tried to hit them aside with his staff, but they raced on to the log stockade, where they tumbled, howling and snapping at each other. Up at the fortress halls, an old guardsman and several servants began shouting.

"The fjord, Queen," Paalo said. The thin man pointed toward the south.

She stiffened. Though the Vikings returned to Tunsberg every autumn, the blur of red sails still gave her a stab of anger. She squinted, waking the wrinkles of age that creased her high, pale forehead. Her eyesight was no longer as sharp as it had once been. She could not make out individual ships. "Is Halfdan among them?"

"There is a black sail."

She should be glad her son had returned. But nothing hurt her more than the knowledge that Halfdan, for whom she had sacrificed so much to gain a kingdom, had chosen to become a Viking raider like his father Guthroth. How was she to fulfill her vow to destroy the Vikings when her own son had grown up to become one of them?

"Add your herb to the welcoming ale, Paalo. Tell the serving men to meet us at the beach with the wagons."

"You will walk, Queen?"

The steep footpath to town would be more refreshing than the wagon route. "We will walk."

In the Great Hall, Asa found the ladies of the court already bustling with nervous excitement.

"Oh, I hope Kolbein finally brings ermine," one young woman exclaimed, wrapping her shoulders in pale cloth. "Just look how my worsted cloak has faded in a winter."

"Just so they didn't spend the summer beating each other's shields in Ireland again," said another, untying and tying her long, golden hair in a loose overhand knot.

"Thor! Not Ireland," a third woman groaned, coloring her eyelids blue. "Then Thrain will just bring more spears—no beads and no trefoil brooches."

A young woman lacing her ankles gasped. "Do you think? I promised my father a slave for his metalworks—certainly not another mess of red-haired shepherds. Sometimes I think Mord takes anything with legs."

Spirits ran so high that Asa had to clap sharply several times before an embarrassed serving woman scurried to prepare her. Asa selected her traditional oval brooches and a regal purple cloak of her own weaving. She wore her keys as always, but shunned the stylish needleboxes and decorative scissors that the younger women—who had learned almost nothing about sewing!—pinned above their breasts in a jangling, ostentatious display. After forty-five winters, Asa knew her beauty relied not on dazzle, but on authority.

It was galling how little actual authority she retained.

Despite the care she had spent on Halfdan's upbringing in Agthir, he had rebelled almost from the first. The stocky, black-haired youth — an uncanny reflection of his father — had devoted his childhood to weapons practice, falling at times into dark fits of rage and often loudly envying the free-booting life of his half-brother Olav. At nine Halfdan had thrown himself into hunting, the only practical use Asa allowed for his weapon skills. He had won his name "Halfdan the Black" by killing a black bear with his dogs during a summer visit to his foster brother Sigurth Hart in Hringariki's forests.

Asa had long known Halfdan would not be the champion she needed to end the ways of the Vikings. But how could she have anticipated the changes he would wreak when he assumed Agthir's Dragon High Seat? Halfdan had hardly taken his place between the dragon-head posts at his debauched coronation feast when he announced that Agthir would henceforth be ruled as a mere province. He would build a copy of the Vik in his portion of Vestfold. There he would found an even greater market town than Skiringssal and erect even stronger defenses. Finally, to Asa's horror, he declared that he would join forces with Olav in the Vikings' summer raids.

Since then a dozen frustrating winters had passed. Never before had the Vikings' barbarity spread so wide. In their first summer together, Olav and Halfdan sailed farther up the Seine than Norsemen had ever dared, finally sacking and burning Paris itself. When King Otto the Bald amassed the Knightish army against them on both sides of the river, the Vikings docked on one shore and crushed half the army first, hanging a hundred captives in trees while the other half of the army watched from the opposite bank, helpless without ships. Otto the Bald had finally paid seven thousand pounds of silver to convince the raiders to leave.

Word of that exorbitant, extorted treasure had spread through Norway's thirty-one kingdoms like a plague. Restless young men, infected by greed and glory, had vanished from farms overnight to swell the ranks of oarsmen beneath the red sails. In Agthir, where resentment of the Vikings' raid against Harald Granraude still smoldered, Halfdan had forcibly conscripted troops, demanding ships as taxes.

Meanwhile, in the remote western fjordlands, several kingdoms had launched their own raiding fleets, copying the Vikings. Even Eirik of Horthaland, Asa learned with dismay, had "gone Viking" with his three young sons to the Shetland Islands for a summer. Only the inland kingdoms—and perhaps those in the far north, near Throndheim— seemed immune to the lure of Viking battle life.

Asa's faith had nearly failed in long nights of despair, when she had wondered how one woman could hope to start healing Norway of its barbaric disease—particularly when her own son was the most virulent carrier.

Certainly Asa had few tools for the task. Though Halfdan meticulously granted her the courtesies due a queen mother, he allowed her no real power. For sixteen winters she had been sole monarch of Agthir, but now she was allowed no more challenging task than organizing the court's servants. Her suggestions for trade or treaties, however insightful, fell on deaf ears.

Nor could she take command of the kingdom in the summers when Halfdan was gone. Halfdan, thirty winters old but still unmarried, simply appointed a summer regent—a fat jarl named Bork. Too slovenly to sail with the others, Bork ruled from the Round Hall on Jarlsberg.

As a result, Asa's only responsibility in Halfdan's absence was to oversee the fortress compound. With the troops gone, the place was little more than a boarding house for Halfdan's spoiled dogs and his newly ennobled jarls' wives.

"The wagons are gone!" one of the ladies cried from the courtyard.

Asa waited until the other young noblewomen rushed out aflutter. Then she calmly stepped through the hall's doorway. "I sent the wagons ahead with the ale. The serving women will bring the apples and flatbread with us, down the footpath."

"But our trains! We'll tear our dresses on the brambles."

"You will hold each other's hems and follow me," Asa commanded. She enjoyed the young women's discomfort as they formed a line behind her. One by one they submitted to the humbling order and stooped to hold the train of the dress before them.

"Paalo?" Asa asked.

The Lapp was helping an aged guardsman unbolt the heavy stockade gate for the women's procession. "All is in order, Queen. I'll wait for you here."

As Asa led the ladies down through a steep field of stumps, she surveyed the approaching red sails on the fjord below. Sixty-five had sailed in the spring. The fleet now seemed somewhat smaller. Already she could hear a crowd gathering noisily along the shore, anxious to learn which men had been lost and what had been gained. The blue-and-white blurs she saw by the docks would be the sails of the merchant sailors from Agthir. She knew they would be raising their masts and hoisting their canvas to clear the beach for the king.

When Asa reached the first streets, most of the townspeople had already left for the harbor. A one-legged crone peered fearfully from the doorway of a thatched hut. Two dogs snarled at each other, springing in vain at a slaughtered pig that hung from a yardarm. In a carpenters' yard, chisels and axes stood where they had been abandoned in half-hewn boards.

Only at Thorleif's smithy did the return of the king apparently arouse little interest. Asa heard hammers clanging within. The old goldsmith slave Bhaldec hobbled out the smoky doorway to dunk a glowing horseshoe into a water barrel. Half hidden by the steam of the iron's hiss, he wrinkled his shiny brow into a solemn wink. Asa returned a slow nod. Thorleif's move from Skiringssal had given her valuable informants—friends who knew to recognize and avoid Olav's spies.

As they neared the clamor at the beach, one of the ladies excitedly dropped her hem and ran ahead. Asa's frown froze the others at her side. She led them sternly through the crowd toward the jetty.

The log streets behind them drummed with hoofbeats as women on horseback arrived from the outlying farms to learn the fates of their husbands. Dogs barked. Seagulls cried. Barefoot children squirmed through the crowd and ran along the water's edge. "There's Papa! See his striped shield?"

In the fjord, the sleek Viking warships had lowered their sails and sprouted oars, but had become jumbled as the Agthir merchant ships tacked out between them to make room in the harbor. Impatient Viking oarsmen slapped arcs of spray across the Agthir ships as they passed.

Unaware that Asa stood close enough to hear, a farmer laughed, "Nothing makes the Vikings madder than being outsailed."

A man beside him whispered tensely, "Shh, friend!" Then he added loudly, "The best sailors, but the worst fighters. Serves the Agthir fishermen right."

As soon as Halfdan's and Olav's banner-ships had jockeyed to the royal berths along the stone dock, a roar rose from the other warships on the fjord. At once their oarsmen strained at their work, jamming the ships toward the beach in a headlong rush. Oars snapped as the long-ships careened onto the strand, sending a wave over the crowd's feet. Before gangplanks could be thrown overboard, Vikings sprang from the prows and vaulted over the gunwales open-armed.

The men's hair was stringy, their cheeks thin, their malodorous clothes dingy and stiff, but they swept up squealing children and hugged wives with relief. Hungrily they gulped the traditional apple slices and flatbread while at the same time attempting to share news of the past four months.

Elsewhere in the crowd, distraught women sought their husbands, interrogating returned men until they learned the truth. Before long, a sorrowful collection of flatbread and apples bobbed where it had been cast into the fjord. The warriors who had been lost needed to know that they were not forgotten. Every widow knew that the compassionate Freya, with prayer, might be persuaded to carry such an offering of food to a husband in Valhalla.

"Toulouse!" Halfdan bellowed proudly, popping bits of Asa's flatbread into his mouth with his thumb.

Over the past twelve winters Asa had become far more knowledgeable about European geography than she wished. Every summer Halfdan's raiders spread farther, no longer sacking only monasteries, but laying waste entire cities and islands. Europe's river towns, fortified for centuries against land-based attacks, lay helpless before the Vikings' fast, shallow-draft longships. York, Hamburg, Tours, Bordeaux, Limoges—all had fallen and burned. Now, Toulouse.

"Even brought back a Knightish princess. Time I had a queen." The black-bearded king turned to curse at a pair of sailors stumbling with a heavy chest. Then he dismissed his mother with a command over his shoulder. "See the ale's opened before I start the gifting ceremony."

But Asa hesitated. Halfdan's startling announcement had put an awkward twist in her plans. And now the sight of the stolen princess—the only female slave on Halfdan's ship—filled her with new anger. The poor girl hardly looked twelve winters old. A strangely cut blue silk gown hung straight on her childish form. Long, raven-black hair fell loose from her upturned head. Asa knew only too well the kind of terror hiding beneath the girl's defiant mien. Had her family been slaughtered too? And why had Halfdan found it necessary to bind her hands?

"Ssff! Can't stay, Halfdan. Ssff!" Old Olav limped heavily down the dock, hissing and stiffening with pain at every other step. Even though he had shed his armor and used his ax as a crutch, the damp sea voyages and cold winters had left him crippled with an excruciating ailment in his left leg that no wizard seemed able to mend.

"What's this? You'll miss the feast." Halfdan frowned.

"My men are eager for their own feast at the Vik." Olav clapped him on the shoulder. Then he added in a somber tone, "And I should tell you, next summer you'll sail with Rognvald." He had decided that morning—with raging regret—that this would be his last summer raid. The most brilliant swordsmanship was of little use if one could not walk. At least, he considered, his son Rognvald was old enough to start commanding the jarls in his stead.

Halfdan nodded grimly. He had been expecting this since the storming of the Toulouse citadel, when Olav had opted to guard the ships. Olav had missed the better part of the booty—the castellan's armor, the cathedral's gold, and the bishop's wondrous, iridescent-feathered bird. Now Halfdan glanced down the dock and noticed young Rognvald pacing with an unaccustomed swagger. When the strapping lad turned, Halfdan saw he already wore the Vikings' famed sword, Fenris.

"Olav. Take the peacock." He knew even such a magnificent gift could not begin to compensate the aging Viking for what he was losing.

Silently, Olav unpinned his much envied camel-hair cape and gave it to Halfdan with a nod. His lips tightened. Perhaps it would have been better to die in the flames of Toulouse.

"Ssff!" Olav painfully limped aside—and stopped at Asa's proud gaze. Asa! The hateful woman had always been a thorn in his side. Never could she be watched too carefully. The jarls had kept her on a short chain until now. But would Rognvald understand how dangerous she was?

Halfdan scowled, "The ale, mother." He turned to his bodyguards, a pair of jarls lolling on the ship with their laughing wives. "Modolf! Thorkel! Escort the Queen Mother so that the ale may be opened. And secure Ship Hall for the rewards."

Asa left the dock before the jarls could free themselves from the embraces of their women. Even if Olav were weakened by age, she knew his network of jarls remained as powerful as ever.

For a man with so little political acumen, Olav had devised a masterful system of terror. But perhaps she herself had given him the idea. Long ago, when Guthroth had died, she had threatened him with the judgment of the people's law-courts—the "Things." She should have known a simple man like Olav would resent the complicated, ancient system of Norse law. Even the wisest of the law advocates had lost cases by overlooking technicalities in the old laws. It took three days at the annual Thing gatherings for the Law Speaker to recite the entire code of Norse law by memory—a task that had been handed down for untold generations so that nothing would be forgotten.

She guessed that Olav scorned the courts even more because their sentences were not carried out by the sword, but rather by an intricate system of fines. A stolen bull was worth two ounces of gold; a killed slave, twenty; a murdered freeman, two hundred. The cruelest punishment was not death, but outlawry—banishment from home and country. Olav preferred the simplicity of battle.

Soon after Asa had left the Vik, word had come of young Olav's bloody razzias against the law courts. Throughout Vestfold, law speakers and advocates had been tracked to their homes and murdered. The sacred meeting places of the Thing courts had been destroyed. To the borders of his kingdom, Olav had demolished the old law. In its place, he decreed that Vestfold would be ruled by the Vik's brutal military justice. To carry out his order he created titles for hundreds of new jarls—crude warriors without a drop of noble blood—and sent them throughout the kingdom, spying on the populace and settling disputes with their swords.

The reign of terror had not diminished when Olav later split

Vestfold with Halfdan. The Viking jarls in Halfdan's realm were only nominally Halfdan's subjects. In truth their first allegiance still lay with the Vik. Asa knew it was no coincidence that Tunsberg was flanked by two of the Vikings' most powerful strongholds, Jarlsøy and Jarlsberg. The jarls not only suppressed rebellion among the resentful farmers, but stood ready to overthrow Halfdan should Olav command it.

If only Halfdan could be made to listen, Asa thought! He was too caught up in the Vikings' glory to see he was their puppet. Hope lay in the lands outside of Vestfold. But saving her son against his will might take more ingenuity than even she could muster.

When Asa had made her way through the crowd to the wagons, she saw with surprise that one of the ale barrels had already been opened. A cluster of rough men were brazenly dipping their drinking horns into the open barrel. The men wore the jarls' distinctive, puffy pantaloons—ludicrous, knee-length Arabian pants that would have been laughed out of Norway had the jarls not forbidden them to commoners.

"Which of you dared to open the welcoming ale?" Asa demanded. She shoved her way through the jarls with surprising strength. In the midst of the jarls, perched on a board across the barrel's rim, sat the grinning, obese mass of Jarl Bork.

"Who dares to ask? The Little Chieftain perhaps?" Bork idly dipped his horn and drank, dribbling froth down his puffy cheeks.

Asa's struggled to control her voice. "By Viking tradition, the Queen must serve the ale—and it should go first to those who have voyaged farther than Jarlsberg."

Bork belched at her. "I hear we'll have a queen someday. Knightish, too, and pretty." The jarls chuckled, but the crowd of common sailors and farmers beyond was quiet.

Asa turned to the crowd. "Open the other three barrels for freemen! The jarls may have this first one for their own, though I fear it's the dirtiest of all." Then, with a sudden lunge, she grabbed Bork's foot and hurled herself against his flank. The overweight jarl flailed, but could find no grip. With a splash he fell backwards into the ale, nearly plugging the barrel with his bulk. The throng erupted in shouts and laughter.

Asa strode on, her head high. The small victory had given her the beginnings of a new plan. As Queen Mother, she had one other ceremonial right at her disposal today. And Halfdan, for all his failings, respected ceremony.

The guards at Ship Hall nodded dutifully as Asa entered the huge double doors. The building was the largest of the twenty boat sheds on the shore. Today the hall was being readied for the only Viking celebration to outshine Yule — the distribution of the summer's booty.

Down the middle of the hall, long boards on trestles already sagged with treasure. Helmets, many of them decorated with precious metals, stood stacked like cheeses. Looted halberds and spears leaned perilously against each other across tables. Stirrups, combs, candlesticks, game boards, jewel-encrusted Skiring book covers, belts, ivory boxes, and gold crosses lay jumbled along the boards as if at Europe's greatest market. Beneath the tables, a row of iron-bound trunks gaped at their own wealth of gold and silver coins.

Asa passed by the treasures, pausing only to examine a display of glassware — something the raiders rarely brought. The sea-green goblets stood on delicate glass stems. A large glass bowl had been blown in the shape of a grinning face, with ears for handles. Beside this was an entire tray of the rare glass beads so hotly desired by Viking wives. Clearly Toulouse was nearer to the source of such glass wonders than the Vikings had yet come.

When Asa took her position in the high seat opposite Halfdan's familiar dragon throne, she could see the new slaves huddling in the shadows along the wall, bound by chains. The little Knightish princess sat apart from the others, flanked by heavily armed jarls. Her hands were still bound only with rope. Her head was bowed and her eyes were closed. Evidently exhaustion had overcome the girl's defiance. But then Asa noticed that the girl must not be asleep after all, for her delicate lips were moving silently and the palms of her hands were pressed together.

"Your pardon, Queen." An elderly serving woman stooped before Asa with a bowl of warm water, a whalebone comb, and an embroidered washcloth.

"Not now," Asa said, annoyed. Then she stopped. "Wait. Bring these to the girl by the wall."

The old woman followed Asa's nod. Her eyes grew large. "To the slave? The one with bound hands?"

"Cut her ties."

"But Queen—"

"Do as I say. She will want to wash after her voyage."

The old woman sighed at her mistress' whim and hobbled across the hall.

Though Asa feigned interest in the final arrangement of the treasure tables, she watched with satisfaction as the old serving woman argued with the two burly jarls guarding the girl. First the serving woman berated them with her hands on her hips. Then she wagged her finger as if at disobedient grandchildren. Finally she brushed past the guards, cut the girl's ropes, and presented the toiletries. The astonished girl responded by speaking rapidly in a high, musical voice. But the old woman simply put a hand to the girl's mouth to show her language was not understood. Then she pointed to Asa and withdrew to other duties, shaking her head. The girl gave the queen a bewildered but grateful look. Then she threw her black hair over her shoulder and bent to the washbowl.

The low, mellow tones of spiral lur horns sounded the length of the hall. All heads turned to watch the entrance of the king.

"Allow the crew of the banner ship to enter first," Halfdan ordered, striding down the hall to the Dragon High Seat. A page hurried behind him with an enormous musk ox horn of ale. As the sailors filed in—all of them jarls in black pantaloons—the king emptied the horn.

He wiped his dripping beard with an arm. "The best ale in Europe. Well done, Asa." Then he addressed the men. "Hail Thor for bringing us home."

"Hail Thor!" the men roared back.

"You have served well and deserve gold from your king. I've watched you fight and know to value your effort. Just as my father, Guthroth the Generous, lavished gifts upon the Vikings, so will Halfdan the Black."

Murmurs and nods from the men showed their approval.

"Following the tradition of Guthroth, and of his father Halfdan Whiteleg, the first gift will be for the ranking queen, to thank the gods for the safekeeping of our homeland." He signaled across the hall to Asa. "Choose."

Asa stood and slowly walked to the tables.

Halfdan noted pointedly, "We managed to bring back some particularly fine glassware this summer."

"That is true," she answered. He was not always an insensitive son. The glassware was attractive, and preserving such fragile treasures through the sea voyage must have been a challenge. "Still, I think I will leave the glassware for another."

"Well, then?" The king impatiently rapped his fingers on the dragon head. "What will you have? And be quick about it."

Asa faced him squarely. "I need younger serving women for the court. I choose as my gift a slave."

He wrinkled his brow. "We took plenty of Skirings, if that's all you want. How many?"

"Only one." She pointed to the girl who had just finished combing out her long hair. "The Knightish princess."

Halfdan stormed to his feet. "What! Choose the glassware, woman! The girl was not brought for you."

"I choose only the girl."

The king balled his fists and reddened with rage, but he knew even this treacherous choice was within his mother's traditional rights. "Are you so jealous of a younger queen?"

"I've heard ill luck and dishonor follow those who take their queens by force," she said.

The allusion to his own father made Halfdan more cautious. He feared ill luck as much as anyone. And it was true, several jarls had warned him that a Skiring wife might offend Thor. "Dishonor? You yourself have said a man's honor is his heirs. Honor requires that I take a wife."

"What would you know of honor, my son? There will only be shame and ridicule for a man who would leave his own brother's murder unavenged."

There were murmurs in the hall at this unexpected accusation. Halfdan himself found the conversation's sudden twist disorienting. His brother Olav was old, but certainly not dead. "My men know I would gladly lay down my life for the honor of my brother."

"Do you swear to that?"

"By all the gods. But you saw yourself Olav is alive."

Asa raised her head. "Your half-brother lives, yes. But your foster brother, Sigurth Hart, is dead."

The king ran his hand over his beard. Sigurth had been a childhood friend and remained, technically, a foster brother. But their paths had parted winters ago when Halfdan joined the Vikings and Sigurth became king of Hringariki, an insignificant inland realm. Was Sigurth really dead, or was this another of Asa's tricks?

"Why has no one told me of this?" Halfdan demanded.

"Your jarls think only of distant lands. They are blind to the dangers on your own borders."

"How did Sigurth die?"

"A berserker named Haki attacked with forty men when Sigurth was hunting in the forest ten days ago. Sigurth killed four men and wounded twelve before falling. Haki himself lost an arm."

Halfdan let out a long breath. Then it might be true after all. Berserkers were capable of such madness. He himself had succeeded in harnessing the awful energy of Vestfold's berserkers by forging them into Viking crews. But he knew that many more of the Odin cultists still lived in the backcountry. Their name came from the bear *serks*, the crudely tanned bear skins they wore. They ate spotted mushrooms to whip themselves into frenzies, impervious to pain. In their rage they sometimes bit the edges of their shields and tore out the hearts of their enemies. That they had now banded together and killed a king was unwelcome news. That Sigurth had fallen was uglier yet.

"And where is this Haki now?"

Asa sensed she had nearly won. "The berserkers overran your brother's estate on Lake Tyri, taking his children hostage. There is a son of eleven winters, Guthorm, and a daughter of twenty, Ragnhild. My informants say Haki will marry her and declare himself king of Hringariki as soon as his wounds heal."

Halfdan frowned. His mother had thoroughly spoiled the celebratory mood of the gifting ceremony. "Page! Bring us more ale!" The brew had a peculiarly soothing flavor. Had she added some new spice? He felt he needed the ale's benumbing strength now.

Asa pressed on. "Will the king uphold his oath of revenge?"

"Warships can't sail over moors." He waved her away with a hand. "I'll take a force there on sledges after the hard freeze. Banner-ship forecastlemen, step forward!"

A faint smile crossed her lips. "Yes, that will do. As long as I come with you."

* * *

Wind hurled dry snow across the dim ice. Dark, fringed shawls whipped from the two figures on the frozen shore.

"*Mamere!*" The dark-haired girl pointed to the sky, huddling closer to Asa. "What is?"

Red and blue spears of light stabbed above the mountains, disappearing among the faint stars of dawn like rippled cloud reflections on water. For a moment the glowing spears stopped in mid-flight — blue, then red, then blue again. Then the aurora faded altogether.

"It is our gods, Mari. They fight our battles in the sky."

The girl nodded fearfully. In this dark, northern land of terrors, she could believe that even the gods were warriors. She hugged the tall woman, knowing she would protect her if anyone could. "In Knightia, god battle here," she said, tapping her heart with her fist.

Asa looked at the child sadly. She was learning Norse. But she was a flower plucked from a world of sunshine and sweet fruits. It hurt to teach her the hardness of the North. Asa tapped her heart. "In Norway, *women* battle here."

The bitter wind gusted again, and they leaned against it together, their eyes closed.

When Asa looked up, the wind had blown dark arcs across Lake Tyri. As if through a tunnel she saw black smoke above a fuzzy spark on the far shore. The hall was burning. If only her eyes were clearer! "Mari, can you see them?"

Mari peered across the frozen lake. "*Cabale!*" She made a galloping motion with her hand. When Asa did not appear to understand, Mari remembered that Norse ponies did not gallop. Instead she moved her hand across her cloak in a trot.

"Horses! At last. I will wait alone now. Go to the house. Build up the fires."

"Yes, *Mamere*." Mari kissed Asa on the cheek and ran up the snowy field to a stone hut.

For nearly an hour Asa stood by herself, watching the dots grow across the ice. A cold ray of sun skimmed the lake, firing the swirling ice crystals with glints of blue and yellow. A reindeer ventured from the woods and pawed at the lakeshore in the hopes of a drink. Then it snuffed toward the shapes on the lake and bolted.

Finally Asa could make out the silver gleam of helmets and the white of the wagon's tent covering. A dozen horse-drawn sledges followed, along with a troop of men poling on bone skates.

"Aunt Asa!" A young woman with drawn features and pale yellow hair called out from the wagon's opening.

"Ragnhild! Are you all right?" Asa had not seen Sigurth's daughter for several winters. She hardly recognized this mature, care-worn face.

Halfdan reined in the ponies, and the ceremonial wagon's wooden wheels rolled to a stop.

"Oh, help us, Aunt Asa," Ragnhild said, cradling a young boy's head on her lap. "My brother Guthorm won't wake up. He was knocked senseless when the warriors burst into the hall. I don't know what to do."

Halfdan turned. "I'll drive him up to the house."

"No," Asa announced. "It's too rough. We'll carry him. Ragnhild, stay by his head." She signaled several warriors to help.

In a minute they were walking up the rocky path to the hut. Blue smoke rose only a few inches above a gap in the sod roof before the wind whisked it away. Asa pushed the door open. The room was redolent with smoke, dung, and hay. Mari stood up from the fireside to greet them, but she caught her breath when she saw the limp child they carried.

"Lay him on the bench." Asa rolled her scarf for a pillow. "Mari, fetch water to boil."

After the warriors had set down their load, they stood back awkwardly. One bumped his head on a ceiling beam and cursed.

At once Asa drove them away. "All of you, out!"

Halfdan peered in from the doorway. "I'll take care of—"

Asa shut the door on her son and returned to the boy. Healers, not battle kings, were needed now. She ran her fingers slowly through Guthorm's thin, brown hair, feeling carefully. The bloodied spot over his temple was not a deep wound. The pulse there was strong. In all likelihood, he could be brought to consciousness with a pungent mash of hot, crushed juniper berries.

When Asa glanced to Ragnhild, however, she saw the young woman was shivering and ashen-faced—perhaps even more dangerously shocked than her brother. She would require treatment, too, but of a different sort. "Your brother's wounds are not serious, Ragnhild. Sit down and we'll make you chamomile tea. You are safe now."

Ragnhild nodded, sinking against a pillar by the fire. "Aunt Asa, so much has happened so swiftly." She glanced uncertainly at Mari, who was hanging a pot of water above the fire.

"This is Mari," Asa explained. "She was brought with the Skirings this fall, but I treat her as I would a daughter."

The shivering young woman seemed hardly to hear.

"Ragnhild, tell me what has happened," Asa said.

She covered her face with a trembling hand. "I was so frightened. I woke up to shouts in the dark. At first I didn't know they'd come to rescue us. I thought it was the berserkers again."

"Was it night when the berserkers attacked last summer?"

"Yes. I keep picturing it over and over. First a naked man split open the door and killed our mother with an ax. Another berserker wrestled our overseer to the ground and bit out his throat. Haki came last. His arm ended in a burnt mass at the elbow." She shuddered. "The battle didn't take long. When it was over, Haki said he was going to marry me. I offered to tend his wounds."

"Why?"

"To kill him. I mixed dung in the salve. But I was afraid to use very much, for fear he'd notice. Finally, he began to regain his strength in spite of me. If Halfdan hadn't come, Haki would have forced me to his bed soon."

Asa finished positioning her poultice on Guthorm's wound. Then she sprinkled sweet-smelling chamomile buds into a soapstone cup, ladled hot water, and brought the steaming tea to Ragnhild. "Haki is dead now. Everything will be better."

But Ragnhild turned away, her face buried in her hands. Her shoulders shook as if she were silently crying.

"What is it, niece?" Asa asked.

"It's—Halfdan."

Asa drew back, horrified. "Halfdan? What did he do to you?"

"In the wagon—on the way across the lake—"

"Yes? What?"

"He said—he said that he would marry me."

For a moment Asa felt only relief. Vikings who raped women on summer expeditions sometimes kept the habit when they returned to their homeland. She was glad Halfdan had not sunk so low. Then she began to realize the importance of her son's proposal. The young woman before her could become her daughter-in-law.

"Does the offer frighten you?" Asa asked. "As an orphan, you can give your own answer."

She turned to Asa, her eyes red. "I know. But what should I say?"

Asa was at a loss for words. "You should say what you feel, Ragnhild. Do you find the match attractive?"

"I don't know. I mean yes, Hringariki could use a strong king, but — I'm confused. I had the most peculiar dream last night."

Asa knew the importance of such visions. The gods have few more potent means of warning mortals of the future. Wizards devoted life-times to unraveling the gods' nocturnal riddles. "And what was in your dream?"

Ragnhild sighed, staring into the fire. "I was in a garden when I no-ticed a thorn in my shift. I reached down and plucked it out, but as I held it, it started to grow. It grew down and up at the same time until it became a long twig. One end reached the ground and took root. The other end kept on growing up. Finally it became a tree so tall I could hardly see the top. The trunk was marvelously thick, like no tree I've ever seen."

"Did it have a color?"

"Yes. Red at the bottom, but blue higher up, and at the top the branches were as white as if they were covered with snow. There were many limbs. Some were short, but others were so long that they seemed to spread out over all of Norway."

"All of Norway . . . ." Asa looked into the fire, her mind racing. It had been a powerful dream indeed. Perhaps Ragnhild really was the one she had been waiting for.

"Aunt Asa, what should I do?"

She took Ragnhild's hands earnestly. "Marry Halfdan. But do not name your first son Guthroth, as he will wish." Asa paused, recalling the promise she had made long ago to her father. "Name my grandson Harald."

CHAPTER 12
FALL, 1904

The flap of Kirstin's tent flew open with such violence that she dropped her pen. Magnus strode in, disheveled, his hair wild. His Norwegian wool jacket hung open crookedly. She wondered at once if he had been drinking.

"I've got to talk to you," he said.

She folded her arms. In the weeks since their kiss at Castle Hill, she had kept her distance from Magnus. If word spread that she was romantically interested in the labor manager, her authority at the excavation would crumble. All through her career she had been told that women could not become scientists because females were driven by emotion instead of logic. She wasn't about to give anyone fuel for that fire.

"You've no right to barge into my tent."

"To hell with that. I've got to know what's happened. Why won't you even look at me? Or did I just dream that we sailed to Tønsberg together?"

She looked him straight in the eyes to prove to herself she could do it. The crackle of attraction was there, with the sharp, electric air that preceded a storm. She had been foolish to let down her guard with this unpredictable man. Now the danger itself had become a dark thrill.

"I'm sorry, Magnus. Our work here at the excavation comes first. I won't let anything jeopardize that."

He turned his face as if slapped. "It's still the missing dragonhead posts, isn't it? You think I stole them after all."

"No, of course not." But in truth, a touch of doubt had crept back. No other clues had turned up. Carl and Otto had volunteered to take over Magnus's shifts as night watchman to make sure he was never alone in the excavation. Nearly a month had passed since then, and nothing else had been stolen.

Magnus straightened. "Someone took that crate, Kirstin, and it wasn't me. Look around you. You'll lose your whole damn dragonship if you don't open your eyes."

"What do you mean?"

But he had already turned and left the tent.

She pushed aside the papers on her desk. It was true that the missing dragonhead posts had never been explained. Her "investigation" of Magnus had ended abruptly with a kiss. After that she had let herself be swept up in the work at the excavation. She hadn't even tried to get answers from Otto, and hadn't he been as likely a suspect as Magnus? Now she recalled how easily the German had shrugged off the theft. He had called it a cost of doing business. She decided it was time to restart her detective work.

* * *

That afternoon Kirstin arranged to work with Otto on the foredeck. The excavation of the front part of the ship had revealed an astonishing array of Viking gear—three sledges, a ceremonial wagon, and a collapsible bed frame with bedposts in the shape of horses.

"You know," Otto said, wagging his camel's hair brush toward her. "I'd be suspicious of a queen who took a fancy bed with her to the grave."

Kirstin smiled. "I think the Yngling Saga shows that Asa could take care of herself."

"She took care of her furniture, too. When the excavation runs out of cash we could set up a flea market. A dragon post here, a collapsible bed there—we'd pay off the farmer and the workers in no time."

The comment did not strike Kirstin as funny, and raised her suspicion of Otto a notch. She tried laying a simple trap. "Isn't there an art auction in Hamburg where they don't ask questions?"

Otto replied with a pained smile. "Just kidding, Kirstin."

The trap had been too simple. She set to brushing dirt from the jumble of wooden fragments in front of her. But her mind was not on the work. Otto had both the motive and the knowledge to sell artifacts abroad. "Don't you sometimes wonder where the dragon posts are by now? If they're already in some private collection?"

"Yes." Otto nodded. "When I stand night watch, there's time to wonder about a lot of things."

"It must be tiring to stay up all night." She had volunteered to take one of the shifts, but Carl had forbidden it, saying he would not allow a woman out alone in the dark. It was one time she had not been able to shake his determination.

Otto didn't meet her eyes. "Sometimes. Last night I actually fell asleep."

"While you were supposed to be on watch?"

He waved the question away. "That's why I'm working straight through today. Penance, you know."

It worried her that he treated their security precautions so lightly. "Maybe we should double the watch."

"Perhaps so." He was silent for a moment. Then he chuckled. "No. Let's just lighten my homework load. Makes me drowsy."

"Homework?"

"You know, that copy of the Yngling Saga you assigned."

She hadn't assigned it, of course. She had merely made copies of the saga for Carl and Otto. "So it put you to sleep."

"Actually I enjoyed reading it. There was one part that struck me as strange, though. That verse about Olav, the king who split Vestfold with Halfdan the Black. How did it go?

> "Of yore ruled
> His realm Olav ...""

When Otto faltered, Kirstin continued,

> "Over vast lands
> In Vestfold,
> Till foot-ill
> The king failed.
> Now buried in barrow
> The great battle
> Liege lies
> Alone at Geirstad."

"Right," Otto said. "'Till foot-ill the king failed.' That puzzled me. What kind of Viking king would die of a foot disease?"

"It does sound peculiar for a Viking," Kirstin admitted.

"Well, it made me think of the Gokstad ship. That old dig's been on

my mind anyway since I heard about Magnus's miniature version."

"And?" Kirstin had briefly told Otto about *Skiblathnir*. Of course she hadn't mentioned sailing in it with Magnus.

"Well, I checked with Carl. The skeleton found in the old Gokstad ship burial was removed from the antiquities collection a few years ago for a more modern analysis. Apparently it belonged to a fifty-year-old man severely crippled by gout in his left leg."

Kirstin almost dropped her brush. "Olav!" Her thoughts sped with the idea. Could Olav have died while suffering with gout? The Gokstad ship had even been found in the part of Vestfold where—according to the sagas—Olav ruled. Then caution slowed her. "But the saga explicitly says Olav was buried at Geirstad, not Gokstad."

Otto shrugged. "Where is Geirstad? I looked it up in an atlas. There's no place in Norway with that name now. Anyway, the ship was found between two farms, Gokstad and Gjekstad. Maybe Gjekstad is a corruption of the old name."

It was as nice a piece of etymological detective work—and it strengthened her own argument about the importance of the sagas. Now both Asa and Olav from the Yngling Saga could be linked to actual burial sites.

"You think the derivation makes sense?" he asked.

"Certainly. I also think it makes sense that two monarchs from the same part of Norway would be buried in the same manner. Look at the rest of Scandinavia. Most Vikings were simply burned in their ships."

"I can sure see why. Burying a ship must have been a huge job. It's hard enough unburying one." Otto shook his head. "But why weren't the ships more alike? Every scrap of wood we dig up here is covered with carvings. The Gokstad ship was as plain as a scow. What's so special about this Asa?"

Kirstin pondered this a moment, allowing shadowy memories from her dreams to drift before her. The image that came to mind was of an older, nearly blind woman in a worn cloak, working in a vegetable garden. What had become of the glorious young queen she had seen in earlier dreams?

"I don't know. I really don't know."

"Perhaps Olav was just a minor chieftain," Otto suggested.

"He was more important than that. Didn't the Gokstad burial include a lot of animal remains?"

"True, true," Otto admitted. "I suppose an ordinary chieftain might have been buried with twelve horses and six dogs, but only a king would have been silly enough to take a peacock with him to the grave."

Kirstin and Otto looked at each other and laughed.

They were still smiling when one of the workers called that dinner was ready.

As Kirstin walked down from the excavation, it occurred to her that Otto had distracted her from her investigation as easily as Magnus. Magnus had given her a kiss and a marvelous ride in a miniature ship. Otto had given her a good laugh and a clever saga theory.

She sighed as she headed toward the water tank to wash up for dinner. She wasn't a schemer — unlike the saga queen who stormed through her dreams. She just wanted to finish the excavation.

As she washed her hands she counted the crates stacked by the dusty wagon road. It had become a habit before dinner each day, keeping track of the team's slow progress, converting a shipload of fragments into neatly packed crates.

Then she stopped and counted again. Twenty-nine? Her heart gave an alarming skip. After crating up the Viking bed there should have been thirty.

With her hands still dripping, she walked about the stack. Anger began to swell within her. Of course it was the newest crate, the one with the valuable bed. It had been stacked in the back, where its loss might be overlooked for a time. The ground was so hard she could only make out a few scuffs from the thief's wagon tracks. Then she noticed a dot of gray amidst the brown grass. A pewter button—the sort of button worn on Norwegian sweaters.

Kirstin leaned against a crate, trying to order her thoughts. Magnus had charged into her tent that morning with his sweater awry. She could almost picture a wool thread dangling where a button had been lost. It could have torn loose when he lifted a crate of artifacts onto a wagon.

And Otto—he'd had an oddly serious expression when he admitted that he had fallen asleep on guard duty during the night. He'd said he worked through the day as penance.

Two scenarios spread before her. In the first, Magnus stole the crate while Otto slept—either to sell the artifacts or to hide them from the Swedish government. In the second scenario, Otto stole the crate at the order of the Kaiser's Reichsmuseum. Then he planted the pewter button to throw suspicion onto Magnus.

If she hadn't known these men so well, either story might have been convincing. But something was very wrong. She felt the undercurrent of a deeper evil, a darker lie.

She slipped the pewter button into her dress pocket and headed toward the dining tent.

CHAPTER 13
WINTER, 867

Asa felt her way across the dim hut toward the red glow of the forge.

A weak cough at her feet startled her.

"Thorleif?" She touched the shadow and realized that the old metalsmith was lying on a bench, covered against the evening's drafts. She turned to the young woman at her side. "Mari, let Thorleif's wife and his servant know we have come."

"Yes, *Mamere.*"

The old metalsmith slowly raised himself to an elbow, studying Asa's tattered cloak. Her jewelry was gone. Her embroidered dress was faded. Even her eyes had clouded. All that remained of the regal "Little Chieftain" he remembered from forty winters before were the proud poise, the steel voice, and the quick mind.

Thorleif's voice was raspy. "We have come to dark days, Queen."

She bent to him. "Is it true that you have seen your fetch?"

He nodded slowly. "I heard a single knock at the door. Time is short. When my spirit knocks again—twice—I must go."

"Even on the darkest days the sky must lighten. Today is the start of Yule."

"There are no more Yules," he said, shaking his head. "I did not live long enough to heal the curse I unleashed. The evil of Fenris ran deeper than we knew. It has poisoned the hearts of too many men. Halfdan—"

Though he was interrupted by a spasm of coughing, Asa knew what he was going to say. Her son Halfdan the Black's madness had destroyed their plans to halt the spread of the Vikings. They had had great hopes during the first year of the king's marriage to the gentle Ragnhild.

Halfdan had even stayed home an entire summer, using Olav's funeral as an excuse to skip the annual raid and enjoy the pleasures of his young wife.

But then Ragnhild's baby had been born blond. The black-haired king had raged through the fortress' halls, slaughtering blond male slaves with his sword. Asa had desperately tried to reason with her jealous son. She was sure Ragnhild had been faithful, and after all, blond hair was common in their family. Wild-eyed, he had denounced her as a traitor and had thrown her bodily out the door.

The day after Halfdan's rampage, his fit of passion had ebbed. But life in the Tunsberg fortress was forever changed. With the curt words, "One queen is more than enough," Halfdan had stripped Asa of her honored position. He'd sent her to live in a rude shed below the stockade wall. Ragnhild, outraged by Asa's humiliation, had insisted the baby be given the name Asa had chosen. She named the boy Harald.

In the ten winters since that time, the king had fallen more and more frequently into fits of rage. Meanwhile the Viking jarls had quietly drawn Halfdan's realm more tightly into their grip.

Thorleif was still coughing when Mari returned with Thorleif's wife Groa and the hunched slave Bhaldec.

"Do you have news from the other kingdoms?" Asa asked Groa.

The old woman nodded. "An Agthir merchant ship arrived yesterday from the west. The jarls of Thelamork have disbanded the kingdom's Thing courts in favor of the Vikings' code. The people were powerless to stop them."

Asa's expression hardened. The lawless Viking terror now reigned in twenty of Norway's thirty-one kingdoms, from the western fjords to Östfold. Perhaps it really was too late for her—for anyone—to stop the Vikings. Their brutal jarls ruled most of England. Eirik of Horthaland's three sons had declared themselves 'Jarls of the Atlantic,' conquering the Orkney, Shetland, and Færoe Islands. Even the Swedes, inspired by the Vikings' success, had subdued the Slavs and besieged the fabled eastern capital of Constantinople. Half the world rattled in the Vikings' chains.

It seemed only the gods could help now.

Asa reached into the leather pouch she had brought. Her fingers closed around the hard, heavy squares she had hidden so long. Then she laid the filigreed gold, with its remnants of torn cloak, in Thorleif's hand.

"The clasps!" he exclaimed. "I forged them for Guthroth ages ago. But why—"

"Reforge them for me," Asa said. "You must try again to break Fenris' curse."

His gaze rose wearily to her. "I am too old for this task."

"Look at the patterns you wrought. You showed Thor himself, hammering out the chain that was to bind the wolf-god. The clasps were your first attempt to bind Fenris. They have failed. You must forge another charm."

Thorleif shook his head. "No use. In the legend, even Thor's mighty second chain was too weak."

Groa came forward, her green eye gleaming. "But in the legend, a leash was finally fashioned. A leash that will hold the wolf-god until Ragnarök. A leash that was forged from the footfalls of cats and the breath of fish. A leash that drew upon subtle powers greater than Thor's."

The wizened sorcerer looked again at the clasp in his hands. Blue, red, and green jewels drew his gaze deep into a faceted crystal world. Perhaps a stronger magic than he had yet tapped lay somewhere in that other, ordered universe. But he was too tired to set out on such a quest. He had already seen his fetch. He might only have moments before the final summons. He would die unreconciled, and Fenris would ravage on, devouring the earth before its time.

Thorleif raised a shaking finger to press the clasp's blue stone. As the two halves of the clasp unlatched, a booming double knock resounded from the hut's front door.

A moan of despair escaped the old man's lips.

"Groa," the old sorcerer said, "Come stand by me." He kissed her wrinkled hand and held it to his chest. Then he nodded to Asa. "Unlatch the door."

The instant she lifted the bolt the door flew open, swirling snow across the room in a freezing gust. A tall, gaunt man lurched toward them. A boy at his side cried, "Grandmother!"

"Harald!" Asa exclaimed, gathering the boy in her arms. "Who is with you?"

"It's me, Paalo," the man gasped, leaning against the door.

Asa recognized the Lappish staccato of her medicinalist. "But you and the prince were supposed to be with Halfdan for Yule."

"We were, grandmother," Harald said, short of breath. "The king fell into his worst rage yet. You've got to hide us."

She put her hand to the boy's head. It was wrapped in a sticky rag. "You're wounded!"

The Lapp tore a strip of cloth from his tunic. "Let me change the bandage. The prince took a blow today that saved my life."

"How did this happen?"

Paalo removed the bloody cloth. "I went with the prince to the Yule celebrations in the Round Hall at Jarlsberg this morning. The mead was poured into a hundred horns for the opening toast. But when we drank, every horn was found to contain water except King Halfdan's. His held blood. He became so angry he smashed the table. Then he called me a wizard and accused you of ordering a spell put on his feast."

"Can you change mead into blood?"

"I know of no herb with such magic, Queen."

Asa nodded. "I'll wager there was no magic. Jarl Bork must have planned the trick to spark Halfdan's rage. Go on."

"When I refused to confess, the king drew his sword. He would have slain me if young Harald hadn't stepped between us."

Harald lifted his chin. "I told my father he couldn't kill my friend. He made me stand up in front of everybody. Then he swung his sword at me."

"The prince didn't flinch," Paalo related proudly. "At the last moment the king twisted his sword so it hit with the flat of the blade."

"I woke up in a bed with nobody around." Harald balled his fists. He had long known that his father did not love him. But until today he had respected the king out of fear. Now that he had dared to confront his father, everything had changed.

Paalo tied a fresh cloth around the boy's head. "The prince found the room where I was locked away. The guard had fallen asleep from his Yule ale. The prince cut my bonds. We ran through the forest to the fortress. A slave there told us we might find you in the village."

"You have both shown great bravery. But none of us is safe here." Asa rapidly weighed their few options. The guards would soon discover Paalo's absence. When Halfdan learned his son had aided in the escape, his rage would be more terrible than anything they had yet seen. The only ones who might calm him were Queen Ragnhild and her brother Guthorm—but they had sailed to Denmark for Yule. "Paalo, how serious is Harald's wound?"

"For such a heavy blow, there is little bleeding. But head wounds can be far more dangerous than they appear. He needs rest."

The boy stood back. "I can't stay here, no matter what. If the king finds me now he won't use the flat of his sword. He'll kill me. And Paalo and you too, Grandmother. We have to go somewhere far away."

"But hundreds of jarls will be looking for us." Asa knew the Vikings would be only too eager to help Halfdan eliminate the kingdom's sole heir.

"The jarls are sailors," the boy countered. "Let's go somewhere they can't follow in their ships. Maybe out with the farmers. They hate jarls."

Asa admired the ten-winter-old boy's thinking. "Yes, a small group on foot might escape inland."

The old metalsmith, recovering from the shock of the unexpected visitors, cleared his throat. "Perhaps I know a place you might stay. Five days' walk into the fjells, beyond the forests of Skrim, are the bogs where the iron ore I buy is secretly dug. The chieftain Jarnskegg fires the smelters there. He is loyal to our cause, and his hall is hidden."

"I want to go there," Harad said. "I don't care if my head hurts."

Asa asked, "How will we find this chieftain's hall, if it's so well hidden?"

Groa advanced to the glow of the forge, her green eye gleaming. "I know the way."

Paalo looked at the crone with concern. "Is it wise for you, in winter—"

"Let my wife go," Thorleif interrupted. "She might not survive here. Halfdan will be in Tunsberg soon, looking for revenge. He is no threat to me, a dying man. Bhaldec, with no tongue, can tell him nothing. But Groa should be spared. She has strengths you may not suspect."

Paalo turned to Asa. "And you, Queen? Can you undertake such a journey?"

Asa recognized the care in his voice. "It is true, I am nearly blind. But if we travel by night, sight is no advantage. I will need only a stout staff."

A gargled cry startled her. Bhaldec hobbled across the room and began climbing a rickety ladder. Soot fell from the poles of the loft as he rummaged through the bundles stored below the thatched roof. Finally he cried out again and descended the ladder carrying what appeared to be a large walking stick. When he stamped it on the ground before Asa, shaking the soot free, a tattered blue cloth unfurled.

Asa ran her fingers along the black dragonhead in the weaving, overcome with memories. "The old banner of Agthir."

"We found it among the discards when Halfdan moved your things from the Great Hall," Thorleif said. "Take it now. Go, all of you, and hurry. Bhaldec will come for you when it is safe to return. May the gods be with you."

Groa urged them out the back door, already organizing the expedition. "Mari, help me fetch provisions from the house. Paalo, catch the pony in the courtyard. Harald, you can help Asa pack blankets."

Once they were gone the old sorcerer closed his eyes, exhausted. Only then did he realize that Asa's jeweled clasps still lay in his hand.

* * *

The travelers had trudged most of the night through the snowy, moon-shadowed forests before Harald noticed the first of the trolls. A small, warty face leered a moment from an oak trunk beside the trail.

Harald shook his bandaged head, sending an arc of pain across his brow. He was exhausted from the long night's march, and his wound burned like a demon in his head. He glanced to Paalo, but the Lapp showed no sign of having seen a troll. Even the pony Paalo was leading merely plodded through the snow without flaring its nostrils.

I must be more careful, the boy thought. *Troll people only catch the unwary.* He had heard of village children who played too near the fjord and were pushed from behind. Shepherds said that those who ventured too far into the fjells were sometimes tripped on —

A thin, hairy hand reached from a huckleberry bush toward his cloak.

Harald jerked away with a small cry.

The women on the trail ahead turned toward him. Asa asked, "What is it, Harald?"

His head was reeling, but he managed to make his voice sound nearly normal. "Nothing, Grandmother."

"We're all tired. A safe farm isn't far."

When they continued, Harald's breathing had become fast and shallow. His eyes throbbed as he scanned the forest for the shadows of trolls. He fell several steps behind, walking beside the pony. Groa had said the pony had been led over this trail countless times, bringing iron ingots to town and returning with sacks of grain and cheese. It was reassuring that the pony knew the forest so well.

A shape flicked in the dark, and one of the pony's sacks quietly slid to the snow. Harald stooped to pick it up, but was surprised that he couldn't. It was much heavier than any sack of provisions should be. He strained again, but could hardly drag it. A small voice cackled.

He looked up with alarm. Paalo and the pony were gone. "Grandmother!" he called, abandoning the sack and staggering ahead into the woods. Suddenly a root sent him sprawling into the snow. He dragged himself to his feet, his head a ball of pain.

A grinning, waist-high man crouched in the path before him, twitching a snake-like tail.

"Out of my way!" Harald reached for his dagger. But when he tried to brandish the weapon, he saw with astonishment that it was nothing but a broken twig.

The stocky troll gave a laugh like an ungreased hub. At once the shadows stirred among the huckleberry bushes. A dozen ugly little men began emerging onto the trail. Harald backed away, horrified. The trolls had impossibly long noses, warty skin, and toothy grins. Several wore huge gold rings in their sagging ears. Some were so hairy that they wore no clothes at all.

Harald turned. Behind him was a throng of even more grotesque troll women, with claw-like fingers and wrinkled breasts that sagged to their waists. In the forest on either side, more dark shapes were moving.

Harald gave the battle cry he had learned from the jarls. With his last remaining strength he ran at the wall of troll men and jumped as high as he could.

Sharp fingers grabbed his feet. He fell into the writhing pack. Powerful hands pressed him face-first into the snow, bound his legs, and tied his arms behind his back. When he was finally rolled face up, bearded trolls surrounded him like goats at a trough.

Harald spat the snow from his mouth. "I haven't done anything wrong! What do you want with me?"

A one-eyed troll poked him with a crooked finger. "Is this the one?"

Another grabbed a shock of Harald's blond hair. "It's him. Look at the wound. He's almost dead. Take him to Trunt."

"Let me go! Grandmother! Paalo!" He closed his eyes tightly, hoping that this was a nightmare he might will to end. How could everyone have left him so far behind?

A dozen trolls hefted him to their shoulders and carried him down the trail. Harald could see they were following the same route Asa and the others had taken. His hopes rose. Any minute now Paalo might notice his absence and come back for him.

The trail bent at a granite hillside. Here the trolls paused while a large troll man waved his hairy hands and muttered at the sky. For a moment, all was still. Then a deep rumble began to shake the snow from the cliff. A black rift appeared in the rock. Slowly, a rough portal opened.

Harald bucked desperately, trying to wrench free, but the trolls gripped even harder, carrying him onward. His shouts echoed into the black opening ahead. Finally the boy twisted so hard that one of the trolls stumbled. Harald's bandaged head thudded on the rock wall. A violent flash of pain lit the world, and then all was dark.

* * *

When he opened his eyes, Harald no longer could tell whether he was being carried through a nightmare or a hellish reality. The trolls had begun a gruff, echoing chant as they jolted him down a tunnel. A flickering torch shivered spiny shadows across the icicled ceiling. At intervals, echoless voids along the walls suggested labyrinthine side tunnels.

Harald resisted the urge to struggle. The fact that his head no longer hurt made him suspect that he had been carried a long time down into the earth. Even if he were free, he might not be able to find his way back to the portal alone. Certainly he could never open the rock gate without proper magic. If only he had stayed closer to Asa and Paalo!

A cold wind in the tunnel made him shiver. Fearful thoughts crept upon him like spiders. Had trolls overcome the others, too? He stiffened at the thought of his blind grandmother in such vile hands. And what did trolls do with the people they caught? Eat them? Then why hadn't they killed him at once?

After several turns the tunnel widened. Two large trolls with spears stood warming their hands before a iron brazier. Farther on were hunchbacked trolls pushing ore carts. They stopped to stare at Harald

130

with red, bulging eyes. Then several barefoot children ran up the tunnel, pointing and squealing, "Look! It's him!" At first Harald mistook them for humans. Their faces, though dirty, were no uglier than some he had seen in the village. But the stubs of little tails twitched from holes in their ragged clothes.

Finally he was carried into a hazy cavern. The floor had been paved in a dragon-shaped pattern of gold coins. Where the eye of the dragon should have been, a coal hearth smoldered red, filling the room with the stench of rotten eggs. Two rows of heavily armed trolls sat on wall benches, as if in a Viking hall. On the golden high seat before the hearth sat the largest and ugliest troll of all.

The trolls dumped Harald on the floor and beat their chests. "Hail, King Trunt!"

The king stepped down from his bench. He kicked Harald to roll him onto his back. The boy gasped at the blow. The king was nearly as tall as a man, but twice as stocky, with powerful, bear-like limbs. A gold ring hung from his protruding nose like the knocker on a grotesquely carved door. White hair sprouted from warts on his head and arms. Jeweled rings covered his fingers down to their thick yellow nails.

"At last, my son," the troll king said. Then he waved to his underlings. "Cut the prince's bonds."

"I'm not your son!" Harald protested. A guard in chain mail slit his ropes with a halberd.

"You will be soon enough."

Harald stood free, rubbing his wrists. "What do you mean?"

King Trunt signaled with a nod. A young troll stepped forward into the glow of the fire. With horror, Harald saw that the troll's face was his own. In fact, only the creature's hairy hands and tail showed that this was in fact a troll, and not a mirror image of himself.

"My son Runt is preparing to exchange places with you," the king explained. "Your human shell is dying, Harald. As its power ebbs, Runt grows stronger. Soon he will be your changeling. Then he will go out into the world to become the prince."

Harald gritted his teeth. "That thing can't take my place!"

The troll king laughed. "Oh yes, that's what changelings do. Believe me, no one will notice at first. But in his heart Runt will be different—a force of magnificent evil. One day, when he becomes king, he'll spread terror and violence throughout the land. He will eat the heart of Norway from the inside out."

"I want to go into the forest, grandmother," the changeling said, mimicking Harald's voice almost perfectly. "I don't care if my head's hurt."

The trolls roared with laughter.

"But what about me?" Harald asked.

"Why, you'll stay here and become my son," the troll king said. "We have found that human royalty adapts very quickly to our ways. You have already begun to join us."

"I'll never be like you!"

The troll king threw back his head and laughed. "Look at yourself, my son. You are a prince indeed. A common boy, without blue blood, would take a week to grow such a fine, strong tail."

Harald gaped at the tufted tail behind his trousers. With a flash of horror he realized what happened to the people trolls caught. The longer he stayed in their realm, the less hope he had of escape.

The dragon pattern on the floor gave him an idea. He pretended to see something at the dark end of the cave. "Look! A dragon!"

The instant the trolls turned to look, Harald bolted for the passageway. He raced past the first guards and was nearly in the tunnel itself when a hairy hand caught his foot and sent him sprawling. Before he could get up, a pile of trolls pinned him to the ground. They dragged him, kicking and struggling, back into the hall.

King Trunt stood with his arms crossed. "Did you think we would be so easily fooled? The days of Jormundgand are gone forever."

Jormundgand! Harald had heard the legends of the ancient dragon-god. His grandmother had told him that Jormundgand, the serpent of Midgard, was the protector of the world. Hadn't she said a ship's prow had been carved in its image once? Then another thought struck him.

"This is the dragon's cave, isn't it?" Harald demanded. "You've killed him."

"It was your own people who killed Jormundgand. No one has seen the dragon since Halfdan the Black joined the Vikings. " The king spoke sharply to the trolls holding Harald. "Bring the boy to the eye-fire. It's time for his exchange."

The trolls held Harald opposite the king at the hearth of glowing coals. "Let me go!" Harald cried.

The king spoke to an armored troll. "Did you bring the banner?" The troll silently handed the king a tattered rag. The blue cloth was embroidered with a black dragon's head.

"Grandmother's flag!" Harald exclaimed. "That was her walking stick."

"Oh, we've left her the pole," the troll king laughed. He held the banner over the coals. "But this—this was her dream. And when it dies, your human shell will die with it. Then Runt will be the prince of men, and you will be my son."

The troll king draped the banner over the coals. Harald tried to cry out, but his throat had tightened, as if he were being strangled by an unseen hand. The banner began to smoke. Patches of black spread across the fabric. Harald looked at his hands, and saw with horror that they were rapidly growing bonier and hairier. A weight in his chest seemed to be crushing his heart.

"Burn!" the troll king commanded.

Harald collapsed to the floor, gasping. "Jormundgand!" he whispered toward the smoldering cloth. "You can't die yet. Help me!"

With a whoosh the banner burst into flame.

The trolls cheered. "Hail Trunt! Hail Trunt! Hail Trunt!"

Harald groaned in despair. But then he noticed that the cloth was burning with a strange red flame. A crimson glow lit the air, not like a proper fire at all. Stranger still, the ground had begun to move. All about him, the pattern of gold coins bulged and writhed. A rumbling grew within the earth. The floor was not paved with gold coins at all, but rather with scales.

Trolls tumbled to all sides in confusion. Harald dragged himself to hide behind the troll king's high seat. There he watched as the pattern on the cave floor rose from the ground, swelled into an arched neck, tore open a mouth, and roared.

"The dragon!" King Trunt drew his sword. "Stand your ground, trolls, and strike it down!"

A row of trolls gathered at the entrance tunnel, holding their halberds in trembling hands. The dragon pulled a leg from the ground, gaped his jaws toward the troop, and scorched them with a blast of fire.

Meanwhile King Trunt had stepped forward. He swung his sword at the underside of the dragon's leg, where there were no scales for protection. The dragon roared with pain, its eyes glowing. Green blood welled from the wound. Before Trunt could swing again, however, Jormundgand's gigantic jaws snapped him up. The dragon shook Trunt like a toy, then bit him in half. The troll's legs fell against the wall bench.

Harald cowered behind the high seat, terrified by this sudden battle. The remaining trolls ran for their lives. Harald wanted to run, too, but he didn't dare leave his hiding place behind the throne. He hardly dared to breathe.

The dragon licked the blood from its wound, rumbling uneasily. Then it suddenly stopped, sniffing the air with flared nostrils.

Harald froze. His hands were damp and his mouth dry. He was about to make a dash for the passageway when the dragon yanked its golden tail from the ground and slapped it against the wall, blocking the entrance.

Jormundgand slowly craned its neck over the troll's high seat. A red eye fixed Harald curiously.

"I—I'm only Harald," the boy stammered.

The dragon snorted soot.

The fact that the dragon had not yet killed him gave him hope. There was even something reassuring in its glowing red gaze. "Thank you for saving me from the trolls."

The dragon rumbled. After a long pause it sat back and began licking its wound.

"I'm sorry you were hurt." Harald touched his own forehead. "I've been hurt too. Do you know the way back to my grandmother?"

Jormundgand whipped its tail, splintering a bench, and spat a golden flame toward Harald. The boy cringed behind the high seat once more. But the flame did not burn him. Neither did it go out. It hung flickering in the air before him like a torch. Then it floated across the hall and out into the passageway.

Harald hesitated only a moment. He followed the flame. For what seemed like hours he walked and climbed through caverns and fissures and mine shafts, following the glow. Exhaustion weighed upon him more and more heavily. Finally, when a crack of daylight widened, it took all his energy to pull himself through and to open his eyes.

* * *

"Queen!" Paalo motioned urgently across the courtyard. "Come quickly! The sunlight is helping."

Harald rolled his head. "Where am I?"

Asa nearly stumbled in her hurry. She knelt beside him, holding his hand. "You're with your grandmother at Jarnskegg's hall."

"Jarnskegg?" He wrinkled his eyes, trying to remember where he had heard the name.

"At the iron smelter."

"But how did I get here?"

"You were hurt, remember? We were walking through the forest and you fainted in the snow. We brought you here on the pony, fearing for your life. Paalo gave you herbs that lowered your fever. He's treated you day and night for over three weeks."

"Three weeks!" The boy sat up with a start. Could the entire ordeal in the trolls' cave have been a dream? He felt his head circling like a seagull. The sun was high and the snow was gone. Gingerly, he touched his head. The wound, too, had vanished.

He looked about him as if at a strange, new world. Black, unfinished ax heads and sword blades lay stacked in piles among the plank-roofed halls. In the stumplands beyond, heaps of charcoal smoldered.

Mari helped Groa walk to the boy's side. The old sorceress asked, "Have you dreamed?"

Harald looked from face to face. The battle had seemed so real. It was hard to believe that the worry in these friends' faces came from a different fear. "I suppose it was a dream."

He told them of his capture by the trolls and his escape with the dragon's help. When he had finished he looked to the old sorceress. "Do you know what the dream means?"

Groa closed her mismatched eyes. For a long time she was silent, her brow furrowed in concentration. Finally she said, "Yes. Your father will die before you. But your trials will be far from over. You will only defeat the forces of evil that rise against you by following a golden dragon."

"How can I do that?"

The old woman shook her head. She was about to speak when a man's cry resounded from across the courtyard.

"Run!" the bearded man shouted, sprinting toward them.

"What is it, Jarnskegg?" Asa demanded.

"King Halfdan is coming! His Viking horsemen are riding up the valley. Run for the forest. I'll help carry the prince."

"No!" Harald stood up from his bench. "I won't run from my father anymore."

The chieftain stared at him, bewildered that the boy was awake. "Prince, he has twenty armed riders."

"I'm not afraid to meet him. Lend me your dagger. I've lost mine."

The chieftain handed him the hilt with a shaking hand. "Then I'll die beside you, Prince."

Hoofbeats drummed on the trail beyond the garden. Four abreast, the riders rounded the stone wall at a full trot, their red shields and spears poised.

An image flashed in Harald's mind of the troll army he had faced. Were Vikings so different? They too lured men with greed and barbarism. And the longer one stayed among the Viking jarls, the more one became a monster oneself. The boy defiantly held up his little dagger toward the mounted troops.

Miraculously, the horsemen slowed. A man in the front rank, his face hidden by a helmet with eye slits, raised his spear in the air. With a clatter of armor and weapons, the riders came to a halt.

"Hail Harald!" the helmeted leader shouted.

The troop joined his cry. "Hail Harald!"

"It's Guthorm," Asa exclaimed. The young man's voice was unmistakable. In the ten winters since Ragnhild became queen, her young brother Guthorm had grown into a capable warrior—perhaps the only fighter respected both by the jarls and by Asa's camp. But how had he found them here?

Guthorm dismounted and pulled off his helmet. Sweat matted his brown hair and dripped from his beardless chin. For a moment he hesitated, obviously regretting the demands of honor. The child was so thin and pale and weak. But an oath was an oath. He drew his sword and extended it hilt-first to the boy. "I've come to offer my loyalty to the new king. King Harald."

"King?" Harald took the sword mechanically. "Then my father is dead?"

Guthorm nodded. "Five days ago he was crossing Lake Tyri in

his sledge, still looking for you. The ice was weak where the farmers had penned their cattle in the winter. Several of the sledges broke through."

Asa turned away, tears welling in her clouded eyes. She had not wanted to outlive her son. She had always fought to save him—first from Eirik, and then from the weakness within himself. It seemed that all her efforts had only driven him farther from her reach.

Harald stared at the ground, surprised that he felt neither sadness nor relief. Even the death of the troll king in his dream had aroused more immediate emotions. All he felt now was an empty numbness. He had steered his whole life by his father—either trying to please the king or trying to avoid him. Without that rudder, the course ahead was unclear.

Mari shook her black hair and boldly stepped forward. "How did you find us here, Guthorm?"

Guthorm's expression softened at the sight of Asa's young serving woman. "When everything was turning upside down in Tunsberg, an old goldsmith swore to me that his slave knew where you were. The slave couldn't talk, but he showed us the way well enough."

The words jolted Asa from her tears. "What do you mean, 'turning upside down'? What has happened?"

"I'm afraid there's trouble over the succession. When news came of King Halfdan's death, you understand, the prince had been missing for several weeks. Many people think he was dead."

Asa knew which group hoped the prince was dead. "How many Vikings have claimed Harald's high seat?"

"Two, mainly. Jarl Bork from Jarlsberg and King Rognvald from the Vik. When I left, their fleets were gearing for battle. Jarls throughout the realm were declaring for one side or the other."

Harald angrily stuck Guthorm's sword in the dirt. "And what about Tunsberg? How many of the warriors there are still on my side?"

Guthorm let out a deep breath. He glanced to the men behind him. "We came as soon as we could, King."

Asa sank to the bench. No amount of political cunning could save the kingdom with just twenty warriors. Harald was a boy of ten—too young to lead an army. And she herself was a blind old woman who no longer had the strength to reconquer kingdoms. The Viking jarls had been waiting for Halfdan to die so they could reclaim Vestfold. Now they ruled not only in all of Vestfold, but in Agthir and Hringariki as well. It seemed the only question left unanswered was whether Jarl Bork's network of Viking terror could hold the realm against Rognvald's Viking pirates.

Harald asked, "What would you do, Guthorm, if you were in my place?"

Guthorm pulled the sword from the dirt and slipped it back into his leather scabbard. "You have no ships, King. Your only hope is that Bork and Rognvald will deplete their fleets by battling each other at sea. Then you'd somehow have to trick the winner into a fight on land. And even then you'd lose without a large army." He glanced again to the troop behind him and tightened his lips. "I will tell you the truth, King. You would need at least a thousand men as devoted as these."

"A thousand men!" Harald swallowed hard. The easiest course would be to stay in hiding, hoping that the Vikings would simply forget about him. But he didn't want to run away anymore. And weren't there other people who hated the jarls?

"What about the farmers?" Harald asked.

"Farmers?" Guthorm frowned.

"Everyone knows the farmers don't like the jarls. Maybe they'd help me."

Asa caught her grandson's arm. "Yes, Harald! The farmers would help—if you promised to bring back the old Norse laws. In every district that joins, you could throw out the jarls and reinstate the Thing courts."

Guthorm shook his head. "You can't fight Viking jarls with plowmen. Even if you could drum up a thousand farmers, they'd have to be organized, armed, and trained. A ten-winter-old king can't hope to run a campaign of that scale."

Asa listened to Guthorm's voice with growing conviction. He was a shrewd, persuasive military man. After all, not many men could have convinced a score of warriors to abandon the jarls and pledge their lives to a crown prince who was widely thought to be dead. "Guthorm—" she began, then suddenly cut herself short. "Guthorm! Your name!"

The warrior humphed. "'God's worm.' A sorry name."

"Not at all. Your name means 'dragon.'" She turned to Harald. "Do you see? That's what your dream was telling you, about the golden dragon. Appoint Guthorm your field marshal. He can train the warriors you need."

Harald caught her enthusiasm. He looked up to Guthorm, his eyes shining. "You were the best of the warriors at Halfdan's court. Would you lead my army?"

"If you will it, King, I'm at your command."

Harald climbed to the bench and raised his arms to the small gathering. His boyish voice was high but clear. "As your king, I proclaim that my uncle Guthorm will be the leader of the realm's forces. I will march with him in every battle, and wherever I rule, the Vikings will be driven out and the old Norse laws will return."

He looked to his grandmother proudly. "And I'll carry a new banner — the Golden Dragon, which I swear to you will never fall."

CHAPTER 14
FALL, 1904

"Kirstin?" The excavation leader stepped up from a trench amidst the ship's ribs, his tall black boots caked with dirt. "Could you come give me a hand?"

"You'll be on watch tonight, Carl. You should be resting."

"Not yet." He wiped his brow with a sleeve. "I've almost got this pole loose. Here, I'll hold it while you take a look. I'd like your opinion before it's moved."

"Of course." Kirstin couldn't help thinking that it had taken her nearly three months to win this kind of respect from Carl. Finally he valued her as a professional. It seemed a small victory in the face of the expedition's looming difficulties. They were running out of money, and the ship was only two-thirds excavated. Worse, winter was hardly a month away. Otto believed a hard freeze might damage the ancient wood they had exposed, turning the ship's timbers to mush. And they still didn't know what had become of the two missing crates of artifacts.

"Look at this," Carl said, pointing to the pole embedded vertically in the side of the trench. "It doesn't make sense."

It *was* a curious pole. They had found its top four days ago, protruding above the ship's rear deck. Although the mound had been settling for a thousand years, leaving most of the wooden artifacts bent or crushed, this post stood almost perfectly upright. Now it was exposed from top to bottom. Kirstin stepped down into the trench and brushed dirt from the base of pole. "That's odd. It's not connected to the keel either. It's just standing there."

"You see, it can't be a second mast," Carl said. "Could it be another oar rack?" They had found the remains of two wooden forks that once must have stored oars above head height.

"With the fork missing? No, it doesn't look like anything's broken. Besides, it's the wrong shape for a rack support." She stepped up from the hole to examine the pole's top. "It tapers a little on either end. Like a cutoff oar, perhaps."

"Well, it's another riddle, then. I'm afraid we don't have time to solve them all now. You catalog it. I'll wrap it with rags for the crate. This good weather won't last forever." Carl glanced to the chilly autumn sky. Then he took the pole in both hands, gently pulled it loose, and began lowering it onto a bed of rags.

A strange fear shot through Kirstin as she watched the ancient pole sink toward the ground. Or was it fear? She had seen this pole before, held proudly in a small white hand. There had been a crisp cloth snapping in the wind then, and crackling through her like a fire, the glorious, terrifying feeling of defiance.

Carl gave her a startled look. She had caught both his wrists. "What is it, Kirstin?"

She took the pole from him and turned it so that he could see. "There are runes."

"Good Lord, you're right."

Kirstin began brushing dirt from the symbols on the back of the pole. "It looks like a variant of the sixteen-sign futhark alphabet."

"Can you make them out?"

As she freed the letters from the dirt she spelled aloud. "L—I—T— I—L—U—I—S—M—" She cleaned the pole farther, but the wood was uncarved. She looked up. "That's all. 'LITILUISM.'"

"Litiluism?" Carl frowned. "What's that supposed to mean?"

Kirstin shook her head. The word resembled nothing she had seen in all her years of translating runic inscriptions. "I don't know."

"Does it connect with something in the sagas?" Carl asked. "A name, perhaps?"

"Litiluism?" She struggled with the strange word, but it awoke no memories at all, either from dreams or Viking literature.

"Well, it's bound to be something significant. These are the only runes we've found in the whole burial." Carl wrinkled his brow. "What the devil was this pole for, anyway?"

"I'm not sure." She held it upright, with the inch-tall runic letters at her shoulder. Now she saw that the upper, flattened part of the pole

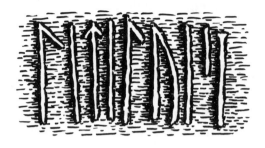

bore a shadow, as if from some long-since rotted fabric. A cold wind blew the loose strands of hair from her face. "But I think it carried the banner of the Oseberg queen."

* * *

After dinner that evening, Carl stood in the dining tent and rapped his fork on a water pitcher for attention.

Kirstin already knew the bad news. She had dropped enough hints that the others would not be wholly unprepared. Now she looked about the lamplit tent. She had come to know these men well in the past months, and could read the worry in their faces. Magnus shoved aside his plate and crossed his muscular arms. Otto nervously polished his spectacles on his shirt. The dozen workers from Tønsberg—bearded whalers with callused hands, wrinkled eyes, and well-worn caps—glanced to each other.

"I'm afraid I have an announcement," Carl began. "First I'd like to acknowledge how hard all of you have worked at half pay, and how much we've accomplished so far. Nearly all of the site's loose artifacts have been cataloged and crated, and much of the ship itself has been unearthed. I think this has been a labor of love for us all."

No one interrupted this sunny praise, waiting for the storm to come.

"But now the university's archeological funding for the year has been exhausted. I'm afraid we have only enough left for another week's wages."

Several of the workers sprang to their feet, talking at once. "One more week? What'll we do then? And when are we getting our back pay?"

Carl held out his palms apologetically. "I know it's short notice, but the money simply isn't there. We'll have to tie up loose ends as best we can in the remaining days. I'd like to finish work on the loose artifacts and build a framework to shelter the ship itself through the winter."

"A framework?" Now it was Otto's turn to object. "Why not just rebuild the mound? A layer of clay protected the wood in there for a thousand years. If the ship's planks freeze they'll lose their structural integrity."

Carl sighed. "I'm aware of the German Academy's theory, Otto."

Kirstin recognized the hidden message behind this reply. Carl didn't believe freezing would damage the ancient wood. He suspected the German theory was merely a ploy to make the expedition accept financial assistance from Berlin—and send the ship there as repayment. She herself wasn't sure how much of Otto's evidence had been skewed by that motive.

Magnus leaned forward. "What about the stolen crates?"

Carl cut him with a cold gaze. "That's another good reason to finish up with the loose artifacts as soon as we can. As you know, the Tønsberg police have found no evidence that could lead to an arrest. As a result, we have to assume the looter is still at large."

Again Kirstin had no trouble reading between the lines. Magnus remained a prime suspect. She flushed to think she had withheld the one solid piece of evidence against him—the pewter button from his sweater. At first she had hidden the button so that no one would jump to conclusions. After all, it could have been from someone else's Norwegian sweater. Or Magnus might have lost it while working near the crate on another day. But now she had begun to wonder if her attraction to the Norwegian labor manager had clouded her reasoning.

"I know all of us are disappointed not to finish the dig this fall," Carl went on. "Next year we'll have a new budget to work with. I'm hoping all of us will be back here in May. Then we can finish excavating the ship, move it to the Tønsberg railroad station, and send it off on a flatbed car by mid-July."

"Send it where?" It was Magnus again, his big arms still crossed. "The longer we take moving this ship to Kristiania, the likelier the Swedish government is to get a hold of it."

"That's right!" A squinty-eyed worker behind Magnus gave a jerky nod. "You tell 'im, Cap'n."

Carl looked to Kirstin, as if for assistance. Normally, she would have been pleased by this acknowledgment of her authority. But this time she was in an awkward position between two stubborn men, Carl and Magnus. She cleared her throat. "It's possible that six months would give us time to negotiate with the Swedish government to keep the ship in Norway."

It sounded weak, even to her.

Magnus met her gaze so steadily that she felt her face begin to flush. It was all she could do not to look away.

"All right, then," Carl announced. "Get a good night's rest and we'll see you all in the morning."

* * *

That night, for the first time since arriving in Oseberg, Kirstin seemed to have won the upper hand over her strange dreams. Sleep overwhelmed her like a drug. No Vikings, no ships, no trolls plagued the darkness. Even the mysterious runic inscription—which she had half expected to confront in another tumultuous dream—made no appearance. She floated through the night like a seed on the wind. If troubled farms or cities lay below, they were invisible. Only once did she hear the suspicious caw of a distant raven. And later she heard the faint nicker of a horse.

A horse?

Unwillingly, she opened one eye a slit. From the dim glow of the tent roof, she could tell it was nearly dawn. She had another full hour left to sleep. Why had she suddenly awakened this early?

Then she heard the horse nicker again.

The expedition kept two horses in the field across the creek—far enough away that she rarely heard them. And even then, they had a different tone. This was an eager little sound. A greeting.

She pushed back her down comforter, her heart pounding. If a horse had arrived at this hour, it might well be pulling the wagon of a thief.

The air was so cold her breath came in white puffs. She pulled on her khaki pants, slipped into a shirt and coat, and quickly laced her workboots. Then she peered out from the tent flap into the dim pre-dawn.

A thin sheet of fog hung above the frosty fields like a blanket. There were no people, and no lights. She crept around the base of the mound, walking carefully to keep her boots from crunching in the frost. Before long she could make out the shape of a flatbed wagon and two horses in the entrance road.

A faint sound of scraping wood came from the crates. Evidently the thief was still there, hidden behind the stack. The watchman must have fallen asleep. She considered calling out to wake him or to rouse the others in camp, but knew this might give the thief time to escape.

On an impulse she crept past the camp's woodpile and took an ax from the chopping block. In a dozen quick, crouched steps she had reached the stack of crates. Beyond were the backs of two men, stooped over a box. With her heart in her throat, she stepped out before them. "Stop where you are!"

The Oseberg farmer gaped up at the ax-wielding woman and let loose a yell, staggering backwards as if he had seen a ghost.

The other man dropped his end of the crate. "Kirstin! God, you gave me a scare."

"Carl?" she asked, bewildered. "What are you doing?"

The expedition leader stood and straightened his back. "I'm on guard duty, of course. We're just moving the crates up to Mr. Hansen's barn so they don't freeze. I didn't want to wake you. I know the trouble you've had getting a good night's sleep."

The farmer edged back toward them uncertainly. "It's not—it's not the curse?"

Carl laughed. "No, not in so many words. It's my colleague. She'll help out."

Kirstin did not lay the ax aside. "The crates don't need to be moved, Carl. We've had frost on other nights. Besides, I thought you said cold weather wouldn't hurt the artifacts."

"It's never gotten this cold, Kirstin. At two in the morning I noticed it was already five degrees below freezing. By four it was even colder. That's when I got worried. So I hiked over to Mr. Hansen's farmhouse to see if he could help."

Carl's reassuring tone made the explanation sound simple. Yet doubt had already begun to spread in Kirstin's mind, opening doors to ominous, dark rooms. She looked to the farmer, a thin man with a patched shirt and suspenders. "This isn't the first time you've moved crates, is it?"

Now that the farmer had recognized her as one of the archeologists, he jutted his chin. "As long as I own the rights to this mound, everything that's dug up is mine."

"Trust me, Kirstin," Carl said evenly. "I have this under control."

Anger filled Kirstin with a heady strength. She narrowed her eyes and took a risk. "You've been lying all along. You blamed Magnus for the missing artifacts when you were stealing them yourself."

"Kirstin, honestly. Nothing's been stolen. I wanted to spare you getting involved. But since you insist on knowing, all of the missing crates are safe in Mr. Hansen's barn."

Carl's matter-of-fact admission stunned her. She had expected him to deny her charge, whether or not it was true. Yet here he was, calmly acknowledging that he had helped hide all of the "stolen" artifacts. That meant he had been persecuting Magnus unfairly for months.

"Why are you doing this?" she asked.

"I have excellent reasons."

"Start naming them."

"Kirstin, you've no right to question my —"

She turned to the farmer. "What did Dr. Söderfelt tell you he was going to do with the crates?"

Mr. Hansen shrugged. "He said he'd be putting them secretly in Norwegian museums."

Kirstin looked sharply to Carl.

"All right," Carl sighed. "I got the idea at the chest-opening ceremony, when we heard the Swedish government wants to take most of the artifacts to Stockholm. It occurred to me that by hiding the most important pieces and offering them quietly to museums in Norway, we could not only keep the finds in the country but also generate enough funds to pay Mr. Hansen for the excavation rights."

"The main thing," the farmer put in, "is that I get paid and the damned Swedish king can't get his hands on anything from my farm."

Kirstin considered this new twist. The explanation obviously appealed to the farmer. In fact, it seemed tailor-made to satisfy the farmer's twin passions, greed and patriotism. But how could she believe Carl? Within a matter a minutes he had run through two entirely different explanations for the missing artifacts, each accompanied by a straight face and an irritating "trust me" tone. What might he have told her in the morning if she had not awakened early? That he'd fallen asleep during his watch when the crates disappeared?

At that moment Otto ran up from his tent, still buttoning his jacket. "I heard the commotion and came as soon as I—" He stopped, wrinkling his brow at the strange tableau in the dim light of dawn. Kirstin was holding an ax. Carl stood before her, hands on his hips. Behind them the Oseberg farmer was idly opening a crate while a horse-drawn wagon stood at the ready.

"*Mein Gott,*" Otto muttered.

Carl smiled. "Here, Kirstin. If you don't believe me, ask Otto. He knows about the plan to store artifacts with Mr. Hansen."

"You do?" Kirstin stared at Otto.

The German archeologist ran his hand through his hair. He looked about at the crates and the wagon as if grappling for words. "Well, perhaps."

"Perhaps?" Kirstin could hardly believe this was the same man who had shared confidences with her through a tent wall each morning for months. Her anger made the words pour out. "Well then perhaps you lied about falling asleep on your shift the last time a crate was missing? Or did you actually help Carl load up the wagon that time? And I suppose you're the one who planted a pewter button from Magnus's sweater here to throw suspicion onto him?"

"Planted evidence?" Otto drew himself up. He turned a reproachful glare at Carl. "I knew nothing of that."

"Nor I," Carl countered quickly. He raised an eyebrow at Kirstin. "But it confirms what I'd suspected about your relationship with Magnus. Otto and I simply wanted the Swedish government to believe the artifacts were stolen. You, on the other hand, apparently withheld evidence from the police that would have pointed to Magnus as a suspect."

Kirstin flushed with a touch of fear. A moment before she had been trapping Carl in his own tangle of deceit. Now he had cast the net back in her face. How had she let him take the offensive so easily?

Carl shook his head. "What would your colleagues at Cornell say if they knew you'd sheltered the expedition's labor manager from the police?"

His threat struck a spark of inspiration. Kirstin hefted the idea cautiously as if it were a sharp blade. Its edge cut into the tangle of lies all too easily.

"Blackmail," she said. "The wrong weapon against me, Carl. Not quite enough leverage to shut me up." She turned to Otto. "But it worked on you, didn't it?"

Otto tightened his lips.

"What did he know about you?" Then she caught herself. "No, it doesn't matter."

Otto looked down, deflated. "It does matter."

Carl laughed. "Don't be fools, either of you."

"I've been foolish too long." Otto looked to Kirstin. "Carl came across a copy of the doctoral dissertation I'd written as a student. He recognized that I'd borrowed much of my data from unpublished papers found in the estate of a little-known Swedish archeologist. Of course if the university in Heidelberg knew they'd revoke my title."

Kirstin felt her heart sink. "But Otto, that must have been fifteen or twenty years ago. You've built a career full of original work since then—your theory of King Olav, for example."

"Built on sand," Otto said. "While Carl's career was founded firmly on Reichsmarks. He's the one with the contacts in the German Academy, not me."

Carl crossed his arms. "Throw it all away if you wish, Otto, but you can't drag me down with you. I've broken no law by storing artifacts in Mr. Hansen's barn. Remember, he is the legal owner of everything we've unearthed."

"Oh, very good, Carl, very good. You've kept your fingers clean. Just as you did when you sold the Gokstad swords to the Kaiser. But I think I've learned how your art dealership in Stockholm turns such a nice profit."

Kirstin, livid with indignation, confronted Carl. "You were going to sell out the expedition! For you, Oseberg was a treasure hunt—just another dig you could rob to keep your art dealership supplied with trinkets."

"Kirstin, there's no proof for any of this." He straightened his cuffs. "If you two are intent on challenging my reputation, perhaps we can't work together at all. It would serve you right if I simply withdrew from the expedition."

She stared at him, appalled. How had she worked with this man for so long? She raised the ax part way, a bladed barrier between them. "Get out. There's no room here for a thief."

The corner of his mouth quivered. "Of course without me you'd have no legal authority here. The two of you could hardly run the excavation anyway—just a girl and a German plagiarist."

"I said *get out*." She began advancing toward him.

He stumbled slightly as he backed away. "You understand that your attitude will be responsible for the loss of the ship? And if you try raising any allegations about me or my work—"

"If you are not gone in fifteen minutes," Kirstin said, her voice low, "I'll call in the newspaper reporters for a ceremony that will make the Oseberg chest opening look like a tea party. You're the one who's made false reports to the police, calling them in to investigate thefts. That's enough of a crime to have you thrown out of Kristiania University."

Carl brushed the dust off his sleeves with all the dignity he could muster. "Very well, I'll leave you to your folly. I've no desire to stay here with the two of you anyway." He turned and strode away in silence toward his tent.

As they watched him go, the black form of a raven sailed out across the morning sky with a screeching laugh.

Otto put his hand to his forehead. "Now what, Kirstin?"

"Oh, we'll do without *him* well enough." She lay the ax aside.

"I guess I should start packing too."

"You, Otto? No, I hope you'll stay."

"After everything that's happened?"

She nodded. "That trouble with your dissertation was ages ago. Carl will be too scared of you now to say anything about it. Besides, we're going to need all the help we can get."

"Then—you're serious about continuing the expedition?"

"I think we should try. Didn't you and Carl originally invite Dr. Williams as co-leader?"

"Well, we meant that to be your father." Otto gave an odd laugh. "But you're as much a Dr. Williams as Leland ever was. Technically, I suppose that leaves you in charge."

"Otto, it's up to us to finish the job."

He held up his empty hands. "But how? The expedition's run out of everything—time, workers, money."

"Then who's going to pay me?" It was the Oseberg farmer, who still stood beside the opened crate.

Otto shook his head. "You see? On top of everything else, Mr. Hansen still owns the rights to every artifact we've unearthed. It's time to give up, Kirstin."

"No it isn't, damn it. We'll just deal with things one at a time."

"Then you'd better deal with me first," the farmer demanded.

"All right, let's talk about you." Kirstin sized up the old man. She had known Norwegian farmers in America, and was familiar with their thrifty, methodical ways. What she needed was an argument he could understand.

"You want to be paid for what we've dug up on your land?"

"That's right."

"Well, suppose instead of finding a Viking ship you'd planted potatoes here," she said. "When would you have gotten paid?"

The farmer scratched his white hair. "At the harvest, I suppose. But that's how farming works. It's a business."

"Well, archeology is a business, too, Mr. Hansen. It's just that our harvest isn't over yet. A third of the crop is still in the ground."

The farmer took out a pipe, filled it with tobacco, and lit it while he mulled this over. He let out a puff of smoke. "Most farmers around here have their potatoes in the barn by now."

Kirstin sighed. "But not all of them, right? We're doing our best. Just give us a little more time."

He cleared his throat. "Maybe. But nothing leaves my farm until we work out a cash deal. I want five thousand crowns."

"Agreed." She didn't have a clue how she would come up with that kind of money, but the agreement gave her time.

The farmer nodded. Then he climbed into the seat of the wagon and shook the reins.

"Wait!" Kirstin called, suddenly realizing that the wagon still held a crate of artifacts. "Aren't you going to leave us the box?"

"No ma'am." The farmer blew a puff of smoke over his shoulder as he drove on. "I'm keeping my eye on these potatoes just to be sure."

Kirstin blew out a breath. The crate contained the runic pole—the one artifact that puzzled and enticed her most.

"Nice try," Otto said. They started walking back around the base of the mound. "But the farmer wasn't your biggest problem anyway."

"What is, then?"

"Finishing up before winter."

Kirstin stopped. "You're going to tell me we should accept money from Germany because you want the ship sent to Berlin."

"Not at all. How could I? I never had an offer from the German Academy in the first place."

"What!"

Otto sighed. "I'm afraid that was another of Carl's inventions. He had me say I'd telegraphed Berlin so he could throw off suspicion by rejecting the money. The truth is, he was planning to auction the three missing crates of artifacts in Hamburg after the fuss had died down."

"Good God." Kirstin could hardly believe how easily she had been misled.

But then another thought struck her. "Does that mean the danger of freezing is true?"

"I tried to tell you. Carl cared about the artifacts he could sell, not the ship. The crates and rags insulate the smaller artifacts pretty well, but a hard freeze really will ruin the ship. They had the same problem at the Gokstad excavation."

"Then we've got a month at most." Kirstin sighed, her hopes sinking again. Then she looked up and saw Magnus striding toward them from the tents. Magnus, she now realized, had been innocent all along.

"Morning." Magnus pushed back his captain's hat. "What's going on? Söderfelt hauled me out of bed to drive him into town, but he won't say why."

Kirstin felt like hugging Magnus for his honesty, but with Otto on hand she stifled the urge. "I've accepted Carl's resignation. It seems he's been moving crates to the Oseberg farmer's barn without telling us."

"So that's it." Magnus glanced back at the tents. "I never did trust him."

"I know Carl was hard on you," she said. "I'm sorry I didn't do more—"

"I can handle myself, Kirstin. I'm just glad he's leaving. If you're taking over we've got a chance to finish the excavation."

Otto threw up his hands. "The way you two talk you'd think it was possible. Carl had funding for another week's worth of wages. He won't write checks from Stockholm. Without him, we can't pay the workers to lift a shovel."

This additional blow gave Kirstin pause.

Magnus, too, was quiet for a moment, his brow furrowed. Then he cleared his throat. "Actually, the workers got together last night. I talked to them about the situation. They're good Tønsberg men, fishermen who've seen hard times before. None of them wants to see

Stockholm to get hold of our dragonship. They agreed if you try to get the ship to Kristiania before winter sets in, they'll work without pay."

Otto scratched his beard. "Incredible."

Kirstin asked, "Without any pay at all?" She remembered how upset the men had been the night before, demanding back wages. "That must have been quite some talk you gave them."

Magnus gave a small shrug and quoted,

> "No great things
> Need you give a man;"

Kirstin picked up the saga verse, still a little bewildered by the easy luck of this man.

> "With half a loaf
> And a half-drained cup
> I won me oft
> A worthy friend."

Otto shook his head. "This is madness, you know."

"Then you won't help?" Kirstin asked.

"On the contrary. Madness has always been my long suit. Count me in, Napoleon."

Now even Kirstin laughed. She put her arms on the two men's shoulders. "All right, gentlemen. Let's get this ship out of the ground."

CHAPTER 15
SPRING, 872

Forge fires lit the Tunsberg metalsmith's hut with a flaming glow. Gold dripped and rune scars ran. Molten metal, honey of Hel, gathered in the glowing iron beaker.

"Go now," the old metalsmith's hoarse voice croaked from the gloom. "You have done all you can."

Bhaldec bowed his sweat-streaked head. The slave's hand made its familiar cross-shaped motion on his chest. Then he closed the door behind him.

"Bolt the—!" But Bhaldec was gone.

Thorleif shakily raised himself from his bench. No man was meant to weather ninety winters. Why had his fetch left him to suffer so long? Five years had passed since Asa asked him to reforge the Vikings' magic clasps into a new charm. Since then Asa had accomplished much on her own, without his sorcery. She had helped young Harald reconquer Tunsberg. She had even seen a prophetic vision about a mysterious girl. But Thorleif knew none of that would matter if he himself failed. The secret power of the Vikings' curse remained unchecked. None of the charms he had yet cast had bound Fenris, the evil behind the Viking sword. He had invoked no deity more powerful than Thor.

Summoning the little strength he had left, he stood once more before the forge. Three jewels caught the coals' dimming glow. Still they did not tell him which stone to choose, what runes to write.

He lifted the clay mold, still redolent of wax, and bedded it in the ashes. He paused for breath. The smoke and heat made his head heavy. Then he tilted the crucible to cast the gold for one last try.

With an erratic double thump, his heart echoed the knocks from the door. His fetch! Thorleif willed his hand to hold steady. A sudden wind whirled ashes into his eyes. But Thorleif kept on pouring.

The door flew open and a hurricane howled in. Sticks and straw blew about the hut, clattering like hooves. Sparks rose in a jerking red column to the smokehole, as if to an unstopped sky-drain. By clutching the firepit's rim, Thorleif managed to keep himself upright until the blast subsided. When the wind stilled, the jewels were gone. He turned to face his fetch empty handed.

There was no one in the door. Huge dark wings swept the hut's shadows with the chill breath of the spirit world. An eagle swooped from the rafters, glided to the floor, and folded back its feathers. The bird had only one eye.

"Are you—?" Thorleif began.

The bird hopped forward, cocked its head, and opened its beak in a screeching cry. The cry deepened as the bird grew, until it became the derisive laughter of the brawny, black-bearded god, Odin. A red socket glared where the god's right eye should have been.

"I am *everyman's* fetch," the god roared. "Go now. You have done all you can." And he laughed a gale.

Soot swirled before Thorleif's dimming eyes. When the darkness began to clear, he gasped to glimpse a city of vaulted stone, where an endlessly tall tower rose above a hall so broad that it seemed a thousand men might enter at once by each of its thousand doorways.

Odin took the clay mold from the forge's ashes, shaking his head.

A roll of thunder boomed in the distance. Odin scowled. The troublesome thunder-god, Thor, was never far behind. Odin quickly drew his dagger and smashed the clay mold with its hilt.

Raindrops through the smokehole began to pelt puffs of sooty steam from the coals. Odin gripped the dagger blade in his hand and carved stick-shaped runes in the hot, soft metal.

Lightning burned sudden shadows across the floor. Undaunted, Odin pried the red jewel from a ring on his finger and held the stone before his empty eye, studying the darkness with solemn intent.

One of Thor's thunderbolts crashed to earth just outside the doorway, shaking the hut's timbers.

Odin took the warm gold and pushed the stone in place. Then he laid the finished clasp in the dead smith's palm and closed the withered fingers over it. "You have done well. But another is still needed—someone Thor will not expect."

154

Odin smiled to himself. "The mortal they call Gytha."

* * *

"Gytha?" the franklin called, squinting through the forest as he wandered among huckleberry bushes near the Vik's beach.

The young princess of Horthaland giggled as she watched her foster father from the branches of a pine tree. He was usually such a good sport. After all, what was the point of coming to a king's coronation on the Viking's home island if she couldn't run off and flirt even a little?

"Of all the vexatious—!" Ragnar, the franklin of Valdres, rested against a pine trunk and sighed. He had never imagined a daughter could be such trouble—especially someone else's daughter. Maybe his wife was right. She had warned him not to bring the thirteen-winter-old girl to a coronation feast so far from home. But what could he do? Old King Eirik himself had sent a messenger explicitly asking him to take the girl "to represent Horthaland" at the crowning of the new Viking king. Some representative!

Stifling a giggle, Gytha leaned from her perch. She reached down toward her foster father with a long twig.

Ragnar swatted a tickling at his left ear. What a nuisance these spring gnats were! And now Gytha was lost somewhere in the woods just as the last guests were arriving. How could she get lost on an island? Particularly on a fortress island like the Vik.

He humphed, thinking about the Vikings. Why should he care which jarl was king down here anyway? Rognvald the Glorious, Hadd the Hard—all the same breed of sea battlers. Served Rognvald right, after all those summers sailing the high seas, to drown in an Irish lough.

He sighed again. The girl had probably wandered back to the halls, following the noise of Hadd's coronation feast. By now people could probably hear the racket halfway to Constantinople.

Ragnar began to walk back through the huckleberry bushes, but was suddenly stopped by the beautifully melodic trill of the elusive *fagurfugl*. He turned and squinted into the forest. Could that fabled bird live here too, and not merely in Valdres? If only he could see it clearly once—even just once—and describe the bird that poured out such a longing call, perhaps his wife would believe him.

But of course the trees were empty. He shook his head and went on.

Gytha swung out from behind the pine trunk, wooden flute in hand. For a moment she regretted teasing him so much. She loved her gentle foster father dearly. But then she hadn't come here to be towed about. This was the Vik, capital of the Vikings! The wild smell of the sea was in the air. There was more excitement here in a day than in Valdres in a year.

Even now, as she looked to the beach, ships from distant kingdoms were arriving. The very idea of ships excited her. With their limitless possibilities they were like the wishes she sent out with dandelion puffs, seeds upon the wind. Valdres was so far from the sea, and King Eirik so rarely allowed her to visit the western fjordlands where she had been born. Still, she knew more about sailing than people suspected. She had spent many a winter evening imagining voyages in the little carved models her older brothers had once sent as toys from their Atlantic jarldoms.

The latest ships to have landed, billowing blue-and-white-striped sails, obviously belonged to some minor chieftain. One was an old, low-sided dragonship, complete with a laughably quaint spiral dragonhead on the prow. The second carried a gold banner but was a sorry flagship—just a refitted, wide-bottomed merchant tub. No wonder this chieftain arrived late, with such a fleet!

She jumped down from her branch and skipped toward the beach, thinking mischief. She rounded a juniper thicket and ran smack into a white-haired old woman hobbling along on the arm of a thin Lappish man. "Oh!"

"Watch where you're going!" the Lapp cried. He helped Asa to her feet, explaining, "It's only a girl, Queen."

"Forgive me!" Gytha gasped. She had no idea which of Norway's many queens this might be, but from the way the aged noblewoman stared past her with white eyes, she was obviously blind. "Are you hurt, Queen?"

Asa managed to give the girl a gracious smile. After not setting foot on the Vik for forty-five winters, she had mentally prepared herself for almost any attack—but the girl from her vision? Evidently Kalf had been right that blindness could open eyes to second sight.

"Nothing appears to be broken," Asa said, straightening. She felt for the hidden pocket in her purple cloak to see if Thorleif's reforged clasp had fallen out. Just as the vision had foretold, the golden clasp was gone. She fought the temptation to tell Paalo and the girl to search for it in the grass. The hardest part of a charm was letting it go—letting the magic runes do their work. Instead she turned to the girl. "People say it's lucky to hear a *fagurfugl*, even if you never actually see one."

Gytha reddened. Had this noblewoman really heard her flute? Or had she hit upon the topic by chance?

"Tell me your name, child."

"Gytha. Gytha Eiriksdottir of Horthaland."

Asa's smile dimmed. Of all possible girls, did it have to be Eiriksdottir? The name stirred an acid sorrow deep within her. Perhaps if the Vikings had never been, she would have married Eirik and had a Horthaland daughter of her own. Yes, and perhaps her own daughter would have been just as dangerously impetuous. It was the curse and the allure of Eirik's line.

Asa sighed and took Paalo's arm again. "Pay attention to your path, Eiriksdottir. And may the gods watch out for you better the next time." Again she felt the pull of the golden clasp, and the urge to retrieve it. There was still time! But she walked on without turning. The gods would not give her another such chance. Eiriksdottir it would have to be.

"Yes, Queen." Gytha kept her head humbly lowered until the old noblewoman was out of sight on the forest path. Then she jumped to the juniper thicket to peer out again toward the beach.

The newly arrived crews were definitely not Vikings. The sailors straightening ropes on the ships had none of the usual battle gear of warriors. Several of the men on the beach actually looked seasick. Most were far too old to be of interest. But two of them were young. The two were standing beside a pole with a peculiar golden dragon banner. Or no—now that she looked closer, only one was really young. A good-looking boy with bright blond hair. Probably a courier, she thought, just a few winters older than herself.

As she watched, the boy signaled to the men, hitched up his cloak, and began to stride her way, as if to catch up with the old queen.

Gytha ducked behind the thicket. With a sudden inspiration she sprawled in the grass, looking as dead as possible. She closed her eyes, held her breath, and waited.

* * *

Harald strode angrily from the beach. What could his grandmother be thinking? The Vik was no place to wander off without a full bodyguard. If anyone knew the danger of ambush on this infamous island, it should be—

He stopped short at the twisted body beside the trail. "By the gods—" The girl showed no wound, but lay as if cast aside from a struggle, her pleated linen shift rumpled nearly to her thighs. He quickly knelt by her side and pulled back her thick blond hair to check her neck for a pulse.

The girl's eyes flickered weakly. Harald gave silent thanks that she was alive. She was so beautiful, with broad, ruby lips and a delicately dimpled cheek. "It's all right. I'm here to help you."

To his astonishment the girl sat bolt upright, hands on her hips. "Can't a princess nap in the sun without some lout disturbing her?"

Harald drew back. "I beg your pardon, Princess. I only thought—"

"I *know* what you were thinking." Gytha indignantly straightened her shift so it nearly covered her knees. "Just look at you. You already have your cloak undone."

Harald held the loose cloth together with a hand. "I swear to you, Princess, I thought you were hurt. And I just lost my cloak-pin on my ship."

She laughed. "Oh?" A glint in the grass caught her eye. She leaned over and handed him the metal clasp. "Then what's this? Lost on your ship indeed!"

He stared at the clasp—a golden dragon with a single red-jeweled eye. From the weight, he knew its gold must be solid. Every curve of the finely wrought treasure was covered with intricate, intertwined reliefs. "But this isn't mine! I've never seen it before. I swear."

Gytha clicked her tongue, enjoying every moment of the handsome youth's discomfort. "So many oaths! The clasp matches your cloak. It even has the same pattern as your ship's banner."

The similarity was indeed baffling. But he couldn't rob this girl of her find because of an unlucky coincidence. "Princess, I'm sorry for the misunderstanding. But I can't take this clasp from you. Vikings have been carrying looted jewelry up this path for generations. Any one of them could have dropped this. Since you've found it, it belongs to you."

Ignoring his outstretched hand, she stood and walked several paces away. She straightened her hair with a proud shake. The boy was obviously no courier. Only a nobleman could afford such a heavy gold clasp, and only a very clever lad would invent such an ingenious way to avoid the gift taboos. "My father is strict about traditions," she said, and began idly braiding her hair. "I'm afraid he wouldn't let me accept a gift from a young man. Even jewelry I happened to find at my feet."

The coy glance she cast over her shoulder left him sublimely confused. The girl's brown eyes were wide as a fawn's. Her red lips had spoken, but now he could hardly remember what she had said. To be sure, her white linen shift was hardly tautened by the curves of a woman, but something in the girl's saucy stance—was it a provocative turn to the hip? A cocked shoulder?—lit a strange, sweet warmth in his chest.

The weight of the clasp in his hand brought him part way back to his senses. "I honestly can't keep jewelry that belongs to you."

"Then you'll have to buy it from me," she teased. "I think it's worth—one good secret."

"A secret?"

"A good one. Something about royalty. Come on. Tell me a secret and it's yours."

He wanted so much to please her, but what secrets did he know? He had never been devious. Then he remembered his grandmother, and a sobering story sprang to mind. "Swear by the gods you won't tell."

His earnestness made her curious. "By the gods, then. What is it?"

He hesitated, suddenly doubting his confidence. He didn't even know this girl's name. Was she a princess, as she claimed, and if so, from where?

She drew closer, looking into his eyes. "Yes?"

"Hadd the Hard," he said quickly. "His sword Fenris is charmed. It can't be broken."

She laughed gaily and pushed him away with her finger. "That's no secret! Everyone knows Fenris will swing at Ragnarök."

"Wait, there's more." His heart pounded, drowning caution. "Whoever holds the sword can't be hurt by the steel of warriors."

Gytha cocked her head. He seemed so serious about this fantastic claim that she almost wondered if he was telling the truth. Such a determined, intense boy. She felt a little sorry for him.

"All right," she said. She straightened his cloak and pinned it in place with the clasp. Then she stood back and surveyed her work appreciatively. "What's your name?"

"Harald," he managed to say. "And yours?"

"I'm Gytha." She rose to her tiptoes and kissed him quickly on the lips. Then she was gone, running down the beach.

* * *

King Hadd the Hard clanked out of the hall in heavy breastplate armor and spurs. His bare arm rested nonchalantly against the golden hilt of Fenris. "You're late, cousin."

The Viking's voice wrenched Harald from his reverie. Before him a pock-marked face hulked in a mass of glistening black hair. Harald's throat tightened. He had not known what to expect from this sudden cousin. The skalds knew no verses about Olav's illegitimate son. And Harald had not wanted to believe the rumors about this unexpected heir to the Viking crown.

"A poor welcome, kinsman," Harald replied. "My men agreed to come to the Vik with your promise of friendship." He tipped his head to the broad-shouldered warrior at his side. "My marshal, Guthorm."

Hadd acknowledged the man with a nod. "I've heard of your uncle's luck."

"And we've heard of the Vikings' generosity," Guthorm replied, his sarcasm unmistakable.

Hadd's arm tensed beside the hilt of Fenris. He had long since discounted the boy-king's peasant uprising—without warships, they were no threat to the Vik. But this brawny marshal was a man to watch. One of these days the Vikings would have to retake northern Vestfold. Perhaps this autumn, after the summer's attack on England? Harald's kingdom was insignificant in itself, but the Vikings never should have let it slip away.

"There's still mead in the hall," Hadd said. He turned gruffly, remembering now the full humiliation the Vikings had suffered at these men's hands. Six winters ago, when Harald had first become king, two groups of Vikings had claimed his kingdom. The rival fleets of King Rognvald and a rebel jarl named Bork had fought a series of terrible sea battles. When Bork's weary crews finally sailed up Tunsberg Creek to repair their ships, Harald's army of farmers had emerged from behind Slagen Hill. The mob blockaded the creek with logs, set fire to the trapped Viking ships, and captured Tunsberg.

Hadd shook his head at the memory. Why hadn't Rognvald attacked Harald then? The farmer uprising would surely have crumbled before a fresh attack from the sea. For some reason Rognvald had ignored the slap for six winters. The Vikings deserved better from their king.

Hadd scowled as he ducked through the hall's outer doorway.

Harald followed into the dark vestibule and began to unbuckle his sword. Guthorm caught his arm. "Keep your sword, King. The Vik has its own traditions."

When the inner door opened, the roar of drunken Vikings hit them from the huge, torchlit hall. Men staggered along the benches. Rows of red shields lined the walls, glinting firelight from their iron bosses. Massive pillars rose into the smoke. Looted gold ornaments hung from the rafters, obviously booty from alien lands — ghoulish children with wings, pale mothers with sunburst heads, and starved men spiked to crosses.

A slave girl brought the visitors horns of mead. Harald hesitated to accept the drink, not wanting to upset decorum. Properly, only a queen should welcome a visiting king with mead. He asked Hadd, "Is your mother ill?"

Hadd cupped his hand to his ear. "What?"

"Your mother, the queen!" Harald shouted over the hall's din. "Is she ill?"

The Viking only laughed. "Queens don't belong in a warrior's hall. They only cause trouble. I'm living proof you don't need a queen for anything."

Hadd raised his horn to drink. Warily, Harald and Guthorm joined him.

Guthorm asked, "Are you building Rognvald's burial mound on the Vik, or near Olav's grave at Geirstad?"

Hadd belched. "Didn't you hear? My half-brother drowned in his armor. Fell overboard in a squall. Sank like a stone in a bottomless Irish fjord. I figure Ireland's a big enough grave mound for him, no matter how glorious he was."

Hadd reached up and took one of the red shields from the wall. Then he pulled Fenris from the scabbard at his side and clanged the wavy-edged blade against the shield. The hall gradually quieted.

"Jarls, get your horse goads and prepare to wager! Slaves, bring the stallions to the courtyard! Everyone with a lust for sport, outside."

Grinning, the Viking sheathed his sword. He asked Harald, "Did you bring a stallion for the fights?"

"No." Harald despised the Viking sport of goading horses.

"Too bad. I'd hoped you upland farmers might breed tougher stock. But I suppose a boy-king would have only foals." Hadd laughed as he strode away.

Harald angrily started after him, hand on his hilt.

Guthorm stopped him with a firm hand. "Let him go, King."

"Did you hear his insult?"

"Neither of us heard it, King. Remember where we are. If Hadd can tempt us to fight, he'll have the excuse he wants."

Harald clenched his fists, but let himself be restrained. Of course his marshal was right. "Yes. We came to seek peace, not to provoke battle."

Outside, a terrified horse screamed. The distant sound of thudding hooves and cheering men drifted into the hall. Guthorm said, "Seeking peace is a difficult task with Vikings. Remember how hard it was to appease Rognvald?"

"Rognvald was a tame dog compared to this wolf." Harald sank onto a bench and stabbed at the remains of a roast duck, recalling their fragile peace with the Vik's rulers. Six winters ago, after their heady victory against Bork, word had come that Rognvald was readying his fleet for a fresh invasion. Guthorm, Asa, and he had spent a long night in the Great Hall, debating how best to respond. Harald had wanted them to meet the Vikings with arms. But Guthorm had argued they stood no chance against a fleet of eighty ships. Finally Asa had come up with a very different idea. "My nephew Rognvald does have a weakness," she had said. "He is vain. Let us make use of that."

And so, on the day King Rognvald had planned to sail against Tunsberg, a strange group of sailors arrived at the Vik in a skiff. At once Vikings surrounded the intruders, but were puzzled to find that the men were completely unarmed. They were skalds, they said, and had been sent by Harald. When the poets were brought before Rognvald, they announced that Harald had chosen to give his cousin an honorific title, "Rognvald the Glorious," along with a naming gift in verse, the Yngling Saga. This three-hour epic proved to be an artfully worded history of the Vestfold kings, tracing Rognvald's lineage back to the legendary Yngling kings, and beyond that, to Odin himself.

After the performance, the skalds had been clapped in chains.

Rognvald the Glorious had sent Harald no reply. But neither had he sent his fleet.

Guthorm lowered his voice, for the hall was nearly empty. "I agree. Hadd seems a far more dangerous man than Rognvald."

"No protocol," Harald mused.

"I beg your pardon, King?"

"Say what you will about the Vik's kings, they have always respected royal protocol. When Olav died, Rognvald honored him with a ship burial befitting a great king. It worries me that Hadd has done nothing for Rognvald."

"But the body was lost."

"Then Hadd should have built an empty gave mound." Harald tightened his lips. "I wonder if the rumors might be true?"

Guthorm looked at him sharply. "That Hadd is a fraud?"

"How can anyone know if Hadd really is Olav's illegitimate son? The old king has been dead for years."

"They both have black hair, a rare enough trait in the North."

"Hadd's black hair is curly," Harald noted. "Olav's was straight. To find black hair like Hadd's, you'd have to look among the Skiring slaves."

Guthorm drew closer. "Are you suggesting that Hadd's mother bore the child of a slave?"

"Certainly a woman with a bastard son would never admit the father was a slave."

"Yes, but to claim the father was a king?"

"The boldest lies are the most readily believed."

Guthorm frowned. "If there was proof that Hadd is an impostor, you would be Rognvald's rightful heir. You're his cousin."

"Which is why the Viking jarls don't question Hadd's claim. They know I've thrown out the Viking's military law in Tunsberg. The jarls would rather die than be on equal terms with farmers again. They'd support any Viking against me."

Guthorm let out a long breath. "Then it's good you have no solid evidence against Hadd. If you did, he'd have to kill you."

"And the Vikings would back him regardless." Harald spun an empty horn on the table, thinking. "You know, Guthorm, sometimes I think Asa's right. There may never be peace until the Vikings are gone." He marveled that this conviction seemed to have jumped out at him so forcefully since his arrival at the Vik. He had always belittled his grandmother's ancient, hopeless vengeance against the Vikings.

"We can't wish them away, King. And with such a small army ourselves, we'd be hard pressed to defend against attack. Your subjects support you to a man, but after six winters of peace, they think of themselves as farmers again, not warriors. Even the law administrators you've appointed —"

Harald banged the table with his fist. "And why, by all the gods, should my subjects have to be warriors? All I want is peace in my kingdom! Just peace."

The animal screams of the horses outside had been growing weaker. Now, finally, a triumphant cheer went up from the men.

Guthorm fell silent. This was evidently not the time to press for new armaments, though the need for defense was greater than ever. How did Harald imagine he would guarantee the peace he wanted so badly? And now the king was daydreaming again!

Harald spun the mead horn absently. "Tell me, Guthorm. Do you know of a royal house with a child named Gytha?"

"Pardon, King?"

"Does Norway have a princess named Gytha?"

Guthorm scratched his beard, wondering where this new topic had come from. "Gytha? Not that I know of. Or wait—maybe out in Horthaland."

"Old Eirik's realm? I thought he only had sons." Harald knew the skalds' verses about the three famous sons of Horthaland. The brothers had founded ambitious jarldoms in the North Atlantic's islands. Last fall all Norway had mourned when the three promising young men had died in a single unlucky battle against the Scots.

"Oh, there's a daughter, all right, though I guess Eirik wishes there weren't. She was born a dozen winters after the boys. Queen Astrid was so old that the birth killed her. Eirik blamed the baby—made no secret of it. Right away he packed her off to Valdres with some unknown franklin as foster father. They say the man's so lax she's grown up like a wildcat."

Harald mused, "But now that Eirik's sons have died, she's next in line for Horthaland's high seat."

Guthorm chuckled. "Well, I suppose she is. Hadn't thought of it before. Wonder what old Eirik thinks of that?"

* * *

"Gytha! I've looked all over for you." Ragnar took the girl in his arm. He was so relieved to find her that the scolding he had planned evaporated. "Where were you?"

"Just down looking at the ships. Didn't I tell you?"

The franklin gave an exasperated sigh. "Ships. I should have guessed. Well, come along. They've already started the swimming challenge."

"What fun! Can I try?"

"No! The competitions aren't for women. It's bad enough I've let you run loose in a shift. If Eirik heard you swam he'd have me skinned and tanned."

The road from the halls led to the strait that separated the Vik from the mainland. Here Viksfjord ran deep but narrow. A rock thrown by a good arm could hit the far shore. When Ragnar and the girl arrived, the bank thronged with nearly a thousand coronation guests.

"Perhaps we could see better from farther away, up on the hill," Ragnar suggested.

Gytha took his hand and pushed straight into the crowd. She squirmed onto a rock ledge where the bank nearly overhung the water. "Here. Who's that swimming with Hadd?"

The Viking king and another naked, large-shouldered man had jumped from the bank and were splashing toward the blue-black waters in the middle of the strait.

Ragnar managed to make his way behind her. "I don't know."

"Fellow named Guthorm," a man beside them offered. "From Tunsberg. Hadd challenged."

"Ah, the Vestfold marshal." Ragnar nodded.

The swimmers each raised a fist, then ducked underwater. Gradually the water stilled.

"What are they doing?" Gytha asked.

"They hold each other down," Ragnar explained. "The one who has to come up for air first loses."

A minute passed, and still there was no sign of the swimmers. Gytha asked, "Do they wrestle under the water?"

"They can."

Finally a brown head broke the surface with a thrash. Then the king's black-haired head appeared, grinning, his fist in the air. The men on the bank roared their approval. "Hail Hadd!"

Guthorm slowly swam back with one hand, covering a bloodied eye with the other. Harald helped him onto a flat rock. The marshal lay with his chest heaving.

"Father, who is that?" Gytha pointed to the young man she had kissed.

"Guthorm organizes the military for —"

"No, not Guthorm. The boy with the gold clasp on his cloak."

"Don't you know Harald? That's Rognvald's cousin, king of Northern Vestfold and — what else? — Hringariki."

Gytha raised her eyebrow. She had guessed the youth might be noble, but would never have thought him a king. Too bad, she thought, that his realm was such an insignificant backwater. Otherwise, she might have been interested in him. "Oh. I met him down by the ships."

Ragnar stopped her. "You talked to Harald?"

"Yes, he seemed nice enough."

"Stay away from him!"

Gytha turned, startled by his stern tone. "Why?"

Ragnar hesitated, unsure how much to tell her. "Call it a family feud, if you like. All you need to know is that Eirik would be angry."

"But you just said Harald and Hadd are cousins. We're friendly with the Vikings."

Ragnar's voice dropped to a whisper. "I said Harald and *Rognvald* were cousins. There are rumors about the new Viking king."

She frowned at him. "Do you mean —?"

"We can't talk about it here. And just stay clear of the boy. Harald's grandmother once insulted Eirik so badly that he doesn't want any reminders — not from you or Harald or anyone. Understand?"

"All right. Fine." She shrugged. The ban wouldn't really limit her. There were far more interesting men at the Vik. But it did make her curious. Ragnar set so few rules.

A voice from the shore called back news to the crowd. "Harald challenges King Hadd!"

The crowd responded with whoops and jeers. Someone shouted, "Beware the beardless boy battler!"

Gytha watched with new interest as the two men prepared for the contest. Hadd flexed his bear-like muscles, bulging his huge chest. The dripping black curls of his beard seemed to blend with the mat on his chest and descend in a funnel to the black bush about his knobby, cold-shrunk genitals.

Harald, by contrast, prepared as unpretentiously as if he were disrobing for a sauna. He unpinned his cloak and carefully placed the clasp in Guthorm's hand. Then he shucked his tunic and trousers with a fluid motion.

The smooth skin of his young body made Gytha think again of their meeting by the beach. Had she really kissed this same boy? He stood in the sun like a blond god—tight-muscled, narrow-hipped, with a wisp of light hair that hid none of his manhood. When his blue eyes swept the crowd, she almost felt as if he were searching for her.

At a signal the two kings sprang into the strait and swam to deeper water. The crowd yelled final words of encouragement. Then the two men raised their fists in the air, and they dived.

A minute passed in near silence. Gytha tried in vain to imagine the struggle taking place beneath the still fjord. A foot briefly broke the surface with a small splash. The crowd shouted, but quieted again when the ripples stilled.

Another half minute passed. A patch of white bubbles bloomed on the water. The ripples stilled again. Would neither of them admit defeat and come up first?

Finally a head erupted from the fjord in a fountain of foam.

It was Hadd, grinning, with a fist raised in victory.

Guthorm jumped to his feet. "If you've killed him, Hadd, I'll—"

Hadd, still catching his breath, managed a short laugh. "Didn't have to! Drowned by himself. Hardly touched the boy."

A murmur ran through the crowd. This was no outcome to cheer.

Gytha's heart lurched. Though she hardly knew the boy, and had not expected him to outswim Hadd, she had not thought that he would die.

"Let's get some divers out here," Hadd ordered. "See if you can't fetch up—"

But the Viking's words ended in a gargle as he disappeared into the dark waters, pulled from below.

For a moment the onlookers were too stunned to react. Hadd clawed his way back up, choking. Then Harald's blond head splashed to the surface nearby with a spurt of water and a tremendous gasp. When the young king managed a grin, the crowd broke into laughter and cheers.

Gytha threw back her head, laughing at Harald's prank. If ever there was a grim old man who needed a comeuppance it was Hadd. And who better to play the trick than a backwoods boy no one would suspect?

* * *

The games, the flirting, the coronation—all the revelries at the Vik passed far too quickly for Gytha's liking. Within a week she was back at Valdres, mired in the tedium of a country estate. Spring yawned, greening the beech woods in the valley with tiresome deliberation. The farm plodded through its routines. Cows were milked, fields were plowed, wood was chopped.

Incredibly, her foster father seemed glad to be back.

Gytha couldn't even pursue her usual amusement—setting up pranks for her foster brother Ulf. He was too busy fishing, now that he had mastered that art. Finally, when her foster mother Hildirid began to nag her for moping about the hall, Gytha took her flute up to the old stone wall at the top of the high field. There she played a melancholy tune to the trees and wished all manner of things.

One day while sitting beside the high field, Gytha caught sight of three horseman trotting up the valley toward the estate. Her tune stopped in mid-note. She squinted. The riders wore shining helmets and carried officious blue shields, unlike any visitors to Valdres she had ever seen. She hopped off the wall and ran down through the fields to see who they were.

Ragnar stopped her when she reached the hall's vestibule. "Gytha."

"Who are they, father?" She reached for the inner door.

He blocked her way. "Don't go in!"

"Why not?"

Ragnar wrestled for words. He had never had trouble discussing serious subjects with Ulf, but Gytha was different. His foster daughter had always seemed so young. He had wanted to protect her—both from the anger of her father Eirik and from the cruelty of the grown-up world. But now she was a woman, and he had no words to prepare her.

Finally he managed to say, "Messengers. They're messengers from Harald."

"Harald?" Gytha puzzled a moment about the various Haralds they knew. None of them seemed likely to have sent so formal a delegation.

"The young king we saw at the Vik."

"*That* Harald?" Gytha's tone revealed her disappointment. "What does he want?"

Ragnar braced himself. "To marry you."

Gytha gaped. "Marry! Him?" Then she threw back her head and laughed. As if the heiress of Horthaland would marry a boy with a half-acre realm!

"Shh!" Ragnar gestured toward the closed door. "You'll offend the messengers."

"Oh, they deserve it."

"Gytha, a marriage offer is a serious matter. Eirik will have to be informed." He shook his head. "I don't know why Harald didn't send his messengers to Horthaland in the first place."

"Because my father would just send them away."

"I suppose he would. Eirik's grudge against Harald's family goes back longer than I can remember. I just wish they wouldn't drag me into it."

Gytha peered through a crack in the door, already sorry that this bit of excitement soon would be over. The messengers stood before the hall's empty high seat, waiting solemnly. They were richly dressed noblemen with fastidiously trimmed beards. To think they had ridden three days from Vestfold for her sake! Had she really impressed Harald so strongly? He had seemed so—how could she say it?—so reserved, even when playing his marvelous joke on Hadd at the swimming competition. The thought gave her a mischievous idea.

"Let me answer them myself," she said.

Ragnar frowned with his eyebrows. "That is your father's task."

"Oh, he's so far away, and you've already said he'll just refuse them. What's the difference if I send them home?" She straightened his tunic and looked up into his eyes, bending her knees a little to make herself seem smaller.

He wavered. When she pouted, dimpling her cheek and looking at him through her lashes, it was difficult to deny her anything. And the truth was, he had been dreading confronting the messengers himself. "You promise you'd just send them away?"

She nodded earnestly.

He sighed. "All right. But be quick about it—and no nonsense. I'll be getting their horses ready."

She kissed him on the cheek and quickly slipped through the door. As Ragnar walked to the stables he shook his head, thinking that this impetuous child would doom him yet.

The three messengers stiffened when Gytha entered. Without giving them a glance she walked to the center of the long hall and sat boldly in the franklin's high seat. Then she turned her eyes upon them loftily. "You have brought a message?"

The oldest of the men, with streaks of gray in his beard, gave her a dignified nod. "A message for your father on your behalf, Princess Gytha."

She lifted her head. "My father permits me to speak for myself on this occasion."

The oldest messenger cleared his throat uncertainly. Although this did not follow tradition, it would simplify his task. Even the foster father might have caused problems, but this country girl, raised in the Valdres woods, would know how lucky she was to be offered a match with a Vestfold king.

"Very well, Princess. We have come bearing the compliments of King Harald, who seeks your hand in marriage."

"Harald!" she scoffed. "He's not much of a king. He doesn't even dare to claim his rightful inheritance."

The messenger wrinkled his brow. "What do you mean by this, Princess?"

She shrugged. "Everyone knows Hadd the Hard is only pretending to be Olav's son. Why, he even murdered King Rognvald. And Harald does nothing."

"These are serious charges, Princess." The second messenger spoke, a sharp-boned man with fiery red hair. "But there is no evidence of treason at the Vik. King Rognvald drowned in a sailing accident in Ireland."

"If Rognvald drowned by accident and sank because of his armor, as Hadd says, then how did Hadd get his famous sword, Fenris?"

The messengers looked at each other. No one had thought to ask such a question before. Hadd brandished the legendary Viking sword at every opportunity. But if Rognvald had fallen overboard by accident, Fenris would have been lost. Then the rumors were true! Hadd the Hard really was Rognvald's murderer. And the Viking jarls who supported his phony claim to the Vik's high seat merely wanted to forestall Harald.

The oldest messenger collected his wits enough to divert the conversation. "Harald's realms are extensive without such claims. He rules northern Vestfold, Agthir, and Hringariki."

"Petty districts!" Gytha chided, enjoying the consternation she was causing these stuffy messengers. "Norway is full of tiny kingdoms, and Harald's is one of the tiniest. In other lands, men are ambitious. Look at the Swedes—they're ruled by a single king. Look at the Knights— they were united by Charlemagne. Tell Harald I'll marry him the day he rules unchallenged as king of all Norway."

The gray-bearded messenger drew in his breath at this insolence. The girl was as foolish as she was spoiled. "Princess, there are thirty-one kings in Norway! No one man could conquer them all."

Gytha tossed her head, hiding a smile. "You have my answer. Now go your way!"

CHAPTER 16
FALL, 1904

A disturbingly mismatched pair of eyes glared from the doorway. "Go away! I wasn't summoning *you*."

Kirstin, standing on the rainy cobblestones before the Oseberg farmhouse, was taken aback. "Mrs. Hansen, I just came to pay a visit. Can't we at least talk?" Kirstin had been hoping to work out a compromise about leasing the excavation site. Now she wondered if talking would help.

The old farmwife squinted up at the rain clouds. "How do I keep getting this wrong? Could the rain be slowing things down?"

Kirstin picked up the topic. "The rain's stopped our work on the excavation for a few days. That's partly why I came."

"It is?" Mrs. Hansen's eyes narrowed. "Well, come in, then. I'll set up the loom and see what I can do about it."

Kirstin followed Mrs. Hansen into a crooked room dominated by a green-tiled woodstove. Dim light from the stormy afternoon filtered through circles of hand-blown glass. A candle sputtered with little effect on a cluttered trestle table. With some surprise, Kirstin noticed that an ancient wall loom—of a design she had otherwise seen only in museums—was leaning against the room's far wall. A row of doughnut-shaped rock weights held the strings taut over the wooden frame's crossbars.

Mrs. Hansen pulled out a chair. "Here, sit by the stove."

Kirstin hung her wet coat beside the stove and sat down. She surveyed the paraphernalia on the table before her with some amusement. Among the old books and bottles were several bones—evidently horse bones, judging from their size. She had known Mrs. Hansen was superstitious. But this equipment suggested more than a passing interest in the old beliefs. Kirstin wished she had come to discuss folklore instead of excavation rights.

"Please sit down, Mrs. Hansen. We need to talk."

"Just let me weave a pattern." Mrs. Hansen picked up a shuttle of black yarn and slid it through the loom's strings. Her lips moved rhythmically as she added lines to the blue runner. With a twinge of alarm Kirstin realized what the old woman had in mind. She was attempting one of the oldest rituals of Nordic witchcraft—weaving a spell. The pattern taking shape on the loom was dark and jagged. It looked to Kirstin as if it might be meant to represent an eagle, the symbol of Odin.

"There!" Mrs. Hansen suddenly exclaimed, ramming the thread tight and whirling about.

When she saw Kirstin, her face fell.

"There?" Kirstin asked uncertainly. What had the old woman expected? Even in the sagas, woven spells seldom worked.

Mrs. Hansen approached as if to examine her. "You're a stubborn one, aren't you? But I've dealt with all kinds." She took up the largest of the bones.

Kirstin stiffened but did not draw back, confident that she could defend herself against whatever nonsense Mrs. Hansen attempted.

Mrs. Hansen turned the bone over. The bottom had been sawed off. She removed a plug and aimed the hollow end at Kirstin, saying,

> "Spell-doomed sending,
> Drive away lies!
> Demon sending,
> Pluck out eyes!"

The curse was delivered so intensely and the formula sounded so convincing that Kirstin nearly expected the enraged spirit of a bottled-up sending to come howling out of the bone. But there was only a faint, intermittent buzz.

Finally a housefly crawled to the lip of the hole. It paused there a moment as if getting its bearings, and then circled toward Kirstin.

Mrs. Hansen raised her eyebrows. But the fly merely circled on, bumped several times against the window, found a crack beside a loose pane, and disappeared outside. Mrs. Hansen yanked the window open. A gust scattered raindrops across the floor. She swore and struggled with the window, trying to slide it closed again.

Kirstin watched this performance with a touch of pity. The old woman had followed the methods of Norse sorcery with professional rigor. No doubt she sold her spells to the townspeople. A provincial whaling town like Tønsberg would always have men who feared cursed ships, and women who wished to communicate with drowned spirits. Woven spells and fly-sendings had served such purposes well enough in Viking times. Yet the poverty of the Oseberg farmhouse showed that the market for witchcraft in the twentieth century was slim.

"You really don't need to be alarmed by my visit. I only thought I'd stop by because of—"

"I know," Mrs. Hansen cut her off. "Because of the dreams."

The accusation caught Kirstin off guard. Her nightmares had indeed resumed, and were more vivid than ever.

Mrs. Hansen pointed at Kirstin. "Despite everything I've done, the dream escorts have been helping you. *Why?*"

"I've studied a lot of legends, but I've never heard of dream escorts. Are they supposed to protect graves?"

"That's why you came here, isn't it? Looking for secrets. And don't think I haven't noticed about the people in town. They wouldn't stay away from me this long unless they'd found someone else."

Finally Kirstin understood. The old woman had mistaken her as a rival. "Let me assure you, I haven't been offering anyone magic."

"Then how do you know about spells?"

"I research folklore for my university work. The reason I'm in Norway is to see the Oseberg ship safely preserved. I'm hoping you'll help."

Mrs. Hansen frowned. "Who are you?"

Kirstin sighed. Talking with this woman was a constant battle. "I am an archeologist."

"My ring says otherwise."

"Your ring?"

Mrs. Hansen held out her fist. "My first husband made a ring to protect against sorcery. Feel it yourself."

The snake-shaped band on her finger had a rough garnet as its eye. As soon as Kirstin examined the worn patterns of scales on the silver, however, she knew the old woman was lying. The ring was a thousand years old, obviously looted from an ninth-century burial site. She turned the ring with her fingers. "It is a beautiful artifact."

Mrs. Hansen angrily yanked her hand away. "What have you found in that ship grave? A magic ring of your own?"

Kirstin looked at her evenly. "No."

"A runic stone?"

The question made Kirstin pause. "Not a runic stone. The only runes we found were on a pole."

"A pole? What did its runes say?"

"If you're interested, you're welcome to look at them." Kirstin unfolded a paper from her pocket. She kept a copy with her to study whenever she found time.

Mrs. Hansen stared at the drawing a moment in silence. Then she looked up at Kirstin with a peculiarly baffled expression.

Kirstin realized her error. Obviously the woman couldn't read the futhark alphabet. "It says 'litiluism.'"

"Litiluism?"

Kirstin nodded. The word itself sounded like an admission of failure. In the past weeks she had tried hundreds of etymologies, none of them convincing. Perhaps Otto was right that it was simply a vanished place name or part of a lost spell. But—an idea clicked—then the old woman actually might be able to help. Place names and spells could be preserved locally in an altered form, just as Asaberg became Oseberg. She looked at Mrs. Hansen with new interest. "Does the word suggest anything to you?"

"Yes."

"What?"

"It suggests that you're not who you say are."

Kirstin's patience was wearing thin. "All right then, tell me who you think I am. A troll? Maybe I should cast a spell and make you serve coffee. Then we could talk like reasonable people."

Mrs. Hansen laughed—a hearty, friendly laugh that made Kirstin feel a little more at ease. "I guess we've both been unfair. But there is something unusual about you. Something even you are not seeing."

"Oh? What?" Kirstin wished she really would bring coffee.

"You're from America?"

"Yes, New York."

"But you speak Norwegian. The accent doesn't sound like it's from southern Norway either."

"It's from Bergen."

"Hordaland!"

"My mother emigrated to America when she was about my age. She ended up marrying an archeologist."

Mrs. Hansen's manner again grew intense. "Have you ever asked why?"

"Why she married an archeologist?"

"No. Why your mother left Norway. What was she running from?"

"Nothing, I assume."

"Oh? Look at me, girl. Where have you seen me before?"

Kirstin turned away, concealing a touch of panic. The old woman's ungodly gaze *did* strike a familiar chord from the nightmares. She had seen those mismatched eyes before, one blue and one green.

"Yes, you know. Can't you feel why you were called here? Why your mother turned aside, and her mother before that?"

Kirstin groped for words. Only a moment before, Mrs. Hansen's superstitious talk had been merely ludicrous. Yet now it led down a dark corridor into her own past. Her mother had in fact refused to talk about her Norwegian heritage. Kirstin herself had turned to archeology and to the sagas, trying to fill that void. Even her decision to join the Oseberg excavation had been part of that drive.

"We hardly know each other, Mrs. Hansen."

"You're a weaver, aren't you?"

Kirstin hesitated to admit that she had woven decorations for her dresses.

"If I'm right, your task will be more difficult than mine. You will need to weave a net from the footfalls of cats and the breath of fish."

Kirstin seemed to be getting nothing from this old woman but riddles. The thought gave Kirstin a touch of warning. Con artists won confidence by startling their victims with vague coincidences. Fortune tellers and circus magicians used the same trick. Anyone might guess from Kirstin's accent and clothes that she had a Norwegian parent and knew how to weave.

She decided to get to the point. "I'm not here to talk about spells, Mrs. Hansen. We need to discuss the excavation. If the ship isn't moved before winter, all the uncrated artifacts will be ruined. I want to see the artifacts preserved, and I think you do too. Can't we work together on this?"

The old woman studied her, unblinking.

"What we need are the rights to the site," Kirstin continued, hoping for the best. "The university is able to pay only half of what your husband wants, and the money can't be budgeted until next year. I'd still like to come to an agreement. What do you think?"

Mrs. Hansen took Kirstin's raincoat from its hook by the stove. Her intensity seemed to have evaporated. "Weren't you told? Thorvald's already been paid."

"He's been paid? How?"

"Against my advice. That's why I set to work on the spells." Mrs. Hansen held out Kirstin's coat.

"But I don't understand."

"No, obviously not. It's time you got going. I helped to call you, but I can't do anything for you now."

Kirstin took the coat uncertainly. "Who paid your husband?"

Mrs. Hansen pushed her to the door. "You won't need a dream escort to figure that out."

Kirstin nearly stumbled on the steps outside. Wind gusted across the courtyard, and the door slammed behind her. For a moment she stared at the farmhouse, angered by the old woman's sudden rejection and her confusing talk. It seemed impossible that anyone could have secretly donated the five thousand crowns the farmer had been demanding. She would have to come back to negotiate when Mr. Hansen was home. He didn't talk much, but at least he made sense.

She set her hood against the rain and trudged across the cobblestone courtyard. She had only gone a few yards when a voice behind her called through the rain, "The runes are wrong!"

Kirstin spun about. But the windows were closed and no one was in sight.

* * *

The empty ship arched in the pit, as if it were struggling against the storm. Now that there was no danger of the ancient wood drying, the rags had been removed, exposing dark, glistening carvings. Kirstin walked along the gunwale, thinking.

The whalers had made steady progress until they were stopped by the rain. The decking and nearly all the dirt from the interior had been cleared, baring the ship's wooden ribs. In its day it had been a light, fast vessel, with a thin hull designed to flex with the waves. Although the planks had been overlapped and riveted to each other in clinker fashion, the boards were not nailed to the ribs. They had been tied to the inner framework with flexible willow withes, as if the shipwrights had believed the vessel were alive and had to be allowed to breathe.

"Kirstin."

The voice made her start. In the rain she hadn't heard Magnus approach. Now he stood beside her, hands in the pockets of a large yellow raincoat. Part of her was glad for his company, yet part of her was on guard. Since Carl had left, Magnus had found excuses to work near her. To be sure, she was attracted to the rugged sailor. But her responsibilities at the excavation had grown in recent weeks. This was no time to risk developing an uncertain relationship.

She pointed to a framework of wooden beams. "I see you've started work on a support."

"We'll need something to help move the ship in one piece. I wanted your advice, but you were gone all afternoon. Where were you?"

She wrinkled her brow, remembering her odd visit. "At the Oseberg farmhouse, trying to make headway on the lease problem."

"And?"

"The farmer wasn't in, so I talked with his wife. A peculiar woman. She finally threw me out."

"She's odd, all right," Magnus chuckled. "Always has been."

Kirstin looked at him with surprise. "You mean you knew about her before?"

"Oh, everyone in Tønsberg knows about the Oseberg witch. I grew up on stories about money goblins and elf bridles — all kinds of tricks she was supposed to have."

"You might have warned me."

"I assumed you knew. She makes no secret of it."

"Do the townspeople believe in her spells?"

"Not many. The priests don't even bother to denounce her. Odin's no threat to them these days."

"Why Odin?"

"Well, that's who she says gives her powers. You know, 'All-Father,' with the eight-legged horse that rides to the land of the dead." Magnus winked one eye shut and raised his arm.

"Careful where you point," Kirstin chided. "You'll change us all into frogs."

He cast his arm toward the ship's prow, but the wooden carvings merely dripped rain as before. He shrugged. "The old gods have fallen on hard times."

"If it's any consolation, Mrs. Hansen didn't have any better luck with me. Maybe Odin's spells only work on Wednesdays now."

"Wednesdays?" Magnus asked.

"You know, 'Wotan's day'. Wotan is the English name for Odin."

"Oh, right. I keep forgetting, you're the word expert."

"Well, Odin wouldn't have much luck on Thursdays, would he?"

"No, definitely not on 'Thor's days.'" Magnus put his arm around her shoulder, and she allowed the comfort. The evening was cold.

"Tell me about your visit with Mrs. Hansen. Did she talk about her spells?"

"That's all she talked about." Kirstin paused, but then realized Magnus was the only one at the excavation she trusted telling about her visit. "Do you still have the dreams?"

"Sometimes. Don't you?"

"Maybe. I don't know. The queen I used to dream about is gone. There's a different girl now, and everything is confused. I still don't remember much."

Magnus shook his head. "Then maybe you're right. We think about Vikings so much during the day that we end up dreaming about them too. It's not that surprising, really. Did the witch ask about what we'd found in the dig?"

"Yes. And she reacted very strangely when I showed her a copy of the runes."

"Oh?"

"I think she said the copy was wrong. But I don't see how it could be. I made it from a rubbing."

"She's probably just envious you found the runes first. Runes are part of her spells, you know. She always tells people Odin traded his right eye to give runes their magic."

Kirstin smiled. "Then she's muddled her mythology. Odin traded his eye for a drink from Mimir, the spring of knowledge. To win the secret of runes he had to hang himself in a tree for nine days."

"There you have it. Odin's practically part of our team."

"Why's that?"

"Hanging himself for knowledge, you know. The original self- sacrificing scientist."

They laughed together, and it felt good. The night rain held a hint of ice, and she drew closer to him. The raucous laughter of the sailors drifted up from the camp's tents as if from a different world.

Magnus pulled her gently against him. The large hoods of their raincoats nearly touched, creating a single dark vault of warmth. The urge to yield to him was almost overpowering. But when his lips neared hers—and for an instant the thrill and danger of their kiss on Castle Hill flashed before her—she turned her head aside.

"What is it, Kirstin?" he asked.

"I'm sorry, Magnus, I—I need time."

"Time?"

"Don't misunderstand. You're very important to me. It's just—" she let out a breath, unsure how to explain. How could she tell him she needed time to discover herself? For years she had been overshadowed by her father. It seemed women were always being defined by the men around them. Now was her chance to explore her strengths, find her weaknesses, be herself.

At length she said, "It's just I have my responsibilities to consider, now that I'm running the excavation." It was also true, and easier to admit.

He nodded without looking at her. "You're worried about the ship."

"I won't really be able to relax until it's paid for and safe in Kristiania."

"Then the Oseberg witch didn't tell you?"

For a moment she was uncertain. "About what?"

"About the ship."

Kirstin went on slowly. "The old woman said something about the lease being settled."

He sighed. "Then she can be trusted for some things at least."

"What are you saying?"

"The witch swore to keep the source secret," Magnus said. "I want you to do that, too, even after the rights are transferred to the University of Kristiania. The farmer has promised to return the missing crates tonight."

Kirstin stared at him, astonished. "You did this? But the money—"

"I sold *Skiblathnir*."

"God, no." She recalled the beautiful, miniature Viking ship. It had cost Magnus years of painstaking work. "You loved that ship. You should never have sold it."

"Was it such a bad trade, a model for a full-size dragonship?" He met her eyes. "I thought you would be glad, Kirstin. You have one less worry."

She tried to grasp the enormity of Magnus's sacrifice. He had had no income for months, yet had given up his greatest possession. She had always known he felt strongly about preserving the Oseberg finds. But the scale of his donation, and the way he had kept it secret from everyone but her, seemed aimed at her.

"It may be years before the university can afford to pay you back," she said.

He shook his head. "It's not a loan. And keep it anonymous."

"Magnus, are you doing this for my sake?"

His face darkened.

"If that's your reason," she said, "I won't allow it—I'll see that every crown is returned. Love can't be bought." She regretted these final words even as she spoke them.

He raised himself to his full height. "Neither can a man's pride."

"I didn't mean—" she began, but he cut her short.

"Sleep well, Dr. Williams." Then he turned and strode into the night.

She felt like kicking herself. How could she have been so insensitive when he had given so much? She hurried after him across the dark excavation site. But she slipped on the rain-slickened clay. She caught herself with her hands, splattering mud the length of her coat. When she managed to stand up, wiping her face with the back of her hand, he was gone.

"Magnus!" She stared into the night. Sleet stung her face.

What had she hoped to say? What had she feared to lose?

Suddenly the whinny of a horse spun her about. Unseen hooves pounded past her in the half-frozen rain and drummed into the night.

CHAPTER 17
FALL, 872

Hooves drummed through the forests of Valdres. Horsemen raced across the fields, throwing torches onto the thatched roofs of the estate's freshly filled granaries. Then, lowering their spears, the warriors rode down bellowing cattle and screaming slaves, charging toward the central halls.

Gytha, playing chess with her foster father, was about to strike a daring blow deep into his ranks. But she paused, chess-queen in hand, at the odd clamor outside.

Ragnar, too, looked up from the board. He had never heard such a commotion on the estate. "I—I guess the game will have to wait." He found a sword behind his bench, strapped the weapon on with some difficulty, and ducked through the doorway to the courtyard.

Gytha followed as far as the porch pillars. Then she froze.

Men were actually fighting on the road beyond the stables. As she watched in horror, the smith and the stable hands—armed only with sickles—were beaten back and hacked to death by a troop of horsemen in chain mail.

She fled back into the hall, terrified. Who were these attackers? Valdres was a harmless, remote farm. There had never been need for defense—in fact, most of the men had gone salmon fishing that day with Ulf and her foster mother Hildirid. Certainly the franklin had no enemies. He was a gentle, peaceable man. And there had been no warning. The estate had received neither visitors nor messengers for weeks.

The last messengers had been in spring, from Harald.

A chill ran through her at the thought of the young Vestfold king. Could this be his work? From behind the door, she peered out

183

fearfully at the battle.

Her foster father stood in the courtyard, the sword in his hands, as the first of the horsemen trotted in. The helmeted leader reigned his horse and demanded, "Where's the princess?"

In reply Ragnar swung his sword two-handed. The warrior parried with his shield and smashed a club against the franklin's head, knocking him senseless to the ground.

"Father!" Gytha grabbed a firewood ax from the vestibule and ran toward the attacker with all her might.

The warrior calmly dismounted on the far side of his horse, signaling his riders to circle the girl. In a moment she was surrounded by shields.

"Pack her up and let's move out," the warrior ordered.

"You won't take me without a fight!" Gytha swung the ax, but it crunched uselessly into a shield. Before she could draw her dagger the men were gripping her arms.

"Tie her." The helmeted leader brought a rope.

She spat in his face. "I'd rather die first. A curse on you and King Harald!"

The leader laughed. "Harald, is it?"

One of his men chuckled, "I told you."

The leader smacked the man across the face with the back of his hand. Then he turned to Gytha. "We're not from Harald."

"Then who are you from?"

"Your father, Eirik."

She gaped at the man. Could her *father* have sent these barbarians? "Why?"

"To bring you to Horthaland. And to punish the franklin for breaking his fostering oath."

"But Ragnar never broke his oath!"

"That's for King Eirik to decide." He raised one hand to the men and waved to the west. "We've another journey ahead of us. Let's go."

The men tied Gytha onto the back of a horse as if she were a sack of grain.

Gytha struggled against the ropes. "Ragnar's hurt! You can't just leave him. Let me go! You've made a mistake! You'll be sorry!"

Laughing and trading jests, the riders trotted out of the courtyard, past the corpses along the road, and up the slopes to the western fjells.

Lashed across the jolting, sweating back of the horse, Gytha suffered as she never had before. Her face thumped against the animal's ribs with every step. Her long, shining hair—always washed and combed with such pride—dragged in the bushes and pulled painfully when it tangled.

She yelled at her captors until her chest ached and her voice grew hoarse. "A princess is to be treated with respect! I command you to untie me!"

At the top of the valley's slope the troop headed south. When they turned, Gytha could see black columns of smoke rising from the burning buildings far below. The awful reality of the destruction of Valdres hit her, and she began to cry.

She thought of Ragnar, defending her with such bravery. He seemed more like a real father to her than Eirik—a distant king she had met only a few times in her entire life. How seriously had Ragnar been hurt? He had been clubbed, but only once. Surely someone else had survived the attack—the dairy slaves at least—and they would come to his aid.

Then she thought of Ulf, her shy foster brother. She liked the boy and often teased him. Tonight he would return from the salmon falls with Hildirid. He would find the estate in ruins, most of the slaves slaughtered, and his father perhaps dead. Hildirid would not be sorry Gytha was gone. Would Ulf?

Tears ran down Gytha's forehead as she dangled upside down on the horse. Was it possible that she was really being taken to Horthaland? A journey of that scale would take a week or more! At least there her captors would face certain punishment. Eirik was a powerful king. He would be furious at the men's error, mistreating his only child. Eirik would set all to rights.

After a long and painful day's ride, the troop finally stopped for the night in a pine forest. When the men untied Gytha she slid from the horse in a heap. Her chest and stomach ached as though they had been crushed by boulders. She had neither the strength nor the tears left to cry.

"That's better," one of the soldiers said. "Knocked some of the noise out of you." While checking her ropes he noticed the hard cross of a small dagger hidden under her shift. He reached under her dress and pulled out the knife.

"How dare you!" she gasped. "Give back my dagger! It has the Horthaland seal of royalty."

The man raised an eyebrow. He turned the blade in his hands, admiring the inlaid black eagle welded there. "A pretty toy. You'll have it back when we reach the king's progress at Stavanes. Until then we'll trust you better without it."

He left her shivering on the ground, tied hand and foot. Then he joined the others at their camp chores, seeing to the horses and building a fire.

Night fell early under the pines. A chill wind mocked Gytha's thin linen shift. She knew this was her chance to escape—to chew through her ropes like the heroes in sagas. But where would she go? She had never been alone in the forest at night. The fire shook troll-like shadows among the dark trunks. What she wanted most was to get help from Eirik, and despite the cruelty of these men, they claimed they were taking her to him. With her hands and feet still bound, she squirmed through the damp huckleberry bushes toward the warmth of the fire.

The troop's leader spotted the bedraggled white face in the firelight. "Ah yes, our cargo. Hungry?"

She wanted to spit at him, but the day's ride had left her mouth too dry. Her voice was a weak croak. "You'll suffer for what you're doing."

"I'll take that as a yes." The warrior pulled his acorn-shaped helmet from his sweat-matted hair and disappeared into the shadows toward the sound of a creek. When he returned he stood the dripping iron helmet before her, using three small stones as supports. Then he tossed her a leathery stick of dried cod and a coarse chunk of flatbread.

The smell of the sun-dried cod nearly brought her stomach to her throat. "Can't I have a wheat loaf instead?"

"A wheat loaf!" About the campfire, several men laughed. The impossible request spoke entire verse-epics about the girl's sheltered upbringing. Only the aristocracy could afford to bake with imported wheat—a grain too delicate to grow in the North.

For the rest of the evening the hardened warriors ignored her, telling stories and bits of poems around the fire. But in their tales of giants and gods, all it took to start the men laughing again was for someone to mention the words "wheat loaf."

After the warriors had rolled into their cloaks beside the fire, Gytha watched the shadows fearfully. On the few trips she had taken from Valdres she had always ridden in a wagon and had stayed in the halls of great estates. Here the flickering campfire turned the ragged fir trees into a netherworldly grotto. Stars glared through gaps overhead. She tried to pull her knees up under the small woolen bag the warriors had left her as a blanket. Her legs were tight with goosebumps. She shivered, sleepless, long after the fire had died.

In the dew-soaked morning, miserable with hunger, she chewed the dried cod the leader had left for her.

"Cut my ropes," she said, but her voice had lost much of its commanding tone.

"No wheat loaves this morning?" the leader asked.

"Please. Don't make me spend another day tied on my stomach. I just want to get to my father."

He grunted. "We can try it. Although I wonder if you know how to ride as well right-side up."

As soon as he cut her bonds she limped toward the creek, her legs still numb from the night, and washed up as best she could. Her hair was difficult, for she had no comb, but she cleared the worst tangles with her fingers and tied the whole thing up in a single overhand knot. Then, feeling slightly less miserable, she walked to the makeshift corral. She chose one of the small, U-shaped wooden saddles stacked there. She checked the saddle's three interlocking parts to make sure they fit tightly and would not pinch. Then she took a bridle, caught her pony from the day before, and brushed its dusty black coat with her hands. Gently she slid the wooden saddle over its shoulders until the curved wood snugged up about the pony's neck like a collar.

"Huh." The warriors' leader watched her from the side. "Guess they taught you something in Valdres after all."

Gytha jumped into the saddle and trotted the pony before him, controlling it with the pressure of her knees against its shoulders. "And you will be taught something in a week, when we reach Stavanes."

He threw his own saddle onto a horse. "Won't take a week to get you there. Not for me."

"What is your name?" she demanded. Now that she studied the leader's face more carefully, she realized he was older than she'd thought—perhaps as old as Ragnar. The comparison brought a lump to her throat. Her foster father might even now be dying from the blow this brute had dealt.

"My name's Gilling." The leader jumped onto his horse and shouted toward the camp, "Move out!"

The men came at a run. Within moments the other horses were readied and the troop was on its way.

The second day of the journey took them into an unsettled valley. They followed a raging river up to a long lake. Gytha sat straight in her saddle all morning, proudly refusing to show her weariness. She no longer spoke, for it now seemed pointless to waste a princess's words on these men. Instead, the pent-up curses, arguments, and denunciations seethed within her as she rode. She spent her time considering which she would use when they finally reached Eirik.

The morning dragged on without so much as a single rest stop. By mid-afternoon, Gytha had begun to waver in the saddle from fatigue. She had not slept the night before and was unaccustomed to anything more demanding than short pleasure rides.

The warriors who had joked about her so harshly the day before were quieter today. It had been easy for them to feel high-spirited about abducting a spoiled, whining child. But now that the girl rode among them with proud disdain, their sporting mood ebbed. One of the men caught her shoulder when she nodded asleep, drooping perilously to one side. She gave a start and jerked away from the man, resuming her stiff pose with a scornful shake of her head. Her blond hair, which had fallen loose during the ride, shook back from her shoulders. She set her eyes straight ahead and pressed her lips together, unintentionally dimpling her cheek. The man glanced to his comrades and silently returned to his position.

When they finally stopped that evening at the lakeshore, Gytha sat by the fire in a daze. The men skinned and roasted the rabbits their arrows had found along the trail during the day. Gytha numbly ate a little of the meat. Soon the exhaustion of the day overcame her, and her eyelids fell. She leaned against a tree root and was asleep with her knees drawn up beneath her delicate, white shift.

Gilling wiped the back of his hand across his mouth, frowning at the very young and very beautiful girl sleeping beside the troop's campfire. "It's warm here," he grumbled. He unpinned his wool cloak and tossed it aside so that it fell across the girl. Then he turned his back and squatted by the fire with the others.

For a while the men merely stared into the flames, occasionally glancing up at the girl. When at length they did begin telling stories and reciting poems, no one laughed as they had the night before.

Gytha awoke in the morning to find a small whalebone comb lying in the grass near her feet. She looked about uncertainly, but the men were busy readying their gear for the day's ride. Whoever had left her the comb had wanted it kept a secret. She hid it under her shift and ran to the lake's shore, eager to wash and comb her hair properly. The morning sun spilled a wavy stream of gold along the lake, as if even the goddess Sol had chosen this mountain water to rinse her shining tresses.

Gytha waded in the lake while she combed out her hair. When she was nearly finished, Gilling shouted, "Hurry up, we're ready to go."

She dried her feet on the grass and began tying her pointed boots, winding the long laces in crisscrosses up her legs.

Gilling found himself watching the laces tighten on the girl's slender legs. He cleared his throat and dropped a sheet of flatbread beside her. "Here's some breakfast. You can eat it while we're riding, Princess."

She cast a glance up at the leader. He had never called her "Princess" before. Perhaps the nearer they came to Eirik, the more manageable he would become.

"Where do we ride today?" she asked.

"The Wastes."

She tightened her lips. She had known the Horthangr Wastes lay between them and Stavanes, but she hadn't expected to cross those dread barrens so soon. "What is the real reason you took me from Valdres?"

The leader shook his head, as if she had already asked too much. "Come on. The men are waiting."

She followed him up to the troop, where her pony stood saddled. She swung onto the animal's back and winced. Yesterday's long ride had left her so sore that the wooden saddle hurt dreadfully.

One of the men smiled at her discomfort.

At once her expression hardened. "Let's go, then."

The leader nodded, and they started up from the lake.

Every step of the horse jolted her against the saddle. To take her mind off the pain, she chewed the piece of flatbread. It was dry and hard, made of cheap barley. Her teeth crunched on sand left by millstones. She swallowed enough to stave off the worst of her hunger and put the rest away in disgust.

"Princess." One of the brawniest of her captors rode up beside her. He held out a leather pouch.

She took it cautiously. Inside were a jumble of wrinkled orange circles, and the sweet smell of autumn. "Dried apples?" she asked, testing one. The fruit had been deliciously preserved with honey. She looked to the big man with a grateful smile. "I thank you."

He nodded awkwardly, his eyebrows lowered.

Gytha savored the sweet fruit, hoping to make it last most of the morning. And as she rode, she watched the warriors with new eyes. Any one of them might have left her the comb that morning. They obviously had begun to understand that she was a young woman after all. Of course she would make them suffer for their attack on Valdres, but the time for that would come.

Occupied with such thoughts, she hardly noticed the landscape about her becoming more and more forbidding. There had been no beech trees in the forests for a day, but as they climbed higher, even the pines began to struggle, twisting and gripping the rocks as if under attack from an invisible enemy beyond. Then only the white-barked birches remained, shivering in the gullies, dropping yellowed leaves in surrender.

Finally a cold wind woke Gytha to the change. They had climbed above the protection of the valley. Now they stood on the edge of a vast heather barrens—the Horthangr Wastes. These were the uninhabitable fjells that formed a no-man's-land between Norway's eastern valley realms and the sea kingdoms of the west.

Sun still lit the dale behind them, but a low, gray ceiling of clouds rolled across the treeless plateau ahead. Beneath the clouds, an ominous blue line of ice capped the horizon.

"Are you sure this is the right way across the Wastes?" She didn't remember much from the few times Ragnar had taken her to Horthaland, but she was sure they had never come so close to a glacier.

Gilling smiled, reading her thoughts. "Women's wagons might take a longer route. We save two days by cutting past the ice."

It bothered her that Gilling seemed in such a hurry to reach Stavanes. Wasn't he afraid of Eirik? Surely her father would punish him for kidnapping her and clubbing Ragnar? Perhaps Gilling wasn't

CHAPTER 17 ~ 872

really taking her to Horthaland at all. Certainly the route along the glacier was new. Could it be that the troop was merely a band of robbers seeking ransom? Robbers sometimes hid in the vastness of the Wastes, and Gilling had refused to explain his "mission" from Eirik. But as she weighed this theory, its flaw became obvious. Robbers would have looted the Valdres halls before taking a hostage. They must be misguided Horthalanders after all.

For the remainder of the day they rode in silence toward the ice cap. Time and again the horses had to circumvent lakes or cross bogs.

By nightfall the ice mountain loomed into the clouds, a white wall fractured by dark blue crevasses. Gilling finally called a halt beside an iceberg-dotted lake. He set the men to piling rocks for a windbreak and a crude corral. Gytha wearily climbed from her horse. She huddled in a borrowed cloak while the shelter's walls slowly rose.

"Where is the firewood?" she asked.

"Look around," Gilling said scornfully. "See any trees?"

"Then how can we cook?"

"No need to cook dried cod."

"Won't we have *any* fire?"

Gilling shook his head and was about to go check the corral, but the princess's look of despair made him pause. At length he grumbled, "Well, we could use a small fire for light. Go on, then. Gather some heather branches before it's too dark."

A week before, Gytha would have laughed at the idea of obeying such a command, but with darkness settling about their camp on the Horthangr Wastes, firewood collecting suddenly seemed very important. She stumbled out of the shelter. She pulled at the tough, mat-like bushes until her tender hands were scratched and torn.

She returned with a small armload of twigs only to find that Gilling had already gathered a heap five times as large. He inspected her contribution dubiously. "Green wood won't burn. Dead bushes like these are better." Then he handed her an iron striker and a palm-sized flint from his belt. "All right, light it."

She looked at the flint and iron. "I—I've always left that to the slaves."

Gilling laughed. "Well you won't find any slaves here." He took her shoulder so that she knelt beside the brush pile. "I'll show you how. Stack a few of the smallest twigs around a piece of dry lichen.

191

That's it. Now hold the flint close and take a strike."

She had seen it done a thousand times, but it proved much harder than she had thought. First the flat piece of iron would not spark at all against the stone. Then her hair fell in the way, knocking the tinder pile apart. But finally a spark lodged in the mesh of lichen. She blew quickly, and was delighted when a tiny flame appeared.

"That's it," Gilling said, adding twigs. Before long the small fire lit their crudely walled enclosure. He turned to the men piling stones. "That's high enough. Come on in."

The rough warriors climbed over the wall and gathered about the blaze. This time Gytha remained among them for the campfire circle. Wind swirled smoke about the group, forcing one after the other of the men to turn away or close his eyes.

Out of the darkness, a deep rumble boomed across the still lake.

"What was that?" Gytha asked.

Gilling frowned. "Frost giants. They live in the ice mountain."

"And you had us camp *here?*"

The brawny warrior who had given her the dried fruit earlier in the day now lifted a heavy necklace over his head. "Take mine, Princess."

She held up the chain. A pewter amulet in the shape of a hammer dangled in the firelight. She viewed the man askance. "Do you all have these?"

The men nodded.

"If you're really Eirik's men, you wouldn't worship Thor. Everyone knows Thor once tried to curse Horthaland."

Gilling grunted. "Odin serves well enough in the fjordlands. But in the Wastes, you want a good hammer at night." He nodded toward the dark glacier. "Only Thor can battle the giants."

The brawny warrior added, "And Thor's power is growing."

Gilling flashed the man a warning glance.

"What do you mean?" Gytha demanded. "Is Eirik in trouble?"

The man mumbled with some confusion, "I didn't mean anything like that, Princess. I just meant Thor used to get fooled by the giants a lot. Thor's smarter now."

Gytha tossed the amulet back. "Thor has never been as smart as Odin. Only traitors wear hammers."

"We're loyal enough to Eirik," Gilling said.

The brawny warrior suggested, "Tell her about the time Thor

crossed the Wastes. Then she'll understand."

"Thor has crossed here?" Gytha asked.

Gilling nodded. "That was before he got angry at Horthaland. They say he was passing near the edge of the ice, not far from here, when night fell. He thought he was lucky to find a large hall with an arched roof and five rooms. Thor stayed there, but in the morning he was shaken out of the entrance. Then he saw he'd spent the night sleeping in the glove of the frost giant Skyrmir."

"Are frost giants so large?" Gytha asked. The shadows had crept closer as the little campfire dwindled. She added the few twigs that remained.

"Some are," Gilling replied. "All of them are powerful."

"What do they do?"

"I can tell you what Skyrmir did to Thor, if you want a tale."

Gytha considered this offer. She was curious about the giants and enjoyed tales, but the closeness of the glaciers made her uneasy. "All right. Tell your tale."

Gilling held out his hands, as if to ready himself for the gestures the story would require. "When the frost giant realized Thor had slept inside his glove he laughed at how small the thunder god was. That made Thor so mad that he threw Mjöllnir, his hammer, right at the giant's forehead."

"So the giant's dead?" Gytha asked.

One of the men scowled at her, as if to say she should know better than to interrupt. She replied with a defiant look, but did not speak again during Gilling's recitation.

"No," Gilling said, "the giant just laughed and asked, 'Did a leaf fall on my head?' When Mjöllnir flew back to Thor's hand as always, he threw it again even harder. This time the giant said, 'Was that an acorn I felt?' Thor had never seen anyone survive such blows from his hammer. He strapped on the belt that doubles his powers and defiantly challenged the giant to any test of strength the giant chose.

"Skyrmir agreed and led Thor to a hall deep inside the glacier. There he showed Thor a huge bowl filled with mead. 'Among my people,' Skyrmir told him, 'a man is considered worthy if he can drink this cup dry in one draft. Some take two drafts, but even the poorest can finish it in three.' Thor gripped the bowl and took an enormous drink. When he finally had to stop for breath, the mead hardly seemed much lower. He took a second drink, and a third, but the level in the bowl had only gone down a little. Skyrmir laughed, 'From your fame, I'd expected better of you, Thor.'

"Thor replied, 'Perhaps giants are strong drinkers, but few would choose to wrestle with me in my anger.' Skyrmir said, 'From what I've seen of you, Thor, I can't think of any man among the giants who would think you're a worthy challenger. But perhaps my grandmother would wrestle with you. She's a little shaky, but she's brought down greater men than Thor, I think.' At that, a withered old hag limped into the room. Thor reluctantly took her on. To his surprise, he couldn't

budge her. The harder he tried, the tighter the old woman held her ground. Finally, she forced him down to his knee.

"Thor lowered his head with disgrace. He left the hall and was led by Skyrmir to the edge of the ice. There Thor admitted that he'd made a poor showing. But as soon Thor was off the ice Skyrmir backed away. 'No, Thor,' he said. 'If I'd known how powerful you were, I would never have let you near my hall

in the first place. I won't allow you there again if I can help it. I've been tricking you with magic. When you threw your hammer at me, I put a mountain in front of me to take the blow. Now when you ride down to the fjords you'll see a huge canyon in the side of the fjells. That's where your hammer hit. Then, when you drank from the mead bowl in my hall, you didn't realize the bowl was actually connected to the oceans of the world. I was terrified when you lowered the level of the water. Now, as you ride down to the fjords, you'll see how much the sea has retreated. From now on that daily ebb tide will be called Thor's draft. And finally, the grandmother you wrestled was none other than Old Age herself—who conquers all men if they live long enough.' When Thor heard how he'd been tricked, he hurled Mjöllnir at the giant. But Skyrmir vanished into the air by his magic."

"The giants have feared Thor's hammer ever since," Gilling

concluded, lowering his voice. In the silence that followed, the last of the campfire's twigs flared and died. Tiny, worm-like orange coals writhed a moment in the cold wind before they too disappeared in the starless night.

Gytha gave a start when a finger touched her shoulder.

"Keep it, Princess." In the darkness she recognized the voice of the shy, brawny warrior. The hammer amulet and chain dropped into her hand with a thin clank. "Eirik doesn't need to know everything you do."

She held the charm in her fist and huddled lower under her cloak. Soon she heard the snores of the men. But sleep came only fitfully to her on that long night.

The morning of the journey's fourth day dawned bright but cold. The sun's first rays glinted pink on the great ice cap beyond the lake. In the night, Gytha had imagined the glacier's crevasses opening like the doors of a crystal cavern, loosing shaggy white giants to forage for flesh. But now, by daylight, she scoffed at such fears. Even in the legends, frost giants did not eat people. The giants were too busy battling gods to trouble themselves with humans, whether they wore little hammers or not. Besides, she had other concerns now that Stavanes was close, and she certainly was never going to camp near the frost giants again. She returned the amulet to the big warrior, saying simply, "I won't tell Eirik if you keep it."

In reply the big man pulled out the eagle-crested dagger that he had taken from Gytha on the first night of the trip. He handed it to her hilt first.

Gytha returned the little dagger to its hiding place inside her shift. Then she quickly combed out her hair and readied her horse. By now she knew the fast-paced routine of the troop, and did not want to keep them waiting.

They rode across the heather all that day, with the glacier dwindling behind them. Streams flowed ahead of them now, first across rock-strewn plains, then between rounded hills, and finally through a gorge cut from the uplands—the gash of Thor's hammer. Eagles circled in the canyon, watching for salmon in the river's cascades. Warm sea breezes gave promise of the still unseen fjords beyond.

Gilling led the troop along the canyon rim until the first pine trees appeared. Then he called a halt, although the day still had several good hours of sunlight. The men dismounted and began gathering the horses as usual. Gytha wanted to ask Gilling why they had stopped early, but when she looked for his familiar, rugged face among the men, he was already gone.

As sunset neared, Gytha walked entirely around the camp, curious what had become of the leader. She had nearly given up when she finally saw him sitting by himself on the rimrock overhanging the canyon. The warrior was staring at the waterfalls far below.

"Gilling?" she asked.

He wiped his face with his rough hand and turned away.

"Is something wrong? Why have you camped early?"

"If we'd gone on, Princess, we'd have been in Stavanes by twilight. Nightfall's a bad time there. Eirik may be old, but he's dangerous when drunk."

Gytha smiled. "You *are* afraid of meeting him."

"I was afraid for you, Princess."

"Me?"

"Eirik's ruled Horthaland longer than I am old — and I've got grown children of my own. I've never questioned his command as king. But now I wonder about him in other ways." Gilling looked at her again and furrowed his brow. "You're not what we were told to expect."

"What were you told? Why were you so cruel in Valdres?"

Gilling sighed. "I'm sworn not to answer."

"I think you're afraid because you overlooked the difference between 'escort' and 'ambush.'"

"Tomorrow, Gytha, you'll see."

"Tomorrow *you* will see!" She turned away and stalked back to the camp. How dare the man address a princess in such a manner! After just four days together on the trail, these crude warriors were calling her 'Gytha,' as if she were a comrade in arms! Now, with the king's court just hours away, it was time she reasserted her position.

"Give me your cloak," she ordered the first man she met in camp. The warrior hesitated, but Gilling appeared from the shadows and gave the man a nod. Silently, the man unpinned his mantle.

She snatched it from him and strode on to the others by the fire. "You, and you! Bring me a portion of the fire for my own, near the trees." The men glanced at Gilling, and obeyed. For the rest of the evening Gytha sulked by her lonely fire, thinking of all the indignities she had suffered in the past days. She recalled the destruction they had left behind in Valdres. She fell asleep thinking of Ragnar and Ulf and Hildirid, wishing that all could be as before.

Gytha awoke early, anticipating the day. She combed her hair, wove it into thick braids, and tied it with a purple ribbon torn from the borrowed cloak. She washed herself in a creek and scrubbed the dirt from her white shift. When she appeared before the waiting troop, riding her pony with her chin set high, she looked as regal as the journey's difficult conditions allowed.

"Hail, Princess," Gilling said. Then he nodded to the men, and the troop set off from the camp.

An hour later they emerged from the forest at a high bluff. Before them the green shoulders of the fjells parted like an army standing aside for the passage of its sovereign. The shining waters of Horthangr Fjord paved that long, winding gap with a path of silver nearly to Gytha's feet. The sight struck her so strongly, and she was still so high above the fjord, that it took her a moment to notice the ships.

"Eirik's fleet has grown," she observed.

Gilling grunted noncommittally.

As they switchbacked down toward the halls of the Stavanes estate, Gytha had time to count the ships more carefully. Eirik commanded only sixty warships, yet here were nearly a hundred — many of them much larger than Eirik's sixty-oar vessels. Could he have built so many in just one summer?

Then she spotted red banners among the familiar white. The sails too, though furled on the decks, were dark red. She lifted an eyebrow. Eirik's allies, the Vikings, must be visiting. She recalled Hadd the Hard, the pock-faced Viking king. It seemed unusual for him to be in Horthaland in autumn. After the Vikings' summer raids he usually returned directly to the Vik.

Still, she was glad the Vikings were at Stavanes. Once she had settled the confusion about Valdres with Eirik, there would be several days before her return trip could be arranged. The Vikings would provide a diversion, no doubt with tales from their much-heralded plan to conquer Wessex, the last corner of England to hold out against the Norse. Certainly the young jarls had outdone each other with verses and sword stunts last spring at the Vik, trying to impress her.

Where the road widened at the upper edge of the estate, Gilling commanded, "Columns!"

The troop broke into a double line with their spears high in the air. Gytha rode proudly at the fore of the warriors' honor guard. Though she kept her eyes straight ahead, she was aware of the workingmen, ladies, and sailors who put down their burdens, whispering to each other as the young noblewoman passed.

Gytha rode to the long, central hall and dismounted. Her heart was beating faster at the thought of meeting her powerful father again after so many winters. Guards with halberds confronted her before the hall's low door. Gilling said, "Let the princess pass," and the men stepped aside.

She ducked through the dark vestibule into the hall. After her journey, the smoky gloom inside was stifling. At first she could see only the servants stooped before the hearth. Then she made out the shapes of the men sitting on benches among the pillars. Finally, she recognized the white-bearded, balding king on the high seat. She was startled by how much Eirik had aged. His arms were still muscled, but his skin was wrinkled and thin. The bones of his cheek and jaw stood out sharply.

Gytha stepped forward and announced, "Eirik, your daughter has arrived."

The old king glanced at her impatiently. "Very well. Bring her to me."

She flushed to think he could mistake his own daughter for a simple handservant. "Father, I am Gytha."

Eirik looked at her more carefully. Could this tall, slender woman really be the child who had caused him so much grief? He studied her features and began to recognize the imprint of Astrid—the full lips, the dimpled cheek. Gytha's birth had killed his wife fourteen years ago. Now it was as if the girl had not merely stolen Astrid's life, but her beauty as well. The old resentment surged back.

Eirik looked away, and his glare fell on Gilling. "Your orders were to bring her bound, to prevent any further mishap."

The troop leader lowered his head. "I thought we would make better time if—"

"Enough! You will stand night watch until you learn obedience."

"Yes, King."

For a moment Gytha was too stunned to speak. Gilling was to be punished for treating her *too well?*

"Father!" she cried. "Do you realize what this man did? He burned the granaries at Valdres, murdered innocent men, and left Ragnar unconscious—for all I know, he's dead!"

Eirik was unmoved. "Ragnar only reaped the anger he had grown. I gave him Valdres against his sworn word. No fosterer of Eirik's kin dares break oaths like laces."

"Ragnar didn't break his oath! He's done everything a foster father should."

"A fosterer has no right to promise another man's daughter in marriage."

"Ragnar never did!"

"Ask Harald of Vestfold."

"*Harald?*" Gytha felt like laughing and crying at the same time. "Father, this is all a mistake—a terrible mistake. I answered Harald myself. I sent his silly messengers back with insults."

Eirik leaned forward and held his fist before her face. "Ragnar should never have let such a foolish child speak for herself. Harald swears you've agreed to marry him on the condition that he conquer all of Norway."

"Isn't that the same as saying no?"

"Evidently not to Harald. The boy has vowed neither to cut nor comb his hair until he fulfills the pact."

"But—but that's ridiculous."

"Nonetheless, 'Harald the Unkempt' has captured the Vik."

Gytha paled. "The Vik? Impossible!"

"We all thought so."

"But how could he? The Vik is a fortress!"

Eirik grunted. "The boy and his marshal Guthorm built floating bridges. Their farmer troops stormed the island while Hadd the Hard was in England. Then they waited for Hadd's ships to return, attacked them on the beach, and burned half the fleet before Hadd could escape."

Gytha's head spun. The fabled Vik, stronghold of the invincible Vikings, had fallen to *Harald?* If a skald had invented such a preposterous tale he would have been jeered. But she herself had seen the Viking ships in Horthangr Fjord. Now she realized they were not merely visiting. They were fleeing the defeat of the Viking homeland.

"Why didn't Harald attack Valdres instead?" she asked. "It was unguarded."

"Because that wasn't the challenge you gave him. And Harald seems as foolishly particular as his grandmother. Now his army is marching on Thelamork, under some kind of cursed dragon banner that never falls." Eirik pushed angrily from his high seat and began pacing the dirt floor.

Gytha had time to collect her thoughts. In a way, she found Harald's bold determination thrilling. And it was flattering to think he had finally dared to stand up to Hadd the Hard because of her. But it was sheer foolishness for him to think he could go on. Norway had twenty-nine other kingdoms, many of them eager to expand on their own. Viking allies all over the North would be targeting the boy for vengeance. They must know he would be vulnerable, with his forces weakened from the battle at the Vik. She was a little sorry Harald's triumph would be so short-lived.

"Surely you're not afraid of a boy's luck," she said.

"A boy's luck, no. But this whole campaign reeks of a different luck altogether. Wherever the boy goes, the Viking jarls are replaced with Norse Thing-courts—popular, of course, with the commoners. I've even heard that several of the old jarl noblemen have gone over to Harald voluntarily. Apparently he makes them local administrators, raises taxes, and promises them more income than they had before. The scheme's clever—far too clever for a boy. It's the work of the Little Chieftain."

Gytha looked at him questioningly. "The Little Chieftain?"

"Harald's grandmother, Asa."

Gytha couldn't help laughing. She remembered the blind old queen she had stumbled into at the Vik. "Who would give a feeble grandmother a powerful title like that?"

Eirik stopped his pacing, his back turned to Gytha. "She was almost as young as you when I did it."

"*You* named her, Father? Why?" She recalled Ragnar's warning about an old family feud between Asa and her father. Enemies sometimes gave each other titles, but they were never as laudatory as "Little Chieftain."

Eirik sighed. "It was a different world then—both simpler and greater. We *lived* the sagas in those days, instead of merely reciting them. Norway will never be so glorious again."

For a long time he was silent. Though he faced away, she could see the old king put his hand to his face. He wiped his hand as though it were wet. Could there be tears? Perhaps age had left her father weakened by sudden moods. Either that, or the hatred between her father and Asa must still be intense.

But Gytha wasn't about to let Eirik's old disagreements destroy her life. Nor could she wait any longer to bring up the subject that mattered most. "Father, about Ragnar—"

"Curse your Ragnar!" Eirik burst out, suddenly turning on her. "The man was a simpleton. And I was a fool to think I'd be free of your mischief while you were in Valdres."

With a chill, Gytha realized that her father might not let her return to Valdres at all. For him, Ragnar had been merely a pawn, a hired jailer who had failed to keep her locked away.

"You act like I'm a runaway slave instead of your daughter! I've lived with Ragnar all my fourteen winters. Don't you care at all what I feel?"

"Gytha." He spoke as though the words cost him great effort. "You are the heiress of Horthaland. The future of the kingdom depends on your safety. Ragnar can no longer be relied upon for your protection."

"And so you'll lock me up here with you!"

"No. There is a better way to stop Harald's troublemaking." The old king signaled to a guard by the door. The man nodded and went outside.

An ill-defined panic began to spread through Gytha. "What are you going to do?"

Eirik watched the door. From somewhere outside came a faint, rhythmic clanking. The sound grew louder as it neared the hall. Gytha drew back. The ominous clanking already echoed in the vestibule.

Suddenly Hadd the Hard threw open the door, his swarthy, pock-marked face distorted by a gruesome laugh. In his heavy iron armor—breastplate, chain mail, spiked gauntlets, and sword—he looked to Gytha like some monster from the tales of Giantland. He swaggered forward and slapped Eirik on the back. "So you've decided?"

Eirik turned to his daughter. "King Hadd has asked for your hand, and I've agreed."

"No."

She had merely breathed the word, but it was enough to send Eirik into a rage. "By the gods, child, it's not your decision! This marriage is vital to the future of Horthaland. We need a young battle-king. Think of the security the kingdom will have, united with our allies, the Vikings."

Hadd grinned. "Harald the Unkempt can grow his hair as long as he wants. We'll cut him down to size."

Gytha shrank from the leering face, desperately thinking of escape. It was no use complaining that the man was repulsive. Eirik obviously cared nothing for her wishes. And Hadd would hardly withdraw his offer; he clearly saw this match as revenge on Harald. But she suddenly thought of a different approach.

"King Hadd has just lost his lands," Gytha objected. "Can he offer me a fair and equal wedding gift?"

Hadd scowled. "Who told you about England?"

It had been a luckier argument than Gytha thought. "The skalds say you're penniless," she lied.

"It's not true!" Hadd growled. "I still have a boatload of silver, more than all Horthaland can boast. And I'll have the rest next summer when we beat King Alfred back to Wessex."

Gytha pushed on. "Empty promises!"

"No one expected the English to build ships of their own and meet us at sea. We'll change our attack strategy next summer."

"To what? Floating bridges, like Harald used to defeat you?" Gytha tossed her head. "That won't reconquer England. I think I can find more promising suitors."

Eirik gripped her arm. "Listen, child! Only a father can choose suitors. Hadd brings with him precisely the things we need: forty ships, the best fighting men in the North, and the allegiance of kingdoms from Ireland to the North Fjords."

Hadd unsheathed his sword with a clang. He held out the wavy-edged blade for her admiration. "And I have Fenris, the blade that can never break, for it will swing at Ragnarök."

She gave a short laugh. "Not only that, but it also—" She caught herself. It was Harald who had told her the sword was charmed, making its bearer invulnerable to the steel of warriors. Harald had made her swear an oath—to the gods!— that she would not tell. Could the secret have been true? And if it was, did Hadd really not understand the power he held in his hand?

"But it what?" Hadd demanded. The blade gleamed, highlighting the wolf engraving and the row of runes.

She fell back on a line from the Yngling Saga. "But also 'Fenris vests the Vikings' fate.'"

"Yes, yes, we've heard that too," Eirik said, dismissing her with a wave. "Now we've had enough talk. Hadd and I have pressing matters to discuss. You'll need to rest after your trip and get ready for the marriage feast tomorrow."

"Tomorrow!" she gasped. Did she have so little time to think of a way around Eirik's will?

"The sooner this agreement is sealed, the better off we'll be." Eirik signaled two guardsmen. "Escort the princess to the log hut. I'll send slave women to see she's washed and dressed. Guard her at all times. Do you understand?"

"Yes, King." The men took Gytha firmly by the arms.

"Father!" she cried. "Don't do this! Please!"

He spoke to the guards. "She's to be brought back here tomorrow noon, rested and properly attired."

Gytha's fury roared in her head like a storm wind.

"No!" She struggled as the men dragged her away. She hated Eirik—how could he condemn her to marry Hadd the Hard? Before the guards pulled her out the door, she saw a terrifying, animal-like gleam in Hadd's eye. Suddenly she believed the horrible stories she had heard at the Vik. It was rumored that the only women Hadd had slept with were the Skirings he chained and raped in England. This same monster was the murderer who had lied his way to the Viking crown. And to think she had hurried to Stavanes, hoping Eirik would understand!

In desperation, without even knowing how she would use the weapon, she grabbed her hidden dagger. But a powerful hand quickly caught her wrist. The guard squeezed until her fingers blanched and the blade dropped. Then he slipped the weapon into his belt and yanked her onward across the courtyard.

The guards shoved her through the low doorway of a block-shaped hut and threw the bolt closed behind her. She pitched forward onto a wooden floor. Crouching there, alone in the near darkness, she cried. Her fears crowded down upon her like a hundred jeering faces. How could people treat her so cruelly — her, the heiress of all Horthaland? She put her hands to her face and rocked on her knees, wishing there were a spell that could take her back to Ragnar. He had always treated her the way a true father should. He was the only one who had ever really loved her.

Except possibly Harald? Her thoughts drifted back to the Vik. She saw her meeting with the handsome boy again as if she were watching from a distance. She had laughed and kissed him on the lips. He had stood there, staring at her as if struck by Thor's thunder. Could he really be so committed to her that he would take her impossible challenge seriously? Would he keep attacking kingdom after kingdom until he was killed? Didn't he realize the ruin his devotion already had caused — that he had brought about her impending marriage to Hadd the Hard?

Finally she dried her tears. Her head had cleared, and one goal remained before her — escape. If only she could get back to Valdres, Ragnar would help her hide.

She looked about the bare cell's windowless walls. There was no encouragement here. The hut was built with a far more solid kind of construction than she had ever seen before. Instead of the usual vertical, split staves, the walls were made of logs, stacked horizontally and fitted together at the corners. The hut even had a solid plank floor. At first Gytha thought the hut's builders had taken this unusual measure just to keep prisoners from tunneling out, but then she noticed barley kernels in the cracks, and realized the room would also serve for threshing grain. There were only two openings to the hut: the bolted door and a tiny smoke hole in the high roof.

She studied the smoke hole, thinking. It was too small for a man, but might a slender girl pass? At once she set about trying to climb the walls to reach the cross-beams, a spear's length above her head. The wall logs had been hewn so smooth, however, that no footholds remained. She walked about the room, trying to climb in countless different places. Always she slipped back when the rafters were still out of reach.

Before long, the guards opened the door to let in Skiring slave women with washtubs, and Gytha was forced to abandon her attempts. As the women started to undress her, she noticed the shorter of the two guards still standing inside the door.

"Leave me," she ordered. "I will bathe."

The guard grinned. "My orders are to watch the princess day and night."

She hurled the clasp of her shift at his head. Then she turned her back, shucked the shift, and stepped into the tub, vowing that one day she would teach such men respect.

After her bath the slaves left, and Gytha was able to refocus her attention on escape. But the guards were relentless. Even when they escorted her to the privy, she was watched. Finally they threw a straw sack on the bare floor and told her to sleep.

The sack of straw gave Gytha had the inkling of a plan. She folded her arms defiantly. "A princess cannot sleep on the floor."

"Why not?"

"I will only sleep in a bed. Eirik's orders were that I should be properly rested for tomorrow's feast. Bring me a bed."

The guards looked at each other. The taller said, "Nobody uses beds. Even the king sleeps on a dirt bench."

"If you do not bring a bed, I will not sleep at all."

The shorter of the guards shoved her toward the sack. "You'll sleep on the floor, all right."

She faced him, chin high. "You are used to forcing people to do things, but you cannot force a princess to sleep. When I last visited Stavanes, Eirik gave me a bed. Bring it now."

The guards began arguing with each other about whether, and how, they could make the girl sleep in order to fulfill Eirik's order. Finally the taller one shrugged and set off to look for the bed. An hour later he was back, carrying a bundle of carved boards. He assembled the bed, grumbling. When he was done, Gytha promptly climbed in and closed her eyes.

For a long time the guards stood outside the door, talking. Occasionally one or the other would open the door a crack to check that she still asleep. Eventually the taller guard yawned. "Who's taking the first shift?"

"Me," the other replied. "Ingi's coming."

The taller guard chuckled. "I'll be inside. Call me when it's my turn." The two men poked each other for a while, and made obscene remarks. When Gytha finally heard a woman's voice, the door opened. The tall guard ducked inside, still chuckling. She could hear the door being bolted from the outside behind him. For a moment she was afraid that he might try to get into her bed. But the tall guard merely threw a hide on the planks and curled up against the door. Soon he was snoring.

Gytha waited several minutes, her heart racing. Then she stepped from the bed. She laid the blanket and the straw tick on the floor. Carefully, she lifted the foot of the bed into the air. When it was standing on end, she climbed to the top. The wooden joints creaked agonizingly. Then she crouched and sprang into the air.

The bed teetered below, clunking with the rhythm of a big, slow heart. Gytha clung to one of the hall's rafters, terrified that the noise might alert the guard. But he only smacked his lips and turned on his side.

When all was quiet again she swung her legs until she caught a second rafter. Then she pulled herself up and stood atop the two rafters. For a minute she eyed the smoke hole over her head. Then she jumped, catching the hole's rim. She began pulling herself up toward the small, sooty square. Her head had almost reached the hole when the strength in her arms gave out. She dropped back with a small gasp. She hung from the edge of the hole, her feet kicking for the rafters out of reach in the darkness below.

She fought back a wave of panic. She couldn't give up now! Once again she began swinging legs. She swung higher and higher, until finally her feet caught a beam on the underside of the roof itself. With that foothold, she shoved herself upward through the sooty hole, squeezing her shoulders one at a time into the night air.

She sprawled atop the shingled roof with relief. She was free!

But then she lifted her head and saw the dark fjells crowding the fjord. She might be free from her prison, but she was still very far from Valdres. A gibbous moon shifted behind clouds, casting a ghostly shimmer across the water. Even with Gilling's fast-paced troop the trip had taken five days. Now she would have to cross the Horthangr Wastes alone. Could she remember the way? And what about food?

Suddenly the immensity of the task loomed before her. With Gilling she had traveled as a captive princess. This time she could not be a princess at all. In the morning Eirik would send out his troops in search of a lone noblewoman. She would have to travel in disguise. But what disguise?

A hoarse voice panted from the bushes below, "Ingi! Ingi!"

Gytha smiled vengefully. She crept down the roof and jumped lightly to the ground. Beyond a fringe of bushes the naked backside of the guard pumped up and down in the moonlight. His clothes lay jumbled in a pile near the door. She slipped to the door, gathered up his clothes, and tiptoed away. She nearly giggled at the thought of the naked guard trying to spread the alarm. With any luck, they would think him drunk.

In the breezeway of a storage shed Gytha examined her borrowed disguise. The long-sleeved woolen tunic was of the commonest kind, with an attached, knee-length skirt that was drawn tight at the waist by a sword belt. She took off her shift and tried on the coarse garment. The sleeves were a little long, but with the cuffs rolled, it fit well enough. When she buckled on the sword, the skirt's hem fell below her knees — far too long for a guard, but just the right style for a shepherd. Very well, she thought — she'd be a shepherd boy.

Enthused by the novelty of her role, she pulled on the guard's stockings — thick woolen tubes that reached from ankle to knee. Copying the style of men, she held the stockings in place by wrapping them with linen bands. Then she tied on the guard's leather shoes and turned about, admiring her disguise. For once she was glad her chest lacked much of a profile. The disguise seemed perfect.

Except for her hair.

A shepherd's hair would never reach even to the shoulders. She ran her hands down her shining, waist-length hair, and swallowed hard. Dressing up in men's clothing was no longer a game. Her golden hair was her proudest possession. Cutting it short would be like casting aside a crown. For the first time that night, her resolve wavered. She thought bitterly of Harald, who had sworn not to cut his hair until he conquered Norway. It seemed a cruel irony that his vow should force her to an opposite, perhaps more difficult sacrifice.

Lacking shears, she reached inside the tunic for the guard's knife. To her surprise, the dagger was her own. Then she remembered that the guard had taken it from her that afternoon — although the incident seemed ages ago. She held the silver blade, feeling the welded eagle of Horthaland's royal insignia. If she had to lose her hair and become a common shepherd, at least she promised herself that she would never again lose her dagger. When the time of troubles passed, that royal mark would prove who she was.

The hair pulled painfully as she sawed it short with the blade. The night breeze raised goose bumps on her bared neck. With tears in her eyes she gathered the fallen tresses in her linen shift and tied the sleeves to make a bag. Even when the guard had watched her bathe she had not felt so naked.

Blinking back her tears, she carried the bag to the door of the storage shed. She had to have food for her journey. Inside, the room was so dark she left the door open to help her find her way among the barrels and sacks. There was no dried fruit. The raw grain was of little use to her. In the end she filled her bag with the same dried cod and flatbread that had revolted her on the first journey.

She had hardly ducked out the door when a spear tip jabbed her tunic.

"Prepare to die, thief!"

Gytha fell back with a small cry. "I'm the princess!" she gasped. The blade had cut her breast.

"And I'm King Alfred." The warrior poised his spear for a final thrust.

In that instant the moonlight caught the warrior's bearded face. Of course — Eirik had ordered him to take the night watch as a punishment.

"Gilling!" she cried. "It's me, Gytha!"

He hesitated. "Gytha?"

Her heart beat wildly. After the scorn she had heaped upon this man during their voyage, there seemed little hope of mercy.

"I've cut my hair and I'm running away from Eirik. He wants to make me marry Hadd the Hard, but I'd rather die first."

Gilling furrowed his brow. "What's in the bag?"

She choked a laugh. "Dried cod and flatbread. Just what you always gave me, and I always hated."

He ran his hand over his face. For a long time he said nothing. Gytha shivered silently, afraid that anything she said might unleash his revenge.

Finally Gilling reached to his belt, slipped his flint from its strap, and held out the worn stone. "You'll be needing this, Princess."

She jumped forward and kissed him on the cheek.

He pushed the flint into her hands as though he hadn't noticed the kiss. "You do remember how to use a flint?"

"Oh, yes! I remember."

"Then don't stand around dawdling." He unpinned his cloak and tossed it over her shoulder. "You'll find the horse you rode in the corral behind the hall. Now go on, get out."

Gytha clutched his gifts and ran into the darkness.

The warrior shook his head after her. "We'll both be needing luck after tonight."

CHAPTER 18
WINTER, 1904

Kirstin pointed to the road from town.

"Who the hell—?" Otto muttered. Though the black carriage was still distant, it did not bode well. Only royal officials traveled with a mounted guard.

"Dödkvist," Kirstin said, the word a puff of fog in the frosty morning air. Her cheeks flamed red above the thick wool collar of her winter work coat.

"And we were so close to moving the ship."

"That's why he's here." She drew her coat tighter and walked down from the mound. Ever since Magnus had paid off the Oseberg farmer she'd put all her effort into a race against the calendar, trying to finish the excavation before the snows. Even her misunderstanding with Magnus had been laid aside with a simple apology. She had needed to concentrate on work. No wonder she had not wanted to think about the Swedish king's claim on the ship. The memory of Dödkvist's disastrous first visit at the chest-opening ceremony still stung.

To be sure, no one could ignore the Union's deepening political crisis. The whalers brought bold-bannered newspapers from town nearly every day. In Kristiania, the Norwegian parliament had demanded greater independence, but had been rebuffed by the Swedish king. Rumors spread that Norwegian army units were on alert—that the border with Sweden was secretly being fortified. At the excavation, the men argued long into the night about the prospects of war. It seemed to Kirstin that the country's political storm had grown fiercer with every artifact unearthed from the Oseberg burial mound.

The black carriage bumped across the ruts of frost-stiffened mud. A coat of arms gleamed beneath shiny lacquer. A guard in a blue-and-yellow uniform dismounted and opened the door. Secretary Dödkvist ducked out of the opening, holding his top hat in place. He stood squarely before them and took a deep breath. Then he broke into a broad smile, extending a hand to Otto.

"Dr. Hoffman! I've been reading your articles in the German Academy's journal. Remarkable what you have here."

Otto managed a smile. "Well, thank you, I—"

"Stockholm may seem far away in these troubled times, but the Ministry of the Interior has been keeping a closer eye on your work than you might think." Dödkvist adjusted his spectacles, then grinned again, spreading out his hands. "So show me this ingenious framework you've devised for fitting the ship onto a railroad flatcar."

Otto searched for words. "First I should tell you that I am not in charge of this excavation."

"Oh well, technically I suppose Dr. Söderfelt is still leader, but since he's in Stockholm, you—"

"Dr. Söderfelt has been replaced," Kirstin interrupted coldly. "The University at Kristiania has officially appointed me expedition leader in his place."

"You?" The Swedish official frowned at her. "A woman?"

Otto cleared his throat. "I suspect Dr. Williams knows she is female. She also knows a great deal about handling excavations."

Dödkvist thought a moment. "I'd heard the expedition had invited some sort of famous American archeologist, but I'm sure it was a man."

Kirstin clenched her teeth behind a smile. "Perhaps you're thinking of Leland Williams, my father. His age prevents him from traveling much these days, so I was invited instead."

"You speak Norwegian." His tone turned the statement into an accusation.

"My mother was from Bergen. I am an American citizen."

"Nice place, America. You know, I spent a year in Baltimore when I was younger. Oyster cannery management. Have you been there?"

"Baltimore? No."

The man seemed to lose interest in her. He turned to Otto. "Well then, Hoffman. Let's take a look at the ship."

As they walked up the mound Otto glanced apologetically to Kirstin. She shook her head to reassure him he was blameless. If they could tolerate Dödkvist, he might be cajoled into dropping the king's claim. If that failed, they would need to convince him the ship wouldn't be ready to move for a week. That might give them time to send it by rail to the university in Kristiania.

The workers had been singing as they completed the wooden framework beneath the ship. They fell silent when the bureaucrat climbed to the excavation.

Dödkvist straightened his spectacles. "Now this end would be the stern."

"The bow," Kirstin said.

"Yes. Beautiful. The whole thing seems so enormous now that it's unearthed. Big enough for an army."

"With thirty oars, we estimate she carried a crew of thirty-five," Otto said.

"Absolutely incredible. Perfectly aquadynamic lines." He held out one hand as if to pluck an invisible fruit. "The real mystery — the magic, if you will — of a ship like this is how our Viking ancestors could design it so perfectly without the use of paper. And then — to build it without proper tools. Don't you think?" He looked to Otto.

"Well, yes, I suppose," Otto said. "We think they built models of the ships to plan them."

Dödkvist nodded. "They were axemen. Fighters who used the same weapons to build their warships as to slay their enemies."

Kirstin couldn't help intervening. "Of course the carpenters used more than just axes."

"Oh? It's my understanding from Dr. Hoffman's articles that the planks were split, not cut, from logs."

"True. But the planks were smoothed with adzes and grooved with hand planes. They had augurs for drilling the rivet holes. They used saws, too, to cut the boards to length."

Dödkvist frowned. "Saws?"

"If you have questions about construction of the ship, perhaps you should ask Mr. Andersen. Our labor manager once built a working model of the Gokstad ship using only technology from the Viking Age. Magnus?"

The big Norwegian had been working nearby. Now he slowly put down his hammer, pushed up his sleeves, planted himself in front of Dödkvist, and looked down at the man. Magnus's fists clenched.

The Swedish official paced several steps as if thinking. Then he stopped beside the uniformed guardsmen and turned. "Hoffman, you've done an excellent job of preserving this ship so far. That's why I want to help you now that your work is in jeopardy."

"In jeopardy?"

Dödkvist unfolded a piece of paper from his pocket. "Telegraph reports say a front is moving in from the North Sea, with a hard freeze and heavy snows."

"*Mein Gott*, that would ruin the ship."

"How much time do we have?" Kirstin asked.

"Only twenty-four hours, I'm afraid." Dödkvist allowed a moment for this news to sink in. "Is it possible you could have the ship ready for transport by tomorrow?"

Kirstin studied the bureaucrat warily. His expression drooped with condolence, but she thought she recognized a gleam of satisfaction in his eyes. He must have been waiting for this opportunity to play his trump card.

"Thank you for the report, Mr. Dödkvist. We hadn't planned to move the ship for another week, but we'll step up our efforts. I'll see that the freight wagon from Tønsberg is here ahead of the storm."

The Swede gave a slight bow. "Understanding the urgency of this matter, I've taken the liberty to make the arrangements."

"I'm sure we can handle the situation on our own," Kirstin replied. Dödkvist was shrewder than she had thought. Obviously he had discovered that the railroad had only one freight wagon large enough to move the ship to the depot.

"Oh, I have no doubt of your abilities. It's the railroad people I thought would need assistance. Cuts in subsidies have left them understaffed, you know. I've placed a small military detachment at their disposal to assist in transporting the ship."

Kirstin reddened. If the Swedish military controlled when and how the ship was moved, they would control where it was moved. "I suppose you've arranged for the railroad flatcar, too."

"Yes of course," he smiled. "The Ministry of the Interior has reserved a special train for the project. Tomorrow afternoon."

Magnus stepped forward menacingly. "This ship isn't your property. It was bought by a donor for the University of Kristiania. The train will stop in Kristiania."

Dödkvist shook his head. "The donation you mention was frivolous, since the artifacts already have been deemed property of the king. The train will steam directly to Stockholm, Mr. Andersen. And you can be sure there will be no revolutionaries tomorrow on His Majesty's railroad." Then he tipped his top hat to Otto. "A pleasure seeing your work, Dr. Hoffman. You may expect the freight wagon here first thing in the morning. Until tomorrow then." He turned and walked with his bodyguard to the waiting carriage.

Kirstin and the others walked down after him in a daze. They watched the black carriage drive away. Even the Oseberg farmer, who had been driving a rake in a nearby field, stopped his team of horses and came to lean against a fence post.

"Damn!" One of the whalers spat. "I say, fight 'em. There's more of us than those damned guards."

Otto shook his head. "If we refuse to move the ship, we'll lose everything to the freeze."

A sailor tossed a wrench aside. "If the Swedes run the railroad, what's the use? We may as well walk away and let the king fetch the boat himself."

Magnus looked to Kirstin, his lips tight. "I'm sorry, Kirstin. I thought we could do it. I gave it all I had."

She looked at the whalers — a beaten crowd of angry men — and she

looked back to Magnus. There had to be more! If she had learned anything from the months of tumultuous dreams it was never to give up.
Where was the cunning of Queen Asa now that the ship needed to sail
one last time?

To sail! She caught Magnus's arm. "Why do we have to move the
ship by land? Couldn't we take it by sea?"

"By sea?" His eyes widened with a new hope. "If we could get it to
the docks, we probably could find a barge. It's worth a try."

A sailor put in, "Larsen's got a tug he ain't using, now that the
whaling fleet's gone south."

"Wait a minute," Otto objected. "Even if you could get a barge up
Oslo fjord, the university's not near the waterfront."

"But the Akershus fortress is," Magnus replied. "It's full of
Norwegian troops, guarding the capital in case the trouble with the
Swedes blows up."

"Would they let us store the ship there?" Kirstin asked.

"Oh, they'd welcome the Oseberg ship with flags waving," Magnus
said. "The problem would be getting launched in the first place. We'd
have to move the ship framework to the Tønsberg dock by tomorrow
morning. Dödkvist has reserved the only wagon big enough. We aren't
going to drag that ship framework very far on our own. It weighs fifteen tons."

The men grew solemn again at these words, but Kirstin had already
glimpsed another way. She walked through the group to the fence at
the edge of the fields. "Mr. Hansen! Cold weather coming, they say."

The old farmer chewed on his pipe. "So I hear."

"Then you've heard, too, that the Oseberg ship may be taken by the
king."

His wrinkled eyes flashed. "Swedes."

"To keep the ship in Norway we'd have to move it to the docks tonight."

He sized her up. "Move that whole thing in a single night?" Then
he blew smoke out the side of his mouth. "If you're looking for magic,
talk with the wife."

"I don't think even she has spells to move ships."

"No, suppose not."

For a while the two were silent. Mr. Hansen puffed, looking
off across the fields. Kirstin gave him plenty of time. Finally she

commented, "You have a flatbed hay wagon."

He snorted. Then he pointed the stem of his pipe at the mound. "Listen, it'd take *five* wagons like mine hitched end to end to move that contraption you've built. And what with all the crates, you'd end up needing twice that many and ten-fifteen teams of strong horses besides. You'd have to go borrow stock and wagons from damned near every farmer in the valley."

She looked at him steadily. Behind her, the crowd of sailors had grown silent.

Mr. Hansen sucked on his pipe, meeting her gaze with a frown. "It'd be a hell of risk, and farming's risky enough."

Kirstin lowered her head. "This ship is our crop. We've got just one night to bring in the harvest before the freeze. We need help."

The farmer looked back to his team of horses, running a hand over his stubbly jaw. Finally he sighed and knocked his pipe against a fence post, scattering sparks. "Well, come on, then. We'd better start asking before it gets dark."

Magnus grinned and several of the sailors whooped.

Kirstin was more careful to contain her optimism. Even if they could rally the other farmers in the valley, there was so much to do before the dawn, and so many ways the scheme could fail. She turned to the excavation team. "Magnus, ride to the docks and see about the barge. Otto, stay here and help the workers finish up the framework as best they can. I'll try to be back by dark."

Then she allowed herself a sigh. "And get the kerosene lamps ready. I'm afraid we've got a long night ahead of us."

CHAPTER 19
FALL, 872

It seemed the night would never end. Though the moon had vanished hours before, Gytha urged the exhausted pony up the steep trail from Stavanes to the highlands. Turbulent emotions charged Gytha's spirits — pride to have defied her father, excitement for the adventure ahead, and worry about Ragnar. Even if her foster father had recovered from his wound, would her home in Valdres ever be the same?

At the first gray of dawn she rode away from the trail and pulled her weary horse into a birch thicket to camp. Hidden by a vault of white branches, she arranged her few things as if she were in a little hall. But the dew had been so heavy she had trouble starting a fire. For nearly an hour she struck sparks with her flint into the damp tinder, growing impatient and angry.

Then she heard hooves. As she watched through the branches, a troop of the king's horsemen trotted along the ridge beyond her camp. How foolish she had been to stop this close to the trail! She reddened to think she had tried to build a fire at all. Smoke would have been a signal flag. No matter how cold it became, she could have no fire.

All that first day Gytha cowered in the thicket, peering out in astonishment at the seemingly endless stream of soldiers passing along the ridge. She had expected a search party — but an army? She dared not sleep, afraid her horse might slip its tether and give her away.

By twilight Gytha was fighting drowsiness. Night would be her only chance to travel unseen. She let the horse browse a few minutes on huckleberry bushes. There was no grass. Then she set out again, this time riding through the much rougher terrain away from the trail.

Twice she saw the flicker of a campfire through the trees, and circled wide, her heart pounding. Once she was startled by the whinny of a horse where there was no light. She remembered Gilling, who sometimes camped without a fire. She might stumble onto soldiers anywhere in the darkness. Instead of making her more cautious, the thought drove her on faster. Her heels thumped against the horse's sweat-soaked flanks. What would Eirik do if he caught her? Was her escape treason? Eirik might claim she was aiding Harald—not her intent at all!—and then what? Could there be any punishment more horrible than marrying Hadd the Hard? She closed her eyes tightly against the thought.

Suddenly branches crashed and the world vaulted.

Gytha groaned in the dark, her face burning and raw. When she rolled over, lightning shot through her right shoulder. She gritted her teeth, trying not to cry out. When she touched the spot she felt a ragged hole in the tunic at her shoulder, already warm and sticky with blood.

The horse was on the far side of a fallen tree. Gytha had been thrown through the snag's branches. The stub of a knot had caught her shoulder in the fall. A rock had scraped her cheek raw.

Gytha eyes dampened. How far she had fallen from the bright days as a princess in Valdres! Hurt and alone, she felt as though she had lost everything—her foster family, her servants, and even her long hair.

A tear ran down her cheek. But when the salt touched the scrape on her face, a flash of pain jolted her back to clearer thoughts. She quickly wiped her eyes. Then she sat up straight, commanding herself in a stern whisper, "Gytha Eiriksdottir! Stop feeling sorry for yourself! If you are a princess, act like one."

She ordered her legs to stand. To her surprise, they obeyed. In fact, even her arms could move freely. Though painful, the gash on her shoulder had broken no bone. She knew she would need to wash the wound. And she was so thirsty. The most important thing, she decided, was to find water. She crawled back through the fallen tree's branches to the horse. This time she didn't try to ride. Horse and girl walked onward together into the night.

The sky had lightened—it was the second dawn of her journey back to Valdres—when she reached a canyon with a waterfall. The falls arched like a sail and pounded into a misty pool. Gytha put her lips to the cold water and drank. Then she leaned back in the moss and was instantly overcome by sleep.

* * *

In the dream her father crouched beside the water, as if he were hiding some ancient secret. She crept up behind a rock to watch. He seemed so old, and yet there he knelt, playing with bits of bark in the water like a boy with a toy fleet. Or were they pieces of bark after all? When she looked closer, she saw they were diamond-shaped boards, such as love-sick youths sometimes float to sea, asking the gods to grant an unlikely match. Each board bore a blue spiral. Gytha came out from behind the rock, puzzled. The King of Horthaland, in love with a woman he couldn't marry? He had shunned women since her mother's death.

"Father?" she asked.

When Eirik looked up, his face melted from grief to rage. Gytha shrank back. The face was no longer Eirik's at all. As she watched it changed into the hideous, pock-marked mask of Hadd the Hard. Red wings unfolded from his back. His massive arms, bound with spiked gauntlets, gradually lengthened into talons. Terrified, she turned and ran into the forest. The shadow of giant wings followed. On and on she fled, stumbling in her fright. Out of breath, she finally burst into a shepherd's hut, bolted the door, and leaned against it. She closed her eyes with relief.

Then a low laugh issued from a dark corner of the hut.

Gytha spun about. A blind old woman in a richly woven dress sat on the wall bench.

"Come child, you will be safe in time."

"How can you know that?" Gytha asked.

The blind woman tilted her head toward a small window in the back wall. "Look. Use your inner eyes."

Gytha stepped to the window. She saw with surprise that it did not open onto forest at all. Far down a grassy hill lay a valley patched with farm fields. In one of the fields, flying a golden banner, a full-sized dragonship was rolling along on dozens of wheels.

"I—I don't understand." Gytha turned, but the blind woman had vanished. Only a low laugh echoed through the dark.

* * *

After Gytha awoke she lay for a while in the ferns, puzzling about the meaning of her strange dream. But her shoulder ached and daylight was fading. There was no time to waste. She would have to travel again with the coming night.

With some difficulty she rose and began washing the gash on her shoulder in the waterfall's pool. It was a painful job, for the wound was deep and unclean. She knew the ragged puncture should have been treated much sooner, but that couldn't be helped now. She made a bandage from a strip of her linen leggings. Every movement sent a fresh flash of pain through her shoulder. Then she rinsed the blood from her tunic and did her best to tie the torn fabric together left-handed. Only when she was finished did she give in to the gnawing in her stomach and get out the food sack. Then she led the horse out of the canyon and rode on toward the moonlit Wastes.

Stars shone throughout the third night of her flight. She no longer saw soldiers' campfires—perhaps because there was so little firewood in the Wastes. Neither did she see the luminous blue ice cap that had been Gilling's landmark on the route from Valdres. She was glad to avoid the frost giants of the glaciers, but wondered if she had gone astray.

Now she wished she had paid more attention to the lessons Ragnar had given her on clear winter nights, reading the sky above Valdres. She remembered the troll's eye was supposed to be in the north—but which star was it? All she could recognize was the triple-starred sword of Dofri, king of the frost giants. She followed that cluster, hoping it lay in the east.

When a red dawn streaked the sky, the horizon slowly solidified into a distant valley with a glint of water. Which valley was it? Dozens of dales descended from the Wastes. Was it a lake or a salt fjord? She wanted to find out at once, but was too tired and weak to continue. Besides, it would be foolish to ride in daylight.

A cold wind cut across the plain. At a point of land between two creeks, Gytha slid down from the horse. There were tufts of grass here for it to graze. Boulders provided some shelter. She lay down to sleep, but cried out in agony at the pressure on her shoulder. She untied the bandage in a daze. Ghastly red flesh puffed between the linen bands. The wound was worse.

Night had fallen when the throbbing in her shoulder wrenched her awake. To take her mind off the pain she reached for the food sack. But the provisions were gone. Animals had emptied the bag while she slept. She kicked the bag angrily into the bushes. Then she pulled herself onto her horse with her left arm, and she rode on, hungry.

Thick clouds rolled in, blotting out the stars. Even the moon dulled and died, leaving the Horthangr Wastes a terrifying, directionless void. Gytha rode blindly down through the black seas of heather, hoping the creek would lead her to the valley she had glimpsed the day before.

Again she spotted campfires, and she shivered. All along the creek were the taunting, flickering lights. How many hundreds of warriors had Eirik sent after her? Dark shapes seemed to be everywhere. Every snapped twig and sigh of the wind made her stare wide-eyed into the night. She tried to close her mind to everything but one thought: she must find Ragnar.

When dawn grayed, she realized the campers could not be Eirik's men after all. She was still high in the valley — too high for farm settlements — and yet the fires were ringed with farm wagons and cattle. There were even children.

Whoever these travelers were, they undoubtedly had food. And they could tell her the way to Valdres. Wearily, she rode toward one of the fires.

"Halt! Who goes there?" A red-bearded man barred her way with a spear.

Gytha lifted her chin. "A shepherd. I fell and lost my way."

The man laughed. "Some shepherd! Where's your flock?"

"It — it was brought down to the farm by the others. I got separated. I think I'm lost. Which valley is this?"

A second man came up from the fire. "What you got, Svein?"

"Oh, some runaway boy. He's stolen a horse."

"I'm not a runaway boy!" Gytha insisted. At least that much was true. She lowered her eyes. "And the horse is mine. I've just lost my way."

The second man snorted. "Well, that's for sure, if you're heading toward the trouble down in Seterdal."

Seterdal? That was in Thelamork! She had reached the eastern side of the Wastes, but was several days south of Valdres.

The red-bearded man nodded down the valley. "It's all the Mop's."

"The mops? What are they?" Gytha climbed down from her horse, but her knees buckled and she staggered to the ground.

The red-bearded man glanced to his comrade. "Maybe the kid really is lost." He unbuckled the sword belt she had taken from the guardsman in Stavanes. Then he slid out the sword to inspect its blade. It was sharper and longer than a shepherd boy would need. He motioned for her to follow. "Come on then."

The two men led the way to a campfire where women bent over cooking pots. They looked up when the men approached. A woman in a modish, imported kirtle asked, "Well?"

The red-bearded man shrugged. "We found this boy spying. Says he's a lost shepherd."

The woman sucked in her breath. "Why, it's just a *child*. He's hurt—and looks half-starved. You fools wouldn't know a spy from a goose." The men retreated before her glare.

The woman dipped a ladle into a pot and filled a bowl. "Here, eat this."

The warm porridge smelled so wonderful and Gytha was so hungry that she tipped the bowl to her lips without waiting for a spoon. When it was gone she set the bowl down, suddenly embarrassed by her greed. "Thank you, madam. You are kind."

"And you're as hungry as an oarsman, child." She took the bowl, filled it with sour milk curds, and handed it back to Gytha—this time with a spoon. "That's a nasty wound. Have you been in a fight?"

"No, " Gytha said quickly. "I was thrown from my horse."

"Where are you from?"

Gytha paused, thinking. Someplace close, but not too close. "Do you know Hemsedal?"

The woman nodded. "It's gone now too."

"What do you mean, gone? And why are all you people traveling so late in the year?"

"The Mop, of course."

"What's the mop?"

"The Mop's not a what. It's a who, child. It's Harald. Harald the Unkempt."

Gytha repeated the name in disbelief. "Harald?"

The woman's eyes flashed. "We Vikings are the rightful jarls in this country. We were good to the people. We were fair. And then this—this—*boy* marches up from some backwoods kingdom with a snake flag and half the farmers turn traitor. Now he's taken all of Thelamork and he's marching on Uppland. Haven't you heard any of this?"

Though Eirik had mentioned Harald's success, the story had

seemed as distant as a saga myth. "I — I was in the Horthangr Wastes."

The woman sniffed. "Well, that's where we're all headed now. Over to King Eirik, where Viking jarls are still free. It's a bad time of year to cross, and we've got a lot to carry. But in Horthaland we can get ships. Then we'll set sail for new shores. There's a place they talk about — Iceland, with grass as deep as a horse's withers." She cocked her head at Gytha. "Maybe you should come with us to Eirik."

"No! No, thank you, really. I have to go home."

"Home." The woman looked away, down the valley shrouded by the mists of morning. "Even a shepherd is luckier than we are. You still have a home." She had a wistful smile. "You know what started all the trouble with the Mop?"

"What?"

"A girl." The woman laughed. "A princess no one had ever heard of. Harald asked to marry her, and she says, 'Not unless you're king of all Norway, I won't.' Can you *believe* her nerve?"

Gytha lowered her head. "I guess I can't."

"I'm told by people who have actually *met* this girl that she's so beautiful men literally go *mad* when they look at her. She has this golden hair that hasn't been cut since she was a baby — that's why Harald won't cut his hair now, either, you see?"

"Oh."

"Of course the best joke is that the Mop's been cheating on her for years."

Gytha looked up sharply. "What makes you say that?"

"Well, he's already married."

"What!"

"That's why he's done so well. It's more than just battle luck, I'll tell you that." She leaned forward and lowered her voice. "Harald's father-in-law is *Dofri*, the frost giant!"

For a moment Gytha almost believed her. But then she remembered meeting Harald at the Vik. He was just a boy, not some mythic hero who dealt with giants. The claim was ludicrous. She tried to show concern nonetheless. "Really?"

"Oh, yes. Harald's real father died years ago, you know. Who do you think taught the boy about battle and law?"

"I don't know. His grandmother?"

The woman rolled her eyes. "No, the frost giants, you goose. When

Harald was little he found the cave where Thor had tied up Dofri. Harald cut Dofri's bonds, and in exchange Dofri gave him his daughter in a secret marriage. The frost giants have been helping him ever since."

Gytha's eyelids began to sag. She had finished the curds and suspected she would learn nothing more of value from the garrulous woman. "I'm sorry, I've been riding all night. Thank you for the food."

The woman smiled. "You're welcome—what did you say your name was?"

"Oh, I'm—I'm Ulf." It was the first male name that popped into her mind.

"Ulf? Really? The same as the hero of Valdres."

Instantly Gytha was awake. "What about Valdres?"

"Well, that's where Harald's princess lived."

"Yes, I know, but—"

"You do?"

Gytha blushed at her error. "I mean, I know it *now*. What happened in Valdres?"

"Nothing. That's the strange part. You think it would be the one place Harald would go. Maybe he knew the princess was already safe in Horthaland." She shrugged. "Everywhere else, folks see this golden dragon banner coming, and then the Mop's marshal, Guthorm, demands they swear an oath of allegiance. Some people do, some people leave, and some stay to fight. But not at Valdres. Harald's whole army just detours around the valley like it was full of trolls."

"But what about the hero?"

"Well, the franklin and his wife were so panicked they simply took off across the hills. But their son Ulf—the boy couldn't have been much older than you—*he* rallies fifteen men and attacks Harald's army head on."

"Fifteen men against an army? Why?"

"To defend the princess's honor, of course. People say he'd been a quiet boy, too. But he battled like a berserker when it mattered. They say Ulf killed seven men and wounded twenty more before Guthorm finally cut him down." The woman glanced wryly across the camp. "Unlike some warriors."

Gytha covered her face with her hands. Ulf! No matter how exaggerated the story was, her foster brother wouldn't be called the 'hero of Valdres' unless he were dead. How she regretted the times she had teased him! She had loved him as a brother, but she had also treated him unfairly. She had always known Ulf couldn't return her taunts because she was a princess. Now he had proven how much nobler he had been all along.

"Are you all right?" The woman bent to her. "Here, let me look at that wound."

"No! I'm just tired." Gytha yanked her arm away, and a stab of pain momentarily grayed the world. She fought to keep the dizziness from showing. "What's become of Valdres now?"

"Oh, the same thing as everywhere else, I'm sure. The Mop's given it to some phony jarl."

"And the franklin?"

The woman sighed. "Listen, you're hurt. You need rest."

"Just tell me! Please?"

The woman studied Gytha more closely. "If it matters so much, they came south past here. Since they were to blame for starting the war, no one wanted them to stay."

"Where did they go?"

"Oh, they headed south across the Wastes, saying they were going somewhere neither Eirik nor Harald could reach them."

"But where?"

"Who knows? The Wastes are wide."

Gytha's mind raced. Ragnar and Hildirid were all she had left in the world. If only she could find them, everything might be better. But where could they have fled? Somewhere neither Eirik nor Harald could reach them. Not Horthaland, then, nor the kingdoms where Harald's armies marched.

Rogaland! Whenever her foster mother had been angry she had threatened to go back to Rogaland, where Sulki was king. Once, during a long Yule blizzard, Hildirid had reminisced about the farm she had abandoned long ago, before moving to Valdres. What had she said? Yules were rainy there. It almost never snowed. And the farm looked out to the ocean across a fjord named —"

"Soldiers from the north! To arms!" The red-bearded man's cry shattered Gytha's thoughts.

The Viking woman wailed, "Gods, no! It's the Mop!"

But when Gytha squinted at the distant horsemen trotting down into the valley from the direction of Valdres, she knew they were not Harald's men.

In the confusion of battle preparations, no one noticed the ragged shepherd boy slip away and ride up a side canyon that led south into the Wastes.

And when the soldiers arrived, under the friendly banner of Eirik's black eagle, the surprised Viking refugees swore that no one had seen the beautiful Princess Eiriksdottir pass their way.

* * *

Night and day began to blur in a swirling delirium of chills, fever, ice, and hail. Roaring black clouds churned across a hellish landscape more desolate than anything Gytha had yet seen. Huge, rock-rimmed lakes sprawled through endless barrens where even heather could not grow. Time collapsed to the beat of the flaming red wound on her shoulder, pumping a dizzying poison through her veins. She was too hollowed by hunger and exhaustion to care about her pursuers anymore. Only the steel-edged will to find her foster parents kept her struggling onward.

When the storm clouds began hurling snow across the plains, Gytha's horse sank to its knees. Numbly, Gytha dismounted and pulled the weakened animal onward by its bridle. She staggered through a creek and was wetted to the waist. The aching in her feet gave way to an ominous, stony dullness. White flakes covered the side of her face and hair. Finally the horse stopped altogether, its knees locked in defiance. Gytha pulled it until the reins broke and she tumbled backwards into the snow.

She lay in the freezing drift, gaping into the howling white sky full of wrathful gods. In an instant of clarity, she knew it was Thor. It had been Thor all along. More than once she had heard it said that Eirik had offended the thunder god long ago. Now she would pay for his crime—whatever it had been. If only she had kept the hammer amulet Gilling's men had given her!

She folded her stiff hands upon her tunic, dimly hoping to preserve the last of her warmth. Beneath her shirt she could feel the hard cross of her dagger—the dagger with the royal Horthaland emblem of Odin's black eagle. Had she been wrong to put her faith in such an awesome prankster? All-powerful, but treacherous. The god of battle, and of poetry. The god whose one eye saw the world's demise, and who therefore saw no wrong in abandoning even his most devout worshipers on a whim.

She pressed her eyes closed, praying with all her heart that Odin might let her live. She was only fourteen winters old! There was so much she had yet to do, so many wrongs she had yet to right.

Her horse nickered nervously, rattling its bridle. Gytha struggled to lift her head to look. The dizziness worsened, spinning her on the edge of blackness. But the wind had eased. Had Odin heard her after all?

Suddenly a black spear pierced the horse's neck. As Gytha watched in disbelief, the animal stiffened. Its eyes stretched wide. A trickle of blood ran down its shaggy coat from the weapon's shaft. Gytha opened her mouth soundlessly. The horse tilted and collapsed to one side.

She turned to stare one last time into the dimming, whirling world. Before her stood the frost giants — huge, white, and faceless.

CHAPTER 20
WINTER, 1904

An icy wind whistled past the five farm wagons rolling the Oseberg dragonship toward the sea. Eight teams of steaming draft horses leaned into the traces, pulling the massive wooden framework up the last rise before Tønsberg. Dawn left the ship's prow a spectral silhouette against the sky's churning grays.

Otto nodded ahead to the fjord, his face lined with exhaustion from the night's work. "Whitecaps. Is it possible to sail in such a wind?"

The gale whipped Kirstin's blond hair and fluttered the cuffs of her khaki pants. "We don't have much choice if we're going to outrun Dödkvist."

One of the whalers pulled his cap tight against the wind. "If we get Per Larsen's barge, you can bet he'd steam through hell. Why, I remember when the *Baldur's* crew was so drunk they ran aground on the outer skerries with a full load of black powder. It was Per Larsen who pulled 'em in to harbor. Wasn't his fault, neither, when the *Baldur* blew up and took out half the docks."

Shouts from the wagons turned Kirstin's head. The sixty-foot ship had slowed to a crawl where the road took a right-angle bend at the edge of town. The Oseberg farmer stood to one side, yelling instructions, while other farmers led the horses in a wide arc. Wheels groaned as the five wagons, hooked end to end like railroad cars, twisted beneath the weight. With sixteen horses pulling toward town, the last wagon rounded the corner from the north, its rims screeching against the curbstone. Overhead, the framework of the ship cleared a log building's eaves by inches.

Now hooves and wheels began to clamor down the city cobblestones with increasing speed, rumbling like a rockslide in the fjells.

Shutters flew open from the wall of clapboard houses crowding the narrow street. Alarmed faces pressed behind panes, mouths caught half open by the monstrous ship lurching headlong through the town. The dragon seemed drawn by the salt tang of the fjord, as if nothing mattered more than to quench its long-denied thirst. Faster and faster it rolled, until the horses were trotting to keep ahead of the wheels.

"It's going out of control," Otto cried, hurrying as fast as his limp would allow. "*Mein Gott*, can't we use more of the brakes?"

Suddenly Kirstin realized what they had overlooked. Although each of the five wagons had a hand brake, the driver in the lead could operate only the first wagon's lever. Unless the wagons could be slowed, the entire assemblage would wreck on the town's steep streets.

"Climb on and pull the brake!" she called to a farmer jogging beside the last wagon, but he did not seem to understand.

"Damn it!" She sprinted ahead. With a jump she managed to catch the protruding end of the ship's framework.

For an instant, as she clung to the beams above the blur of cobblestones, she regretted what she had done. She was Kirstin Williams, after all, and not some hero from the sagas. What had she been thinking?

"Kirstin, let go!" Otto's voice called.

It was just the motivation she needed to hang on. She swung her feet forward onto the wagon's bed. Then she crawled beneath the rocking framework of the ship to the front of the wagon and pushed the ratcheted handle as far as it would go.

Brakes screeched iron against iron. Sparks flew as the wagons careened across the church square, tearing out a lamp pole as if it were a straw. A wide-eyed delivery boy whipped his horse, jolting a bakery cart toward a side street. Bread loaves spilled across the cobblestones.

The ship ripped through a hedge and crossed the harbor boulevard before it began to slow. Wagon wheels rumbled onto the wooden planks of the wharf. Kirstin leaned still harder against the brake handle. Just short of the harbor's waves, the chain of wagons finally stopped.

Kirstin climbed down and sagged against a wheel with relief. She put her head on her arm to catch her breath. She had come to Norway to test herself, but now she felt as if the ship were testing her.

"You all right?" Magnus had run up from the direction of the wharf cranes.

She nodded. "Sorry I'm late."

"It looked like you were going to launch the framework, wagons and all."

"We nearly did." She wiped her forehead with her sleeve. "How about you? Could you find a barge?"

"Larsen will loan us his barge sure enough, but that won't help now."

Otto and the others were hurrying onto the wharf. Already a crowd of onlookers was gathering along the waterfront. Men stood in twos and threes, lit their pipes, and watched silently.

"Kirstin!" Otto said, puffing. "You could have been hurt."

"I'm all right, but Magnus says we've got a problem." She turned back to the big Norwegian. "What's wrong?"

Magnus nodded toward the fjord. "We can't put out in this gale. We'll have to hold off."

"We can't wait either. Dödkvist has probably already figured out where we are."

"Kirstin, Oslo Fjord's reporting fifteen-foot seas."

"Well the waves aren't that high in the harbor. Let's load everything onto the barge and wait in a sheltered spot until the wind drops."

"That might help keep the artifacts from freezing, too," Otto suggested. "Isn't air warmer over the water?"

"Yes, it is," Magnus nodded.

"Then let's get underway." Kirstin surveyed the confusion on the dock. "I'll want to talk with Mr. Larsen. In the meantime, Magnus, you can see about getting the barge loaded. And Otto—"

But the German archeologist held up his hands. "I'm no sailor, Kirstin. Plan on me staying behind this time."

Kirstin studied her friend. "You've worked on this find since it was a hill in a field. We can't arrive in Kristiania without you."

He sighed. "Maybe I'll make my way to Kristiania after things have settled down. You don't need another archeologist on the barge. You need someone here in Tønsberg to straighten out the mess you're leaving behind."

"You mean Dödkvist?" she asked. If Otto stayed, he would face the wrath of the Swedish king's representative.

"And me, I'm afraid." He lifted his chin. "I've decided to tell my university the truth about my dissertation."

Kirstin stopped short. She and Otto had thrown so much of

themselves into their work that she had nearly forgotten the threat Otto still faced from his plagiarism long ago. The look in his eyes told her that he had found the strength to face his own personal demon, even at the cost of his career. In a sense he was showing greater courage than any of them.

"If there's anything I can do, Otto, count on me to stand up for you." She put an arm around him and hugged him. Much might change before she saw him again. "Good luck."

He touched her hair a moment. Then he closed his eyes, as if he were drawing strength from her nearness. "We'll both be needing luck after tonight."

A double blast of the tugboat's horn shivered through the wind. Kirstin looked up to see the dragonship lift into the air and sway, as if it had opened unseen wings and caught the gale. With a rush of steam and a giant growl of engines, the wharf's crane turned its steely beak, slowly twisting the Viking ship toward the fjord.

Kirstin kissed Otto on the cheek and hurried to the throng of men at the edge of the dock. Suddenly a gust of wind caught the prow, rotating the ship in midair with ponderous grace. A corner of the ship's protective framework caught one of the empty hay wagons, splintering it to kindling. Men shouted and ran across the docks. But as the gust subsided, the ship began twisting back in slow motion. The crane growled forward again, lowering its load as it straightened. The dragon settled onto the slowly rocking barge with a screech of bolts against iron—as if its claws had gripped this floating nest, and the dragon was eager to sail once more.

At once sailors scrambled onto the framework, freeing the cables. Then the crane growled again to fetch the remaining artifacts.

"Where's Mr. Larsen?" Kirstin shouted to one of the men over the roar of wind and motors.

"Which Larsen?"

"The barge owner."

The man jerked his head toward the tugboat.

Crouched at the back of the tug stood a red-shirted sailor, swearing violently while he wrestled a heavy snake of rope as thick as his leg. He was hefting the rope over the tug's railing, obviously trying to secure it to a cleat on the barge's rim. To lend a hand, Kirstin leaned across the gap between the pitching iron decks. She grabbed the loop of rope and helped pull until it dropped about the cleat.

Instead of thanking her, Per eyed her dubiously. He spat into the sloshing chasm between them.

She put out her hand. "Kirstin Williams. I've heard you'll be helping us move the Oseberg ship."

Per grunted in reply. He took her hand in his callused paw as if to shake it. Instead simply pulled her across the gap onto the tugboat. Per's grin revealed teeth as crooked as a row of derelict pilings. He sized her up, saying, "So you're Magnus's woman?"

She yanked her hand free. "I am *not* Magnus's woman."

"Don't burst your boilers, Miss. It's just what the others say." Per turned and limped toward a ladder. "May as well come on up."

She followed him up an almost vertical stairway to a balcony in the full blast of the wind. Per held a rounded metal door open against the storm. She stepped inside to the tug's bridge—a tunnel of salt-streaked glass. Per let the hatch slam closed with a clang, suddenly cutting off the tumult of the wind and the dock. A deep throb remained, rumbling through the hull of the ship like a heartbeat.

Through the aft windows the harbor seemed as distant and still as a Turner canvas in a gallery. Beyond the barge with the Viking ship, the bay arced past a row of rust-stained fishing boats. The town itself stood faceless in the feeble dawn, a rim of shapes about the shoulder of Castle Hill, lost in low clouds. Kirstin turned to look toward the fjord, but the fogged front windows left that view ethereal. She wiped the glass with her sleeve and still could discern nothing but grays and whites.

"Coal up, Svend," Per shouted into a metal tube. "We'll need plenty of steam for the run to Kristiania in this gale."

"We're not going to Kristiania yet," Kirstin said. "The waves are too high."

"Sure, we'll take on some water, but we'll get through, I reckon."

She chose her words carefully. "We're proud of you, Per, for donating your skill and your ship, but the cargo we're transporting is delicate. We will wait in a sheltered place for better conditions."

Per's jaw worked as though he were chewing this new concept—a polite command from a woman on his own bridge. The idea must have left a sour taste his mouth, for he noisily cleared his throat and looked out the aft window. "I reckon it figures."

"Pardon?" She crossed her arms, expecting the worst.

The tug captain scratched his jaw. He eyed her from head to toe — the high white forehead, the cool blue eyes, the khaki pants outfit. "I've known Magnus since before his Pappy died. A boy like him could have had his pick of women in a dozen ports. All those years, nothing. Not interested, he says. And then — *this*."

"She's all steamed up, Cap'n," a tinny voice at Kirstin's elbow cut in, leaving her momentarily wordless. The pipe gave a raspy hollow cough, as if the disembodied engine were trying to suck air through an unwound tuba. "Need me up on deck?"

Per looked out the window and bared his crooked teeth. Then he hissed a long, fiery curse — an ear-singeing concoction of body parts and unspeakable acts from Portuguese, Dutch, and several languages Kirstin did not recognize. "There's your goddam Swedes. What now, Admiral?"

Kirstin followed his gaze with alarm. Dödkvist's black carriage was indeed rolling through the town, led by a troop of mounted soldiers. But the crowd in the streets was slowing their progress. And the last crates were already on board.

"We've got our cargo," she said. "Let's sail."

The tug captain yanked a handle. An ear-splitting blast wailed amidst a white rush of steam. For an instant all heads on the dock turned their way. Then sailors began casting off the ropes.

"Full ahead, Svend," Per yelled into the pipe.

The ship shivered. White water boiled up beside the barge. Sailors jumped to the dock as the horsemen arrived. A forgotten rope sang taut and snapped across the pilings. Frightened horses reared and whinnied. One of the guards managed to dismount and raise his pistol skyward.

But the tug was already under way.

CHAPTER 21
FALL, 872

The darkness chanted Odin's dread names:

> *Grim, Gangleri,*
> *Herjan, Hjalberi,*
> *Thekk, Thrithi,*
> *Thuth, Uth,*
> *Helblindi, Har,*
> *Sath, Svipall,*
> *Sanngetall.*

Valhalla rolled and jolted. First came the haunting, cold stench of rotting flesh. Then there was a muffled stomping and snorting. Gytha's arms and legs were immobilized, unfeeling. Her body was wrapped as tightly as a stored cheese. She was afraid to open her eyes.

She was dead. She knew that. She had glimpsed the frost giants while freezing in the Horthangr Wastes. She had defied her father and run away in search of her foster parents, and now the angered gods were taking their horrible revenge. She was dead.

But what did Valhalla look like? And why did she still feel the wound on her shoulder as a dull ache? It was less painful than when she was alive, but in Valhalla wounds were supposed to vanish altogether.

Cautiously, fearfully, she lifted her eyelids. A strip of blinding white flapped before her. Or no—it was a wrapping of dark hides that flapped. Beyond, through the opening, was sun-brightened snow. And animals. Gleaming, round eyes watched her. Wet noses snuffed steam. Shaggy brown heads tossed in the air, raising great racks of antlers.

Reindeer?

Gytha had several hours to puzzle about the reindeer. Evidently she was not dead, but instead was being dragged through the snow on some kind of travois in the midst of a reindeer herd. It was also clear that several hours—perhaps entire days—had passed. The weather was different. Her shoulder was definitely better.

What had become of the frost giants? Or was this strange bondage one of Odin's ghastly jests? If so, she might be dead after all.

Twilight fell before she heard the giants' voices. Deep and gruff, they spoke in a rattling language she did not know. The reindeer stopped. Boots crunched through the snow. She wanted to run or call out, but could neither move nor speak.

An enormous, white-furred arm reached before her, loosening the leather straps that bound her in the roll of hides. She stiffened.

"*Mika teita vaivaa.*"

A huge, shapeless head loomed before her. Gytha caught her breath.

Suddenly the frost giant's head covering flopped backwards. Inside the big fur hood was the wrinkled face of a man. He ran a fur glove over his short black hair. His eyes squinted at her. The nostrils of his nose flared.

"Rokalanti?"

Gytha's voice cracked in response. "You—you're not giants."

"Rokalanti!" The man jumped backwards, gesticulating and shouting in a rapid, unintelligible clatter. Soon another fur-coated man was helping to peel back the hides from Gytha's head and arms.

"Are you Laplanders?" she asked. She had never met anyone from that northern race, yet many sagas told of Lappish magicians and their reindeer. When the men did not respond, she simply nodded toward them, asking, "Lapps?"

The first man wrinkled his face. "Lapps?" He looked to the other man and they laughed, exposing gaps in their crooked teeth. He shook his head, pointing to himself and his companion. "Samelats."

"Samelats?" Gytha repeated. What kind of people were they? Without their fur coats the men were actually quite small—no taller than herself. It must have been the fever that had made them appear as giants.

The man pointed to Gytha next and said, "Rokalanti."

"I am Rokalanti?"

The men laughed again. After they had finished untying Gytha, she tried to stand—and found her legs were as wobbly as a newborn colt's. The two men helped her to a nearby rock. Then they went about the business of setting up camp.

First the men unbundled the poles that had made up Gytha's travois. Next they stood the poles to make a conical framework. Finally they covered the impromptu structure with hides.

The men were building a fire inside this tent when a second herd of reindeer appeared on the crest of a rise. The lead animals lifted their heads, sniffed the air, and trotted down to join the first herd. Half a dozen drivers followed, dressed in thick white furs.

Gytha managed to stand up to meet the newcomers. To her astonishment they were even shorter than the first Samelats. Some were hardly waist high.

"Rokalanti! Rokalanti!" the littlest ones cried, pointing. One of the larger figures shushed the children with a sweeping arm motion. Then she flipped back her hood, revealing a weathered face and shoulder-length brown hair. "Better today?"

"You speak Norse!" Gytha exclaimed.

"Some."

The words rushed out. "You saved me from freezing. Who are you? I thought I was dead. I'm grateful for what you've done, but I don't know where you're taking me or—"

The woman repeated the arm motion she had used to silence her own children. "Herbs. Then food. Then talk." Abruptly she turned to help set up camp. Gytha was left standing by the rock, her fleet of questions drifting slack-sailed.

The men unpacked a second tent. Children fetched water and branches from the edge of a pond. Two of the women lured a reindeer close with handfuls of lichens. Then one woman held the reindeer's head while the other squatted by its restless rear hooves, reached for the reindeer's teats, and squeezed milk into a bowl.

The woman who could speak Norse was cutting meat and arranging soapstone bowls on rocks beside the fire. Gytha walked unsteadily to the tent, drawn by the warmth and the aromas there. Never had she felt so dependent—so helpless. She could not command anyone. She owed these strangers her life, and they owed her nothing. They had food and shelter. They knew where they were traveling. Even if she had the strength to run away, she could not leave. She could only beg.

Gytha lowered her head. "I'm hungry. May I please have something to eat?" Smoke from the sooty tent made her eyes damp.

The woman kept on working. The tent was so warm that the woman had stripped to the waist. Her breasts swung back and forth as she sawed at a bone in the meat. "Herbs," she said. "Then food."

The first Samelat man was squatting on the far side of the fire. He held a large, oval container that looked like an upside-down drum. He motioned for Gytha to sit on a hide beside him. When she crawled across the tent he placed a small bone, a black feather, a white rock, and a shell inside the drum. Then he began tapping the taut skin on the bottom. The drum was painted inside with intricate blue-and-red zigzag patterns. The objects in the drum had been positioned at the intersections of patterns. Gytha wondered what the device was for.

As the man tapped, the rock, shell, and bone danced out of place, slowly circling the black feather.

"*Outo. Parempi.*" His eyes wrinkled. Gytha wasn't sure if this meant he was pleased or worried by the result of his effort. He picked up the shell, dipped it full of boiling water from a pot by the fire, and added green flakes from a leather pouch. Then he held the shell to Gytha's lips.

She looked to the Samelat woman for help. "What is he trying to give me?"

The woman ignored her. Gytha sighed, took the shell, and drank. The brew left a repulsive, moldy taste in her mouth.

As soon as Gytha set the shell down, the man grabbed the skirt of her tunic with both hands and pulled it over her waist.

"Don't you dare!" Gytha cried out, fighting him with her weakened arms. The man pulled back, frowning. Gytha crawled to the woman by the fire, her voice quavering. "Who are you people? What in the name of Odin do you want?"

The woman glanced up from her work. "You need herbs." She touched Gytha's shoulder and made a motion indicating the tunic must come off.

Gytha retreated from them both, sulking at this additional humiliation. She was at their mercy. And the truth was, their medicine must have helped her shoulder heal. Reluctantly she loosened her belt and lifted the tunic over her head.

Naked except for her leggings, she sat straight, trying to muster her pride. But there was no hiding the fact that she was a girl, despite her shepherd clothes and mannish haircut. Her white skin betrayed a childhood sheltered from work and weather. Her waist and arms, already delicate, had thinned alarmingly from her journey.

She turned her eyes away while the Samelat man washed the scab on her shoulder. Then she quickly pulled her tunic back on, straightening its ragged skirt with exaggerated care.

Soon the Samelat woman called the children in from their chores for the evening meal. Each child received a piece of roasted meat and a small cake of pressed seeds. Gytha was so hungry she could hardly wait her turn. When she was finally served, she bit into the meat like a starving animal. Never had food tasted so wonderful. She gnawed the bone clean and begged for another.

"Good?" the woman asked.

"Delicious!" Gytha replied.

The woman nodded. "Your horse."

Gytha's hand stopped in mid-air. "My horse?" Her stomach tightened at the thought of the shaggy pony that had carried her so far. A fearsome memory flickered back from her delirium in the snow — the image of a spear in the pony's neck.

Her stomach knotted. She returned the second piece of meat. It was time to find out who her rescuers really were. "You promised we would talk after I had eaten. Now I have eaten."

"Good." The squatting Samelat woman leaned forward. "*Who are you?*"

The question left Gytha momentarily wordless. It was precisely what she herself was about to ask the Samelats.

"You dress like man. You are woman. Who are you?"

Gytha was unsure how much to tell these people. It didn't seem fair to lie to them after they had rescued her. On the other hand, if she admitted her father was a king they might ask for a reward — which she couldn't pay. "My name is Gytha. My father wanted me to marry a man I hate, so I cut my hair and ran away."

"Here?"

"I got lost on the way. I was traveling to stay with my foster father in Rogaland."

The black-haired man perked up at this last word. "Rokalanti!"

Gytha glanced to the Samelat woman questioningly. "Do you know

Rogaland?"

The woman nodded. "We winter in forests near Rogaland. But we do not go near giants."

"Frost giants? I don't want to go near them either."

"No frost giants," the woman laughed. "Frost giants are children's story. I mean giants like you. You are giant."

Gytha raised an eyebrow. These people considered her a giant. In their eyes, she was a monster. Perhaps it was only fair. She had once thought they were monsters too. "Then why did you stop to save me?"

"We killed your horse. Every loose horse, sheep belong our people. When we saw you, we understood horse was not loose. We were sorry. We gave you reindeer milk. You say Rogaland."

"I spoke while I had a fever?"

"Rogaland—Rogaland." The Samelat woman imitated the fretful moan they had heard. "We want take place your horse, take you home."

Now Gytha could fit the pieces together. These rugged herdsmen killed whatever unguarded Norse cattle strayed onto the sparse mountain pastures that they claimed for their reindeer. No doubt the Norse shepherds considered the Samelats thieves. But the Samelats' moral code was obviously strict. When they killed a horse and then discovered the owner nearby, they did their best to replace the animal.

"How many days have you been traveling with me?"

The woman held up the fingers of both hands.

Gytha looked at the number in astonishment. Could she have been dragged, delirious, behind a reindeer for so long? "And how many days away is Rogaland?"

A single thumb went up. "But we do not go near giants. It is good you can walk now."

So she would have to walk down from the mountains alone. And then how would she find Ragnar? Gytha took a long, thoughtful breath. Rogaland was nearly half the size of Horthaland. The kingdom was split by scores of fjords, each with dozens of isolated farms. She couldn't even remember the name of the fjord her foster mother's old farm was on.

While she was lost in thought, the Samelat man and woman had been speaking to each other in their rapid, rattling language. At length the woman put a wrinkled hand on Gytha's arm and said, "My man is good magician. He says you not worry. Giant-woman has powerful luck."

Gytha smiled to them both. "I suppose I must have powerful luck, if people such as you have found me." Then she remembered the question she had wanted to ask from the first. "Aren't you Lapps?"

"Lapps?" The woman rocked back, suddenly shaking with laughter. Even the little children giggled and hid their faces.

"Did I say something wrong?"

"No, no. Lapps are what we call Samelats who are taken as slaves by giants. Everywhere, giants capture Samelats and make them Lapps. But you—you are giant captured by Samelats."

Gytha laughed with them a little. It felt good to be able to laugh again. But the more she thought of their bittersweet joke, the harder it was to smile. All her life she had assumed that slave races were morally inferior to Norse royalty. Now, sheltered by a people the Norsemen hunted as slaves, she realized how unfair the assumption was.

She had been captured by the dreaded frost giants, and had found them a worthier folk than the Vikings she had fled.

* * *

In the morning Gytha was disappointed that more of her strength had not returned. Shaky from the long days of illness, she could only walk with a staff.

The Samelats talked among themselves for a long time. Finally the woman announced to Gytha, "My man take you Rogaland."

"How? I can hardly walk, and there won't be enough snow for a sled down in the forest."

The woman nodded toward the reindeer herd.

Puzzled, Gytha followed the woman's gaze. Creeping among the animals was the black-haired Samelat man. Suddenly he lunged at the neck of one of the largest reindeer. It stomped and pawed in outrage, but he hung on tightly, looping a rope over its muzzle. A second man took the rope. Together they half-dragged, half-led the reindeer toward Gytha.

"Surely you don't expect me to ride a reindeer!"

The woman looked at her with genuine surprise. "Did you not ride horse?" She took the rope, taking care to stand clear of the reindeer's tossing antlers.

"A horse is different," Gytha protested. "This is a wild animal."

The Samelat man had already gone back to the herd. He wrestled a second reindeer, swung onto its back, and stampeded past the tents, shouting, "Rokalanti!"

He yanked the bridle to one side. His reindeer circled back at a trot and stopped before them, panting steam from flared nostrils.

The woman shook her head at Gytha. "Reindeer not wild."

Gytha bit her lip. The Samelats obviously thought nothing of riding the animals they herded. But it was just as clear they knew nothing of saddles, stirrups, or bits—refinements she had always taken for granted when riding horses.

"You go Rogaland?" the Samelat woman asked, holding out the rope.

How else was she to reach civilization?

"I hope so." Gytha stroked the warm, coarse fur of the reindeer's shoulder. The animal tensed. But she kept stroking, and its muscles seemed to relax under her soothing hand.

The Samelat woman's voice was low. "You are good, giant-woman."

Gytha smiled to her. "You have been good to me, too. I wish I could pay you back for all you've done."

"You bring strong luck. That is powerful gift." She held the reindeer's head by its fur and handed Gytha the ends of the rope.

Gytha took a deep breath, gathering her strength. Then she pulled herself onto the reindeer's back.

Before she could sit upright the animal bolted loose, jolting her across the snowfields at a gallop—faster than her Norse pony had ever raced. Her fingers gripped desperately at the shaggy mane, dangerously close to the swinging antlers. The lakeside bushes flashed by in a blur. She struggled to pull herself higher. The fur smelled of sweat and musk. When she finally straddled the reindeer's back, the skirt of her tunic had blown to her waist.

"Rokalanti!" the black-haired Samelat man laughed, pointing ahead as he jolted past.

Gytha gripped the reindeer's ribs tighter with her knees. The animal sped across the snow, following the first reindeer into a long valley. Even when they reached the forest her reindeer hardly slowed, dodging branches and jumping logs in stride. Each sudden shift in direction left Gytha grasping for balance. No matter how hard Gytha yanked on the bridle rope, her reindeer insisted on keeping up with the frantic pace of the rider ahead. They splashed across a creek, climbed the far bank, and flew on.

When they finally slowed to a walk Gytha pleaded, "Can't we rest? I've never—"

But the black-haired man cut her short with an emphatic wave of his arm. He frowned, listening ahead into the forest. Then he tapped his fur boots against the reindeer's flanks and continued at a cautious walk. The reindeer snuffed the warm, heavy air suspiciously. Even Gytha could smell the tang of sea salt.

Finally the Samelat man stopped. Nervously, he motioned Gytha closer. Through the trees ahead she could see gray dapples of water and a faint haze of smoke.

"Rokalanti," he whispered, his eyes narrowed. He leaned over and took her bridle. Then he motioned for her to dismount.

She slid down from the reindeer with relief.

Instantly the Samelat jerked the bridles and cried, "*Nopeasti!*"

Hooves pounded as the man and the reindeer vanished into the woods.

For a moment Gytha stood bewildered by their sudden flight. Which of Rogaland's fjords might this be, that the Samelat man was so frightened? She peered down through the trees at the flashes of water. In a settlement there would be fruit and cheese and flatbread—and all the other things she had done without for weeks. Here the people would owe allegiance neither to Eirik nor to Harald. Perhaps someone would even know where her foster parents were. She could admit to them that she was a princess again.

Then she remembered her clothes and her short hair. No princess would look like this. Until she could find her foster parents, she would have to remain a shepherd boy.

She sighed. Then slowly, unsteadily, she walked down through the trees.

To her surprise, the steep, forested slope dropped directly into the fjord. There were no estate halls, no farm fields, no clearings, no signs of civilization at all. Waves curled against jagged rocks on a shore banded with dark green seaweed. Ahead, the choppy gray waters narrowed between immense highlands—cliff-edged mountains shrugging long waterfalls from their shoulders. The fjord bent out of sight below a snow-capped horizon, obviously still far from the open sea. The fjord seemed lost to the world—hardly the kind of "strong luck" suggested by the Samelat woman.

Then where had the smoke come from? Gytha scanned the desolate shore. Nearly a mile away, a thin gray streak drifted along the water's edge. But she could see no clearing even there. She broke a small branch to serve as a walking staff and began to make her way over the wet rocks lining the shore.

It was late in the day before Gytha neared the crude shed that was the source of the smoke.

"Hello?" she called.

At once the crooked door banged open. A black animal bounded out. It wriggled on the stone step, sniffing the air with the whiskered snout of its seal-like head. Then it shot toward Gytha, somersaulted, and walked the last three steps on its hind legs. A long pink tongue drooled excitedly. A joyous tail wagged.

"If you're a dog, you're the strangest one I've ever met." Gytha held out her hand for it to sniff. The smooth, furry head wiggled closer. Then she realized what looked so odd about this black dog. "Why, you don't have any ears. What's happened to you? Where are your people?"

The earless dog bounded away from Gytha, fetched a bone from the bushes and dropped it at her feet.

She laughed. "Is that all you left of them? Such a fierce watchdog!" She petted its shiny black coat. "Clever too. Particularly if you've learned to build fires by yourself. Come on, let's take a look inside."

She peered through the low doorway. A rough hole in the hut's thatched roof let in light. Smoke curled from a smoldering log on the hearth. The room had only one short wall bench, strewn with dried grass. The dog jumped to a corner of the bench and thumped its tail against the wall staves.

"All right, we'll wait here until your people come home." Gytha joined the dog on the bench to wait. She noticed a block of wood hanging from a ceiling beam by a thick wooden chain—a chain that had evidently been whittled from a single pole. But this afforded little entertainment. The dim, smoky room left her drowsy. Soon she lay down on the bench and fell asleep.

* * *

"Oh, fickle are the nights in fall,
With fair and foul
Ere five suns flee,
And more within a fortnight."

Gytha awoke to a melodious, mumbling verse. Daylight had faded to evening, and a bald man was squatting on the floor of the dark hut, with his back to the bench, rebuilding the fire. The earless dog nudged his arm urgently, but the man only roughed the hair on the dog's head.

"Andar! Three herrings caught me today. Ouch! Like that. They only let me go when I invited them into the boat to read. And the troll missed again! Now, with just one link left—"

The dog nudged him again, harder.

"Oof! A fist I fear
'Neath every furry coat."

The dog whined.

"What is it, Andar? Enunciate! I can teach you to listen without ears—better than men who have them, trust me—but if all you do is mutter, you'll never learn to waft 'midst the wondrous word-winds.

"When lame lizards rain
And lewd lambs snow,
I'll tie my tongue
To a mast-top."

Gytha stifled a giggle at this preposterous verse.

Instantly the bald man flattened himself against the far wall. His eyes bulged. Now that Gytha could see his wrinkled face, rimmed with a thin white beard, she realized how very old he must be.

"I didn't mean to startle you. My name's Ulf. I'm a shepherd." She gave him a disarming smile to patch up any offense. She needed his help. The easiest route out of this remote fjord was clearly by boat. And judging from what the man had said, he was a fisherman.

The man trembled. "Rogue doesn't see you! Rogue didn't let you in! How did you find this place?"

Gytha was taken aback by the intensity of his raving. Suddenly he seemed like a different, far more dangerous person.

"I just followed the smoke. A storm in the highlands made me lose my way. When I got here your dog practically invited me in." She hoped he wouldn't ask about her home. She still couldn't remember the name of Hildirid's fjord.

The man shook his head. "No! Rogue hears a lie. You have no pack. You have no sword. You have no horse. You're not a shepherd. No boy could cross the Rogaland highlands alone. No one ever comes to Lysefjord. Tell the truth! *What are you?*"

Gytha felt a flash of panic. Her deception had been sliced to pieces by this hermit's frenzied, verbal knife-thrusts. She quickly gathered her wits and tried to parry from a different angle. "All right, you may have the truth. I am Princess Eiriksdottir of Horthaland."

The bald man's face stretched one way and then other, as if he had to chew Gytha's statement. A guffaw bubbled from his lips. He looked at the dog. Another chuckle rose and burst. Then he laughed out loud. "Andar! The ghost thinks we are fools!"

Gytha folded her arms. "Stop it. I am not a ghost."

He squinted one eye, making the other eye bulge even more. "Clever ghost. Rogue *is* a fool. But even a fool knows King Eirik has only sons."

"That's not true. I am his daughter. Besides, my brothers died in Scotland three summers ago."

"Ah? Don't try to trick Rogue. He guesses what you are, just as Gizur once guessed Rogue's secret. Gizur always envied Rogue because the king trusted a fool more than a wizard."

"What are you talking about? Who is Gizur?" By now she felt certain the man was mad, but she couldn't help trying to make sense of his ramblings.

"Who is Gizur?" The man laughed again, tensely. "Tell the ghost about your swim, Andar, when you found Rogue in Boknafjord. Who would need a dog's ears but not a dog? Only a wizard who knows the spell for hearing thoughts. Only Gizur, who wanted revenge."

"I don't know anything about your secrets or spells. Do I look like a wizard's revenge?" Exasperated, Gytha held out her thin, white arms. Then she cocked her shoulder and pouted her lips. This flirtatious pose had always worked for her in the past, melting men to her wishes. "Do I act like a ghost?"

The old man paled. "Yes! You tempt Rogue exactly as before! Gizur waited all these links for this night, didn't he, ghost? Gizur waited until he could raise the boy's corpse and send it after Rogue. What shape did he change you into to get here? A fly? A bat? An eel?"

"Perhaps I flew here as an eagle," Gytha chided. "If you believe I'm a sending, you should be more careful not to cause offense."

"Yes!" The old man dropped to a cautious crouch, as if he expected Gytha to attack. He took a fish from his wooden bucket and laid it in on the end of the bench. "Eat a share of Rogue's herring. Sleep on the bench by the fire. Rogue will sleep in the boat where he is safer."

He backed out of the hut, accompanied by the earless dog,. He shut the door firmly.

Gytha started to go after him, but then hesitated, afraid she might frighten him away altogether. If he abandoned her in this remote fjord, another boat might not happen by until spring. She watched through a crack in the wall as the two shapes moved down toward the oblong shadow of the boat at the edge of the starlit fjord. She could hear the old man talking to his dog. Strangely, his voice was suddenly as calm as it had been before he discovered her in the hut.

"You see, Andar, I was right about Eirik's luck, and he was right about mine.

> "Far too late
> To some feasts I come;
> To others, far too soon.
> The beer is drunk
> Or still unbrewed.
> Have I ever hit it right?"

The boat sent star-sparkled rings across the water as the old man and his dog settled in for the night.

Gytha returned to the fire, thinking about this odd, two-faced hermit. When he was with his dog he was witty, speaking in riddles and confusing verse. But with Gytha he became a haunted sufferer, speaking of himself only as "Rogue." What was the secret his enemy Gizur had learned? And what could he possibly know about Eirik's luck?

Gytha roasted the herring on a stick. Too hungry to wait, she ate the hot flesh before the jelly-like center had cooked white. Then she discovered the entrails—she had never had to clean a fish before—and dropped the remainder into the fire with disgust.

* * *

The earless dog was licking her face when she awoke. She pushed him aside, laughing. Then she remembered where she was. Daylight streamed through the hut's smoke hole. She rushed to the door. Far down the fjord a tiny sail tilted in the shadow of cliffs.

"I guess you didn't wake me soon enough, Andar," she sighed. "At least if you're still here, your master is likely to come back tonight."

As she was ducking back through the doorway she noticed a small wooden pot filled with huckleberries and dried fish. She shook her head to think of Rogue gathering these gifts. He obviously believed she was an angry sending in need of appeasement. She sat on the sunny doorstep and ate her sacrificial breakfast.

Andar lay his head on his paws, watching every bite.

"All right, all right." She broke off a piece for him. "Rogue thinks you talk. It almost seems like you do. Why don't you tell me about the wizard who cut off your ears? Do you suppose he really used them in a magic spell for hearing thoughts?"

She sighed. "I guess I never cared much about knowing other people's thoughts. You don't need to when you're a princess. That's everybody else's job. They're supposed to look at your expression, the way you frown, the way you move your hand, and guess what you want."

She stroked the dog's black fur. "Even without your ears you're better at hearing thoughts than I am, Andar. If only you could teach me, maybe I'd know what to do about Rogue."

When she scratched his nose, the dog licked her hand.

"You know I'm not a ghost," Gytha mused. "Maybe what I need to do is convince Rogue."

For the rest of the day Gytha set out to demonstrate she was not a ghost. She knew sendings delight in wrecking houses, so she swept and tidied the little hut until it was meticulously ordered. Because sendings often spoil or spill food, Gytha picked huckleberries and honey mushrooms until she had filled all the buckets she could find. And since sendings often steal firewood, Gytha set about chopping and stacking branches — although this proved difficult because she had very little experience handling an ax.

Toward evening, when the sail appeared at the far end of the darkening fjord, she washed herself with water heated over the fire. Then she sat on the bench and waited with the door ajar.

Soon Andar bounded down to the gravel shore, somersaulting and walking on his hind legs as joyously as he had when Gytha arrived the day before. The boat sailed past the little landing site while Rogue surveyed the hut. Then he lowered the sail, rowed ashore, and tied the boat to a rock.

"Found by a flounder, Andar!" the bald man exclaimed. Then he lowered his voice. "Should I have shown it past the troll?"

The dog ran around in a circle, his tongue flying to one side.

Rogue caught him and roughed his fur. "Ah, you're a handsome hound.

> "If a fair face oft
> Makes fools of the wise,
> Imagine the danger
> For genuine jokers."

He glanced up grimly at the hut. "Let's go see what damage the ghost has done."

Rogue walked toward the door but stopped short when he noticed the newly stacked woodpile. More cautious now, he leaned over to look through the doorway. For a moment he stared at the crackling fire, the buckets of food, and the carefully swept floor. Then he gripped his head and wailed as if his eyes had been burned. He sank to his knees and cowered, crying like a punished child.

Gytha had prepared herself for almost any reaction but this. What tormented this poor, lonely man? The schemes and arguments she had rehearsed that day suddenly dissolved. She knelt beside him and put her arm on his shaking shoulder.

The old man did not resist. Nor did he look up from his tears. Finally he sobbed, "Rogue thought he had paid enough for his crime. Twenty-four links! Rogue thought you would leave him in peace."

"Please, tell me why you are so afraid. You're mistaking me for someone else—I don't know who. Can't we help each other?"

He drew away, wiping his eyes. "Gizur sent you empty of memory?"

"You can believe that, if it helps. How can we know it isn't true? Maybe the gods have changed all our memories. What I remember is running away from Eirik in Horthaland. What do you remember? Will you tell me?"

Rogue's face darkened. He turned his back, crouched by the fire, and began whittling on the block at the end of the wooden chain.

"Rogue remembers running away from Eirik, too," he said stiffly, his eyes fixed on his work. "In those days Rogue was so young he had a different name. That name is forgotten now. He was Prince Eirik's favorite skald. The night Eirik became king the skald saw a grand saga poem in a dream. Never had there been such a poem, full of prophecy and power! It was to be the completion of Eirik's Saga. In the morning he recited it proudly. And in return, Eirik gave the skald a new name."

"A title? Eirik gave you a naming gift?"

"Eirik named the skald *Rogue*, the greatest fool in the thirty-one kingdoms of Norway!'" The old man's knife slashed across the block, peeling a curl of wood into the fire. "Then came the naming gift, just as appropriate. Banishment of Eirik's Saga from the lips of men, and banishment of the poet from the kingdom."

Gytha lowered her head, embarrassed to have dragged this story from him. For once she believed Rogue. She too had felt Eirik's sudden anger—both from the king and from within herself. Her impetuous spirit was a troublesome inheritance. It seemed she hurt everyone who came near her—her brother Ulf, her foster parents, and even Gilling, the one warrior among Eirik's men who had taken pity on her. Now here was Rogue, a refugee like herself. He had suffered Eirik's anger for most of a lifetime. She did not want to hurt him too.

"I'm sorry," she said quietly.

"Sorry. No one is as sorry as the goat who eats his master's ring. Rogue earned his name."

"Banishment is the hardest of punishments. Where did you go?"

The bald man cocked his head. "Rogue? To Rogueland, of course! If you're the greatest fool in Norway, you can be a jester in almost any king's court. At first, life was better for Rogue, too. Before, no one had known whether to laugh or cry when Rogue recited verse. At the King of Rogaland's court, they knew his verse was nonsense, so they all laughed. Rogue's foolishness was his strength."

He sighed, and then added, "Everything was simple until Rogue met *you*, Prince."

"Me? You think I'm the ghost of a Rogaland prince? But Sulki is the king of Rogaland, and he doesn't have any sons."

"No, but before Sulki became king he had a brother—an older brother. In those days the crown prince—fear your name, ghost!—was called *Valgard*."

Rogue spat the word as if he expected Gytha to shrivel.

Instead she merely shook her head. "I didn't know. Prince Valgard must have died a long time ago."

Wearily, Rogue held up his wooden chain. Carefully whittled beasts writhed around the wooden loops. "Twenty-four links, twenty-four winters. Rogue's dreams said he would be safe behind twenty-five. He tried to carve every demon's face—and fell one short."

"What was Valgard like?"

"Look at yourself, ghost! Valgard was everything his brother was not. While Sulki practiced with weapons, Valgard gathered mushrooms and berries. While Sulki was tough and dark, Valgard was soft and fair. While Sulki learned spells from the wizard Gizur, Valgard spent his time with the court fool."

"But if he spent so much time with you, surely you can see I'm different."

"Different? Not so different, ghost. Rogue knew the crown prince was a woman at heart. The prince tempted him night after night. And since Rogue was a fool, he finally gave in."

Gytha caught her breath. She had heard of men who loved other men. Vikings, on their long womanless journeys, saw no shame in using young men as if they were women. But the men who submitted were horribly ridiculed. And to think a crown prince — a future king — had done such a thing!

"This was not your fault, Rogue."

"No, it was Gizur's. The wizard favored Sulki. He wanted Sulki to have the high seat of Rogaland. The younger prince always listened to the wizard. So Gizur cast a spell on Valgard. That's what tore the crown prince apart. His heart pulled one way, his head another. He couldn't be the warrior his father wanted. Yule came. Rogue gave Valgard a colorful belt, just as the prince had wanted."

The old man lowered his head. "That night they found him in the hall rafters, hanging from Rogue's present."

"Oh, Rogue!"

"No one knew why. But Gizur! How he grinned at Rogue! Gizur guessed! Rogue had to hide! Rogue fled and started his chain! Too late, too late!"

The bald man huddled on the floor, his hands against his face, his knees pulled close.

Gytha's eyes filled with tears. She knelt and put her arm around him as he rocked back and forth. "Oh, Rogue — all these things have probably been forgiven and forgotten many winters ago. I'm sure time has healed everything. Haven't you ever gone back to find out?"

He whimpered, "Beyond the troll, Rogue is only safe in his boat, guarded by the runes. Only fish can get at Rogue in the fjords."

He chanted as he rocked, "Hugsfjord, Frafjord, Idsefjord, Gandsfjord, Hafrsfjord — "

But Gytha heard no more. Hafr — *oats*. Hildirid had said the weather was so mild at her old farm they could grow *hafr*. That was the name — Hafrsfjord!

Now she knew where to look for Ragnar and Hildirid. For an instant she wanted to run to the shore, in the dark, and push off in Rogue's boat at once. But if she stole his boat he couldn't catch fish. He and Andar would starve. Her mind raced, searching for a way to reach Hafrsfjord without hurting Rogue. Every path seemed to end at the boat. If only she could convince Rogue she was not a sending! Or maybe she could convince him to take her *because* she was a sending.

"Rogue, if you want to be safe from ghosts, take me to Hafrsfjord."

"Hafrsfjord?"

"My foster father lives there. If you take me I'll stay with him and not bother you again. I swear."

"Gizur!"

"My foster father's name is Ragnar, but—oh, what does it matter? Just say you'll take me there."

Rogue's eyes darted about, as if he were expecting her to change shape and attack. "Ghosts can't pass the runes on the boat."

Gytha groped for a counter argument. "Your chain! You've started carving the last link. Your house is safe—the whole fjord's safe. The only place left for me is in the boat."

He looked at her, his eyes red and wet. For a moment she thought his madness had passed, that he'd smile and apologize for thinking she was a ghost. But then a growl began deep in his throat. Suddenly he jumped toward her with his wooden chain.

Startled, Gytha fled outside. The door slammed behind her. When she reached the safety of the first trees of the forest, she collected her thoughts. For a long time she watched the hut's door. It stayed tightly shut. Finally she crept down to the shore.

The boat was a tubby *færingr*—a four-oarer, much like the smallest of the toy models she had once treasured in Valdres. She had never sailed a boat by herself. Still, she had imagined it so often that she was confident she knew how. Up at the hut, firelight flickered from the stave slits, orange bars in a cage of spirits. Rogue was dangerous. No one would blame her if she left him.

She put her hands on the edge of the boat, and shivered to feel the grooves of Odin's stick-figures—the runes. Everywhere the boat's woodwork was filled with the strange scratchings. There must be thousands of runes! Had Rogue really succeeded in cursing, or perhaps charming, his boat with the magic symbols? She would have to face that risk if she wanted to get to Hafrsfjord.

Gytha began to untie the mooring rope. But how could she abandon Rogue? Perhaps if she waited until morning, the hermit really would take her to Hafrsfjord. So she climbed into the boat and lay down to sleep. A chill wind snuffed the stars with unseen clouds. She pulled her cloak tight, but still was cold. No matter how she turned, the boat's ribs pressed against her own. The whittled runes roughened every strake and plank.

Rogue's tale haunted her. Skalds were among the most honored retainers of a king. According to Rogue, he had once been her father's favorite skald. The more she thought, the more curious she became. What was the prophetic poem that Rogue had recited the morning after Eirik's coronation? She'd never heard that her father had a saga written about him.

When dawn came she was lying in the beached boat, her eyes finally closed.

"In, ghost, in!"

Gytha jerked awake.

The bald hermit danced on the shore, waving an ax toward the open end of a hollow bone.

"What on earth are you doing?"

"Get in, ghost!"

"Rogue, I can't fit in a bone."

"Change into a fly! It's the only way Rogue will let you past his runes."

Gytha was tempted to get up and walk away from the boat just to prove his runes were powerless. But what if he took the opportunity to shove off without her?

"No, the only way I'll leave this boat is if you take me to Hafrsfjord."

"If Rogue does this, will you swear to leave him alone forever?"

"I swear by all the gods."

He weighed this oath for a moment. Then he dropped the bone and called over his shoulder. "Andar! Into the boat. Rogue has thought of another way to put this ghost to rest."

The earless dog jumped in, panting. Rogue stowed a large stone in the prow of the boat. Then he untied the rope and pushed off, ax in hand.

Gytha could hardly contain her excitement. Dark clouds in the north sent a brisk wind that caught the sail. Rogue steered with an oar in the stern. The prow plowed a bubbling wake through the waves. The thought of her foster parents brightened all the dark omens around her — the storm clouds, the runes, the ax, the looming mountain cliffs.

"What mountain is that?" She pointed to a square-topped cliff that towered a thousand feet above the fjord's narrows.

"The troll's high seat." Rogue hunched his shoulders and steered so close to shore the cliff rose nearly overhead. "Wise sailors say, 'Only a fool would sail past the troll.' That's why Rogue is alone in Lysefjord.

He is a fool." The boat glided under the precipice and into a larger fjord. Rogue turned to starboard and reset the sail.

"Have you ever seen the troll?"

Rogue shook his head.

"Then I don't think you're a fool, Rogue. I bet there is no troll up there. The others are just afraid." For a while she looked across the waves, thinking that soon she would be in civilization. She would never have another chance to ask about her father's saga.

"Rogue, what was the poem you told after Eirik's coronation?"

"The Eirik's Saga? Banished! No one may speak it."

"But you can tell about it, can't you? What's in it?"

He lips tightened into a strained smile. "You are."

"Me? *I'm* in the saga?"

"As long as you're in the boat." His hand swept along the runic carvings covering the inside of the vessel. "This is Eirik's Saga. Rogue was forbidden to speak the verses, so he saved them in wood."

"I don't understand."

He stroked Andar's back, reciting,

> "Cattle die,
> Kinsmen die,
> Kings and knaves
> Will die alike.
> But saga fame
> Will never fade
> For one who
> Wins it well.

"A skald sees many things. Before Rogue was Rogue, he met a Skiring holy man from Ireland who had a stack of white leaves. Each leaf bore rune-like markings, and each marking had a name. The slave swore the markings told a long, powerful Skiring saga. Rogue forgot the slave and his markings for many winters. But later, when Rogue was spying on Gizur to learn his spells, he discovered that the sixteen runes of Odin have names, too. Each one remembers a different sound. Then Rogue thought—runes can remember the forbidden saga! So Rogue carved the entire saga onto the boat. That way anyone who reads runes can understand the verse without speaking it. Do you see?"

Gytha frowned, unsure if this nonsense was simply more of the hermit's raving. "You've carved so many runes, you must think they protect you."

He sighed. "Fools are protected by foolishness. Poets are protected by verse. Rogue has both, and still is lost."

The fjord had widened into a broad bay with low, forested islands. Tilted hard by the wind, the boat lurched across the swells toward a gray stripe of open sea. From the north, black clouds were closing a slanted curtain of rain.

Gytha returned to her question. "What was in Eirik's Saga that made Eirik banish you?"

"Rogue's dream. Everyone knew that Eirik had offended Thor, but no one knew how. Rogue's dream explained it all."

"And how did Eirik offend Thor?"

Rogue sighed and told her story of Eirik's Saga—about the coronation feast where Eirik had unwittingly offended Thor by eating the marrow of his goats' bones, and how the gods had responded by giving Eirik both curses and gifts.

Gytha listened carefully as Rogue described the gods' decisions in the saga. Thor had condemned Eirik to die in despair. But Odin had weakened Thor's curse, declaring that Eirik would first rule for fifty prosperous winters as Horthaland's king. Odin had given Eirik the gift of the *Skaldskaparmal*, the mead that lets men compose poetry as fast as they speak. But Thor had decreed Eirik would never remember his poems. Then Odin had countered by granting him three famous sons. But Thor had sworn they would all die without offspring. Finally Odin had promised Eirik one great, life-long love. And Thor had cursed him that his great love would never share his bed.

When he had finished with his tale, Rogue scowled across the tossing sea. "As Kalf, the great skald of Agthir, once said,

> "Halfway wise
> Or a full fool be.
> Beware of being too wise.
> Tormented, the man
> Who foresees his fate.
> Better to be blind!"

Gytha considered the prophecies one by one. They suggested that

Eirik would remain Horthaland's king for many winters to come. Certainly the predictions of Eirik's poetic gift and of her three brothers' fates had come to pass. But what of the great, life-long love? Rogue had been cut off from the rest of the world for so long that he didn't know his saga was outdated.

"Rogue, you were banished for a fiction. Your dream wasn't true. Eirik has no life-long love. His queen, Astrid, died when I was born. He hasn't allowed a woman near him since."

Lightning boomed from the hills. Rogue steered hard to port, riding a wave through the narrow inlet of a fjord. Sheep raced in panic across the clearings on either hand. With a gust, the rain burst upon them, lashing the water into a froth. In the narrowest neck of the fjord entrance Rogue lifted the stone from the ship's prow and dropped it overboard. Then he steered onward, his clothes already dripping with rain.

Rogue spoke over the roar of the storm. "Astrid was never Eirik's great love."

A bright bolt crashed into a headland nearby, shattering rock across the waves.

Gytha gripped the edge of the boat, cringing at the storm's sudden wrath. "That's not true. Who else could he have loved?"

"Asa, the Little Chieftain."

"What! Harald's grandmother?"

"She is King Granraude's daughter, Princess of Agthir, Queen of the Vikings. Asa has always been Eirik's one great love."

Lightning lit the clouds, casting Rogue's face a ghastly white. His words were so confusing, yet so earnest. Could her mother have been Eirik's second choice? Could Eirik hate Asa's grandson, Harald, out of jealousy? It seemed to Gytha that Rogue was trying to turn everything inside out. "How could you know who my father loved?"

"Rogue knew too much," he said. "Eirik's Saga began before Eirik was king, when Asa was to be his bride. When the wedding grew near, all Horthaland readied to greet the new queen. A royal estate in the east, at Valdres, was to be the marriage present. Eirik also ordered another gift — a woman's dagger, forged by the best smith in Skiringssal and inlaid with the black eagle of Horthaland. But once the Vikings took Asa to Vestfold, all was lost. The saga twisted toward ruin."

The boat drifted in the middle of the storm-swept fjord with the sail luffing madly. Rogue raised the ax over his head. "The truth made Rogue a fool! Rogue was crowded with ghosts! Death to the saga! Death to the ghosts!" He swung the ax, splintering the boat's seat. He swung again, chopping hard into the floor strakes.

"Stop! You'll sink the boat!"

He chopped again. Saltwater began leaking between the boards. "The ghost swore it could be laid to rest in Hafrsfjord. Rogue plugged the fjord's mouth with a stone. Drown with a fool, ghost!"

Gytha scanned the rainy shore. She could swim that far if she had to. Even the dog might make it. But the old man would die.

In desperation she hurled herself against him, knocking him backwards. He managed to raise the ax with one hand, but she slapped him so hard across the face that he staggered against the mast. Before he could regain his footing Gytha pulled the hidden dagger from her tunic. She held the blade before him as if it were a charm against demons.

"Rogue! I am not a sending."

"The Horthaland dagger!" The old man gaped. "How—?

"Queen Astrid was old when I was born. She died at my birth. I inherited the dagger of Horthaland from her."

Rogue squinted into her bright brown eyes as if he could see through them to someone—something—else. "Then who are you?"

"I am Eirik's daughter."

Gradually the tension that had tautened his aged frame gave way. He slumped back. "Eirik's daughter?"

The earless dog splashed across a growing puddle in the boat and licked rain off the old man's face.

Gytha smiled, relieved that his madness seemed to have ebbed. "You see, even Andar trusts I'm not a ghost."

"Eirik of Horthaland's *daughter?*"

She tore a sleeve off her tunic and stuffed it into the damaged hull. Then she emptied fishing gear from a wooden bucket and began to bail. "Your boat can still sail, but it leaks pretty fast."

"It's not the boat," Rogue said, still dazed. "It's the saga. The saga is leaking."

"What do you mean?" She turned the boat with an oar. A rainy gust stretched the sail toward shore.

"Eirik's Saga says the sons of Horthaland will die childless."

"They did."

"But Thor intended the curse to end the Horthaland line. He didn't think of a daughter."

Far back in the hills, a bolt of lightning zigzagged from the passing clouds. Rogue drew back, as if he only now realized how dangerous the thunderstorm had been in the open fjord. "It's Thor!"

She nodded. "I know. The gods keep on battling, playing their horrible, huge game. Sometimes I feel like a pawn, about to be sacrificed for a whim."

"But you haven't been sacrificed. You've been overlooked while they were fighting elsewhere on the chessboard."

"Maybe it's worse to be overlooked." She touched the ragged hems of her humiliating shepherd's tunic.

"Not in this game, Eiriksdottir. An overlooked pawn can become a queen."

The boat nudged a sandy bottom. Gytha jumped out and began to pull the boat up through the waves.

"No, don't!" Rogue protested. "I never touch land outside Lysefjord."

"*I*? Did you say 'I'? Can you remember who you are?"

Rogue ran his hand over his thin white beard. "My name was — is — Horth."

"Horth?" The old name struck a chord in Gytha. Once a traveling skald had credited a particularly witty verse to the legendary Horth, and the audience's laughter had instantly stilled. She had never understood why. "Were you called Horth because you came from Horthaland?"

"No, it was the other way." The skald frowned out across the fjord, as if it hurt to pull the memories back. "My grandfather, Jarl Horth, helped build the kingdom long ago. Horthaland was named for him. When I was banished for the Eirik's Saga, Eirik decreed that no one would be allowed to bear the name of Horth again."

"You're not in Eirik's kingdom anymore, Horth. You can use whatever name you like. And you don't have to lock yourself away in Lysefjord. Come with me. We'll find Ragnar, my foster father."

"No, please, I can't."

"Why not? You're neither a rogue nor a fool. You're a clever skald — and a skald is always welcome. Besides, I have questions I want to ask.

You're the only one who remembers Eirik's Saga."

The old skald shook his head. He leaned an oar overboard and pushed off into the fjord. "I can repair my boat, but not my verse. I don't want to remember the past anymore. I'm an old man, Eiriksdottir, set in my ways. I only want to live alone with Andar. You promised to leave me in peace if I brought you to Hafrsfjord. Keep your promise."

She tightened her lips. "If that is what you want."

He quoted,

> "One's home is best
> Though a hut it be.
> My hound and my hearth
> Are fiefdom enough."

Andar hung his paws over the side of the boat and gave a single joyous bark.

Gytha held up her hand in farewell, saddened to see him go — this stranger who had told her so much, but who might have told her even more.

As she stood there in the waves, in the wind, she ran her fingers over the inlaid metal of the Horthaland dagger. How odd to think that the dagger had been forged for Asa, not Astrid! In that alternate world, even Valdres would have been Asa's wedding gift. And Harald? Did Harald sense how close they stood to each other in that other world?

With a sigh, she slid the dagger back inside her tunic and turned toward the farm fields lining the shore. Deliverance from the trials of her journey seemed close. At last she had reached a land where she could admit to royalty.

But when she approached a sturdy estate hall overlooking the fields, snarling dogs drove her back. Neither the dogs nor the sway-backed horses seemed right, so she trudged half a mile to a cluster of smaller stave buildings. A thick-browed slave stacking rocks in the rain gibbered angrily at her in a language she didn't know. The names "Hildirid" and "Ragnar" produced no effect, so she kept on walking.

At the third farm — a pathetic collection of thatched stone huts — a stocky farmer sized her up from the doorway.

"Nothing for beggars, boy."

She straightened, wiping the rain from her face. "I am not begging. I only need directions to Hildirid's farm."

He guffawed. "Hildirid's farm? Suits the likes of you, I'd say." He jerked his thumb over his shoulder. "Up the hill."

"Oh, thank you!" Her heart beat wildly as she hurried up the slope in the direction he had indicated. She was almost there!

But the route was much rockier and steeper than she had expected. The sheep trails she followed were muddy and slick from the rain. When the faint paths gave out altogether she stopped to catch her breath. Night was coming, and the farm was still nowhere in sight. She set off again, struggling up to where the hill disappeared into the clouds. As daylight dimmed, the rain gave way to a cold fog.

Finally she stopped at a grassy wall. Too tired to climb any farther, she sagged against the stones. It seemed a good place to rest. It reminded her of the stone walls high on the slopes above Valdres where she used to sit on sunny afternoons and play her wooden flute. The memory was so bright and warm that she whistled the trilling melody of the *fagurfugl* bird into the wind, as if to defy the storm and the night.

"There!" A voice cut through the fog. "Did you hear it?" Muffled footfalls thudded, and a man's gray shape grew.

"Ragnar!" Gytha jumped to her feet. The sound of her foster father's voice flooded her with a wild rush of joy and hope.

"Princess! Could it be?" The franklin came hurrying across the slope, holding out his arms to her in disbelief.

She sprang into his embrace and hugged him as tightly as she could. "Oh, father, I'm so glad to have found you!"

"It *is* you! My princess, I've missed you terribly." He held her head against his chest. "You won't believe this, Gytha. I just came out because I heard the *fagurfugl* sing."

"I heard it too, father. Isn't it wonderful?" Finally she could be herself again—a girl, a daughter, a princess.

"Oh, it is a lucky bird. But how is it possible that you are here? We told no one where we were going, and this place is halfway to the end of the world."

Gytha blinked away the tears in her eyes. "It's been harder than I ever imagined, father, but I had to keep going. I had to find you. You're all I have left of home."

"My princess, I'm glad you've found us too." He leaned back to look at her. "Why, you've gotten drenched in this storm. Come inside and dry off by the hearth."

"Is it far to the hall?"

"The hall? You were sitting on it."

She looked down at the grassy wall where she had rested. Now she realized it was the front edge of a sod roof. But the entire structure was hardly waist high. "This is for the pigs?"

"No, I'm afraid we don't have any pigs. Hardly any sheep yet. Come on, let's show you to Hildirid. Though I should warn you, your mother has changed."

"She isn't ill, is she?" Gytha asked.

"No, she's well enough. But the war has hit her hard. I can't promise she'll be happy to see you." He led Gytha by the hand as if he were afraid she might vanish in to the fog like the mysterious *fagurfugl*.

Gytha was still looking for the real hall when Ragnar descended a step and ducked into the windowless sod shed. The warm stench of sheep dung brought her stomach to her throat. Bleating animals stumbled out of the way as she crouched through the dark.

"Ouch!" Her head bumped against a beam.

"Careful, it's a little low at this end. Follow me."

This wasn't how Gytha remembered Hildirid describing the farm in Rogaland at all. Where was the huge central hall? Where were the rich oat fields?

Finally Ragnar pushed open a low door. Dimly lit smoke swirled out.

"Hildirid, here's someone who needs our help."

The square-jawed woman stood behind the flickering hearth, her arms akimbo. "This is not Valdres, Ragnar. This is my farm, and I'll decide when beggars can stay."

"No, look again. It's our princess."

Gytha lifted her head so the firelight caught her face.

Hildirid drew back in horror. Her voice dropped to a spiteful hiss. "You follow us like a curse, Eiriksdottir."

"I have nowhere else to go. I mean no harm."

"No harm?" Hildirid's eyes flashed. "Because of you, my son is dead. Everything we had was lost. How dare you cross my doorstep?"

"But dear," Ragnar put in, "can't you see the child is —"

"Silence!" Hildirid cut him short. She scowled at Gytha. "Look at you. Your hair's chopped off. Your clothes are rags. You're filthy. You're no more a princess than a slave. What do you want? To ruin us again?"

"No, mother, I—"

"Don't call me mother! The boy I mothered is dead."

Gytha hung her head. Hildirid had indeed changed, and Gytha now realized she herself was to blame. "I loved Ulf too, and never would have asked him to do what he did. I only want to stay a little while, until things are better in Horthaland and I can go back."

Hildirid threw back her head and laughed. "Until things are better! Where have you been? All of Norway is looking for the princess who started the Great War. Eirik has sent out a hundred ships and his entire army. Even King Sulki couldn't protect us if your father learned you were here. Eirik's promised to hang anyone who's so much as given you a piece of flatbread." Her face darkened with suspicion. "How did you get here from Horthaland? Were you followed?"

"No, I'm sure I wasn't. I took these clothes from one of Eirik's guards in the night and fled toward Valdres. Soldiers tried to follow me, but I lost them in the Wastes. I got lost, too, and came out in Thelamork. No one recognized me there because I'd cut my hair to look like a shepherd. When I found out you'd passed that way I guessed where you were going and set off again."

Ragnar wrinkled his brow. "You crossed the Wastes alone—twice? Is this possible?"

"The second time I had help from the Samelats."

"Samelats? Who are they?"

"Laplanders. They can hardly speak Norse. They didn't know about me or the war at all. They brought me across the snow."

"And then?"

Gytha hesitated. She didn't want to tell too much about Lysefjord and Horth. She had made a promise to the old skald to leave him in peace. He valued his isolation.

"A hermit fisherman took me to Hafrsfjord. He hadn't heard about the war either."

"But he'll find out, and then he'll remember about you," Hildirid said, fear in her eyes. "Did you tell him your name was Gytha?"

She had, but it was also true that she had given a different name first. She looked down. "I told him my name was Ulf."

"Ulf!" Hildirid balled her fists. She muttered fiercely, "You've even stolen my son's name!"

Ragnar put his arm around his wife. "Enough, Hildirid. Ulf is gone. Gytha's all we have left. Let's not lose her, too. Let her stay, if only until she is rested."

For a long time Hildirid smoldered, glaring across the hearth at Gytha. Finally she drew in a long breath through flared nostrils. "Gytha may stay in this house only if she is not Gytha."

"Not Gytha?" Ragnar asked. Then he thought he understood, and smiled. "Of course! She'll need a new name so people aren't suspicious. But what name?"

Hildirid shook her head. "More than a name. She must become someone else. There is a debt to pay, isn't there, girl?"

Gytha looked at the flame in her foster mother's eyes and knew which debt she meant.

"*Ulf,*" Hildirid pronounced, aiming her finger Gytha as though it were a spear. "You caused my son's death. Now take his place."

"But how can I?"

"If you stay, you will have to cut your hair even shorter. You will wear men's clothes. You will work in the fields and watch the sheep. The neighbors haven't seen Ulf since he was a baby. You will tell them you escaped from Harald at Valdres after all. You will learn the things he learned and do the things he did. You will be Ulf—and only Ulf— for as long as you remain in Rogaland."

Gytha's head reeled. Had she been such a fool as to imagine her problems would end when she reached Hafrsfjord? How selfish she had been, not to think of the trouble she would bring her foster parents! Even now, confronted with Hildirid's ultimatum, she recognized her first thought as a selfish one—she wanted to grow out her long, beautifully golden hair again. Even the thought of living in a miserable sod hut and wearing shepherd's rags might be bearable if she could comb out her long hair at night and know inside that she was still a princess.

"Well?" Hildirid demanded.

Ragnar gave an encouraging look, as if to say he had done his best.

Gytha lifted her head. "There was never a worthier person than Ulf. I am not fit to take his place, Hildirid. But I'll do as you say. You may call me Ulf, and I'll answer to it. At least then I will be able to call you my real parents. That is what I've always wished I could do."

Ragnar gave a sigh of relief. He was pleased to have Gytha back, even on these harsh terms. And he was glad Hildirid's heart was not so full of revenge that it had no room for sympathy.

"Gytha—"

"Ulf!" Hildirid reminded him.

"Ulf, then. If you're going to be our lost son, returned by a miracle, I say we need to celebrate. I've saved a few wheat cakes and a little mead. Can we spare a lamb, Hildirid? The one with the short leg won't make it through the winter anyway."

The woman glanced from her husband to the girl. "All right. For Ulf."

"That's better. Tonight we'll live high! Come on, Ulf, I'll show you where you can wash up while I see to providing for the feast."

He took Gytha by the arm and led her through a low doorway to a vestibule where there were buckets of water. But as soon as the door was closed he turned to her.

"I'm sorry, Princess," he whispered. "You deserve better than I am able to offer."

Gytha shook her head. "Hildirid is right. I owe you both a debt. You should call me Ulf, father, until it's paid."

He tightened his lips. "Very well, then. Tonight I will celebrate the return of a lost son. But I hope with all my heart that I live long enough to celebrate the return of my daughter."

Gytha hugged him. How she loved him! "You will, father. I swear you will!" And she believed that day would come soon.

* * *

But nine winters passed before Gytha again spoke her own name. Nine winters building sheep pens in the rain and pulling bloody lambs from bleating ewes. Nine winters feigning disinterest when neighbors brought news of the Great War creeping across the land.

Each year the domain of Harald the Unkempt grew. The boy-king conquered Uppland and marched north over the Dovra Mountains. In Throndheim he laid eight kingdoms low. His marshal Guthorm, in a single spectacular summer, was sent to quell an uprising in Thelamork and went on to carry the Golden Dragon banner across Vingulmork, Östfold, and Vermaland to the border of Sweden itself. But the most portentous rumors came from the far north. There, out of reach of the Viking raiders, it was said that Harald had begun building ships.

Each year Eirik's power also grew. He persuaded the kingdoms of the western fjordlands to unite in a Viking alliance spanning the North Sea. Hadd the Hard trained the largest and most brutal army Norway had ever known. Viking jarls from as far away as Ireland and Normandy stood ready to contribute ships and men for a great armada to crush the upstart Mop.

Each year Gytha spoke less. Her hands grew callused and her arms grew strong. Her plump, rosy cheeks tautened, revealing high, noble cheekbones. Day after day she tended sheep in the rocky fields high above Hafrsfjord. She played a haunting, minor tune on her wooden flute as she watched distant sails drift past the fjord entrance on a narrow tapestry of open sea.

After nine winters she had almost convinced herself that Eirik and Harald, caught up in their vast military rivalry, had forgotten her altogether.

And so she was unprepared for the day Eirik's men broke down the sod hut's door.

CHAPTER 22
WINTER, 1904

The door burst open with a clang, jolting Kirstin awake. For a frightening moment she did not recognize the man in the doorway, his raincoat flocked with wet snow.

"Asleep at the wheel?" Magnus asked as he closed the door of the tug's bridge behind him. "Glad we're at anchor."

She sat up from the bench with relief. "Sorry, I must have nodded off."

"I'm not surprised," Magnus said. He hung up his coat and lifted the lid of a coffeepot on the bridge's cast-iron stove, filling the narrow room with the steamy aroma of coffee. "I hear you were out late last night. Something about a date with an old farmer, collecting wagons."

She smiled, glad he was still able to jest about their narrow escape from Tønsberg. They had spent most of the day anchored in a choppy inlet, waiting for the weather to improve so they could sail to Kristiania with the Viking ship and the other excavation artifacts. The tugboat's captain, Per Larsen, had been working in the engine room. That had left her with Magnus on the bridge. The hours together with the ruggedly handsome Norwegian sailor had been an unexpected temptation. Even now, as Magnus stoked the cast-iron stove, she couldn't help noticing how the blue neckerchief he wore at his open shirt set off his full reddish beard and oaken features. She had to make an effort to look elsewhere.

"Do you think the snow is damaging the artifacts?" she asked.

"It's probably the best insulation we could get against the freeze." Magnus poured a cup of coffee. "I've always thought a good snowfall makes things more beautiful."

She took the cup he offered and looked out the window. The snow certainly looked peaceful. It decorated the railings of the tugboat, and lay like a feather comforter on the giant barge tethered behind. Although the Oseberg ship was only half as long as the barge, the snow made its curves stand out in such sharp relief that Kirstin could almost imagine there was no barge at all, and that the snowy Viking ship was sailing on a waveless white sea.

"The snow's so thick you can't even see land," Kirstin mused.

"We're just off the Jarlsberg dock." Magnus pointed into the storm.

Kirstin turned to face him. "You know, a lot of people think it was the Baron of Jarlsberg who donated the money for the excavation rights. If you don't take the credit for buying the ship, someone else will."

"Let him. Only a small man brags."

She sipped her coffee, amused by how easily this sailor could call even a baron small. But then she had been surprised more than once by Magnus over the past months. "You've never thought much of titles, have you?"

"Titles?"

"You know—barons, kings." She slipped him a half smile. "When you're upset with me, you call me Doctor."

"Do I?" For a rare moment he looked flustered. He lowered his eyes. "I'm sorry if I have. It's just I've known people who hid behind titles. Some of the worthiest titles seem to hide the least valuable men."

Kirstin wondered if he meant Dr. Söderfelt, or if he mistrusted university degrees in general. "I suppose you can judge what makes a person worthy?"

"Well, that's a tall order." Magnus set down his coffee. "I'd say the sagas are as fair a judge as any. Look how they weighed a man's worth a thousand years ago. All free men were equals, but fame only clung to a few. The heroes were the ones who best understood what honor means."

"But the Viking heroes were fatalistic," Kirstin objected. "They thought their actions were predetermined by the Fates. How can you do anything about your honor if Urda, Verdandi, and Skuld have already woven your destiny into a cloth?"

"Cloth isn't exactly stone, is it? It can be folded or sewn—or even embroidered with a pattern of eagles, if a person's clever enough."

Kirstin smiled at Magnus's careful wit. He had not only found a loophole in the standard, dreary view of Viking mythology, but he had dropped her a compliment as well. "You don't give the old gods much credit, then."

"Oh, I don't know. Perhaps the gods have been pulling the strings all along. One of these days a voice from the sky might break in and laugh at all our troubles. But it's an impromptu puppet show, don't you think? There must be times when even the mightiest gods are busy elsewhere and a person can take the stage for himself. Gaps in the script, moments of opportunity. Either we dare to take them, or they're gone forever. If we miss that chance, it's like waking up from a dream—and remembering nothing but the loss."

She looked up at him again and found him lost in thought, his eyes turned toward the whitened windows of the silent bridge. No one in the learned world she knew spoke with such matter-of-fact intimacy about these soul-searching dilemmas. It was almost as if Magnus dealt with the gods every day. Or was she able to appreciate his insights only because she had grown to know him so well?

"The dreams, Magnus. You don't forget them entirely either—I know. When you dream, who are you?"

He turned to her abruptly. "Does that matter to you? We don't live

in a world of dreams, Kirstin. Your happiness won't be found any-where but here and now."

"My happiness? You worry about that?"

"Yes I do. I've worried about it since that first night when I drove you in to Oseberg."

Kirstin lowered her eyes. She knew she should stop him, but she wanted to hear him speak these words.

"Maybe you think I'm below you, Kirstin. Well, I am. I'll never be a scientist like Söderfelt or Hoffman. But you'll never find a more honest man — a genuine man — who loves you more. I only ask to be judged for what I am."

He took her hand in his great, strong palm. "Don't you feel it? The gods are napping. Right now, for a moment, you can change the world with a word. By the time we reach Kristiania, the chance may be gone."

"Magnus, I — "

"Tell me now, Kirstin. What do you want? Should I stay with you after all this is over, or should I step out of the way?"

"Magnus, I enjoy your company very much."

"Enjoy? That ship's neither in port nor at sea."

"Can't we just keep things the way they are?" She knew it was clumsy, but she couldn't find any other words.

"The way things are is tearing me apart. You might as well ask a blackberry to stay green. Look at me, Kirstin. Do you want me? Yes or no?"

"What you're asking — I — " Desire and pride battled within her. He stood before her, as powerful and attractive as if he had stepped out of a saga verse. She did want him. Yes, and she had to admit to herself there was more than that. The warmest moments of the past months had been when they were together. Talking with him seemed natural-ly easy, and being near him always gave her a shiver of anticipation. Perhaps she did love him — but she had not fought her way to a doctor-ate through a world of men by letting her emotions gallop unchecked. Now that she was in charge of the expedition, she felt an even greater responsibility to keep her personal feelings separate from her work. Wasn't she strong enough by herself without a man to lean on? Wasn't that the lesson of the dreams? And why did he press her to declare her love now, when the Oseberg ship was still at risk? Couldn't an honest relationship benefit by a short delay?

"I don't want you to leave, Magnus, but I can't say yes—not yet."

The moment hung in the air as they faced each other.

Suddenly a hollow, disembodied voice beside them broke the stillness. "God damn it, isn't anyone on watch up there?"

They both turned to stare across the empty room, astonished by the interruption.

Then Magnus blew out a frustrated breath. He strode to the wheel and grabbed the speaking tube. "Sure, Per. I'm here."

The voice from the tube spoke again. "Well, look the hell out the window, will you? The deck hand tells me a fishing boat's closing like she plans to board. See anything coming?"

Magnus wiped the window and swore under his breath. "It's *Thor's Revenge.*"

"Thor's revenge?" Kirstin's head had begun to throb.

"Knut Lagstrom's boat. Looks like he aims to board, all right."

"Maybe it's really Dödkvist," Kirstin said. "He might have commandeered a boat."

"Not in Tønsberg, he couldn't. Besides, her nets are dripping, just back from the day's fishing." Magnus pulled on his yellow raincoat. "Guess I'd better see what he wants."

"I'll come too." She put on her coat and followed outside.

The sudden cold blasted away any remnant of the romantic atmosphere they had shared. Snow drifted from a leaden sky. Decks and railings stretched shadows beneath a strangely luminous white skin of snow. Wood creaked as the two-masted trawler shouldered the larger tug. The rank smell of fish billowed across the decks.

Per emerged from a lower hatch and walked to the railing. "Knut! What've you caught?"

"A bit of hard news."

"Oslo Fjord's still too rough?" Magnus asked.

"No, the swells have dropped with the wind, but you won't get through anyway, I'm thinking."

"What's to stop us?" Per asked.

"Caught sight of a Swedish gunboat steaming up from Göteborg. She'll be waiting for you at the mouth of the fjord."

Magnus frowned. "So. We gave them time to telegraph."

For a moment, as they thought over the limited options, the only sound was the sloshing of waves.

Magnus looked out across the darkening fjord. Finally he said, "You willing to sail this stretch at night, Per?"

"Hell, I could sail it blindfolded. But that patrol boat will have searchlights."

"Yes, I suppose she will. Still, if you give me a two-hour head start with Knut, I'll keep her out of your way."

"What are you going to do?" Kirstin asked.

"I'm going to get you through in one piece — you and your dragon."

She searched his eyes, wondering if danger lay in his plan; if fate had already come between them. "I wish you could stay."

"But I can't." He held up her chin. "Damn it, Kirstin. I wanted you to love me as much as I love you. I guess some things just weren't meant to be."

He kissed her on the lips — a desperate, all-too-short kiss — and turned to board *Thor's Revenge*.

Kirstin nearly called him back — nearly blurted that she loved him too.

But the moment was past.

She watched numbly as the trawler gunned its engines and canted toward the Tønsberg docks. Before the shape vanished into the snowstorm she heard its ship bell clanging in cadences of three.

"What does the bell mean?" she asked.

Per pressed tobacco into his pipe. "S — O — S."

CHAPTER 23
SPRING, 881

"Gods, what a racket." Hildirid pushed Gytha aside and crossed the room to answer the pounding at the door. "I'll deal with this, Ulf."

Gytha had lived on the farm since the early days of the Great War, hiding from the revenge of her father Eirik. Throughout those nine tormented years she had remained disguised as her foster parent's lost son, Ulf. But she had also become a woman of twenty-three. She knew she should have been considered an adult long ago — if not a woman, then at least a grown man. Hildirid still treated her as if she were a boy.

Fists pounded again on the sod hut's plank door.

Hildirid stopped, hands on her hips. She yelled at the door, "If it's old man Tore's slave, tell your master the black-faced sheep is still ours."

A voice bellowed back, "We're *Vikings!* Open up in the name of King Eirik."

"Eirik!" The name escaped Gytha's lips as a small gasp. A chill ran down her back, as if a window from her past had blown open. She had envisioned this moment so often, and it had always been just this way: the knock on the door, the dread name — just as if her fetch had come to drag her from the land of the living to the halls of Hel.

Gytha took a deep breath and straightened to meet her doom. No punishment could be worse than the one Eirik had set for her — marriage to the ghastly Viking murderer, Hadd the Hard. After nine years of hiding, she was ready to take off the mask of Ulf. Though her hair was short and her shepherd's clothes ragged, she would confront Eirik's men with the honor of Horthaland's heiress.

Hildirid sagged toward a post, her knees suddenly weak. She spoke toward the door, "Wh— what do you want?"

"We know who you've been hiding in there. Open up!"

Hildirid backed blindly across the room. Ragnar caught her by the arm and led her to the edge of her bed closet. "We've done nothing to be ashamed of. We will face them together."

Hildirid stared at her husband as though he were a pillar that had suddenly started speaking. At the door, the pounding gave way to the thud of axes. Metal clanged as an ax caught a hinge. Hildirid crawled into her bed closet.

The men outside began ramming the door with their shoulders. Planks splintered with the blows. Then the door cracked widthwise, and the remnants were ripped from the opening. As soon as the way was clear, six men in chain mail and leather armor strode into the hut, swords and axes at the ready. The leader, a thick-necked young man with a blond beard, surveyed the occupants and grinned grimly. He pointed his sword toward Gytha and announced, "There's the one we want."

"Don't kill us!" Hildirid cried. "We didn't know who it was!"

The blond-bearded leader scrutinized the cringing woman with some puzzlement. "What? You didn't know your own son?"

"My son?"

The Viking looked to Ragnar. "Is your wife mad, then?"

Ragnar stammered, "A-at times. But who are you? And what does King Eirik want with—with our Ulf?"

"I am Svein, charged with conscripting men to serve in the war against the Harald the Unkempt. Under the provisions of the alliance, Eirik has ordered every free realm to build and man warships. We bring a summons for Ulf." He lifted the ceremonial war arrow that hung from his belt. Gytha saw it was indeed the *heror*, the token of a royal summons.

The Viking looked Gytha in the eye. "You are called to serve the king."

Gytha fought back a moment of vertigo. To be sure, she had not been recognized as Eirik's daughter. But was it any less horrible to be drafted by her father to become a Viking?

Time was short and her options were few. She knew the consequences for refusing a royal summons in time of war. Her entire family would be banished, and their property confiscated. Hildirid and Ragnar would lose their farm and be driven from the kingdom.

She could hardly ask her foster parents to accept such disgrace. Besides, where could they go? All of Norway had been divided between Harald's and Eirik's forces.

If she revealed that she was not Ulf, but rather a woman, she'd be exempt from the summons — but then people would start asking other questions. Before long someone would guess she was actually Gytha. Then the punishment for Ragnar and Hildirid would be merciless. Eirik had threatened to hang anyone who aided the missing princess of Horthaland.

If she remained Ulf and agreed to join Eirik's navy, her foster parents would be safe, at least for a while. But how long could she maintain her disguise as a man? In the sheep pastures it had been easy enough to pretend she was Ulf. The pretense would quickly wear thin in a warship full of Vikings. And what if Harald's men killed her in battle, or if she were captured as a slave? It seemed the Fates were catching up with her after all.

She struggled to rein in her fears, knowing the danger of letting them wander now.

"I would gladly serve in your force, Svein, but you can see that my parents are old and our farm is poor. I cannot honorably leave them here alone. Eirik himself is old and must have sympathy for my parents' plight. My father and mother need the help of a young man."

The Viking captain's glance strayed toward Hildirid. He frowned, his determination softened by the obvious truth of Ulf's words. Nonetheless, he shook his head. "Then let them find a slave. We must have warriors for the fleet."

"But Ulf is no fighter," Ragnar objected. "He tends the sheep. We live alone here. We have never taught him to use a sword or a bow."

Svein chuckled. "A warrior among the lambs. If he doesn't practice with weapons, what does he do with his long, lonely hours?"

Ragnar lowered his head as if in shame. "He sews."

At this, all six of the Viking men broke into laughter.

But Gytha did not redden.

When Svein caught sight of her level gaze, his mirth ebbed. To be sure, the boy's face was smooth and his shoulders narrow, but he seemed to possess an inner strength that could prove to be an asset. Moreover, Svein knew his sailors could think of pleasant uses for such an attractive, smooth-skinned boy.

Svein cut the men's laughter short with a wave of his arm. "Enough. The king needs every man he can get. Ulf will come with us. If nothing else, he can stitch our sails."

* * *

Angry and afraid, Gytha trudged down the hillside with the Vikings. She carried a sack over her shoulder with the few things she had been able to bring—her flute, her dinner bowl, the blanket she had woven from the wool of her sheep, an extra pair of trousers in the Vikings' baggy fashion, and a tiny wooden box. The box could unfold to reveal a miniature chess set, a gift from Ragnar the year before. She wondered how long it might be before she could set up those pieces with Ragnar again.

She stared at the ground, trying to think of an escape. If she ran away, the Vikings would punish Ragnar and Hildirid in her stead. If she admitted she was Princess Gytha, she would have to face the wrath of her vengeful father and marry the Viking, Hadd the Hard.

Her fists clenched at the thought of becoming a Viking herself—a still more humiliating role than the shepherd she had acted for nine years. Yet her choices were as limited as a pawn's. It seemed she had always been merely a pawn, trudging square by square. For years she had waited, forgotten, while gods and kings marched about the board. Now she was blindly trudging again, though the endgame raged and the dangers mounted around her.

Svein's troop stopped at three other farms that morning, collecting hands to fill out the crew. Gytha studied each of the new recruits, hoping to find a kindred spirit, an unwilling draftee who might prove sympathetic to her cause.

The first farm they visited was a mere hut amidst hardscrabble fields, and the only inhabitant was a middle-aged bachelor named Gauk. When Svein presented the *heror* as a summons, Gauk's eyes gleamed. He tossed his pitchfork into the sod roof. "Count me in. I say to Hel with scratching oats out of these rocks." Within minutes he had strapped on a sword and had packed a wooden box with his things.

At the second farm they recruited Svip, a gangly lad of fifteen winters. The boy could hardly believe Vikings would accept him at all. "Me? On a by-the-gods-true Viking ship?" In response, Svein chuckled to Gytha, "Well now we've got two beardless boys to train. Don't worry, we'll make men of you soon enough." Gytha tightened her lips.

She felt little affinity with Svip, an awkward, ignorant youth trying to keep the muscles on his skinny arms flexed.

The only other unwilling person the Vikings enlisted was Hosvir, the owner of the third farm. His was a well-ordered, wealthy estate with covered stalls for twenty cows and a separate shed for slaves. Hosvir himself seemed strong and skilled, but was cursed with a re- markable ugliness. The features on his long face sagged unevenly, as though his flesh had melted and run.

"I'm needed here on the estate to oversee the work," Hosvir said. "Why don't you take my slave Edmund in my place? He's the stron- gest man in the district. And I'll throw in a mark of silver to sweeten the deal." While he was talking his young blond wife entered the room. She was as beautiful and casual as her husband was homely and busi- ness-like. Gytha at once understood Hosvir's reluctance to leave this woman on the estate alone.

But Svein offered him no real alternative. "Either you come with us, Hosvir, or we'll take all your slaves and silver."

By late afternoon the four new Vikings were following Svein's troop toward the pine woods on the unsettled end of Hafrsfjord.

Svip, the lanky boy, dogged Svein's steps. "How big is our ship?"

Svein glanced to the other veterans of his troop, and they laughed.

"Is it a full dragonship?" Svip persisted.

Svein spat to one side and walked on.

One of the older Vikings, a man with gaps in his teeth and a torn ear, fell back to scowl at the new recruits. "Until we sail you men are *grubs*, get it? Worms. You don't talk to Svein unless he's talking to you. Any questions?"

After a moment Svip ventured, "Would you be mad if I just asked the name of our ship?"

"We call her the *Naglfar*."

"The *Naglfar*?" Gytha said. "But that's a ship of evil." According to legend, the *Naglfar* would sail only at Ragnarök, when it would join the dread wolf Fenris. The *Naglfar* would carry the dark powers that would destroy the sun, and would slay all gods and men. It was said those evil forces were arduously building their ship from the finger- nails of dead men. Because of this, pious men buried their dead only with carefully trimmed nails, thus delaying the ship—and the inevi- table destruction of the world.

The older Viking frowned. "Our ship is named for power and fate. The seers say she'll sail alongside Hadd the Hard in the final battle against Harald. In that Ragnarök, they say, the unbreakable sword Fenris will win out and put an end to the Mop forever."

The recruits had crowded behind the older Viking to listen to this news. Svip gaped. "Then our crew will help defeat Harald the Unkempt?"

"Yes, and more than that. Because our crew has no royalty and no jarls, our shares will be equal when we divide the booty—silver, slaves, land, women, everything."

Gauk, the middle-aged bachelor, smiled. "I see we've joined the right crew."

"There's plenty of work too." The older Viking directed a sobering glance at the new recruits. "Grubs have to cook and serve dinner for the rest of us."

"What!" It was Hosvir, the wealthy farmer. "Aren't there slaves for women's tasks?"

"Slaves can't be trusted in war. You'll work and you'll like it."

"But you can't expect—"

"Shut your ugly face." The older Viking walked ahead, answering no further questions.

After another mile Svein stopped the troop beside a pebble beach at the edge of a large, stump-filled clearing. Ahead lay a hundred-foot-long arc of fresh wood that resembled the spine of a beached whale. Beyond the unplanked, unribbed skeleton, a campfire smoldered between two rows of tents. A crow cawed and flapped away. Waves lapped the shore with a gravelly voice. From far back in the forest came the rhythmic clang of an ax.

Svein held out his hand to the barren keel. "This is the *Naglfar*."

The recruits exchanged dubious glances. Hosvir spoke first. "What do you mean, assembling a crew for an unbuilt ship?"

"Finishing the ship is part of your training. Men fight harder defending a ship they've built themselves."

"Everyone does this work?"

"All seventy of us alike. By the time we finish the *Naglfar*, you'll know every man on this crew inside out, and trust each other like brothers."

Though Gytha saw the logic of his plan, intimacy was precisely what she feared most. "Svein, I know nothing of woodworking."

"The shipwright will train you. And if that doesn't work, I meant what I said about sewing sails. Everyone has his use." The young leader gave her a suspiciously lurid look.

Then he addressed the group again. "There's an empty tent for four at the end of the row. Choose a corner and keep to it. You'll also find a net of fish tied to the shore and a keg of milk by the firepit. The rest of the crew will get back here about dusk, and they'll be hungry. If you don't have dinner ready by then, wear your swords. I don't make trouble, but I don't stop it either."

With that, Svein led the veteran Vikings off into the forest toward the distant sound of ax blows.

When they were gone Hosvir grumbled, "He can't be serious. Cook fish for seventy men?"

"He's serious." Gauk shouldered his wooden box and headed for the tent. Here in the Viking camp, where similar wooden boxes stood stacked outside nearly every tent, it was obvious that the bachelor farmer had been to sea before. Gytha remembered now that oarsmen traditionally brought their own foot lockers to use as seats on benchless decks.

Gytha followed Gauk toward the tent. But Svip cut in front of her before she reached the tent opening. The boy barred her way. "How old are you anyway, kid?"

"A bit older than you."

His face fell a moment. Then he jutted his lip. "That don't matter. I'm stronger, and I can prove it."

She doubted it. She had wrestled sheep his weight, and always won. But she could see the boy was testing her rank among the crew members. Even in a troop where all men were equal, she knew only one person could be considered the least capable. Among Vikings, she wanted that reputation. A boy as clumsy and immature as Svip presented genuine competition.

Gytha feigned embarrassment. "You're right, Svip. You go ahead and choose your spot in the tent first."

"I will." The boy was about to turn, but he stopped to gloat. "You know, Svein doesn't like you."

"What makes you think that?"

"Did you see the look he gave you when he said you'd sew sails?"

She had, and it worried her. In her experience men only gave that kind of earnest, hungry gaze when they wanted something they didn't dare ask for aloud.

While Svip arranged his gear inside she noticed that all of the tents had totems carved into the tops of their crossed tent poles. The totem for their own tent was a goat. Not a bear or an eagle—a goat.

"All right, kid, your turn," Svip said.

As soon as Gytha looked inside, she knew she couldn't sleep here. The tent was so small that the three recruits were already packed in like pickled herring. If she were forced to squirm amongst them night after night, they would surely discover she was not a man. "With the weather so clear, maybe I'll sleep outside."

"Uh uh," Gauk objected. "You heard Svein. Choose a corner and stick to it."

The trouble was, Hosvir had laid his fancy goose-down bedroll across two corners. Gytha hit upon a little plan. "Tell you what. I'll sleep right in the middle. It'll work fine."

Gauk shrugged. "Suits me. Let's get started on dinner. Hosvir and I can clean the fish while—"

"I will *not* clean fish," Hosvir announced.

Gauk turned to the wealthy farmer. "All right then, Svip and I will clean the fish. You can help Ulf curdle the milk. With a face like yours, you won't need rennet."

Svip laughed at this until tears ran down his face.

Hosvir gave Gytha a stiff nod. As they left the tent together he muttered, "Gods, I wish they let you buy your way out of these cursed crews."

Gytha stopped beside the long, smoldering firepit. The barrel of milk stood open, a white mirror flecked with dead mosquitoes. "We'll have to heat it."

In reply Hosvir began tossing chunks of firewood into the firepit.

She unstacked a pile of iron kettles. "How long do you think they'll keep us?"

"Just through summer. Maybe into the fall. The longer it is, the more I'll worry. A farm like mine can't run itself."

"There's always your wife."

Hosvir gave Gytha a guarded glance as he helped to dip the kettles full. "She's very young. Doesn't know the farm well. We were just married this spring. She's from Sweden."

"Really?"

"A noble family."

Gytha assumed the marriage pact had been concluded before the girl actually saw her husband's disfigured face. Courting at a distance was common among the well-to-do, but hazardous.

While Gytha set up long-legged iron tripods astride the firepit, Hosvir lugged the kettles to hang beneath them.

"So now you know about me, Ulf. You even got to see my estate on the way here. But I haven't heard where you came from."

"Oh, I'm from Hildirid's farm. Up on the hill, an hour's walk from your place."

Hosvir looked at her again. "You're *that* Ulf? Somehow I wouldn't have guessed."

"Why?"

"It's just all that talk a few years back about the 'Hero of Valdres'."

Gytha shrugged, hoping to look casual. "Stories. I was only a child."

"I bet. It's been nine winters since the Great War began. And if I remember right, Hildirid left this district with you a while before that. Quite a while before that." The farmer paused, thinking.

The silence gave Gytha a shot of fear.

When Hosvir continued, his voice was low and deliberate. "You're not really who you pretend to be, are you?"

Gytha's heart beat in her throat. "What do you mean?"

"I mean, the unskilled bungler. I thought there was something about you. Your eyes were too quick, your step too sure. You're older than you let on. What did you do, pluck out your beard?"

She kept her eyes fixed on the steaming milk, afraid to answer either way. Anything she said might lead to still more dangerous questions.

Hosvir chuckled darkly. "Don't worry about me, Ulf. I know your game. I'd play it if I could. But after seeing my farm, no one's going to reject me from the crew for incompetence. Coming from Hildirid's place, you've got the ghost of a chance."

Even as he spoke, the first of the crew members began returning from the forest, jesting and cursing. Gytha was grateful for the diversion.

Gauk hurried up from the beach in dismay, his arms full of fish on sharpened sticks. "For gods' sakes, get that milk off the fire, can't you see it's clabbered? We've got to get these fish roasting, and fast. The crew's coming back."

Svip had run up from the beach, too, but dropped a fish on the way. When he stopped to pick it up, two more slid into the dirt. Gauk was too busy positioning the sticks over the coals to notice.

"At least *we're* done," Hosvir said, lifting the milk kettles aside.

"Not yet." Gytha searched through the tubs and sacks beside the firepit. She handed Hosvir a pot of honey. "Here. Put of a dollop of that in each of the kettles." Then she found a bag of rock-hard flatbread—not much different than the overdone hardtack Hildirid roasted. She cracked the bread into chunks and sprinkled it amid the curds.

Hosvir sampled a spoonful of the mixture. "Not bad. How did such a young boy learn to cook like this?"

Gytha slowed. She had nearly forgotten the danger of doing anything well. "From watching my mother, I suppose."

Bowls in hand, the weary crew members began milling toward the firepit. The first man inspected his portion of curds suspiciously. Then he surveyed the new recruits. "Well, look what I've found here. Four little milk-sops."

"Where's the meat?" another Viking asked.

"Almost done," Gauk replied.

The Viking grunted. "Why, I smell something fishy—and I think it's these grubs. You know what they say, a fast ship can't have slow oarsmen."

Svein made his way to the edge of the firepit. "Where's the fish, Gauk?"

"Here, they're ready. Try one."

Svein took the stick and bit into the side of the sizzling fish. Scalding juice dribbled into his beard. White flesh steamed. He looked back at the Vikings. "I've eaten worse."

As if they had been waiting for this signal, the rest of the crew now pushed forward, holding out their bowls. They ate without talking. Then they refilled their bowls and ate again.

Only when everyone else was done were the new recruits allowed to sit by the firepit and eat. By then night had dimmed the sky. Men gathered around the row of dancing flames in the long pit. Flickering shadows framed a shivering hall of light.

Nearly all the crew sat or squatted in the glow. A few occupied themselves by playing chess on stumps, but most just sat, recounting incidents from the day's work in the woods. Worries and fears suppressed by day found voice here, too, for the shadows lent a feeling of anonymity. Only rarely could Gytha tell which man had spoken.

"I hear the Mop is building ships, too," a voice said.

"In Throndheim. But not near as many as we'll have."

"They say he cheats in battle. Uses sorcery."

"How?"

"If he's losing, he'll turn himself into a whale."

"I've heard if you cut off his hand he simply puts it back on and it grows together with a magic word."

"And he wears horns attached to his helmet."

A silence followed this last suggestion. Svein frowned. "That's ridiculous. If a man put horns on his helmet, it'd catch every sword blow."

"Still, he does. Because he's a berserker."

Hosvir, who had finally finished his fish, now threw the stick in fire, generating a tower of sparks. "Harald doesn't wear horns and he's no berserker. You men talk a lot, but I'll bet I'm the only one here who's actually met the Mop."

It was a bet Gytha couldn't take.

Svein, however, confronted the new recruit with drawling sarcasm. "Hosvir, the only Mop you'll ever meet is the one that scrubs our deck."

Hosvir lifted his chin, perfectly aware that his ugliness made him an easy target for ridicule. "I was called to appear before Harald when I was in Tunsberg early this spring."

"Ha! Harald lives in Throndheim these days, not Tunsberg."

"True, but he traveled overland for a two-week visit at the end of winter. His grandmother lives in Tunsberg, and she was said to be in ill health."

Svein still looked doubtful. "And what were you doing in Harald's realms?"

"I was on my way to Sweden to pick up my bride. I'd paid for passage on a Shetland ship to Gautland. Since the Shetlands weren't allied with Eirik then, we beached at Tunsberg to trade. A prosperous little place it was, too. You wouldn't have known there was a war on, to look at the cloth and cheese we bartered for. We'd been trading half an hour when a messenger asked us to appear before the king. I didn't want any part of it, but the Shetland captain thought it would be wiser if we all went together. So we followed the messenger up the hill to a long hall. Turns out the Mop just wanted to find out how the Shetlands felt about the Viking alliance against him. I don't think he liked what he heard, but he let us go unharmed."

The crew considered this tale in silence, weighing the wealth of credible detail. Gytha was not only certain the story was true, but she wished she could find out more. She had met Harald long ago, when the king was no older than Svip. What kind of man had he become? Hosvir was the first person in years who might be able to tell her.

In the dark, the question might have been anyone's. "So what is he like, this unkempt king?"

"Well, he's no older than I am, and no taller," Hosvir replied. "It's true enough that he doesn't comb or cut his hair. Matted yellow stuff hangs halfway down his back. But he isn't filthy like I expected, either. Just the opposite. Even his fingernails were clean. He wore a brilliant red tunic, and his cloak was pinned at the shoulder with an impressive gold clasp — dragon-shaped, with a red-jeweled eye."

Gytha bit her lip at the news that he still wore the clasp. She often thought about how easily she had found that gold ornament at the Vik, and how convincingly Harald had denied it was his. What if he had been telling the truth? Perhaps she had impressed him because she had traded a treasure so casually for a single secret. Or was the mysterious Asa somehow involved? Gytha remembered colliding with Harald's blind grandmother just moments before the clasp appeared. It was a far-fetched connection, to be sure, but then Asa seemed to be at the bottom of so many mysteries — Eirik's anger, Horth's saga, even Harald's political strategy. What was such an old woman after, anyway? Ambition? Power? Revenge?

"You men had better get to bed," Svein said. "We'll be up at dawn."

"Will you be wanting us to fix your breakfast, too?" Now it was Hosvir's turn to edge his voice with sarcasm.

Svein shook his head. "Each man takes care of that himself."

The crew reluctantly left the warmth of the fire and groped their way across the stump-filled clearing to the ghostly gray tents.

"Where's the latrine?" Svip whispered.

"Can't you smell it?" Gauk replied.

"It's so dark you could fall in!"

"Look, I'll go along."

Gytha heard their arcs of urine pattering into the shallow pit. She quietly circled beyond to find a more private place, deeper in the gloom of the forest. She knew privacy was the key to keeping her disguise. With a bit of planning and stealth, her toilet needs could be kept secret. Securing a private sleeping place would be trickier.

When she returned from the forest the other new recruits were already rolled in their blankets, leaving only a small, nest-like space at the center of the tent. Fully clothed, she lay down in this hole and stretched with a tremendous yawn. In all directions her arms and legs shoved grunting bodies back toward the tent walls. Then she settled with her woolen blanket, waited a minute, and began to snore.

Every few minutes that night one or another of the men would roll back toward the middle of the tent. But she was ready with another stiff-armed yawn, snoring mightily all the while.

When Svein's piercing whistle announced that dawn had finally arrived, the four recruits emerged from the tent bleary-eyed. Gytha yawned one more time. "Gods, I'd rather sleep under a tree."

Gauk grunted. "Be my guest."

Hosvir added, "Please."

After a brief breakfast of hardtack and sour milk, the Viking crew marched through the forest to the pines that were to furnish the ship's planks. Gauk was promptly enlisted to help chop down trees and limb them into measured logs. Hosvir joined the respected cadre of splitters—woodworkers skilled enough to crack the logs into knot-free planks. Much of the splitters' time was spent discussing exactly where the iron-sheathed wedges should be driven to outguess curves in the wood's grain. Svip became a hewer, a backbreaking job that involved stooping over a plank and whittling it smooth with a very sharp ax.

The shipwright, a fat man with massive hands, frowned when Gytha was presented to him for assignment. At length he set her to work with a small two-handled drawknife, planing out long grooves on either side of each hewn plank. The outside groove, he explained, was merely for decoration. The inner groove, however, would keep the ship watertight. When this cavity was later filled with a mixture of tar and animal fur, it would be trapped in the overlap between planks, sealing the seam.

Gytha did not have to feign incompetence. Neither as a princess nor as a shepherd had she ever dealt with drawknives. When she pulled the U-shaped tool along a plank, the handles came off in her hands. She tried holding the handles in place, but then the tool pinched her palms, raising dull red blisters. She gritted her teeth and kept working. For a while she seemed to be whittling out a fairly straight groove. Then the blade caught under a splinter. She tried prying it loose. To her surprise, a deep three-foot-long gouge ripped diagonally across the board.

The portly shipwright, watching from a distance, slapped his hand to his forehead.

Svein put a consoling hand on the shipwright's shoulder. "Ulf says he can sew."

"For gods' sakes, then, take the ninny to the sailcloth."

A hewer nearby cried, "Look at the new boy! They're gonna send him to women's work."

The crew broke into laugher. Svip crowed with a high, cracking voice that Gytha found particularly grating.

"Come on," Svein said.

Gytha set down the drawknife and followed Svein on the path toward camp, pursued by jeers. She had wanted to be a failure, but victory left an angry burn in her stomach.

"Ignore them," Svein said. "They're still stuck back in the days when men rowed boats and only sissies sailed."

"Vikings have used the wind for years."

"Nonetheless, sails are the most neglected part of a ship. They always rip when you need them most."

At the camp, Svein rolled the mast out from under the *Naglfar*'s unfinished ribs. Then he laid a longer pole across the mast-top at right angles. "There. That's the size sail we'll need. Now the cloth." He opened a supply tent and showed her a stack of red fabric.

"Wool?" Gytha asked.

"It's all we can get from the farmers."

"But wool's weak when it's wet. No wonder your sails tear."

"That's why you have to sew in crisscrossing ropes. And remember to leave the rope ends hanging out the bottom so the crew can hold onto the sail."

"Why?"

"What do you mean, 'Why?'"

"Why does the crew have to hang onto the bottom of the sail?"

"So it doesn't flap away, of course."

"But wouldn't it be easier to attach the sail to another pole across the bottom?"

"Another pole?" Svein scratched his blond beard a moment, wondering why indeed the sail wasn't tied to a pole along the bottom. Then he shook his head. "Look, Ulf, don't ruin this with experiments. Just sew the sails."

"Fine." Gytha shrugged. "I'll do whatever you want."

Perhaps it was the nonchalance of her shrug that caught Svein's eye. It was, in fact, the same coquettish gesture she had used so successfully years before.

The Viking leader's gaze was steady. "Whatever I want?" He ran the back of his fingers down her short blond hair and smooth cheek. "What I want, Ulf, is *you*."

Gytha drew back, unsure how to handle his clumsy, dangerous advance. She had suspected Svein's motives from the first. Vikings banned women from their ships, but they sometimes took along compliant boys for sex. If only she could convince him she was untrainable for such a role!

"I warn you, Svein. I'll answer insults with a dagger."

He smiled. "Give it time, lad." Then he slowly walked past her into the forest.

When he was gone she sagged onto a bolt of cloth and let out a long breath. Even before their ship was afloat, life amongst the Vikings was proving to be full of hazards.

At the same time she recognized the irony of her plight. Svein was just the sort of muscular young Viking who would have attracted her as a fourteen-winter-old girl. She had teased a dozen similar swains at the Vik. But nine winters as a shepherd boy had weakened the allure of flirtation. Now she looked at Svein and saw at once the man's hapless crudity.

Gytha covered her eyes with a hand. Life had been simpler when she was a princess and the world had been full of charming men.

* * *

That night the Vikings avoided Gytha as if she were a slave. Only Hosvir, serving stew beside her, muttered, "You've quite a talent for being untalented."

After dinner a crowd gathered to watch sweating contestants wrestle in the dirt, naked but for their shoes and leggings. Gytha, who had been keeping an eye out for Svein, was a little surprised that the Viking leader didn't join the match. Instead he sat hunched over a chess board with the shipwright.

"Checkmate!" Svein laughed. "Five games in a row, by the gods. I say this deserves a celebration." He clapped his hands. "Fetch out the barrel of mead. We'll all drink to the *Naglfar*, now that her crew's assembled at last."

A rowdy chorus of encouragement followed this suggestion. The wrestlers abandoned their sport and thronged toward the barrel. As soon as every man had dipped a hornful Svein tapped the lid closed. He strode before the firepit and raised his silver-handled horn. "To the *Naglfar*!"

Gytha sipped the dizzying brew. Redolent with honey and wild berries, it tasted of autumn outings in the fjells, of winter feasts in smoky halls, of —

"To Eirik!" another voice cried.

Gytha turned the horn in her hand, hesitating. Then, solemnly honoring her vengeful father, she drank again.

"To Hadd the Hard!"

At this name the drink soured in her mouth. She stepped into the shadows and poured what remained into the grass. In fact, only a few of the Vikings had joined this final toast. Most had already drunk their horns dry. One man stood licking his horn's rim. Another stared into the fire and belched.

"Another horn, Svein?" a voice asked.

The leader shook his head. "We'll save what's left for launching the *Naglfar*."

Voices groaned in disappointment.

"Vikings only drink their fill after a victory. You know the verse:

Mead and battle,

The twin thirsts,
Share a single horn.

"If you want more drink," Svein added, "fight Harald for it."

"Or fight you, right?" a voice suggested.

The crew laughed at this anonymous jibe.

Svein gave a good-natured growl. "I heard that challenge! Who wants to try?"

When no one spoke, Svein spun his horn in his palm. "I've said we're all equals on this crew, and I mean it. King Eirik chose me to raise a crew, but not necessarily to captain the ship. That job demands not only strength, but wits." He looked around the ring of faces lit by the flickering fire. "I'll yield as leader to any one of you who can defeat me in both wrestling and chess in a single day. I'll give each of you a try."

For a moment the men were silent, admiring Svein's courage. The thick-necked young leader had clearly won a new level of respect. But each man secretly weighed his odds, too. The glory of captaining a Viking ship was no small prize.

One of the wrestlers rubbed his hands together, his muscular arms glistening. "This is the kind of entertainment we've been wanting. Strip off that tunic, Svein. I'll give you a go in the ring."

Svein growled in reply, unbuckling his sword belt. Men laughed and clapped him on the shoulders with encouragement. Others lit torches and gathered for the spectacle at the wrestling area.

Only a handful of men remained by the firepit—Hosvir and the shipwright among them. Gytha too had stayed behind, and her presence was tolerated by this more sober group. When they began to talk it was not of wrestling, but rather of the more serious battles that lay ahead.

A man with a long white scar across his face spoke solemnly. "I fought against Guthorm five winters ago. We chased his dragon banner out of Jathar, but the cost was great."

"Guthorm is the real danger, isn't he?" another man put in. "My father lost an arm to him in Agthir. The Mop is nothing without his uncle as field marshal."

The scar-faced man nodded. Then he looked to Hosvir. "You were in Tunsberg. Is it true what we hear, that Guthorm has married? At his age, that can change a man, make him give up the warrior's life."

"He'll keep on leading troops for a while at least. The marriage won't be until fall." Hosvir stood a little straighter, glad that the crew now accepted him as a valuable source of information. "And I didn't actually meet Guthorm, though I saw his bride-to-be. She's Queen Asa's Knightish handmaiden, a black-haired woman named Mari."

"A Skiring slave!" The man with the scar narrowed his eyes. "This is the filth that Harald's reign is bringing to Norway. He won't be happy until he's destroyed the sacred Viking traditions and polluted our pure Nordic blood with foreigners."

The heavyset shipwright shook his head, jostling his jowls. "You make this Harald sound so terrible. But you should hear what they're saying in Thelamork. The word there is, Harald's for law and order. If there's one king instead of thirty-one, we'll have less fighting and more trade."

Hosvir studied the shipwright. "You don't sound like a Viking at all."

"I'm not. Svein hired me to build a ship. What you do with it is your own business."

"Then stick to building ships, if that's all you understand." It was the man with the scar. "And look at Knightia if you want to see how an emperor works. Charlemagne's son is so corrupt, warring factions are everywhere. Taxes are high but there's still no defense. We can sail in and sack any city we want."

The scar-faced man turned back to Hosvir. "Now what about Guthorm? He's clever with an army on land, but we'll meet Harald at sea. Guthorm's never been known to sail. Is he collecting warships in Tunsberg like Harald is in Throndheim?"

"We only saw half a dozen ships in Tunsberg, all of them old. And of course the usual fishing boats along the Agthir coast."

The man with the scar smacked his fist against his palm. "Then we've got him. Once we trap the Mop on water, he's doomed."

Gytha had grown more and more restless, frustrated by all the talk of politics and military strategy. Finally she could restrain herself no longer. "Isn't the Great War supposed to be about a princess?"

The men all turned to her. One of them said, "You mean Eiriksdottir?"

"Yes, that one."

"Are you kidding? She's dead."

"What!"

The scar-faced man scowled. "Where've you been, kid? Old Eirik built a burial mound for her last winter. He's made Hadd the Hard his foster son, the new heir."

Gytha paled. Her father thought her dead? Did he actually believe he had buried her, or was this one of his tricks—a ploy to fool Harald? And how could he have promised his inheritance to Hadd the Hard? Now, even if she dared to reveal her identity, she would be second in line for the throne. Sons always outranked daughters. Against the ruthless Hadd, ranking second would be as hopeless as placing second in a duel. Hadd would either murder her as a rival, or worse yet, force her to marry him.

She asked uncertainly, "Where did Eirik find the princess' body?"

"He didn't," the scar-faced man replied. "The grave mound is empty. They figure she died nine winters ago in the Horthangr Wastes. It just took Eirik this long to give up and declare her dead."

Another man added, "I'd sure like to get my hands on that black eagle dagger of hers, though."

"Why?" Gytha asked, suddenly conscious of the small weapon's steely coolness beneath her tunic.

"For the reward, of course. It's worth your weight in silver if you bring it to Stavanes." The man grinned. "You see, even Eirik must wonder what really happened to the princess. Personally, I think the dragons got her and took her to the bottom of Horthangr Fjord."

"And what of Harald?" Gytha asked, bolder now. "Does he care if his precious princess is dead?"

Several of the men shrugged.

Hosvir, however, knitted his brow. "I think he does. I heard a strange tale while in Tunsberg, from an old woman selling jewelry—a peculiar hag I wouldn't normally trust, with one blue eye and one green. But at least part of her story must have been true."

Gytha cocked her head. "Oh?"

"The old woman insisted Harald hadn't come all the way from Throndheim because his grandmother was ill, despite what the courtiers said. Of course we didn't believe the hag at the time. Why else would the Mop attempt such a dangerous journey just when the lake ice was breaking up? But then we saw Asa later at the hall. She was blind, feeble, and seventy winters old, to be sure—*but not ill*. She paraded past us with her black-haired slave woman as if she ate men like us for breakfast."

The shipwright raised an eyebrow. "So why did Harald travel to Tunsberg?"

"According to the old woman, it was because he'd heard Eirik declared Princess Gytha dead."

"That doesn't make sense," the shipwright objected. "You don't visit your grandmother because your girl's dead."

"No, no. He visited Asa because she has second sight—she can see the future."

Hosvir's listeners studied him skeptically.

He quickly added, "That's what the old hag claimed. She said Harald had gone to Asa to ask if the girl were really dead, or if she still lived. To find out, Asa locked herself in an empty hall for two days. When she came out, she told him she'd had a vision of Gytha from the not-too-distant future."

The shipwright mused, "Then by that account, Eirik was wrong. The girl's still alive."

"Maybe and maybe not. You see, the vision was of a shipwreck. The girl was lying among broken planks and corpses on a shore. She was dressed in rags, and her hands were covered with blood."

Gytha caught her breath. "You don't seriously believe this?"

"As I say, I didn't believe it at the time. But it wasn't long afterwards when Harald ordered his Throndheim troops to begin building ships for a final attack on the western kingdoms—an attack to be carried out from the sea, where he must know he's at a disadvantage, and within this year, long before he can expect to launch a fleet to match the Vikings. Anyone can see it's a desperate gamble. I tell you, the Mop believes his princess is still here in the western kingdoms—and he believes she's in terrible danger."

Gytha's throat tightened. Was it possible, after all these years, that Harald would risk so much for her? She turned away from the fire, trying to compose herself. She needed time alone to sort out her emotions. A roar rose from the wrestling ring, turning the men's heads. Gytha used the distraction to stumble across the clearing toward the tents. She collapsed on her blanket, her eyes wet with confusion and despair. Was she dead? Was she loved? Who was she after all? Perhaps the part of her that once had been the beautiful Princess of Horthaland really had died in a blizzard in the Horthangr Wastes. Perhaps what Harald loved was nothing more than a vision, the ghost of a beguiling girl who no longer existed. For the first time in years, Gytha let herself cry.

Then a rustle of the tent flap stopped her with a shot of fear. She quickly wiped her face and sat upright. But no one was there. The tent had merely luffed in the breeze.

She slowed her breathing. Self-pity would gain her nothing. Did she honestly believe the goddesses of fate planned for her to die in a shipwreck? Hosvir might have fabricated the tale to impress the crew. Or the garrulous jewelry vendor in Tunsberg might have invented the story to fool a gullible traveler. Even if it were true that Asa had described such a vision, Gytha knew the 'Little Chieftain' was a devious queen. Asa may have had mysterious motives of her own for prophesying a shipwreck.

Gytha straightened her shepherd's tunic over the waist of her baggy Viking pants. No matter what happened in Tunsberg or Stavanes, she would have to deal with life at Hafrsfjord first. For now, the reward offered against the Horthaland dagger would make her life here particularly dangerous. If the Vikings found the telltale weapon they would gladly deliver her to Stavanes, and Eirik's vengeance would be terrible indeed—not only for her, but for Ragnar. The safest thing would be to throw the dagger into the fjord. But she wasn't about to part with the hidden weapon, either. The inlaid eagle was all that remained of her life as royalty. One day she might need proof that

she was the lost princess. Until then, she would have to redouble her efforts to keep her identity secret.

A new sleeping place! She remembered her plan from yesterday and quickly gathered her things in the blanket. Earlier she had noticed a hidden hollow beneath a half-fallen beech tree. Now she felt her way through the dark forest and spread her blanket there.

For what seemed a long time she lay staring up through the forest shadows, unable to sleep. She was still far too wrought up from the day.

At length she took up her wooden flute and made her way through the woods to the fjord's pebbled shore, where a sickle moon splashed silver stripes across the waves. A single rock stood a short ways out from the beach. She waded out and climbed to a dry perch on its summit. There, with the rhythmic splash of waves as a heartbeat-slow accompaniment, she played the lilting minor tune that had always served to calm her.

On and on the melody carried her, beyond the fears of Vikings and the unknowns of Harald. The tune soared, on soothing wings of time and tone until, when the moon was settling into the hills across the fjord, the song ceased, seemingly unfinished, in the midst of a scale.

Later, when Gytha crept back toward her sleeping place in the forest, she passed within a stone's throw of the tent where she had slept so fearfully the night before. She froze at the sound of Svein's voice.

"Where's Ulf?"

Hosvir answered hesitantly from the tent. "Ulf said he was sleeping in the forest tonight."

"With who?"

"Why—alone, I assumed."

Svein laughed. "Unlikely, isn't it?"

* * *

In the weeks that followed, Gytha felt hunted. She secretly moved her sleeping place in the forest every night. During the day she was afraid of being caught alone with Svein while she worked on the sails. Only the evenings were safe, for then the leader was busy with the challenge he had issued.

The evening competitions soon proved how few of the men could best the stocky, thick-necked Svein at wrestling. Even fewer could outwit him at chess, and no one seemed able to beat him at both sports in one day.

With a bit of luck and a clever leg hold, Gauk managed one evening to pin Svein in the ring, but Gauk was then mercilessly checkmated at the chess stump. At the crew's prodding, Hosvir was the next to try his hand at chess with Svein. The wealthy farmer quickly advanced his pawns into a formidable wedge, but when the moment came to close in on Svein's king, Hosvir suddenly lost his queen to a simple oversight. The crew scoffed that he had thrown the game to avoid facing Svein in the wrestling ring—and Gytha suspected it was true. Svip had shown how dangerous it was to venture into the ring unprepared. Svein had humiliated the boy by pinning him to the ground while holding one hand in the air.

After three weeks of work in the forest, the shipwright announced that they had manufactured enough planks. From then on the Vikings stayed in camp, learning the very different skills required to assemble the ship. Some men served as blacksmiths, pounding lumps of iron into rivets and washers. Joiners fitted the planks along the growing hull, arching each board and riveting it to the plank below. Framers hewed ribs to brace the inside of the hull. Then they pegged the ribs in place with dowels.

Gytha worked alone as before, and although she was taunted for her woman's task, she created a much stronger and finer sail than was the custom. She sewed three layers of wool into the corners to keep them from ripping. Then she cut an extra bolt of cloth into a ten-foot-tall Horthaland eagle, dyed it as black as possible with a foul-smelling brew of bark and berries, and stitched it into the sail's center. By the time she was finished, even Svip—who had taunted her the worst of all—had to admit the *Naglfar* would be a proud sight with such a sail.

For the final fortnight of preparations the summer sun was hot and high. The harried shipwright worked long into the nights, for the sky never grew completely dark and he had many details to complete. He fashioned the mast braces, the bat-shaped rigging cleats, the hinged oarhole covers, and—most important of all—the side-hung rudder, curved so cunningly that the ship could sail straight even if the helmsman were felled by an arrow.

By this time the crew's share of the construction work was mostly done. Svein left only a few men to help the shipwright carve oars and fit the decking. The rest were assigned to ready their weapons.

Gytha and the other new recruits had to build their own shields. "If you make your own," a veteran Viking told them, "you'll blame no one but yourself when it breaks." With this incentive, Gytha did her utmost. She watched the others carefully. Then, following their pattern, she riveted two layers of thin planks into a square, hewed it round, and painted it red. After she had attached the metal parts prepared by the crew's blacksmith—an iron rim, a handhold, and a cup-like central boss—the Viking veterans were surprised to judge her shield as light and strong as their own.

Next, Gytha was taken to the Vikings' weapons trunk to choose a sword. She picked an old, three-quarters-length blade with a leather scabbard. As she strapped on the scabbard's belt she felt for a moment the pride and power of a Norse warrior. But then she remembered seeing such swords slaughter innocents at Valdres, and the feeling of power vanished. The weapon hung as a dead weight at her waist.

"You must carry a second weapon," the veteran guarding the trunk told her. "Ax, spear, halberd, club, or bow. Choose."

She picked a cudgel, knowing it was an absurd choice. The man only shook his head.

A second, unguarded trunk held wooden versions of the bladed weapons, to be used in the daily practice sessions. Hour after hour the men stood in the sun-scorched clearing, battering each other's shields with the toy-like stick weapons. But there was nothing toy-like about the blows. Although Gytha parried and blocked as fast as she could, she was an easy target. Her legs and shoulders soon swelled from countless bruises, and her arms sagged with fatigue. When she finally retreated to rest on a stump, Gauk called across the field to her, "Practice, Ulf. You won't last two minutes against the Mop."

Gytha sat unmoved, her head in her hands. At times it seemed that an honorable death in battle would be the easiest way.

Then she felt a hand grip her shoulder.

"Come rest in my tent, Ulf." It was Svein. "You know what I want. It's about time I got it."

Terror fired Gytha with new strength. If Svein set out to rape her, he would hardly stop when he discovered she was a woman. Once he was finished with her, he might well kill her so he could turn in the Horthaland dagger for the reward.

Gytha yanked free from his hand, picked up her wooden sword, and strode back into the mock battle, slashing at the Vikings' shields as if her life depended on it.

* * *

On the morning of the launch, Hafrsfjord lay like a mirror under the mists. The crew gathered below the ship's curved flanks, thirty-five men on a side, while the shipwright readied rollers before the prow. At his signal the men knocked the hull's props loose. For an instant the dragonship balanced on its keel. Then it listed ponderously to Gytha's side, as if it had long since recognized this woman amongst the crew and was intent upon crushing her. Gytha kept her shoulder to the planks, straining with the others. Slowly the huge wooden shell righted again.

"Forward!" the shipwright commanded.

Gytha braced herself to push, but the dragon had already begun creeping ahead on its own. The rumble of rollers resonated through the hollow flanks like a summer thunderstorm.

"Easy!"

One of the log rollers caught against a stump and snapped. The keel smacked the gravel of the beach but plowed onward. A sheet of water smashed the fjord's mirror. Then the *Naglfar* drifted to the end of its tether, strained a moment, and reluctantly turned back to shore.

Amid the cheers of the crew, the shipwright slapped his palm before Svein. "Built, beached, and delivered."

Svein shook his head. "Our bargain included a sea trial."

The fat shipwright reddened. Then he turned to the men and bellowed, "Fetch the mast and oars!"

Within minutes the crew had carried the remaining gear on board. Even Gytha, overseeing the stowing of the sail, felt the thrill of finally standing on the deck of the ship she had helped build.

As soon as they had cast off from shore, Svein walked the length of the deck to check the rowers' positions. His hand hesitated on Gytha's shoulder as he passed. When Svein reached the aft prow he nodded to the two lead oarsmen. They bent forward, raising their oars. Fifty-eight oars wavered up behind them, trying to mimic the position. Then the lead oarsmen dipped and pulled.

Gytha was not the only one who followed the lead oarsmen's example too slowly. Oars crossed and men cursed. On the second stroke,

Gytha's oar merely skipped across the water flat-bladed. The ship faltered like a beetle on its back. But gradually the slow rhythm of the lead oarsmen caught hold—dip and pull, dip and pull. The *Naglfar* edged across the fjord in the face of a cool mid-morning breeze.

The more Gytha rowed, the longer and heavier her oar seemed. After a mere quarter hour she was tired—and glad when the helmsman turned about. Svein ordered the oars stowed on the forked racks overhead.

"This boat rows like a washtub," Svein told the shipwright. "But it's the oarsmen's fault, not yours. Now try the sail."

Ten men set to raising the mast from the aft deck. Gytha stood on the foredeck, tying the sail to the spar. The shipwright walked about the mast, securing the many stays to the ship's sides. Then the men who had raised the mast pulled together on a rope to hoist the sail. The pulley on the mast's tip screeched as the spar slowly lifted from the deck. The red sail luffed cautiously at first. Then it billowed, arching the black eagle emblem toward the bow. Gytha wiped her forehead with relief, glad that her sail had withstood its first test.

Spirits ran high on the return trip across the fjord. Gauk struck up a bawdy sea ballad. Soon half the crew were singing or thumping the decking planks. The shipwright beamed.

Once the *Naglfar* had beached, Svein weighed out ten pounds of English silver coins for the shipwright. "There's your pay, and well earned too." Then he turned to Gauk. "Now let's fetch up that mead."

"All of it?"

"We'll drink her dry. Your next barrel's brewing in Tunsberg."

It was an afternoon of song and drink. Gytha had planned to skip her share of the drink, but the enthusiasm of the men caught her up. Besides, the others seemed unaffected by the mead.

After Gytha had finished her second horn, however, she felt the ship beginning to roll. By the time she had drunk the third horn she was sitting beside the mast with Gauk and Hosvir, singing with her eyes closed.

It took her a moment to notice when the song stopped. She stood up—too quickly—and caught the mast to keep her balance. The Vikings were shading their eyes, looking past the prow to the fjord. She squinted. A black sail?

At once she wished her mind were clearer. "Is it Eirik?"

She realized she had accidentally spoken her thoughts when a Viking answered, "Not likely, with such a small ship. This one's low and fast."

The ship was very fast. In half the time it had taken the *Naglfar* to cross the fjord, the ship drew so close that it lowered its black sail for the final approach by oar.

"Hail Vikings!" a voice called.

"Hail Horthalanders!" Svein replied. "What news?"

"Orders from the alliance." The sleek vessel shipped its oars and slid alongside the *Naglfar*. A young nobleman with a red silk cloak stood out amongst a crew of more ordinary sailors. He sized up the row of dirty, bearded Viking faces lining the gunwale. "Which of you answers to the name of Svein?"

The leader scowled, for he disliked submitting to any aristocrat, and this one seemed particularly haughty. "I'm Svein."

"And I am Jarl Brynjolf. I understand you were commissioned by Eirik to raise a crew and build a ship."

"She was launched today."

"Behind schedule, then. I should tell you that Harald has already been sighted sailing south from Throndheim."

"So early?" Svein wiped his hand over his blond beard. "How many ships does he have?"

The jarl smiled. "That is not your concern."

"Not our concern?" Svein retorted angrily. "Who in the name of Thor's iron balls do you think is going to fight him?"

"All of us in the North Sea alliance will fight him."

Svein grumbled, "Then what's our plan?"

"The alliance intends to draw Harald as far away from his home ports as possible. This will give us time to reconnoiter and to gather our forces. Alliance ships are already crossing the North Sea. They should arrive in a day or two on the coast of Jathar, where they'll be met by Hadd the Hard. You are to sail south to join them there."

"We'll need to load our supplies, but we could leave by tomorrow morning easy enough."

"Good. Have you chosen a captain?"

Svein hesitated a moment out of pride, and hit upon a little jibe. "Lacking a jarl, we decided instead to choose a captain with wits and strength."

Brynjolf smiled. "And was there such a man among you?"

"Well, yes," Svein said, a little flustered by the jarl's smooth reply. "We held a competition. I told the crew anyone who beat me both in wrestling and chess in a single day would lead the ship."

"Commendable. Then everyone has challenged you?"

"Yes."

Jarl Brynjolf looked at the crew a little sadly. "And they all have failed."

Hosvir objected, "Not yet."

Svein gave the farmer a ferocious glare. "You played at chess and lost. A man with a clumsy queen gets no second chance."

"Yes, I lost. But you haven't yet been challenged by Ulf."

Gytha caught his arm and whispered, "Hosvir! Why on earth?" He was the closest thing she had to a friend on the crew, yet now he was dragging her out for public humiliation.

"It's your last chance," Hosvir whispered back. "Truth is your best friend now."

Gytha groaned. How she wished she could have confided in Hosvir! He still imagined she was a man pretending to be an inept boy.

"Most entertaining," the jarl said. "Where is this Ulf? By your own rules, Svein, you must allow the challenge. And I think we've time for a quick sporting diversion. Which would you care to try first—chess or wrestling?"

Svein shoved his way through the men to Gytha. His eyes narrowed threateningly.

"I choose chess," she said quickly.

"Bring us the board!" Svein growled.

Gytha half wondered if this was all some nightmarish hallucination brought on by the mead. The entire crew gathered around while the chess pieces were set up on a foot locker before her. Even the Horthaland sailors and Jarl Brynjolf climbed aboard to watch. A confusion of men's voices roared in her ears. Faces wove before her, goading. All the insults and humiliations she had suffered from the Vikings mounted into a single swell of anger and shame.

Then she saw that Svein had already moved his castle's pawn two squares forward. It was an idiocy that she and Ragnar secretly called "Hildirid's gambit." Did none of these men know how to play chess? With sudden resolve she pushed forward her king's pawn—the harmless looking opening to a devastating response.

She knew she must lose the game. But first she intended to give Svein a fight to remember.

By the fourth move her horsemen had ripped open his pawn defenses. Svein hunched over the board, deluged with advice from behind. Then he saw his chance to recoup: Ulf had left a pawn completely unguarded. His queen struck and Ulf seemed to retreat. More confident now, Svein slid his queen to snatch an even better prize—an unprotected castle.

The Vikings laughed, holding up the fallen chess piece for the men in the back to see.

"It's a rout," one man said.

"It's a trap," Hosvir corrected.

Gytha's small white hand reached to the back row. Her queen's sorcerer slipped diagonally through the pawns to the center of the board. Suddenly Svein's queen stood exposed on one flank and his king on the other.

"Check."

Svein pulled his king to safety, but the queen was lost.

Vengeance became a delirious toxin pounding in Gytha's veins. Deaf to the clamor of the men, Gytha sent her queen on a devastating foray through Svein's back rank. Then, as a final humiliation, she began advancing her horseman's pawn. Square by square the lowly piece trudged across the board. Her queen raced about, deflecting Svein's every attempt to cut the pawn down.

Still giddy from the mead, she pushed the pawn into the final square. "Make it a queen, Svein."

The jarl behind her said, "A queen? That's checkmate, then."

Gytha looked at the board, terrified. In her maudlin rush for revenge, she had forgotten what havoc the second queen would wreak. She had won the game—and now stood to lose everything.

Svein kicked the chess board aside. His voice was ominously low. "Now we must wrestle, Ulf."

"No!" She tried to back away, but bumped against the side of the ship.

"Strip off that tunic," Svein growled. Let's see what kind of man you are."

Did he already know her secret? What horrors awaited her if this mob saw her breasts and realized a woman had been amongst them all this time?

"Keep away, I warn you!" But words were meaningless now. In desperation, she drew her sword.

The clang of the blade instantly silenced the men.

Jarl Brynjolf raised an eyebrow. "It seems you have an offer to loosen the rules of your wrestling match, Svein."

Svein unsheathed his sword in reply. The men scrambled to make room. Before Gytha could parry, Svein's sword flashed in a swift arc, catching her blade just above the hilt. Her sword flipped harmlessly from her hand and splashed into the fjord.

"Kill him!" several voices shouted.

Gytha was too terrified to know what to do. Should she risk telling them who she really was? Should she leap overboard? Should she stand straight to take the death blow?

"No," Svein said—and his leer sent a chill through her. "I've something else in mind."

He dropped his sword, grabbed her shoulders, and pressed his face against hers, kissing her viciously on the mouth.

She struggled, but he was far too powerful. He had already begun to tear her tunic when her hand finally closed around the secret dagger.

Suddenly Svein fell back, a gaping stripe of red across his cheek. He touched a hand to his face and stared at the blood in disbelief. "The hidden weapon of a girl!"

Gytha slipped the dagger again under her clothes. Had its royal emblem been noticed?

Svein pointed a bloody finger at her and announced in a voice of utter contempt, "*Woman!*"

At first she thought she had been discovered. But when Svein spat at her and turned away, she realized what had happened. He had branded her with the gravest and most degrading insult in the Viking vocabulary—the only obloquy from which a man's honor could never recover.

"Woman!" One of the older Vikings stepped forward, spat in her face, and turned.

She stood unflinching as one after another of the crew spat and turned away. Svip leaned close and laughed when his spittle struck her eye. Gauk spat solemnly at her feet. Even Hosvir made the sound of spitting as he passed, though she alone understood his conspiratorial nod.

Finally Jarl Brynjolf studied her grimly. "A pity, Ulf. I'd have judged you won your wrestling match. But failing to avenge an insult of this magnitude means accepting the consequences of its disgrace."

She said nothing, nor did she lower her eyes.

"Better if you had died than to let your name be so ignobly dishonored," the jarl said. "You are no longer fit to serve Eirik."

"Very well," she said. "Then I will serve him no more."

* * *

Hildirid stopped her in the doorway of the sod farmhouse. "You! What trouble are you bringing us this time?"

"I don't know." Gytha was too tired to argue. She dropped her bundle and sat outside, leaning against the hut's grassy wall.

Ragnar hurried up from across the field. "Thank Odin you're back. Are you all right?"

"I—I'm not sure. Gytha is officially dead. Eirik's built an empty grave mound."

"Then, if no one's looking for her, we could—"

"No, father. Let's not start waking the dead again. But on the other hand—" she stared out toward the distant, darkening fjord. After the long stretch of summery weather, clouds were piling up over the coast. "I don't think you'll want Ulf back either."

Hildirid's suspicions grew. "Why did the Vikings send you back so soon? Their battle hasn't even begun yet. Tell me the truth! How much do they know about you?"

Gytha shifted uncertainly, considering the irony of this question. Though she had been a Viking for over a month, they had learned almost nothing about her. Only Ragnar and Hildirid understood, and they always seemed to suffer for it. "The truth is, the Vikings said I was incompetent and insubordinate. They rejected me from the service of the king and put Ulf's name in dishonor. I'm sorry."

Ragnar wrinkled his brow. "A dishonored name would follow you all your life."

"A dishonored name will follow us too!" Hildirid said, outraged. "I don't care who you are. You can't live here. No one would trade with us. We'd be ruined."

"Hildirid, please. You can't just throw him out. Besides, the Vikings are the only ones who say the name's dishonored. They're not from Rogaland. Once the Mop's defeated, they'll all go back where they came from. Then they'll take this talk of dishonor with them."

Hildirid looked unconvinced. "That could take years. Maybe the Mop won't come looking for a battle at all."

"I'm afraid Harald's fleet has already set sail," Gytha said. "The alliance's ships are gathering off the coast of Jathar. They expect to meet Harald within a week. No one is planning a second encounter."

Ragnar glanced uncertainly toward the fjord, as if it hid a ghostly menace. "Gods, will it come to that? After nine winters, an end to the Great War."

"Odin grant us the troops don't come here," Hildirid said.

At this prayer they fell silent, each thinking of Valdres and the horrors that had swept through their lives at the beginning of the war.

Finally Gytha picked up her blanket bundle. "I won't stay in the farmhouse. It's time to take the sheep up to the high pastures anyway. I can camp with them up there for now."

Hildirid's lips tightened. "And I'm supposed to forget that you have dishonored the name of my son?"

"Surely there's no harm in letting him camp with the sheep," Ragnar objected. "Besides, if the war ends the right way the dishonor won't matter."

Hildirid looked at Gytha again, considering. "All right. We'll wait and see. If they kill Harald, you can stay."

CHAPTER 24
WINTER, 1904

Kirstin still worried about letting Magnus go. It had been difficult enough telling him to wait, after he had declared his love so earnestly. But then he had suddenly left on a fishing boat, saying only that he wanted two hours to clear the route to Kristiania. They both knew the Swedish government had ordered a gunboat to block the fjord ahead. How did Magnus imagine he could change that? For that matter, Kirstin wondered, was it safe for anyone to navigate these rocky fjords at night?

Precisely two hours after Magnus had left, the tugboat captain walked past Kirstin and took the wheel. "Half ahead, Svend," he ordered into the speaking tube.

Kirstin had to make an effort not to interfere. She had taken charge of the excavation because she knew archeology. But she knew nothing of navigation. She had to trust the skill of Per and the word of Magnus.

The snowstorm over Tønsberg Fjord had settled into an eerie silence. Flakes drifted past the tugboat's brightly lit windows and winked out into the darkness below. At times it seemed to Kirstin as if the snow weren't falling at all, but rather that the tugboat's bridge were floating upwards through star-like lights into a surreal world, a world of dreams and myth. Lack of sleep left her hollow and stiff. But the danger ahead kept her nerves taut.

"Jarlsberg dock light to north by northwest," Per muttered. "Heading north by northeast another minute and a half."

All Kirstin could see ahead was snowflakes. She turned and looked back at the snow-draped dragonship, mounted on the deck of the barge behind them. The ship's prows arched proudly into the storm, as if it were ready to sail on without them into the dream world under its own mythic power. The image reminded her of *Skiblathnir*, the miniature Viking ship Magnus had sold to pay the Oseberg farmer. Much had changed since the sunny summer day when she and Magnus sailed this same stretch of fjord in *Skiblathnir*. She had known so little about him then.

The sudden blast of the tug's horn jolted her back to the present. When she turned she could see colored lights dancing upon the waves ahead.

"We've got company," Per pulled a handle to give the tug's horn another short blast.

Through the snowstorm a chorus of mismatched horns and bells began answering the tug's signal—bass blasts and shrill pipes, clanging gongs and tinny bells. Now Kirstin could make out snowy decks and swaying masts illuminated by the red, green, and white lanterns of countless fishing boats.

"Who are they?" Kirstin asked.

"Looks like the whole goddam Tønsberg fleet, that's who," Per replied.

"In a storm like this? What are they doing?"

"Cap'n Andersen must've roused 'em for a little midnight cruise. It's a scheme, sure enough. A few extra boats in the fjord just might crowd them Swedes."

So that was Magnus's plan! The scale of his effort was breathtaking—and so was the Tønsberg fleet's response. "How did Magnus get them to put to sea so quickly?"

Per shook his head. "Must have put out an S.O.S. at the Sailors' Center." As the tug churned through the harbor narrows, vessels of all shapes and sizes surrounded them. Creaking schooners, hulking freighters, shadowy trawlers—perhaps a hundred ships faded in and out of the snowstorm. The lights winking at their sterns showed they were daring to fly Norwegian flags.

"With this visibility, every one of those men is risking his ship," Per said, squinting from his compass to the window. "At least they know the skerries better than the Swedish crew out there."

"Could anyone but Magnus have rallied so many ships on a night like this?" she wondered aloud.

"I don't reckon. Lots of folks are grateful for what he's done since he sold that little Viking ship."

Kirstin looked at Per, surprised that he knew of Magnus's donation.

"Magnus said he was keeping that a secret."

"A secret? Well, he might have tried, but you can't pump five thousand crowns into a town this size without word getting around. He gave away half of what he made selling that ship."

"What do you mean, 'half'?" She remembered the night Magnus had told her about trading his model for the rights to the Oseberg ship. Had he actually earned more than he'd let on?

"I should know," Per said. "I hauled his boat to Hamburg on this same barge. I saw it sell at auction for ten thousand."

For a moment Kirstin was glad Magnus had kept a reserve of money for himself. And she wasn't particularly surprised that word had leaked out about his donation. But then a strange feeling began creeping upon her—the unsettling and yet wonderful suspicion that she had underestimated Magnus yet again. "You say his donation went to Tønsberg? I wonder if we're talking about the same money."

"You didn't know about the cash for the Seaman's Center?" Per studied her with disdain. "I reckon it figures."

"So Magnus was paying the wages of the excavation workers too?"

"How the hell did you think those sailors were feeding their kids? They can't eat glory. Since the factory ships threw so many whalers out of work, there's families all over Tønsberg thanking Cap'n Andersen for keeping bread on their tables."

She looked out the window at the lights of the fleet, realizing in a rush of emotion how much she had loved Magnus all along. How foolishly proud she had been to reject his love, and how callous to doubt his motives! He had given up his beloved *Skiblathnir* not merely for her sake, nor for the money. He had quietly given everything he'd earned to his country and to the people who needed help the most—his comrades in Tønsberg.

Her throat tightened as she recalled the times she had treated him coldly, the times she had suspected him unjustly. She had been so full of her own pride—her head had been so full of her new sense of power—that she had overlooked the truth in her heart.

"I should have known. But I'll make it up to him,"

"That'll be a trick," Per humphed. "I saw you, letting him walk away like he was a bum. And what with the reserves calling him up he'll probably be at sea for a year."

"What?" Kirstin found this sudden news hard to believe.

"Well, aren't you a smart one, Admiral? Everybody knows the Norwegian navy's mobilizing for war. Cap'n Andersen will be leaving for an active command any day."

She stared at him, dumbfounded. It seemed she had known nothing at all about this man. Why had she had never asked the right questions? Had a trace of prejudice lingered, whispering that Magnus was nothing more than a common sailor from a rough Norwegian port? She had been such a fool!

Per shook his head. "Serves you right, getting left at the dock."

Suddenly a brilliant beam of light swept across the bridge.

"What was that? A lighthouse?" Her first fear was that they might have strayed too near the rocks in the dark.

"No lighthouses on Jersøy." Per squinted from the compass to the shapes in the snowstorm. "Reckon all it could be is your Swedish friends."

The searchlight strafed the snowy decks of ship after ship. "Keep up full speed then, Per."

"Full speed, Admiral."

Through the brew of snow and darkness, Kirstin began to make out a ragged line of shapes between the searchlight and the barge's path. There could be no communication among the Tønsberg sailors in this storm, but they had already recognized the danger and had steered close, like songbirds gathering to harass a hungry hawk.

The steady throb of the tug's engines seemed intolerably slow. If only they could sail past Jersøy to Oslo Fjord, the safety of Akershus fortress would soon be in reach. A lit window on the island's shore hung before them, immobile as a star.

The warning moan of a horn sounded from the blockaded patrol boat. Echoes rolled back off the unseen skerries across the fjord.

"The fishermen are holding a line," Kirstin said.

"Sure, but there's probably a Swede out there with a megaphone reading 'em the regs, taking down boat names. There'll be hell to pay."

Suddenly a silent burst of fireworks lit the gunboat's deck.

"What in the—" Kirstin began. Then the thunder of a cannon overtook her.

Per muttered an oath.

"They've opened fire!"

"Just a warning shot," Per said. For a silent minute they watched the ships' outlines. One after the other, the fishing vessels began to sail aside to clear a path for the Swedish gunboat.

Per shook his head. "Can't say I blame them. Fishermen can't fight cannons."

The searchlight swiveled, sparkling off a stripe of open water between the patrol boat and the barge. Twin white curls of wake grew from the prow as the gunboat aimed through the gap. For a moment the searchlight flashed in their eyes. Then it settled on the prize—the curved, snow-flocked hull of the Viking dragonship.

Kirstin slammed the flat of hand against the glass in frustration. "No! We can't give up now. Not after all we've been through."

Per pointed up the fjord. "Looks like *Sleipnir* agrees with you."

"*Sleipnir?*" Kirstin knew the word only as the name of Odin's eight-legged horse—the legendary steed as dark as night and as fast as thought. Certainly the mythic horse of a Norse god wasn't likely to come to their aid. Still, when she peered up the dark fjord she actually could make out an ominous, hulking shadow advancing toward them.

"What on earth?" She wiped the window and squinted into the night. The shape seemed taller and broader than a ship. No running lights betrayed the huge phantom, nor did the speeding patrol boat seem aware of its danger. "Whatever it is, it's heading to ram the gunboat."

"Then the Swedes will be at fault. By naval law, sails have the right of way over steam. Clever lad, Magnus."

"Magnus!"

"*Sleipnir's* his ship, sure enough, since his Pappy died."

Suddenly the patrol boat's searchlight jerked frantically to starboard, sweeping the towering sails of a fully-rigged five-masted sailing ship, a leviathan from the days before steam. The sleek hull curved with the grace of a clipper, but the deck was crowded with the winches and cranes of a fishing vessel. Kirstin stared at the enormous old sailing ship with astonishment and pride. That Magnus had never boasted he owned such a ship made her admire him all the more. If only she had dared to give him the trust he deserved!

The patrol boat's horn bleated, but the wind-driven ship sliced steadily onwards on its collision course.

Per's eyes narrowed. "I hope your Swedish friends don't underestimate the Cap'n's nerve. If he hits 'em broadside at that speed, they'll both sink."

At the last moment the gunboat threw its engines into full reverse. While the patrol boat struggled to churn back, *Sleipnir* silently cut in front of its bow, eclipsing the searchlight's glare.

Kirstin watched Magnus's ship, her heart full of anguish. She wished she could somehow signal to him, admit to him how foolishly proud she had been, tell him that she loved him, ask him for one more chance together.

Per frowned out the window at a cluster of crewmen near *Sleipnir's* stern. "What the hell is his crew doing?" Per was still frowning, deep in thought, when the ship slid away and the patrol boat's searchlight reappeared, glaring past the Norwegian flag at the back of Magnus's ship.

Now the gunboat was so close they could hear the growl of its engines. The Swedish ship began to cross the narrow patch of turbulent waters to the barge.

Kirstin sighed. "Even Magnus could only delay the inevitable, I suppose."

But Per seemed stuck on a different thought. "Those crewmen were on *our* side of the ship, where the Swedes couldn't see them working."

She looked to him for an explanation, but none came. Magnus's ship had already vanished into the night. He was gone, perhaps forever now, and the gunboat was speeding unhindered to overtake them.

Suddenly the growl of the patrol boat's engine dropped a note. The entire vessel wrenched to one side, as if the hull had been grabbed by monstrous jaws from below. Its searchlight tilted crazily, stabbing about in the snowstorm.

"Glad that isn't my ship," Per laughed.

"What on earth is happening to it?"

"She's dead in the water now. Them Swedes should have known better than to cut behind a trawler."

"But why?"

"Cap'n Andersen must've been trailing a steel-cabled fishing net behind him. When the Swedes steamed over it they fouled their rudder and bent their prop. Gods, what a catch!"

CHAPTER 25
SUMMER, 881

"If they kill Harald, you can stay." The words rang in Gytha's ears all that night as she huddled from the rain in the corner of a sheep pasture. Why had she bothered to come back to her foster parents' farm at all? Of course she loved Ragnar—and Hildirid, too, she supposed—but her stint on a Viking shipbuilding crew had opened her eyes. She was twenty-three, quite capable of tackling the world on her own. And she was sick of playing a pawn in the Great War between Harald and Eirik. She wanted to go somewhere far away and start over.

A wet sheep interrupted her thoughts by wriggling under the tarp to join her in the corner of a stone fence. Gytha shoved the animal back with her foot. The sheep bleated and stupidly tried to climb the wall. The tarp pulled loose, dumping cold water onto Gytha's blanket.

She swore one of the fiery oaths she had heard amongst the Vikings.

While she stood in the rain rebuilding her shelter, she made a sudden decision. No matter how the battle between Harald and Eirik ended, she would quit being Ulf. With Princess Gytha Eiriksdottir officially dead, why bother disguising herself as a man any longer? She wanted nothing to do with Harald, Eirik, or Hadd the Hard. She was ready to leave her foster parents behind too. She'd take a new name and escape—perhaps to Denmark. She could become a wandering musician, playing her flute for her supper. And she'd grow her hair long again. Already it hadn't been cut for a month. How wonderful it would be to comb out her long, golden hair after all these years!

A pair of uncertain eyes peered under the tarp.

Gytha sighed at the sheep's persistence. She scratched its woolly nose. "What do you think? Should I become a musician? You've been my best audience up to now."

The sheep lifted its muzzle and chewed tentatively on her hand. Then it drew back and bleated.

Gytha smiled a little sadly. "Musicians don't have a very good reputation, do they?" Nor did women really travel alone, even in Denmark. In her heart, she knew running away would never be the answer.

* * *

Clouds dripped across the hills in the morning. Gytha drove the sheep up a muddy track toward higher pastures, keeping an eye out to the west. Only twice that day could she glimpse the bottle-shaped fjord below. The first time, she spotted the *Naglfar* rowing past a small green island like a caterpillar beside a fallen leaf. Hours later, when

the swirling clouds parted again, the ship had reached the sea and metamorphosed, its tiny red sail-wing already bearing it south to rendezvous with the fleet of the Viking alliance. Although she was glad to be free of the *Naglfar* and its coarse crew, she couldn't help feeling that a part of her was still on board. She had sewn its proud sail. She had served long enough beside Hosvir, Gauk, and the others to know they were men, and not monsters. Most of them had no experience with war. Despite all they had done to hurt her, she found herself worrying about the crew's fate in the coming battle.

The following day the weather worsened. Lightning crashed into the hilltops, scattering the terrified sheep into the thickets of the wooded draws. Wind-whipped rain spattered the rocks and slid down the slopes in sheets. Gytha wrapped the tarp about her shoulders, chasing after her herd. Finally, exhausted and drenched, she collapsed in the lee of a boulder. Painstakingly, she built a small fire before the twilight closed in.

Struggling to keep her smoky fire alive, she thought of the hundreds — perhaps thousands — of men at sea in this storm. She shivered, imagining them rowing in the dark against winds that pushed their wooden boats toward the roar of surf. They would be bailing desperately against the rain while waves slapped over the ships' sides. That night the armies would not be battling each other, but rather the gods.

In the dawn Gytha awoke to an eerie silence. A gauzy mist draped the hillsides, pinkened by a low sun. She ate cheese and flatbread beside the ashes of her fire, slung her bag over her shoulder, and set off to collect the sheep the storm had scattered.

She stopped short, however, at the crest of a rise. The fjord below shone like a platter of gold in the sun. And speckling the strip of ocean beyond, still far to the north, were the sails of ships.

Harald.

She sank to a rock, the sheep forgotten, her heart beating far faster than she wished. For a moment she wanted to go to him — to signal the ships and meet this man who had pursued her for so long. She could warn him of the Viking alliance's massive preparations and save him from sailing into their trap. She would be hailed as a queen, with all the honor and wealth that rank entailed. After the indignities of the past nine years, the prospect seemed both tempting and incredible.

But then she crossed her arms. How could she throw herself

at Harald's feet? Wasn't his arrogance the cause of her suffering in the first place? Because of Harald, her foster parents were paupers. Because of Harald, the new heir to Eirik's realm was Hadd the Hard. She looked at the wet rags she wore, blaming Harald for every tatter. She would rather die as a shepherd than beg from the Mop.

She watched Harald's ships sail south along the coast, clusters of tiny yellow sails against the deepening blue. When they reached the mouth of Hafrsfjord they paused to gather. Then, to her surprise, they turned inland, squeezing through the narrows by threes and fives. She counted as they spread out into the larger bay below: fifty, a hundred, two hundred, two hundred and forty dragonships! How could he have built so many so fast? Could it be enough to match the Vikings?

All the boats seemed identical but one. She climbed a bit lower down the hillside and squinted. Turning in the middle of the fjord was a ship nearly twice as long as the others, with room for perhaps sixty oars on each side. Its painted planking gleamed as bright a yellow as its sails. Its forward prow curled up to the knob of a large dragonhead, while the back prow narrowed into a tail. From the foredeck flew a banner Gytha knew must be the one she had seen so long ago when Harald arrived at the Vik: the infamous Golden Dragon.

While Harald's flagship waited, the other ships cruised along the shoreline, inspecting every corner of the fjord. The sun was already high when the ships gathered again. As if Harald had failed to find whatever he had been seeking, the Golden Dragon turned back toward the narrows.

By then Gytha had long since spotted a blur of red on the ocean from the south—the Viking alliance's sails. Harald, however, could not see the threat until his flagship rowed out to the fjord's mouth. There he stopped, obviously watching and counting the sails.

Gytha counted too, squinting as she ticked off tens with her finger. More than two hundred red sails. Evidently other crews like her own had enabled the Vikings to rebuild their fleet. Behind them were a hundred black-sailed Horthaland ships of Eirik's men. Still another hundred ships carried white sails. Gytha guessed they were Vikings from across the North Sea. Together four hundred ships! If each were like the *Naglfar*, with a crew of seventy, the Viking alliance must have amassed nearly thirty thousand men!

Gytha closed her eyes, wishing a thought to Harald. Run! Escape to the north while you can!

When she opened her eyes, however, the Golden Dragon flagship had hoisted its yellow sail as a defiant announcement of its identity — and had turned about.

She watched with disbelief as Harald herded his fleet back into Hafrsfjord. Was he mad? The fjord ended in two inescapable bays — a southern bight full of low islands and a northern bay of open water. Harald's two hundred and forty ships slowly arranged themselves into a single line across the middle of the northern bay. When the line was complete, she saw that the sailors were lashing the ships together side to side.

Only then did Gytha understand Harald's grim strategy. He did not want to allow his troops a route of escape. With their ships bound in place and their backs against the fjord, his men would either all be victorious or all die.

The first Viking ships followed cautiously through the narrows, as if unwilling to believe their luck at having caught the Mop in such a convenient cage. Long into the afternoon alliance ships filtered through the fjord's neck and grouped in the southern bay among the islands. Gytha climbed lower down the hillside to identify their many banners. King Sulki of Rogaland, King Kjotvi the Wealthy of Jathar, and King Hrygg of the North Fjords flew their flags from red-sailed ships alongside Hadd the Hard. The white-sailed ships bore strange, foreign banners that Gytha knew only from hearsay — Northumbria, the Faeroes, the Shetlands, the Orkneys, Scotland, Ireland, the Isle of Man, and Normandy. Leading them all, amidst the crowd of black-sailed ships, rose Horthaland's black eagle banner. Gytha's throat tightened at the sight of her father's standard. Seventy-three winters old, Eirik was commanding the vast Viking alliance in person. Despite all he had done to hurt her over the years, threatening her and disowning her, she still felt awe and pride for her father's power.

Opposite the many flags of the Vikings flew a single banner. The Golden Dragon fluttered above Harald's half-mile-long phalanx of carved ship prows and gaping figureheads. With lowered sails and set anchors, Harald's ships waited in strict formation for the attack.

Communication was obviously more difficult among the alliance's many units. They jockeyed for an hour, trying out several battle positions. Because Harald's ships effectively spanned the fjord, no

Viking vessels could slip past them to attack from behind. At the same time the Vikings could not directly outnumber Harald in a frontal assault, because the fjord was only wide enough for his row of ships.

Finally the Viking alliance lashed together a line of ships matching Harald's one-to-one. A second, looser row of vessels straggled behind. That the *Naglfar* was relegated to this second row suggested to Gytha that its crew was known to be inexperienced. Nonetheless, she recognized the strategic advantage of these reinforcements. They would be free to help wherever the need was greatest and could plug any gap that developed.

The Viking ships of the front line lowered their masts, letting the ships in back slowly push them toward Harald's anchored position.

Five hundred yards of water still separated the fleets. A flock of ducks splashed into the air, frightened by the gigantic jaws narrowing upon them.

Eirik's flagship lay squarely in the alliance's front line. The *Naglfar* sailed somewhat nearer Gytha's shore and behind Hadd the Hard's flagship, drifting directly toward the Golden Dragon. Even closer to Gytha, a shipful of Viking berserkers in wolf coats were shaking their weapons and shrieking. She watched from behind a boulder, her heart pounding.

At three hundred yards the terrifying battle cry of the Vikings began to roll across the fjord, overpowering the berserkers' screams. To Gytha it seemed the blood-curdling roar of Ragnarök itself.

At two hundred yards the Vikings' first arrows arced high across the gap. Many of these first bolts fell into the water, but as the Vikings closed in, their archers found their range.

Still Harald's troops waited silently, their shields raised. Gytha wondered if they didn't mean to attack at all. Could that be why they had retreated into Hafrsfjord?

Then at fifty yards a massive wave of arrows launched from the entire length of Harald's line. Nearly arcless, the sudden barrage obviously stung hard, for the Viking battle cry wavered. In another moment the long, uneven battle lines began to collide. Planks groaned as the ships strained in their deadly embrace. Spears bristled, jabbing from the prows. Brawny forecastlemen leaned out to hook away shields and careless shoulders with their halberds. Archers aimed death at any man whose shield fell.

Long before there was room for the first swords to be drawn, corpses draped the forward gunwales. By that time few arrows flew. Most of the shieldless archers had already been killed.

Gytha felt sickened by the carnage, but found herself unable to look away.

All that evening the battle raged. As twilight slowly dimmed the sky, the struggle took on a new and gruesome element of terror. Sudden cries in the half-darkness told of unlucky arrows or spears. Fearsome roars told where ships had been invaded by boarders. Gytha stared into the murk, straining in vain to discern which of the banners still stood. Flaming arrows set several of the ships on fire, but these scattered islands of light revealed little about which side might be gaining the upper hand.

When dawn sliced across the hills, Gytha's heart fell. The night had not taken any of the kings, but it had decimated the pawns—and it had left Harald's position desperately weakened. Empty ships littered the fjord. The Vikings had refilled their front-row ships with troops from behind, leaving most of the ships in the second row adrift. Harald, however, had been forced to cut loose fifty emptied ships on either end of his line. With his battle formation too short to span the fjord, he was now vulnerable to attack from behind.

The *Naglfar* was among the first of the Viking ships to spot its chance and slip past Harald's flank, rowing hard. Soon forty ships from the Vikings' second row followed suit and were lining up behind Harald to open the new attack. Meanwhile the Vikings' front row—far longer than Harald's—began folding in around him like the pincers of a gigantic claw.

As the claw closed, the Viking battle cry rose again, more chilling now that the end was near. The *Naglfar* and three other ships grappled onto the tail of Harald's huge, yellow-sided flagship, like angry bees clustering to kill an alien queen in the hive.

Men surged across the gunwales. Gytha stood on tiptoe and squinted. If she had still been on the *Naglfar*'s crew, she might have been face to face with Harald now—or she might already have been dead. She thought of Hosvir and the others she had known. They were facing death even now, in the bloody center of the battle.

Could Hadd the Hard's banner really have crossed from his own ship to Harald's? Certainly Hadd's flag seemed to be waving within yards of the Golden Dragon itself.

A minute passed while Gytha strained to see what was happening, scarcely daring to breathe.

Then the Golden Dragon banner disappeared.

A long roar of victory went up from the ring of Viking ships.

Gytha stared a moment in disbelief. Even against Hadd's invincible sword, she had not wanted to believe the Golden Dragon could fall. Yet Svein's prediction had come to pass. Harald the Unkempt was dead.

She climbed down from the boulder unsteadily. Odin! How could the gods let Harald die after bringing him so far against such odds? Why had the gods fought for him—and tormented her!—all these years, if only to let the saga be drowned out by a Viking battle cry? Of course she hadn't truly loved Harald—how could she love a man she had met only once? Yet now she had to admit his unwavering devotion had left its mark. Without Harald the sun would rise a little duller, robbed of its spark of secret promise. Odin! Treacherous prankster!

She pressed her eyes to shut out the tears. Then, blinking, she lifted her head to face her future, changed now forever.

She had to blink several times. The Vikings still held Harald's ship encircled, to be sure, and Hadd the Hard's banner still flew there. But on the edge of the battle the Golden Dragon banner had somehow risen again—above the deck of *Hadd the Hard's* ship.

While she was still puzzling over this bewildering switch, a bit of movement caught her eye in the west. More Viking ships?

A fresh column of sails was pouring into Hafrsfjord from the south—probably late arrivals from Anglia or Jutland, though she couldn't remember which of those Viking powers colored their sails blue. Nor could she imagine either of them mustering a hundred ships for a battle in Norway. Then who?

As the strange fleet neared she realized it wasn't composed of warships at all. It was a motley collection of ungainly merchant tubs and fishing boats. Of course, blue sails were popular with the simple fishing folk of the southlands. But why on earth would thousands of common fishermen from Agthir and Vestfold sail to war? They knew nothing of battle!

Then she saw the ship at the fore, and she caught her breath. It was the same decrepit, spiral-prowed dragonship she had seen years before when Harald arrived at the Vik.

The old dragonship, still a swift sailor, had dropped its blue sail to half-mast so as not to outrun its cumbrous fleet. Behind it, the deep-keeled fishing boats plowed across the fjord under full sail. Slow and heavy, they bore toward the banner ships of the Viking alliance, splayed out around Harald's diminished force like keys on a ring. The Vikings scurried to meet the new ships with halberds and spears. But the fishing boats showed no interest in playing that game. Instead of dropping their masts to row, the ponderous boats rammed at full speed, straight into the Vikings' line, hitting the sleek Viking vessels amidships. Dozens of the thin-flanked warships buckled open like eggshells.

Vikings cast their halberds aside and struggled against the rising water. Those who had worn chain mail drowned almost at once. The others crawled dripping onto the remaining Viking ships. But the men from the fishing boats were already storming over the ships' sides after them, swinging firewood axes and fishing gaffs.

Eirik's banner was the first to fall. With a touch of panic, Gytha searched the neighboring ships. He had always been so powerful! Surely her father's banner would reappear. But then another of the Viking alliance's flags fell. And another. And still another. Finally an entire wing of allied ships broke away from the fight, raised white sails, and made for the open sea. The flagship of King Kjotvi the Wealthy limped to the southern end of the fjord and beached, allowing the crew to flee overland.

In less than an hour, only Hadd the Hard's banner remained. When it too fell, the sounds of battle finally stilled. For a moment the fjord lay under a solemn calm. Then the chant began, louder and louder:

"Hail Harald! Hail Harald! Hail Harald!"

The name rolled across the fjord and echoed from the fjells, as if they too were hailing the one great king who now ruled unrivaled over all Norway.

Gytha ran down to the beach—though she herself was unsure why. Dead men rolled amid debris in the red surf. Capsized ships ground against the rocks. Ravens squawked and circled. A pair of the big black birds were plucking at the red gashes of a wide-eyed corpse.

"Ulf!" a voice croaked.

Gytha spun about, startled.

"Help me!" The weak voice came from a bedraggled figure struggling out of the waves. His bloody left forearm dangled horribly from the elbow.

Gytha ran to help the wounded man, but stopped when he looked up. A narrow red scab had ripped open on his cheek, dribbling blood into his blond beard.

"Svein."

"Help me, Ulf!" Svein gasped.

Gytha crossed her arms. "Once, in anger, you called me a woman. I would just remind you of that now."

The Viking captain dragged his mutilated arm beyond the reach of the stinging saltwater and sagged onto the beach. He no longer tried to meet her eyes. "Prove that you are a man, then, and kill me."

She withdrew the dagger hidden in her tunic.

He nodded. "Be quick, lad."

"No. I've something else in mind."

"Something—else?" Svein recalled the ominous words as if from a nightmare.

Gytha dragged the Viking up onto the dry rocks, raised the dagger above his chest, and—to the man's astonishment—cut off a long strip of his tunic.

"Wha—" Svein began, but the question melted into an anguished scream.

Gytha had twisted the strip of cloth tightly about his mangled arm. Soon the tourniquet slowed the blood welling from his gash.

"You are going to live. And you are going to tell me what happened."

Svein's head reeled from pain and confusion. "Tell what happened? Where?"

"In the battle. The *Naglfar* attacked Harald's flagship from behind. And then?"

His head began to sag into unconsciousness.

Gytha tightened the tourniquet again.

Svein jerked awake with a sharp cry.

"And then?"

"And then we boarded Harald's ship." Svein's voice wavered, but the words came quickly now. "We waited until Hadd the Hard had boarded from the bow. Then we climbed in from the aft. The fight was horrible. Svip and two others were killed at once. It was Gauk who finally cut down the banner bearer."

"I saw the Golden Dragon fall."

Svein looked at her, bewildered. "Impossible."

"I was watching from the shore."

"But it didn't fall. Harald dropped his sword and dived to the deck. He caught the pole before it hit."

"Then he was unarmed?"

"Why the Hel does it matter?"

"Answer!" Gytha reached for the tourniquet again.

Svein jerked his arm away. The sudden motion made his gray face stiffen with pain. He mumbled a fragment of an oath.

"Answer, Svein."

Svein closed his eyes with exhaustion. "All right, he was unarmed. We would've killed him, but Hadd the Hard ordered us back. Hadd held up the Fenris sword. I'd never seen it before. It has wavy edges on the blade. And magic runes. It can't ever break."

"They say its sorcery runs deep," Gytha said darkly. "What did Hadd do?"

"He told Harald, 'Now Fenris will comb your hair.' But before he could swing, Harald turned up the end of the banner pole and rammed Hadd in the throat."

"Of course—wood!" Gytha exclaimed, suddenly understanding. Though Fenris had protected Hadd against the steel of warriors, it was powerless against wood. Had Harald known the banner pole was his only usable weapon?

"Would what?"

Gytha caught herself. "Of course the Golden Dragon would save Harald."

Svein shook his head. "It was just a lucky blow. Hadd was caught off balance and dropped Fenris. Before we could think, the Mop grabbed the sword and jumped over to Hadd's ship. He planted his banner pole there and started swinging Fenris two-handed. After that, no one could stop him."

"And the merchant ships? Was that Guthorm's doing?"

Svein nodded feebly. "Agthir fishermen. He must have got them to bring his troops from Tunsberg. At least he won't ever help the Mop again."

"Why?"

320

"Dead. I saw him cut in half by a halberd."

Gytha looked away. Guthorm was to have married Asa's hand-maiden that fall. The marshal's death was but one tragedy among thousands from the battle. That year, nearly every family in Norway would have a name to mourn.

"Eirik's banner fell," she said, hesitating. "Do you know how it happened?"

"We'd just spotted Guthorm's ships. Everyone was getting ready for the attack. Then the men started shouting from ship to ship that Old Eirik had died the straw-death. Not a wound on him. His heart just quit. No mead-drinking in Valhalla for him. He'll be in Niflheim by now, bored till the end of time."

Gytha tried to picture her father's last moments. Victory had seemed at hand. But then the lookouts had warned of the coming ships. The stubborn, white-bearded king had turned his wrinkled face to the blue sails. And he had seen his fetch: Asa's ancient, spiral-prowed dragon-ship relentlessly bearing toward him — as if it were Asa herself, come to him at last.

Svein's head began to sag. "At least Eirik didn't have to see our defeat. All the Viking leaders are dead. Hadd the Hard announced that he was the new King of Horthaland — but he was killed within an hour. He had no heirs. The Vikings have no king. And now the line of Horthaland is dead."

"Not quite, Svein." Gytha held out the dagger in her hand.

His eyes widened. "The black eagle dagger!"

She nodded.

"Where did you get this, Ulf?"

"You know me as Ulf. But I am not the son of Ragnar and Hildirid. You called me a woman in truth. My name is Princess Gytha Eiriksdottir."

"*You?* You're the Gytha who sent Harald to war?"

"And spared your life. I'll have few enough subjects as it is."

Svein looked from the legendary Horthaland dagger to her boyish — womanly? — face. The insults he had heaped upon her in the past flashed before him. "Then — then you rule the Vikings. You're my Queen."

"The only Norwegian royalty Harald hasn't bent to his will."

The Viking sank back, finally giving in to the wounds that had drained so much of his strength. His mouth opened silently. Then his lips pulled into a strange grin. "Does Harald know he's fought so hard to win a smart-ass shepherd?"

Gytha drew herself up at this insolence.

But the Viking was already slipping into the realm of a different sovereign. His eyes rolled back in his head. And then he was still.

Gytha shook him by his tunic. "Wake up, curse it all! You have to live!"

But he did not respond.

Slowly she unclenched her bloodied hands from his shirt. Her eyes grew damp with anguish and regret. Though she once had hated this man, she had never wanted him to die. Now she was Queen, but of what? Her only subject lay dead before her. She had reached the end of the chess board. She was a queen. But there was no victory, no checkmate for her here.

Suddenly the sound of voices shook her from the dead man's gaze.

A shipload of warriors had landed further down the beach. They were marching quickly along the shore. No doubt they were searching among the survivors for suitable slaves. She folded Svein's arms across his chest, so that he might at least confront his enemies with dignity. Then she crouched away from the shore and hid behind a boulder. It was too late now to reach the woods unseen. Her best chance was to hope the troop would pass her by.

For a minute Gytha thought the warriors must be running along the beach in pursuit of an escaping prisoner. The wild-looking man in front certainly seemed driven by desperation. But when he stopped just short of Svein's body, the entire troop froze in its tracks. Incredibly, the forty armed warriors simply waited a dozen yards behind him.

And then, with a rush of alarm, Gytha knew.

It was the king.

Harald stormed about the beach, gesticulating and cursing as if he had gone mad. His head was a mass of yellow hair, with beard and mane grown together into a long shag. His dented armor had torn apart at the chest and hung, clattering, from his broad shoulders. He scanned Svein's body and the battle debris littering the beach. Then he clenched his fists, leaned back his head, and let loose a long, despairing roar.

Watching from behind her rock, Gytha felt her skin rise up in goosebumps.

"Why?" Harald shouted at the sky. "Why do you toy with me?" He drew Fenris from its scabbard and aimed the wavy-edged weapon at the clouds overhead. "Stand, gods, and listen! You give dreams — you raise hopes — and then you turn away! All-knowing powers of the earth and sky, haven't I suffered enough?"

His anguish tore at Gytha's heart. He had come for her, following Queen Asa's vision. He had come to rescue a castaway princess. He had conquered all Norway for that dream and now raved at the gods in despair. But how could she step forward? In his rage he would only scoff at a dirty shepherd boy with short hair and bloodied hands. And what right did he have to demand her from the gods, as if she were a prize? Did he think he alone had suffered in these nine torturous winters?

A gust swept across the fjord, darkening the water as it came. Harald braced his legs apart and faced the wind, the remnants of his torn cloak fluttering. He shook his fist. "Laugh, Odin, at the misery of men! One day, even the age of gods will pass."

When the wind grew stronger, Harald gradually lowered his arm.

"King," a finely-armored noble from the crowd of warriors spoke. "The crew you requested is ready to sail. There is nothing more for you here."

Harald nodded to the man. But before he left he slowly ran his eyes one last time across the beach, searching the flotsam and the rocks of the shore.

Gytha's heart was in her throat. She wanted to stand forward — to run to this man like a carefree girl. But how could she, and keep her pride? For nine winters she had been humiliated because of Harald's reckless pledge. Now, at last, she had a taste of her old power.

The gust of wind passed. Harald strode back along the gravel. And the ravens that had swooped away with the breeze circled back above the shore, screaming.

CHAPTER 26
WINTER, 1905

A freezing fog had blown in off Oslo Fjord, portending more snow. Kirstin paced inside the gateway of the Akershus fortress, trying to keep the chill from penetrating the fur trim of her coat.

The longer she waited the more her resentment grew. What did she really know about this tour group, anyway? The leader, a Mr. Theodore Wooten from Minneapolis, had written to her that the group consisted of wealthy Americans who might be persuaded to support the Oseberg ship's restoration. That description had convinced her to make time for the group, even on a national holiday. But Mr. Wooten had already proven himself unreliable by rescheduling the tour twice. Perhaps he had mixed up the dates after all. More likely, Kirstin thought angrily, he had skipped her tour altogether so his clients could get good positions at the parade.

She was tempted to go join the crowds on Karl Johann Street herself, though the new Norwegian king wasn't expected to arrive in Kristiania until noon.

She puffed warm air into her cupped hands, thinking how unlikely the idea of a Norwegian king would have seemed a year ago, when the Oseberg ship had first been brought to Kristiania. At the brink of war with Sweden, the Norwegians had surprised everyone by calling for a ballot referendum. Out of 368,000 Norwegian voters who went to the polls, only 184 had favored continuing the union with Sweden. In the face of such solidarity, the Swedish king had finally relented, granting Norway independence. The Norwegians had invited a distant descendant of Harald Fairhair, Prince Carl of Denmark, to become their new king. Today he would finally arrive.

Kirstin had almost given up on the arrival of the American tour group when she was startled by the sight of a streetcar careening down the avenue, entirely off its tracks. As the speeding vehicle neared and backfired, she realized that it wasn't a trolley it all. It was an *automobile* — as incongruous on the cobblestone streets of Kristiania as a flying machine. Yet this horseless bus would have stood out even in New York City. Eight black tires supported the oversized chassis. Trunks and suitcases teetered on the roof's luggage rack. Splashed across the side panels in the garish style of a circus wagon were the red-rimmed letters, SAGA TOURS.

The bus squealed to a halt in front of the gateway and backfired one last time. A man with a bowler hat and a black eyepatch stepped down from the driver's seat. He strode up to Kirstin, his hand extended in greeting.

"Kirstin Williams! Great to meet you. Theodore Wooten's the name. Call me Ted. Everyone does."

Kirstin was more than a little put off by the man's loud, chummy manner, particularly because he had kept her waiting so long. The eyepatch was also disconcerting, though his good eye twinkled good-naturedly. She had an uncomfortable feeling that she had met this man before in some other disguise. Perhaps in America?

"I was beginning to wonder if your group would come, Mr. Wooten."

"Wouldn't miss it, you bet." The man cranked a handle on the side of the bus. As the door squeaked open he launched into a rapid-fire spiel. "Ladies and gentlemen, this is *Akershus*. The fortress you see here has been besieged on four occasions — three times by the Swedes and once by the Danes — but has never yielded in battle. Today the fortifications house an arsenal and a prison as well as the famous archeological workshops we'll be visiting. If you'll step this way?"

Mr. Wooten herded a dozen middle-aged tourists to the stone gateway. They stood there, looking cold and a little bored.

"Kirstin Williams, the director of Norwegian antiquities, will be showing us the most elaborate of all Viking-age finds, the Oseberg dragonship. We'll be here just forty-five minutes before moving on to the parade, so please try to stay together. Dr. Williams?"

Kirstin surveyed the small group. The women wore large feathered hats and garish brooches. The men seemed half asleep, yet their shoes were shined and their slacks pressed. Wooten had been right about one thing—they were well-to-do Americans.

"Let's move inside where it's warmer, shall we?" she suggested.

As she led the way across the parade grounds she commented to the tour leader, "You know quite a bit about the local history."

"I try to keep up."

"You overstated my title, though. I'm only the acting director of Norwegian antiquities."

"Right. Whatever did become of Carl?"

Kirstin looked at him uncertainly. "You're acquainted with Dr. Söderfelt?"

"Sure. He's the one I first wrote to. That was over a year ago, back when you found the ship." He lowered his voice. "I really meant to get here ages before this. I hope everything's OK. You've no idea how hectic my business gets."

Kirstin wasn't sure if he was apologizing for making her wait in the cold, or for something else.

"Dr. Söderfelt resigned. And since you asked, he's serving a ten-year sentence in the Stockholm penitentiary for smuggling and grand larceny."

"Oh dear. And what about that other fellow? Hoffman, wasn't it?"

"Doing quite well. He's temporarily assumed my place as associate professor of archeology at Cornell University." Kirstin fished an iron key ring out of her coat pocket and unlocked a massive wooden portal.

As the door swung open the tourists murmured. "Wow." "Will you look at that!"

The Oseberg ship, stretching from one end of the brick-floored storeroom to the other, was lit in stripes by windows set deep into the thick walls. The ancient hull curved gracefully from keel to gunwale, from stem to stern—as functional and sensual as a masterfully built cello.

Kirstin knew the storeroom was too small a cage for the dragonship. The ceiling beams barely cleared the broken-topped prows. There was no room at all for a mast. But she also knew the effect this would have on the tourists, making the ship seem all the larger—a blue whale in an aquarium, a ship in a bottle.

"Welcome to the Oseberg collection of the University of Kristiania," Kirstin began. "The ship you see here and all the other artifacts I'll be showing you on this tour were excavated last year from a farm near

Tønsberg, ninety kilometers south of Kristiania. The find has been dated to between 850 and 900 AD, a period from which we otherwise have very few wooden artifacts. That the Oseberg ship survived at all is a result of being buried four meters deep under an airtight layer of blue clay."

"Someone buried this whole thing on a farm?" a man asked, now obviously awake. "Were they nuts or what?"

Several tourists chuckled.

"Not at all. Ship burial was the traditional method of honoring royalty in Vestfold. This particular ship entombed two women. One of them may have been Queen Asa, grandmother of the first king to rule all Norway, Harald Fairhair."

"Seriously?" It was the same man.

She ignored him this time. She had come to admire Asa, and it irked her when tourists treated the old queen lightly. She continued, "We know from signs of wear on the oarholes that the ship was already old at the time of the burial. Probably it had been out of use for years. Some of the most worn-out gear appears to have been hurriedly patched together, presumably so the ship could be sailed up Oseberg Creek for the funeral."

Kirstin pointed to a plan of the excavation site. "After the ship reached the head of navigation it was dragged overland to a shallow pit. As in all ship burials the prow faced south toward the sea. Vikings believed north led towards Hel. However, the Oseberg burial was unique in several respects. For one thing, the ship contained no weapons. Instead it was filled with some of the most beautifully carved Viking woodwork ever discovered. Another difference was that the ship had been tied to a boulder and completely covered with large rocks."

Although Kirstin recounted these facts with a straightforward tone, she herself had often wondered why the ship had been so securely buried. Rocks might be a logical precaution against grave robbers. But why would Harald Fairhair order his grandmother's ship tied in place with an enormous rope? What had he feared?

"Any questions before we move on?"

A woman tentatively raised her hand. "You said a queen was buried with the ship. Where do you have the bones?"

For an instant Kirstin thought of the Oseberg farm wife and her sorcery. But the tourist before her was no eerie-eyed witch. She was a harmless-looking matron with spectacles.

Kirstin replied, "All of the human remains were analyzed and then reinterred in the Oseberg mound when it was being refilled."

"Oh, that's nice."

The woman's response made Kirstin dismiss her doubts. "Then if you'll follow me we'll take a look at the restoration laboratory."

She led the group into a storeroom thick with the pungent, wharf-like smell of creosote. Rows of wood fragments lay arrayed on the uneven brick floor. Ledgers, trays, and brushes cluttered workbenches below the windows.

"Restoration of the bronze and iron artifacts has been relatively straightforward, since we could rely on established procedures. But no one had ever unearthed wood carvings of this age before. If the wood dries out, it shrivels. If it freezes, it disintegrates. After much experimentation we've learned that harder woods such as oak can be steamed and then successfully creosoted. Pine and other soft woods have to be boiled sixteen hours in a solution of alum, dried over a period of weeks, impregnated with linseed oil, and finally lacquered."

"You haven't done all that to the ship?" a tourist asked.

"I'm afraid so. The ship was dismantled, treated piece by piece, and then reassembled."

The tourist whistled. "A heck of a job."

"It was. But we still have much to do. Most of the artifacts had been crushed by the stones piled on top of the ship." Kirstin pointed to a table full of wood fragments, some with bits of finely carved relief. "This sled, for example, was found in over a thousand pieces. And it is only one of four such sleds from the ship."

"This thing here looks in good shape," Mr. Wooten commented, casually reaching as if to pick up one of the dragonhead posts.

Kirstin caught his arm in time. "*Please* do not touch anything."

"Sorry. It looked so fresh."

"Actually it's a reproduction. I commissioned artists to carve copies of the most significant artifacts, including all four of the dragonhead posts."

As always when she saw the dragonhead posts she remembered the night she had discovered them with Magnus. And as always she felt a pang of guilt to think that she had misjudged Magnus so badly.

But how could she expect to understand men, when she couldn't understand a simple puzzle like the dragonhead posts? The Vikings obviously thought these elegant sculptures were significant, but why? She hoped none of the tourists would think of asking what the oddly truncated posts had been used for.

Mr. Wooten fixed her with his one good eye. "So what do you suppose these posts were used for?"

"We're not certain," she said coldly. God, what an annoying person he was! She moved on to the artifacts at next table.

"Here we have our most delicate restoration job, the tapestries found in the ship's grave chamber. All of the linen warp-threads have rotted away, leaving the woolen patterns unsupported and extremely fragile. Looms were small in Viking times, so you'll notice the tapestries are only twenty centimeters wide. But just look at the figures crowded into these fragments—horses, wagons, men with spears, women with long trains. Nowhere else in the archeological record do we have evidence of the colors of Viking life."

"Lovely," the matronly tourist said, studying the tapestry through her lorgnette. "Did this help you figure out the colors of the Vikings' sails?"

Kirstin cleared her throat. The group was asking all the wrong questions. "Surprisingly, none of the tapestries shows a ship. We don't know the color of Viking sails, even from the sagas."

"Oh." The woman's voice fell.

By now Kirstin thought it unlikely she could wheedle much in the way of donations from the group. Still, she had to try or the whole morning would have been wasted. "If you'll come this way, the final exhibit is kept in my office."

She led them down a corridor and up a short flight of stairs to a circular room inside one of the fortress's stone towers. There she gathered them around a table with a glass case. Inside was a model of a cross-shaped building with a tall, arched roof and many windows.

"This is the future I see for the Oseberg finds. We obviously aren't able to display the exhibits properly in our quarters here, and the university's historical museum is already overcrowded. My goal is to build a new Viking ship museum with four wings. The first wing would house the Oseberg ship. The second and third wings could display the less well-preserved burial ships from Gokstad and Tune. Both of those ships have been stored in temporary sheds at the university for over twenty years. The museum's fourth wing would have room for the sleds, the wagon, the dragonhead posts, the tapestries, and all the other artifacts buried with the Oseberg queen."

"Where would this museum be?" a tourist asked.

"On the island of Bygdøy, in Oslo Fjord." Kirstin walked to the tower's deep-set window overlooking the eastern harbor. The snow-storm had finally set in, wrapping the harbor and the fjord in a sheet of speckled gray. A lone, ghost-like ship drifted through the storm. "On a clear day you can see the ferry terminal connecting the city with the island. The National Norwegian Museum has already been built on Bygdøy, funded largely by private subscriptions. A Viking ship hall would fit right in."

She returned to the group, ready now to launch into her pitch for donations.

But Mr. Wooten interrupted. "Hey, you've got runes!" He had discovered the banner pole mounted on the wall beside Kirstin's desk. "Were these in the grave mound, too?"

"Yes," she said, trying to hide her irritation.

"Can you translate it?"

She let out a long breath. It seemed as though her attempt at fund raising had been doomed to fail from the first. "It says 'litiluism,' and no, we haven't been able to translate it."

The tour leader frowned at the inscription. "Litiluism? I'd think you'd at least have a guess."

"There are plenty of theories." The fact was, she kept the pole beside her desk because this was the riddle that bothered her most of all. She knew she had seen this banner pole somewhere in her dreams. If she could only read the runes, everything else might fall into place. It even seemed possible the tormenting dreams might finally end.

"Is this what you're calling a U here?," the one-eyed tour guide asked, pointing. "Couldn't it be a V instead?"

Kirstin nodded cautiously. "Yes, U's and V's were written the same. Do you know the runic system?"

"It's a hobby. Helps on tours to old places. Runes aren't all that tough to recognize. There's only sixteen, and a lot of them look like regular letters."

"I suppose they do."

"So what about these theories of yours? Is the inscription a curse or what?"

Kirstin glanced to the tour group. They seemed almost as interested in the runes as their leader. "Actually, one of the theories does use a V."

"Then you've got 'litilvism.' What's that mean?"

"Nothing, as a single word. But it could be read it as three separate words, all run together. The first part, 'litil,' would be clear enough. In Old Norse *litill* means 'little.' The word *vis* means 'knows'. That would only leave the single letter M, which was called the 'man-rune.' All together, 'litil-vis-m' could mean 'little knows man.'"

"'Little knows man.'" Mr. Wooten grinned. "In other words, 'People don't know much.' Perfect! I like it."

The matronly tourist ventured, "I wonder if a Viking would say something like that."

"I bet not," her husband added.

The tour leader raised his eyebrow. "Then maybe the M doesn't stand for man after all. It could represent something else. Maybe it's someone's initial. What you need to think of is a name that starts with an M. How about that, Doctor?"

Kirstin flushed. She *had* read it that way, torturing herself that the name that fit best was the one she had lost—Magnus. How did the tour guide know precisely which taunts would wound her? Who did he think he was?

Mr. Wooten pulled a handkerchief out of his pocket with a theatrical flair. Then, to Kirstin's horror, he began rubbing his handkerchief on the pole.

She grabbed his arm. "*Please* don't touch anything."

"I was just cleaning things up. Sorry."

She put her hand to her forehead. Not only had the tour guide given her a headache, he had made her lose her train of thought. Perhaps it didn't matter. Now she just wanted some time to herself.

"Well then, if there are no more questions, I think that pretty much concludes our tour." She walked across the office and held open a door that led to the parade grounds.

Mr. Wooten's face fell. "I guess that is the end." He sighed. "Well, it's time we went to see the arrival of the king anyway. Ladies and gentlemen, the bus is waiting." He held out his hand to the door to encourage them.

Several of the tourists made a special point of thanking Kirstin as they passed by. "It was all so very interesting," said the woman with the spectacles. Another woman added, "And I hope everything works out with the museum. Do you think it will, Thorvald?" The woman's husband nodded, "Bound to." Then they pulled their collars close against the snowstorm and made their way back across the broad parade grounds.

Mr. Wooten held back, his face still lowered. Standing in the snow with his bowler in his hand, he suddenly looked very old, and Kirstin felt a little sorry she had been so abrupt. She wondered again if she had seen him before. But the only image that came to mind was from one of the nightmares at Oseberg. And she knew that memory had only been jolted loose because of the man's eye patch.

"I didn't mean for it to end like this," Mr. Wooten said.

"I understand."

"I doubt it. Nobody understands anymore. People think they can do everything by themselves. The wolf's loose again and people don't even hear the alarm."

"Honestly. What are you talking about?"

He looked at her. "I'm getting old and weak."

"Well you can't change that any more than you can change the weather."

"I wish I could change that too."

She couldn't help smiling. "I guess we all wish for things we can't have."

Mr. Wooten considered this a moment. "Yes. Unless one wishes hard enough." He put on his hat. "Well goodbye, then, and thank you for the tour."

"You're welcome." She surprised herself by adding, "If you'd like to bring another tour group, let me know."

"I'm afraid my business won't bring me back this way again for quite some time. Take care, Doctor." As Mr. Wooten turned to go, his good eye fluttered—a blink perhaps, or a wink. "And be careful the next time you wish."

Kirstin watched him fade into the snowstorm, wondering about the peculiar old tour leader. He had been articulate at times and incoherent at others. Perhaps the poor fellow fit in better at home in America.

She had been away from that country too long to know for sure.

She sighed at the thought of America. What was it, really, that held her in Norway? Her parents and friends in New York wrote almost every week, asking when she would return. Even her dean at Cornell kept writing, wondering if he should hire Otto permanently in her place. She told them all she was staying to solve the Oseberg excavation's archeological puzzles. She had told herself the same thing. But now, standing on the edge of the vast, vacant Akershus parade grounds, staring into the oblivion of snow, she had to admit it was only part of the truth.

She had stayed for Magnus. Of course it sounded foolish, waiting for a man she herself had turned away. Yet why else had she chosen an office overlooking the harbor? She had spent countless hours watching the Navy ships come and go, wondering which one might be his. And why else had she led so many tours? In the back of her mind she knew Magnus would come one day to see the ship they had saved. The truth was, the preservation work had settled into a routine. Her supervision was no longer essential. She had stayed in Norway because she had lost something here. She had lost a chance at love, and she knew she was being a fool to wish it back.

But she wished it back all the same.

Then, shivering, she turned toward her office.

She was climbing the steps to the door when she noticed a white figure leaning against the stone wall. In the shadows of the eave, it could have been anything. Except that she imagined it had moved.

"Hello?" she asked uncertainly.

"Hello." The shape pushed off from the wall. It drifted forward, slowly taking the form of a large man. The man wore a white military coat and cap.

"Magnus?" Could he have been standing there all this time?

He looked down at his hands.

"What on earth are you doing here?"

"I—I don't know."

"Well, come inside. You must be half frozen." She paused. "Or did you only come because you're still angry with me?"

"Angry? No, not angry."

"You should be." She gave an embarrassed shrug. "I'm sorry I acted the way I did that night on the tugboat."

He shook his head, his unruly red beard only partly tamed by a military trim. "I wasn't quite fair with you either, Kirstin."

It was so good to hear him say her name that she stood there a moment speechless. She almost wondered if she were only imagining what she saw. Would he vanish if she turned away?

"It *is* cold out here." He began turning up the collar of his white naval overcoat.

"Come in, please." She hurried up the steps and opened the door. "They don't heat my office much on Sundays but I can put some coal on."

While she emptied the coal hod into the heater she watched Magnus out of the corner of her eye. He hung his overcoat on a hook by the door, revealing the crisp dress white uniform of an officer. Then he glanced about the room, taking in the various artifacts and drawings mounted on the walls. Finally he took off his braid-trimmed cap and leaned over the glass display case.

"A model of a church?"

She smiled. "It's a museum I'd like to build for the dragonship."

"Good idea.

"Or should I say, for *your* dragonship?"

He wrinkled his brow. "Kirstin, the rights were transferred to the university almost a year ago. I'd rather people didn't know I was involved in that end of the business."

"You gave up *Skiblathnir* to buy the excavation rights. I know how much that sailboat meant to you."

"I've put it out of my mind. You should too."

"If you wanted me to forget, why did you come?"

Magnus shook his head as if he wasn't sure of the answer himself. He walked over to Kirstin's desk, picked up the old wooden flute she kept there, and turned it slowly in his big hands. "I used to listen to you play, down by the creek at night. I'd be standing watch in the excavation, working by lamplight."

"I didn't think anyone could hear."

"I listened a lot." He smiled wistfully. "One song in particular struck me. An old folk tune that stopped without sounding finished. I've had a lot of time to think, out on the frigate, running coast patrol. I kept hearing that broken-off song, wondering how it's really supposed to end."

"That's the way it's always been, ending suddenly."

Magnus held out the flute to her. In his big hand the wooden pipe looked as fragile as a straw. "Do you think you could make up a different ending this time?"

"If you'd like."

"I'd like."

When she reached for the flute her hand rested a moment in his palm. The warm touch sent a tingle down her spine. Then she lifted the flute to her lips.

Kirstin put her heart into the music, starting each phrase softly but soaring toward the end. The haunting old melody crept through the room, lingering from the curved stone walls. The wooden flute gave the notes a breathy undertone, like an April wind in pine woods.

Magnus closed his eyes, intent. Then he turned, viewing the wall displays as he listened.

When the melody halted abruptly on the second tone of the scale, Kirstin paused only long enough for a quick breath. Then she improvised, flying up the scale, skipping down by thirds, blending in fragments of the old tune. Finally she concluded firmly on the tonic, where she had always known it should end.

"That was perfect. You play like it comes natural to you."

She shrugged aside the compliment. "I don't have much time to practice, what with the work. You've heard, I suppose, how difficult it's been to preserve the artifacts."

"I was just noticing how well you've restored the banner pole. Even the runes are clearer."

"They are?"

"The last one, anyway." He pointed to the inscription. "Without the smudges, it looks more like an 'I' than an 'M'."

She stared at the letter. In sixteen-sign futhark, an 'I' was a single line while an 'M' was a line ending in a dot. But now the dot on the pole looked like an accidental chip in the wood's grain. At once she thought of the tour leader. He had wiped the inscription with his handkerchief. But that couldn't really have affected the runes. The inscription itself was no different. All that had changed was the way she interpreted it.

"Litiluisi," Magnus said. "Not any word I know."

"No, not litiluisi." Then inspiration struck her like a bolt. "But what about *litil visi?*"

He looked at her, eyebrows raised. Then he laughed.

"What's the matter? Why couldn't it be 'litil visi'?"

"Oh it could, it could," Magnus said, still chuckling. "It's just that's the nickname I've always used secretly for you, Kirstin. 'Litil visi' — the Little Chieftain."

Suddenly the walls shook and a deafening roar blasted the air.

She held Magnus's arm for support.

He smiled. "Never heard cannons up close?"

Another blast rocked the fortress.

"For gods' sake, Magnus, who's firing at us?"

"No one." He walked her to the window as yet another detonation rattled the walls. "Akershus is giving a twenty-one-gun salute."

The snowstorm outside had cleared enough that Kirstin could make out a ship beside the bunting-draped dock below. Rows of sailors in dress white uniforms lined the wharf.

"The king." She looked to Magnus. "That's why you're in Kristiania, isn't it? You were supposed to be down there with the others when he arrived."

He frowned, but didn't deny it.

"Why aren't you there?"

"My first officer will have the crew organized."

"But you can't just walk off."

"I haven't been in town for ages. I wanted to see you."

"When every other sailor in Norway is in formation to meet the new king?"

He pressed his lips together. "I'll lose my commission, it's true. But they don't really need me, now that things have settled." He looked in her eyes. "And damn it, Kirstin, I've missed you."

His confession left her light-headed, and a little frightened. His presence had already suffused her office with an intoxicating blend of subtle scents — starched uniforms, ship rigging, and leather. His forthright, broad-shouldered stance had the same attraction she had forced herself to resist during the months of excavation work together.

"Every day I wrote you a letter," he said, "and every day I tore it up. All of them said the same thing — what I'd told you last year on the tugboat. Once a man's love is refused, it isn't fair for him to burden her with daily reminders."

A cannon's boom rattled the window unnoticed.

She drew closer to him, her head lowered. "As soon as you left, I realized how much of a mistake I had made, letting you go." Then she lifted her eyes. "I've missed you too, Magnus."

He folded his arms about her. In a moment his lips were kissing her hair, and then her neck, and then her half-open mouth. His powerful hands slid from her shoulders down along her back, pulling her against him. Distantly she felt the room shudder from the cannons' blasts. It seemed to her as if she were floating in the warmth of this dream — as if the terrors of the nightmares were melting away.

Finally Magnus leaned back with his arms about her waist, admiring her. "I should have known the Little Chieftain would want love on her own terms. You should have been a queen."

"The new king's not my type."

"Then I did right, leaving him at the dock?"

"Absolutely." She leaned her head against his chest. "Let him find another captain."

He stroked her hair contemplatively. "It's time I left the reserves anyway. I have a few business ideas."

"In Tønsberg, I suppose." Her voice fell. Kristiania had been a lonely place to wait for him, but she had had her work. There would be nothing for her in a provincial town like Tønsberg.

"Actually I've been thinking about going into shipping. I fixed up *Sleipnir* and traded for a steamer. It's not big, but I thought I might open a freight route to America."

"With an office in Kristiania?"

"Copenhagen, actually. And New York. I could anchor myself in either of those two towns if you'd like." He tilted his head questioningly. "Would you like, Little Chieftain?"

The last of the cannons boomed, and the crowds outside roared.

Kirstin smiled. She had been given the chance to rewrite her own saga.

CHAPTER 27
SPRING, 882

Fall gave way to winter in the fjordlands, and winter gave way to spring. Petals from the apple trees drifted down the green slopes to land on the lapping waves. Clouds scudded above the waterfalls toward a glint of bluish ice — the fjell glacier, where winter never waned.

A melancholy melody floated past the halls of Stavanes. High on a slope above the old settlement, where dandelions and new grass had begun to cover an earthen mound as large as a house, Gytha was playing her wooden flute. Her blond hair, grown long again, draped about the fur trim of a royal Horthaland cloak. She often climbed to this spot in the hours following the afternoon meal. Ragnar would be napping and Hildirid would be bickering with the slaves. It was peaceful up here, playing her minor tune beside her father's tomb.

Since the battle of Hafrsfjord she had thought about Harald far more often than she wished. Traveling skalds told how the king had cut and combed his hair in Tunsberg to celebrate his victory over the Viking alliance. The sagas related how he had changed his name from Harald the Unkempt to Harald Fairhair, king of all Norway. But none of the verses told of the great king's infatuation with a country girl from Valdres. Perhaps the man had been changed by the magnitude of his success. Perhaps he had never loved her at all. When she thought back upon his tormented search on the Hafrsfjord beach, remembering his every word, it was painfully clear that he had been looking for a missing comrade instead of a princess.

Gytha's melody ended abruptly, as it always had, on the second tone of the scale. She laid the flute on the rock beside her. She told herself she was glad to be forgotten. After all, her father had died in the battle against Harald. Later, after Harald had sailed away, she had been able to bring Ragnar and Hildirid to Stavanes to help manage the home estate she had inherited. To be sure, the land was only a tiny portion of Eirik's former kingdom, but it was enough to support a good life. She even called herself Queen in this small branch of Horthangr Fjord, and no one bothered to dispute her authority. Harald had appointed Gilling administrator of Horthaland — the same Gilling who had helped her escape from Stavanes years before. Now, as a governing jarl, he seemed quite willing to turn a blind eye to Gytha's claims.

She surveyed the curving bit of fjord before her, a miniature kingdom. Why wasn't she happy? She felt no ambition to extend her rule. She had never really cared for governing. At times it seemed as if the torments of the past ten winters had simply pressed the joy out of her, like oil from a seed. Once she had been a wild young girl — naughty, arrogant, flirtatious. Such immaturity would not befit a queen. But did that mean she had to be so miserably staid?

On an impulse she snatched up her flute, stood on top the mound, and blew the wild and beautiful call of the *fagurfugl*. She had teased Ragnar about that legendary bird of fortune so often when she was a child. Now it seemed as though the melodious song represented all the happiness and freedom and love she had dreamed might be hers.

The last of the trills echoed from the fjord's far walls. She stood there a long moment, listening to the music die away. Finally all that remained was the rush of distant waterfalls. With a heavy heart she lowered her head and began walking down the path to the halls.

But then, to her astonishment, a faint trill resounded from high on the valley rim. She stopped and stared up at the forests. Impossible!

Suddenly she grabbed up her hem and began hurrying up the slope. She knew it was madness to think the lucky bird had really answered, but she had heard it so clearly.

Or had she only imagined it? She stopped at the edge of a small, steep meadow and caught her breath. Then she blew another phrase of the melodious call on her flute.

This time there was no answer. Instead she heard a crashing in the forest brush, as if a deer had been startled her way. When the hoofbeats grew clearer, she realized how foolish she had been. Stavanes was one of the closest settlements to the Horthangr Wastes, the refuge of outlaws and robbers. Since the collapse of the Viking alliance, a new breed of desperate men had retreated into the mountains. Her call must have alerted them to an easy target. And now she was too far from the halls to reach help.

She ducked behind a tree, her hand on the dagger at her waist.

Within moments a horseman charged out of the brush and reined his steed in the middle of the meadow. The man had a blond beard, a coarse woolen cloak, and short, wind-blown hair. A long sword hung at his side. His eyes swept the forest about the opening. Then he cupped his hands to his lips and whistled the *fagurfugl's* call.

Gytha watched him, calculating. The robber was smaller than she had expected, and rather young, but his manner was full of purpose.

The horseman listened a moment intently, then sprang to the ground. "I tell you, it's her, Faxi," he said to his shaggy-maned horse. "We're close enough now we'll walk. That's a boy."

He threw his cloak over his shoulder and led the horse across the meadow, almost directly toward Gytha. The tree she had hidden behind was so small she was certain to be discovered. She decided to take the offensive. As long as the man was alone and on foot, surprise would give her an advantage.

When he neared the tree she jumped into his path, her dagger at his chest. "Hands in the air!"

He dropped the reins but kept his hands poised.

"Up, I said!"

He let out a breath of resignation and slowly lifted his arms.

She nodded. "Very good. Now I'll have your sword and your name."

"I have your name first." He ventured a smile. "Only the Queen of Stavanes would assault strangers with the infamous Horthaland dagger."

"I can defend my kingdom as well as any man."

When he began to lower his hands she touched the dagger's tip below his lower rib—precisely where the Vikings had instructed her that a thrust to the heart should begin.

Promptly the hands went back up. "So I see. But how am I to give you my sword with my hands in the air?"

Without reply she unbuckled the scabbard left-handed.

He raised an eyebrow. "You seem well-practiced with men's belts."

"More than you would know. Now state your name and your business in my kingdom."

"My name is Harald, and I've come to give you this." He lowered his left hand just enough to fold the cloak back from his shoulder. Beneath was a gold clasp in the shape of a dragon with a red-jeweled eye.

For a moment she stood speechless. It was the clasp she had given Harald years ago. Or was this an impostor? She studied the trim-bearded face before her. Certainly it bore little resemblance to the wild-haired man she had seen on the beach of Hafrsfjord. But perhaps there really was a dim reflection of the boy from the Vik, changed by age into a strong-featured, high-browed man.

Anger, suspicion, and curiosity boiled through her by turns. Her heart had begun to race, too, and she couldn't say why. She did not lower the dagger. "If you're Harald, where are your ships?"

"I never liked sailing. A weak stomach, I guess."

"You expect me to believe you rode here alone, across the Wastes?"

"I heard you crossed them yourself a time or two."

"But Harald travels with an army."

"I've come to plead my case, not to wage war." He smiled painful-ly. "Of course I hadn't expected the *fagurfugl* stunt. This will be harder to live down than the time you pretended to be dead at the Vik."

Only Harald would know the circumstances of their first meeting.

"Then it really is you," she marveled. His words and his manner were as disarmingly frank as they had been long ago. She realized now that most of the anger she had felt over the years toward Harald had been aimed at a stone-hearted military king—perhaps an image she had invented out of resentment? The young man she saw was not the angry warrior she had imagined.

"Yes. It's me." He hesitated. "Do I still have to keep my hands in the air?"

She considered this, enjoying for a moment the thought that Harald Fairhair, King of all Norway, had probably never stood so defenseless before. Then she put away her dagger—and buckled his sword belt about her own waist.

He lowered his arms. "I've wanted so badly to talk to you again. It seems I haven't thought of anything else all these years."

She tossed her head and began walking on the path down the hill. Would he really have wanted to talk with her during his Great War, when she was suffering as a shepherd boy on a poor farm? She thought it unlikely.

Harald picked up his horse's reins to follow—but the horse was busy grazing after its three-day trip across the barren Wastes. "Come on, Faxi!" He pulled the horse out of the meadow and hurried after Gytha.

When he had caught up he said, "I'd understand, Gytha, if you're angry."

"Angry?" She confronted him, hands on her hips. "You leave me for ten winters, kill my father, rob me of my inheritance, and then ask if I'm angry?"

The horse impatiently bumped Harald in the back, making his apologetic gesture seem all the more awkward. "I grieve for Eirik, too. I never wanted him to die—or anyone else, for that matter. I'm not a berserker. I'm not even a warrior at heart. But once there was an impetuous girl who asked me to conquer thirty kingdoms." He looked her in the eyes. "In a more perfect world, Eirik would have married my grandmother."

She turned thoughtfully and continued down into the burial mound's meadow. "You know about Eirik and Asa?"

"Yes."

"Why didn't they marry? From what I've heard, Asa's first husband was dead by then."

He shook his head. "The gods stood in their way."

"I suppose if the gods make a mistake they don't admit it." She stopped beside the mound, watching the breeze ripple the fresh grass. "Eirik built this mound for me, you know. I hated him then. Ironic, isn't it? Now that he's buried here instead, I come to mourn him almost every day."

"I understand."

"I doubt it." She turned on him, angry again. "If you understand so much, why weren't you here? Where were you when I was burying my dead?"

"I had my own dead to mourn."

She realized she had spoken too quickly. "There was your uncle."

"Guthorm. A great man and a friend."

"He won the battle at Hafrsfjord for you." She had seen how close Harald came to losing that fight. Harald had certainly not conquered Norway on his own.

"I know." Harald lowered his head. "He also brought word that Asa was dying. A week after I reached Tunsberg, she was gone."

Gytha regretted having pushed him so far. "I didn't know that."

"The skalds don't recite sagas about women, even if they shake Asgard," Harald said.

"I met her once. She seemed — subtle."

Harald nodded. "Her subtlety hid more power than anyone will ever know. I buried Asa in her dragonship with all her belongings — her wagon, her weavings, her Agthir banner, her dragon high seat pillars. Even her handmaiden, Mari."

She looked at him coolly. "You killed her servant?"

"No. Mari had been planning to marry Guthorm. She never recovered from the news that he was dead. A week later, after Asa had died, we found Mari on a bluff overlooking the sea to the south. She had eaten the death cap mushroom."

Gytha sighed. "You and I are no longer the children who played games at the Vik."

"An age has passed, an age of hatreds and jealousies. I want to start over."

"And so you ride into my kingdom protected by a magic sword, invulnerable to the steel of warriors. Even now, only a woman was able to disarm you by force."

He shrugged. "If you believe that, look at the sword."

She lifted the gold hilt from the long scabbard at her waist. The blade was beautifully crafted, but had no wavy edge and no runic inscription. It was definitely not Fenris. "Surely you haven't trusted someone else to wear the Viking sword?"

"No one can be trusted with such a weapon. Fenris was buried with Asa. It was her last request."

She nodded slowly, trying to piece together what she knew about Harald's grandmother. "I always wondered if Asa was driven by revenge. How does the verse go? 'Fenris vests the Vikings' fate.' By taking the sword to her grave, she's finished their saga until Ragnarök."

"There's more to it than that."

"The skalds say Asa's father was slain by the first Vikings. Now, a lifetime later, she's used you to settle the score."

"Listen to me, Gytha." He turned her by the arm to face him. "When Asa was dying she told me about the curse behind the sword's magic.

The wolf-god himself helped forge Fenris. The sword was made inde-structible, but at a terrible price. Evil and violence spread among the sword's followers like a disease. Fenris made the Vikings what they were."

Gytha considered this. "Then even my father might have been af-fected."

"Of course. Anyone could be. That's why I not only buried Fenris in Asa's dragonship, I anchored the ship in place, covered it with boul-ders, and built the biggest mound in Norway."

A new fear caught Gytha. "Did Asa tell anyone else about the sword?"

"Only Mari. And I've told no one but you." He unpinned the clasp from his shoulder. "That's why I want to give this back."

Gytha considered the offer. "When you bargain for a secret, you can't undo the trade."

"No, but with Fenris buried, does the secret count anymore?"

She weighed the gold ornament in her hand. "I don't want to owe you for a gift now any more than I did at the Vik. Do you have a hap-pier secret for sale?"

He laughed. "I'm not made of mysteries. That was Asa's way."

"Then tell me one of hers. People say she had second sight."

"She did have visions." He put his foot on a rock and stared past the burial mound. "Once she told me she'd seen her dragonship roll-ing toward the ocean on wheels."

Gytha started, suddenly remembering that once, long ago, she too had had a peculiar dream of a dragonship on wheels. "But—but that prophecy never came to pass."

"No, we rolled the ship away from the ocean, on logs."

"What else did she claim to see?"

"She said that you'd survived the battle after all—that I'd find you here in Stavanes this spring."

Gytha reddened just slightly. She wondered if Harald had made this up, or if Asa had really prophesied their meeting. And if so, had Asa foretold what would happen next? Would Harald be sent back across the Wastes empty handed, or would he be invited into the hall? She herself had not yet decided.

She looked at him askance. "You've yet to tell me a genuine secret. If Asa had visions, tell me something no one else in Norway would know. Something about the distant future."

"The distant future?" He frowned out across the fjord, thinking. His grandmother had talked of ages beyond their own. Strange times, terrible times, and beyond that—

"Well?" Gytha asked.

"She said—" Harald caught himself, unsure if he should go on. He turned to her earnestly. "She said she had seen a time when Fenris and all of its evil was gone from the face of the earth. A time when men no longer studied fighting, and women no longer studied revenge. There were no raids and no wars. There was only peace. Peace, everywhere."

"And do you believe that?"

"Yes. I do."

She studied him—an intense, idealistic, young man. A dreamer who had won an empire on a foolish young girl's dare. Norway might never again know such an unlikely king. In that moment her heart went out to him, and she knew where the future would lead.

"Norway hasn't seen much peace under your rule so far," she chided.

"It's time that changed."

"Then you'll leave the Kingdom of Stavanes independent, despite the challenge I once gave you?"

He raised an eyebrow. "I don't recall ever being asked to conquer the *queens* of Norway."

With a smile, she hooked his arm in hers and led him down the path to the halls.

Epilogue
Spring, 1905

Groa Hansen crouched atop the remains of the Oseberg mound, sprinkling flakes from a bottle across the coals of a small fire. A sword-shaped tongue of fire shot up before her, gleaming in her mismatched, green and blue eyes. The glow hovered a moment like a fiery rune. Then it vanished into smoke. In the distance, the insane, yipping howl of a wolf drifted through the twilight.

Now she knew for certain why grave robbers had tunneled into the mound so soon after the burial. It wasn't for the bones. The thieves had known exactly what they wanted. The wolf-god Fenris was loose.

She sighed and turned toward the dying light of day in the west. There would be no happy ending after all. War after war might drag the world toward Ragnarök before its time.

The old woman frowned. A dark century loomed, and no one was prepared. Nights of restless dreams lay ahead. She would have to begin her long quest all over again.

Acknowledgments

Many museums helped in my research of this book—notably the Viking ship museums in Oslo, Roskilde, and Haithabu (Hedeby), and the open-air museums in Oslo, Tønsberg, Lom, Lillehammer, Trelleborg, Lyngby, and Hjerl Hede. At the annual Viking Meet in Moesgård, Denmark, I rode a Viking ship and watched Viking armies battle. I'm also grateful for those who assisted during my travels—the late Svend and Gudrun Jensen of Vester Skerninge; Lisbet Jensen and Mogens Mikkelsen of Øster Skerninge; Gitte Tvedeskov of Hørsholm; Knut and Janna Haugen of Tønsberg; Randi and Tore Ellertsen of Bergen; and the late Karen Westermann of Laholm.

In the United States, I owe thanks to the University of Oregon library and to the Library of Congress in Washington, DC, where I studied the five-volume official publication of the Oseberg excavation, *Osebergfunnet*. I'm also indebted to Martha Bayless, Talbot Bielefeldt, Barbara Emashowski, Norman Barrett, Lee Kirk, Leslie What, Howard Wade, Paul Hash, Brenda Shaw, and Pat Murphy for reading the manuscript and offering editorial advice.

My biggest debt, however, is to my family, who shared both the mundane trials of a writer's existence and the more adventurous trials of my research. Together with my wife Janell Sorensen and my children, Karen and Ian, I spent a chilly night camped in the Horthangr Wastes (Hardangervidda) and climbed to the windswept edge of the Troll's High Seat (Prekestolen) above Lysefjord. With Janell I backpacked four days across the glacial landscape of Jotunheimen, hitchhiked the length of Norway's rugged western fjordlands, sailed a fishing boat through a storm in Tønsberg Fjord, and skied across Nordmarka in January. In all of my writings, Janell's enthusiasm and fortitude have been a source of strength and inspiration. This book is for her.

AUTHOR'S NOTE

While it would be inappropriate to include footnotes in any historical novel, readers may be interested to know which portions of *The Ship in the Hill* are historical and which are novel.

Throughout the book, Karen Sullivan's pen-and-ink illustrations of artifacts are based on historic photographs of actual Viking-age objects, most of them unearthed at Oseberg.

The story contained in the Viking-age chapters is based on the *Heimskringla*, a saga of the kings of Norway written in Old Icelandic during the twelfth century by Snorri Sturluson. Snorri's saga condenses the harrowing tale of Asa's capture and Guthroth's subsequent murder into a single paragraph. A quotation in that paragraph indicates that this particular story was scavenged from a still earlier (and otherwise lost) work, the *Ynglingatal,* a saga composed by Thjotholf in honor of Rognvald the Glorious.

As in all sagas, poetic license may have led to exaggeration, but Snorri's description of Asa has the ring of truth. I have embellished the tale by giving Asa's servant a personality (Kalf), by suggesting Eirik of Horthaland as a rival to Guthroth, and by inventing the sword Fenris.

The derivation of the word "Viking" is a matter of much debate. I support the theory that these island-loving seamen were originally based on the only Norwegian island named "Vik," located in the protected waters near present-day Larvik. Just three kilometers away, on the mainland, lies the ninth-century site of Norway's earliest market village, identified in this book as the legendary Skiringssal. Excavation has shown that this village had a wealth of imported goods and yet had no defensive structures. Might the village have relied for its defense, and its wealth, on a nearby garrison of Vikings?

The stories of Halfdan the Black and of Harald Fairhair are supported by material in one other work, the *Fagrskinna*, an anonymous prose history from the early Middle Ages. However, Snorri's *Heimskringla* is the more thorough of the two extant histories. Snorri's text tells how Halfdan rescued Ragnhild from the berserker Haki, relates Ragnhild's prophetic dream, describes how Harald fled the enraged Halfdan at the age of ten, explains how Harald defended Vestfold with Guthorm as marshal, and provides an outline of the wonderful tale of Princess Gytha's haughty challenge.

I have omitted a few marriages to reduce confusion. According to both sources, Halfdan the Black was briefly married to another woman before Ragnhild, and Harald Fairhair married dozens of women besides Gytha once he conquered all of Norway.

I have also added a number of incidents to fill out the story. For example, although neither Snorri nor the *Fagrskinna* mentions Asa after the death of Guthroth, it is reasonable to assume that such a strong-willed queen would continue to exert influence, particularly in light of the importance accorded her burial. Similarly, the old sagas mention Eirik and Hadd the Hard only in passing, despite their historical significance. Mari, Paalo, Gilling, Horth, Hildirid, and Svein are my own fictional inventions.

I have handled the chapters set in 1904-05 somewhat differently. A great deal is known about the Oseberg excavation, and I have tried to describe the unearthed artifacts as accurately as possible. However, all of the characters I have portrayed in these chapters are entirely fictional. Ownership of the artifacts was in fact an issue, but it was resolved by a donation of twelve thousand crowns from Fritz Treschow of Larvik. The Swedish king, Gustaf Adolf, was extremely interested in the excavation but had no designs on the artifacts; on the contrary, it was the king's suggestion that led Mr. Treschow to donate the ship to Norway. Nonetheless, it is true that political tensions with Sweden ran high during this final year of the union with Norway.

One of the advantages of a historical novel is that the author can speculate freely about questions that puzzle historians. Certainly the artifacts unearthed at Oseberg cry out for this kind of conjecture.

For example, the four exquisitely carved dragonhead posts had originally been identified by archeologists as "probably" designed for "religious processions of one sort or another." Meanwhile, the sagas tell us that a Viking family's most prized possessions were its intricately carved high seat pillars—posts that were so highly valued they were taken with the family on ship voyages. For years, archeologists claimed that no example of a high seat pillar had ever been found. This book joins those who now suggest that the mysterious dragonhead posts are in fact examples of such pillars.

The interpretation of the Oseberg ship's runic pole also leaves room for speculation. According to a leading theory, we are asked to believe that this pole is an oar with both the handle and the blade broken off, and that the runes were carved by a bored oarsman who wrote "little knows man." However, the end of the pole does not appear broken— it is cut clean and has the kind of small centered hole typically left by a lathe. Moreover, why would an oar have a foot-long, carefully flattened notch on its side? Something obviously fit onto this flat surface. Perhaps a banner?

As for the pole's runic inscription, one theory assumes that the final letter is an M, and that this M is an unusual abbreviation for the word meaning "man." In the runic alphabet used at that time, an M was written as a single vertical line with a circle at the top, or rarely as a line with a well-defined crossbar at the top. The final rune of the Oseberg inscription, however, is a vertical line with a minuscule chip at the top—a chip which could be accidental. If this rune is read as an ordinary I, the inscription suddenly becomes clear: *litil visi*, "little chieftain," an altogether appropriate title for the banner pole of a queen.

Some archeologists have been cautious to connect the Oseberg burial mound with Queen Asa, although the circumstantial evidence is great enough that most museums now subscribe to the theory. As a historical novel, *The Ship in the Hill* is free to pursue the theory and to offer explanations for a number of puzzling questions: Why was the ship anchored so securely? Who was the second woman buried in the grave chamber? What did the tapestries signify? And most intriguing of all, what did the Viking-age grave robbers take when they tunneled into Asa's buried dragonship a thousand years ago?

WILLIAM L. SULLIVAN

The author of three novels and a dozen nonfiction books, Sullivan grew up in Salem, Oregon. He completed his B.A. degree in English at Cornell University under Alison Lurie, studied linguistics at Germany's Heidelberg University, and earned an M.A. in German at the University of Oregon. He reads in a dozen languages, including Danish, Norwegian, and Old Norse. He undertook seven voyages to Scandinavia while researching Nordic sagas and Viking history for *The Ship in the Hill*.

Sullivan is known in the American West as the author who backpacked more than a thousand miles across Oregon's wilderness in 1985. His journal of that adventure, *Listening for Coyote*, has since been chosen one of Oregon's "100 Books," the most significant books in Oregon history. In summer he writes at the log cabin that he and his wife Janell Sorensen built by hand in the wilds of Oregon's Coast Range, more than a mile from roads, electricity, and telephones. The rest of the year they live in Eugene, Oregon, where he volunteers to promote libraries and literature.

A list of Sullivan's books, speaking engagements, and favorite adventures is at *www.oregonhiking.com*.

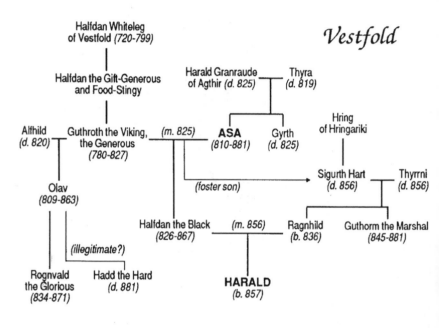

The Royal Lines of Vestfold and Horthaland
in the Viking Age

Vestfold

Halfdan Whiteleg of Vestfold (720-799)

Halfdan the Gift-Generous and Food-Stingy

Harald Granraude of Agthir (d. 825) — Thyra (d. 819)

Alfhild (d. 820) — Guthroth the Viking, the Generous (780-827) — (m. 825) — **ASA** (810-881) — Gyrth (d. 825)

Hring of Hringariki

Olav (809-863)

Sigurth Hart (d. 856) — Thyrrni (d. 856)

(foster son)

Halfdan the Black (826-867) — (m. 856) — Ragnhild (b. 836) — Guthorm the Marshal (845-881)

(illegitimate?)

Rognvald the Glorious (834-871)

Hadd the Hard (d. 881)

HARALD (b. 857)

Horthaland

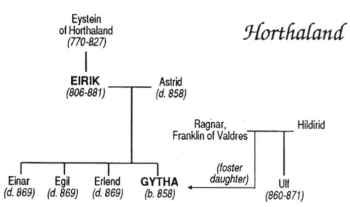

Eystein of Horthaland (770-827)

EIRIK (806-881) — Astrid (d. 858)

Ragnar, Franklin of Valdres — Hildirid

Einar (d. 869)   Egil (d. 869)   Erlend (d. 869)   **GYTHA** (b. 858)

(foster daughter)

Ulf (860-871)